WHEN A ROGUE MEETS HIS MATCH

D0017815

"Why would you want to marry *me*?"

Gideon smiled then, as if he'd won a point—and maybe he had. "I think you're forgetting your enormous dowry."

"No." Messalina shook her head. "I've not forgotten it. Lucretia's dowry is the same. Why me instead of her?"

He looked at her from under his outlandish eyelashes. "Would you *rather* I marry your sister?"

"Of course not." He was trying to distract her and she mustn't let him. She needed all her attention for this fight if she was to persevere. "Answer my question, please."

He was suddenly in front of her, so close he might've kissed her, his black gaze intent upon her face. "Because, Messalina, I want you. I want your wealth. I want your rank. I want the power and influence your family name will bring me. But most of all?"—he cocked his head, bringing his hand up to glide along her cheek, not touching but so close she felt the heat of his fingertips like the ghost of a threat—

"I want *you*."

PRAISE FOR
ELIZABETH HOYT

"4½ stars! Top Pick! Readers will be transfixed by this poignant tale of revenge and redemption."
—*RT Book Reviews*

Duke of Pleasure

"Hoyt once again successfully deploys her irresistible literary triumvirate of marvelously engaging characters, boldly sensual love scenes, and elegant writing brightened with just the right dash of dry wit."
—*Booklist*

"4½ stars! Top Pick! Always unique, wonderfully romantic and highly sensual, Hoyt's stories take readers' breath away."
—*RT Book Reviews*

Duke of Sin

"A complete triumph."
—*Booklist* **(Starred Review)**

"4½ stars! Top Pick! Hoyt delivers a unique read on many levels: a love story, a tale of redemption, and a plot teeming with emotional depth that takes readers' breaths away. Kudos to a master storyteller!"
—*RT Book Reviews*

Sweetest Scoundrel

"4½ stars! Just as enchanting as fans could desire....It is a story that takes your breath away and leaves you uplifted. Hoyt does it again!"
—*RT Book Reviews*

Dearest Rogue

"[This] superbly executed historical romance is proof positive that this RITA Award–nominated author continues to write with undiminished force and flair."
— ***Booklist*** **(Starred Review)**

"Scintillating romance."
— ***Publishers Weekly***

Darling Beast

"Hoyt's exquisitely nuanced characters, vividly detailed setting, and seemingly effortless and elegant writing provide the splendid material from which she fashions yet another ravishingly romantic love story."
— ***Booklist*** **(Starred Review)**

"4½ stars! Top Pick! Wondrous, magical, and joyous—a read to remember."
— ***RT Book Reviews***

Duke of Midnight

"Richly drawn characters fill the pages of this emotionally charged mix of mystery and romance."
— ***Publishers Weekly***

"4½ stars! Top Pick! There is enchantment in the Maiden Lane series, not just the fairy tales Hoyt infuses into the memorable romances, but the wonder of love combined with passion, unique plotlines, and unforgettable characters."
— ***RT Book Reviews***

Lord of Darkness

"Hoyt's writing is imbued with great depth of emotion.... Heartbreaking.... An edgy tension-filled plot."
—Publishers Weekly

"Illuminates Hoyt's boundless imagination.... Readers will adore this story."
—RT Book Reviews

Thief of Shadows

"This one did not disappoint."
—USA Today

"An expert blend of scintillating romance and mystery.... The top of its genre."
—Publishers Weekly (Starred Review)

"All of Hoyt's signature literary ingredients—wickedly clever dialogue, superbly nuanced characters, danger, and scorching sexual chemistry—click neatly into place to create a breathtakingly romantic love story."
—Booklist

"When [they] finally come together, desire and long-denied sensuality explode upon the page."
—Library Journal

Scandalous Desires

"Historical romance at its best."
—Publishers Weekly (Starred Review)

"With its lush sensuality, lusciously wrought prose, and luxuriously dark plot, *Scandalous Desires*, the latest exquisitely crafted addition to Hoyt's Georgian-set Maiden Lane series, is a romance to treasure."
—*Booklist* (Starred Review)

Notorious Pleasures

"Emotionally stunning.... The sinfully sensual chemistry Hoyt creates between her shrewd, acid-tongued heroine and her scandalous, sexy hero is pure romance."
—*Booklist* (Starred Review)

Wicked Intentions

"4½ stars! Top Pick! A magnificently rendered story that not only enchants but enthralls."
—*RT Book Reviews*

OTHER TITLES BY ELIZABETH HOYT

ELIZABETH HOYT

WHEN A ROGUE MEETS HIS MATCH

A GREYCOURT NOVEL

FOREVER
New York Boston

Copyright © 2020 by Nancy M. Finney

Cover design by Elizabeth Turner Stokes
Cover illustration by Alan Ayers
Cover photography © Shirley Green Photography
Cover copyright © 2020 by Hachette Book Group, Inc.

Bonus novella *Night of the Scoundrel* by Kelly Bowen © 2019 by Kelly Bowen

Forever
Hachette Book Group
1290 Avenue of the Americas, New York, NY 10104
read-forever.com
twitter.com/readforeverpub

First Edition: December 2020

Forever is an imprint of Grand Central Publishing. The Forever name and logo are trademarks of Hachette Book Group, Inc.

The publisher is not responsible for websites (or their content) that are not owned by the publisher.

ISBN: 978-1-5387-6356-8 (mass market), 978-1-5387-6355-1 (ebook)

Printed in the United States of America

OPM

10 9 8 7 6 5 4 3 2 1

CHAPTER ONE

*There once was a jolly tinker who tramped up and
down the land selling his wares....*
—From *Bet and the Fox*

SEPTEMBER 1760
ON THE OUTSKIRTS OF LONDON

There is never a good time to be accosted by highwaymen.
However, whilst emptying one's bladder is a particularly
bad time.

Messalina Greycourt froze, the last drops of her urine
tinkling into the pretty china bourdaloue she held between her legs. She stood awkwardly in the carriage, both
her maid, Bartlett, and her uncle's wicked factotum, Mr.
Hawthorne, having stepped out to give her privacy not two
minutes before.

Outside the carriage it was ominously quiet, as if the
shouted order, "Stand and deliver!" had stilled everyone
there as well.

She swallowed as she strained to hear any sound.

Boom! The gunshot broke the silence.

Messalina let her skirts fall.

The carriage door flew open, and Bartlett was shoved inside. For a second Messalina saw Mr. Hawthorne's savage face, his wicked black eyes glittering as he ordered, "*Stay.*"

Then the door slammed shut on the sounds of shouts, gunfire, and whinnying horses.

Bartlett, normally a sturdy, practical woman, looked at Messalina with wide eyes.

The carriage rocked as if something large had been thrown against it.

"How many highwaymen are there?" Messalina demanded.

"I don't know, miss," Bartlett replied shakily. "Over half a dozen, I think." Her gaze dropped to the bourdaloue still in Messalina's hands, and she added more prosaically, "Oh, let me take that."

The bourdaloue looked like nothing so much as a gravy boat. Oblong and with a handle at one end, it was a delicate pink, gilded around the lip. Usually, of course, Messalina would hand it out of the carriage to Bartlett, who would dispose of the contents. Now her poor lady's maid was left standing, holding a china vessel full of piss inside a rocking carriage.

This was all Mr. Hawthorne's fault. If the man had simply let her stop *prior* to nightfall as Messalina had suggested, she—

The door was wrenched open again and a large, filthy man filled the frame, his fleshy lips pulled back in a leer.

Bartlett shrieked.

Messalina snatched the bourdaloue from the maid's hand and flung it in their attacker's face. The china dish bounced off his forehead, dousing him in urine. Messalina pushed him hard.

He tumbled backward out of the carriage.

She slammed the door closed after him and looked at Bartlett.

The other woman's face was white. "That was...erm... quick thinking, miss."

Messalina straightened, trying and failing to control the heat rising in her cheeks. "Yes, well. Needs must."

Outside, someone screamed and was suddenly cut off.

Messalina found herself holding her breath in trepidation.

The carriage door opened, and Gideon Hawthorne climbed inside.

She let out her breath in a gusty sigh of relief before sinking to the carriage seat.

"Oh, thank the Lord," Bartlett said, exhibiting a hitherto unknown religious fervor.

Mr. Hawthorne shrugged. "Or me."

Messalina fought an urge to laugh as Bartlett plopped down beside her.

Then she saw the bloody knife Mr. Hawthorne was holding.

His enigmatic eyes met hers. "I trust you are unhurt?"

He'd killed for her—and himself, of course. "I'm fine."

Mr. Hawthorne nodded and sat. He produced a hand-kerchief and began wiping the blood from the knife, staining the fabric bright red as he did so. Without glancing up, he murmured, "I always clean a knife immediately. The blade can become dull if left...dirtied."

"I'll be certain to wipe the blood from the many knives I carry," she said tartly.

"Do so. Besides," he said with what sounded like perfect seriousness, "blood is ungodly hard to remove from fabric."

She stared at him, appalled.

Mr. Hawthorne wasn't a particularly big man. One

didn't immediately think on first glance, *Here's a fellow I should avoid at all costs if I value my life.* It was the *second* look that did it. Then one noticed the competent, muscled frame, the dangerously economical way he moved, and his sudden stillness, as if he was gathering himself to attack.

And then there was his face.

Mr. Hawthorne had the countenance of a devil. His eyebrows formed a deep V over his eyes, the outer edges winging up in a demonic slant. On his right cheek was a long vertical scar, thin and ominous. He was an intimidating man.

A *frightening* man.

When Messalina could stand the silence no longer, she cleared her throat. "*Well?*"

He glanced up at her. His eyes were gleaming black like his hair. "Well what?"

Messalina's own eyes narrowed. "Are the highwaymen *gone*?"

"Of course." He flicked the knife closed and somehow made it disappear into his coat before standing to knock on the roof.

Hawthorne sat again, watching her unnervingly.

There were only two servants in the carriage box. Even if Bartlett had overestimated the highwaymen, Mr. Hawthorne and his men had been badly outnumbered.

"Did you worry for me?" His sly, rasping voice interrupted her thoughts.

"No," she said flatly.

"You'd prefer a band of highwaymen to me?" His inflection had just a hint of the London streets.

"Yes!"

"Fortunately," Mr. Hawthorne said softly, *ominously,*

"you'll never have the chance to make that silly choice. Not while I have possession of you."

"*Possession.*" Messalina glared at him even as she suppressed a shiver. Why would he use *that* word? As if he *owned* her. "Whatever makes you think you can—" she began, and then she noticed that he had taken something from his pocket.

He held her bourdaloue, pink and dainty, in his hands.

"I think," he said, examining the vessel with unseemly interest, "that this is yours."

Messalina's mouth dropped open.

Bartlett snatched the dish from Mr. Hawthorne's hands. "I never!" she muttered as she put the thing away.

Mr. Hawthorne smirked, leaning back and tilting his hat over his eyes until only his curled lips could be seen.

Messalina turned pointedly to gaze out the darkened window.

A little over a week ago Mr. Hawthorne had waylaid her carriage in the north of England and informed her that her uncle, Augustus Greycourt, the Duke of Windemere, required her presence immediately. So immediately in fact that the duke had sent Mr. Hawthorne to personally escort her back to London. She'd been forced to abandon both her carriage and Lucretia, her younger sister, with whom she'd been traveling. There had just been time for Messalina to indicate to Lucretia that she should go to their eldest brother, Julian, for help before she'd been whisked away.

After that, Messalina had spent a week traveling with the odious Mr. Hawthorne.

She darted a glance at him from beneath her eyelashes.

Mr. Hawthorne was apparently asleep now that the danger was over. His booted feet were crossed at the ankles, his arms over his chest. The carriage lantern threw a glow on a sculpted chin and breathtakingly high cheekbones. His mouth was curved at the corners as if even in sleep he were privately amused at some lewd joke. The upper lip was thin and strictly constrained to a classical Cupid's bow, but the lower lip belied the upper's repression with obscene plushness.

He had the most depraved mouth Messalina had ever seen on a man.

She looked away hastily. Mr. Hawthorne was a *ruffian*. Messalina knew—as did everyone else—that he'd emerged from the worst stews in London. There were rumors that her uncle had found him earning his living by competitive knife fighting. Mr. Hawthorne had been but seventeen at the time. Up until ten minutes ago Messalina had always dismissed that gossip as far too lurid to be true.

She was beginning to revise that opinion.

She eyed the white scar bisecting Mr. Hawthorne's left cheek. It was thin and silvery like the trail of a teardrop. She would do well to remember that Mr. Hawthorne was a man accustomed since youth to savage violence.

Messalina shivered in distaste and turned away again from her guard dog. Instead of woolgathering over Mr. Hawthorne, she ought to be considering Uncle Augustus's purpose in summoning her. Mr. Hawthorne had flatly refused to inform her *why* her uncle wanted her in London. Naturally that had meant she'd spent the past week becoming more and more anxious.

Not that she let it show.

Whether Uncle Augustus had decided to exile her to the American Colonies, present her with a new riding mare, or cut her living expenses entirely, she would meet the news equally phlegmatically.

The Duke of Windemere gorged on fear.

Better to remember the small amount of pin money she'd saved over the last few years. When Messalina had saved enough, she would take Lucretia and disappear into the Continent or the New World.

A place where her uncle could no longer dictate their lives.

"Ah, now we're in London proper, miss," Bartlett whispered, nodding to the bright lights outside the carriage window. "It'll be nice to sleep in a decent bed after so many nights on the road, if you don't mind me saying so."

"Yes indeed," Messalina replied, not bothering to whisper.

Mr. Hawthorne didn't react. He was either still asleep or pretending sleep, the better to spy on her.

Messalina watched out the window as they trundled slowly into the West End, feeling quite weary and ready for a rest.

It was nearly an hour more before the carriage drew up outside the towering classical facade of Windemere House, the London residence of the Dukes of Windemere.

Mr. Hawthorne stirred immediately, sitting upright as alert as if it were morning, damn him.

He looked at her, and for a moment she had the idea that his hard eyes had gentled. He seemed almost as if he wanted to tell her something.

Then the carriage door opened, and a footman handed Messalina down. She glanced up from shaking out her skirts and couldn't quite suppress a start.

Augustus Greycourt, the Duke of Windemere, was waiting at the top of the stairs. He was a jolly-looking man, short and round, with a face that might seem kind if one was unaware of the rot within.

Hawthorne came up beside her and took her arm. She glanced at his hand, confused. He had missed a bit of blood on his thumbnail.

She shuddered.

"Ah, Messalina," Uncle Augustus said. "I was beginning to think you'd be late to your own wedding."

Messalina felt a chill run down her spine. Her *wedding*?

Uncle Augustus continued, smirking, "But how could you be late when your bridegroom is also your escort?"

Slowly Messalina turned her head.

And met Mr. Hawthorne's diabolically gleaming black eyes.

* * *

Gideon Hawthorne had always thought that Messalina Greycourt had the most fascinating eyes. They were gray—a cool, clear gray—with a ring of near black around the iris.

He watched as those intriguing eyes filled with loathing—for him.

Gideon looked away. He'd always known that she'd hate this plan. Still he felt a twinge—a very small twinge.

Gideon's gaze slid to Windemere. What was the old man doing? Messalina was a headstrong, smart, and stubborn woman. The duke knew she wouldn't agree easily to a forced marriage. And yet his words were calculated to make Messalina dig in her heels.

But perhaps that was what Windemere wanted: a fight that could end only one way—with the duke triumphant and Messalina humiliated.

Gideon would have to make sure no such thing happened.

Windemere grinned. "Come, girl," he called to her. "Bring your fiancé inside so we can have a coze in my study."

Messalina's features were blank. Most would have no clue that she was frantically thinking underneath her guarded expression.

But Gideon had spent years watching Messalina's face. He knew he had to prepare both his offense *and* his defense.

His grip tightened around her upper arm. It was unlikely that she'd run off into the dark streets of London—Messalina was no fool—but the old man was doing his best to provoke her. And Gideon would be damned before he lost her now.

His touch seemed to wake her. Messalina blinked and tried to pull her arm from his hand. She glared up at him when he refused to release her.

Gideon let a small smile curve his lips—better a scowl from her than to be ignored.

Windemere interrupted their silent skirmish. "You've declined all the suitors I've put before you, Niece, but you shan't wriggle free from marriage tonight. I've already sent for the bishop. If you want to marry in something other than stained traveling clothes, you'll have to hurry."

Gideon shot a narrow-eyed glance at Windemere.

The duke beamed down on them, damn him.

Gideon leaned close to Messalina, murmuring, "We'd best go in."

"Naturally *you'd* say that," she snapped in reply, but she stepped forward to climb the steps.

As they drew level with the old man Messalina said simply and certainly, "No."

There was his girl. Gideon couldn't help his silent satisfaction even if her stubbornness wasn't to his benefit.

Her flat refusal finally drove the idiot smile from the duke's face. "What did you say, sweet niece? Pause before you speak, for I know you've been hoarding your pin money."

She paled. "What have you done?"

"*I* have done nothing," Windemere replied. "*Hawthorne*, however, has taken your little purse into his possession."

"Of course Mr. Hawthorne did." Messalina's glance at him was searing. "I do hope you enjoyed rummaging in my trunks."

Gideon raised an eyebrow, irritated by both her scorn and her words. "I assure you, I was quite bored."

That for some reason provoked a blush. "You've rifled through that many ladies' possessions?"

Before he could reply, the duke interrupted.

"Enough!" Windemere said impatiently. "Messalina, you have no hope—not even any expectation of hope—of escaping me. Go to your rooms and prepare yourself for your wedding." He paused and then said with studied nonchalance, "Unless you'd prefer to have Lucretia take your place?"

Gideon felt a muscle twitch in his jaw. He'd agreed to marry Messalina and *only* Messalina. He had no intent—or desire—to marry Lucretia Greycourt.

Messalina inhaled sharply as the duke laid down his trump card. She lifted her pigheaded little chin, but the slight tremble in her voice betrayed her. "I will never marry your henchman, nor shall my sister."

Gideon cleared his throat and gave the duke a pointed look. "It is chilly, Your Grace. Would you not like to talk with your niece inside by that fire you mentioned?"

The duke hesitated, clearly not pleased by Gideon's suggestion, but he grimaced and strode into Windemere House.

Messalina didn't move. Her head was held high, but her eyes were wide and frantic. She was obviously shaken by the threat to her beloved sister.

Gideon said quietly, "Will you stay here until you turn to stone out of pride?"

"*You* wouldn't care," she shot back viciously.

"You have no idea," he said truthfully, "how much I'd care."

She stared incredulously at him.

He held her clear gaze. Those eyes would be the death of him. "Better to go in, yes?"

Messalina blew out a breath and muttered, "I don't think I have a choice."

"No," he said gently, "you don't, but I'll make it as easy as I can."

She huffed and went in.

Windemere waited in the entry, his happy mood returned.

Messalina eyed him warily, then said, "I need to refresh myself. If you'll excuse me, Uncle."

Gideon let his hand fall, and she jerked away to hurry up the grand staircase.

He fought a sigh. Now was not the time to tame her. That would come later.

The duke growled, "She'll try to escape out the back."

Gideon didn't bother looking at him. "My men are already guarding the doors, Your Grace."

Windemere grunted. "Good. Come with me."

He turned and walked across the red-white-and-black marble floor of the entry hall, servants falling away before him. Gideon followed silently. A footman pushed open the door to the great library as the duke approached.

"Shut that door," Windemere snapped to the footman once they'd entered. "And make sure no one disturbs us."

The door closed without a sound.

The duke sank into a high-backed chair. Gideon didn't bother taking a seat.

Windemere eyed him with a disgruntled expression, and Gideon felt his upper lip lifting.

It was *almost* funny.

His work under Windemere had been both unlawful and at times brutal. Gideon probably knew more about the old man's dealings than any other person alive, which gave him a certain amount of power over Windemere. But at the same time, the duke knew *exactly* what Gideon had done in his service. Gideon had no doubt at all that the old man had kept records and whatever evidence there might be. The duke could have Gideon hanged with a word or two in the right places—*if* he didn't mind falling with Gideon.

Their past was a double-edged sword neither was particularly anxious to handle.

Windemere grunted. "If she escapes, I'll not offer her to you twice."

Gideon let a mocking smile twist his lips. "Which is why I'll not let her escape."

"You had bloody well better not," the duke growled, obviously irritated by Gideon's insolence. "The wench is worth a fortune. Not only will you lose her as a wife, but I'll take her dowry out of you if she runs."

Gideon didn't bother replying. He'd heard this all before, an endless, dusty rant filled with grievances and threats.

Windemere suddenly smiled, making Gideon come to full alert. "Although if Messalina were to disappear, it might save me much trouble."

"I would protest violently if that were to happen," Gideon replied softly. "You've promised to give me Messalina."

The duke scowled at his threat and then waved his hand. "A fortnight locked in her room with naught but water and pap should make her soften. The gal has never wanted for a meal or anything else. She'll soon come around."

"No doubt," Gideon said carefully. If he showed too much concern, the old man would follow through on his threats, and Gideon didn't want Messalina starving—or worse. "But you said you'd already sent for the bishop. Was that a bluff, Your Grace?"

"No." The duke scowled. "I'll have to send him away again, and the bishop will want his guineas even if he does nothing in return. Churchmen are a greedy lot."

Then it was up to Gideon to convince Messalina to wed him if he didn't want any further delays. He started for the door.

"Where are you going?" the duke called peevishly from behind him.

Gideon turned. "To persuade Miss Greycourt to attend her own wedding."

Windemere snorted. "Easier to find a Wapping Docks whore without the pox than to win over the chit."

Gideon lifted an eyebrow before turning back toward the door.

The duke called behind him, "Just remember: no matter what she decides, you've already made the bargain and given your oath. You're my man and you'll do as I wish."

Gideon paused with his hand on the door handle. His knuckles went white as he tightened his grip. "I'm unlikely to forget. Your Grace."

With that he left the room.

Gideon closed the library door behind him and took a moment to inhale, leaning against the door. Almost a year ago he'd decided that it was past time to leave the old man's employ—both because he hated the tasks Windemere set him and because he wanted to concentrate on his *own* business.

But leaving the employ of the Duke of Windemere wasn't such an easy thing. Gideon's knowledge was dangerous to the old man. He'd rather not end as a corpse floating on the Thames.

So Gideon had waited, judging his exit carefully. When he at last told the duke that he planned to leave, Windemere had surprised him by offering a prize that Gideon simply couldn't refuse: Messalina Greycourt.

But first Gideon had to secure his lady—preferably without the duke starving her.

He straightened and snapped his fingers.

A slight shape slunk into the light, transforming into a disreputable youth with a broken nose and the innocent wide blue eyes of a baby angel. The youth—actually a young man, for Keys was older than he looked—straightened and nodded. "Aye, guv?"

"Where is she, Keys?"

Keys rolled his eyes skyward. "Upstairs in 'er rooms last I checked with Reggie."

Gideon nodded. Now he had to worry that she might try to escape *and* that the duke would follow through on his casual threat against Messalina. "Do the rounds, make sure Pea has his gang in the garden and at the sides. Then come in and stand with Reggie. Clear?"

Keys merely touched a finger to his forelock and slipped away.

Gideon mounted the grand staircase to the upper level, the red marble steps curving back on themselves like a coiling snake. The muscles in his arms and legs felt bunched, ready to spring after quarry. Perhaps it was the excitement of fighting off the highwaymen earlier. Perhaps it was the thought of all he so nearly had in his grasp.

Or perhaps it was *her*.

She'd been only a girl when he'd first entered the old man's service. Young and long limbed, not a child at fourteen, but certainly not yet a woman. He'd made note of her along with all the Greycourt siblings: Julian, the eldest, as trustworthy as his uncle. Quintus, who had been a sot at the age of eighteen, still mourning the death of his twin sister,

Aurelia. Messalina, grave beyond her years. Lucretia, the youngest, pretty and mischievous.

To Gideon, Messalina had been simply one of the aristocracy. Born to lounge about in silks and jewels, eating Turkish delight with soft white fingers while the rest of the world slaved. She was just like every other highborn lady.

And yet he'd watched her, even then. He'd spied from the shadows, a rough St Giles lad, invisible among the duke's dozens of servants. Gideon might be only a couple of years older than Messalina, but they were worlds apart. He'd observed as she'd grown into womanhood, as she donned rustling dresses and put her hair into intricate loops on top of her head. Watched as she laughed at the young fops who gathered around her like wasps drawn to spilled beer.

She wasn't for him, *that* was always clear.

Even so, he'd not been able to tear his gaze away. She made something inside him *want*.

Messalina had been the star he longed for but couldn't reach—and the old man knew it.

Gideon scowled as he made the upper floor. He didn't like the fact that Windemere had been able to read him so easily. His desires and thoughts were his own, and it was simply too dangerous to let others see inside. But fourteen years ago, when he'd first entered the duke's employ, he'd been young—seventeen—and less used to hiding his every expression.

Her rooms lay down a long hallway. Gideon nodded to Reggie, large and looming in the shadows several steps from the door.

"Careful, guv," Reggie called softly.

Gideon shot him a look. He hardly needed a warning from his own man.

He pushed the door open, raising his right arm to protect

his head at the same time. She came rushing at him, a small marble statuette in her hands.

Marble. He couldn't help a flare of admiration. He wrenched the statuette from her hands and caught her. "I see you're bent on murder, Miss Greycourt."

She twisted like an eel, trying to escape, but he held her firmly by both wrists. When she realized she wouldn't be able to free herself, she attacked, kicking at him, even though she was hampered by her own skirts.

He crowded her with his body, forcing her to retreat until her back hit the wall. For a split second he studied her, trapped between the wall and him. Her heavy black hair was uncoiling around her face, her cheeks flushed pink from exertion. She glared up at him with gray eyes that held storms and dire warnings.

But there was no fear in their clear depths, none at all. Something inside him exulted that she couldn't be cowed, even by him.

He bent his head, aware that he was close enough to seize her lips beneath his, and murmured, "Now then, I think we need to talk."

* * *

Messalina stared into Mr. Hawthorne's horrid black eyes. This close she could see how long and thick his eyelashes were, as if his eyes were outlined in charcoal. On any other man they might look feminine.

Not on him. *Never* on him. She could almost smell his masculine musk. Few men had ever stood as close to her as he did now.

"Let me *go*," she growled belatedly, yanking at her wrists to no avail.

One of his sloped eyebrows arched at her struggles. He looked *amused*, damn him! He leaned close to her, his breath tickling her lips. "Will you give me your word not to attack again?"

She nodded once jerkily.

He let go of her arms and stepped back.

She found herself inhaling deeply, as if his presence so close to her had kept her from breathing.

Perhaps it had.

"I'll not marry you," she stated as calmly as she could. "No matter what my uncle says."

The duke might've had Mr. Hawthorne steal her pin money, but there must be other avenues of escape. The threat against Lucretia filled her with panicked nausea. If she could just *delay* Uncle Augustus's schemes, she would find a way.

"Really." He turned his back on her—rather insultingly—and strolled to a table near her fireplace. Someone had placed a decanter of wine there, along with a repast of bread and cold meats. He poured a glass and returned to her. "Even if His Grace offers me your sister instead?"

He held out the glass.

She swallowed, ignoring the blasted wineglass. "He'd never do such a thing."

"Because your uncle is such a very reasonable man?" Mr. Hawthorne's eyes widened mockingly before he took a sip of the wine. "No, His Grace will happily force Lucretia to marry me, both for spite and because he wants to retain my services."

He was right and they both knew it. She lifted her chin, seeking any way out of this trap. "What do your services to my uncle have to do with Lucretia or me?"

"Your uncle wishes me to do a certain task. I refused.

But then he offered a very tempting enticement." His gaze wandered down her frame before that distracting mouth twitched and he met her eyes. "*You.*"

She wanted to strike him. The intensity of the violent urge shocked her. Her words came out in a stutter, she was so angry. "So you'll m-marry Lucretia if I refuse?"

"No." The wine had left a wet stain on his bottom lip, shining and mesmerizing. "I want only you." He shrugged as her eyes widened. *Her?* "I merely point out that your uncle is fickle. If you hinder his plans, he'll punish not only you but everyone you hold dear. He's already suggested imprisoning and starving you. Do you want him to do the same to Lucretia in order to *persuade* her to marry some aged lord?"

"No." Messalina glared at Hawthorne. He was quite correct, unfortunately. Uncle Augustus was a monster who didn't bother with even the appearance of the morals that guided other men. "My uncle is cruel—that I agree with you on, but I don't understand. Why would you want to marry me?"

He smiled then, as if he'd won a point—and maybe he had. "I think you're forgetting your enormous dowry."

"No." She shook her head. "I've not forgotten it. Lucretia's dowry is the same. Why *me* instead of her?"

He looked at her from under his outlandish eyelashes. "Would you *rather* I marry your sister?"

"Of course not." He was trying to distract her and she mustn't let him. She needed all her attention for this fight if she was to persevere. "Answer my question, please."

He was suddenly in front of her, so close he might've kissed her, his black gaze intent upon her face. "Because, Messalina, I want you. I want your wealth. I want your rank. I want the power and influence your family name will bring me. But most of all?"—he cocked his head, bringing his hand up to glide along her cheek, not touching but so close she felt the heat of his fingertips like the ghost of a threat— "I want *you*."

She had to fight to keep from trembling. The intensity in his gaze was overwhelming. Had any man ever watched her like this? As if no bonds of civility or man-made laws could stop him from seizing her in his arms?

She looked him in the eye, this evil, awful man, and said crisply, "You can't have me."

"No?" He stepped away, throwing back the rest of the wine in his glass. "But I think I can." He sauntered to the table where the decanter of wine stood, unstopping it before glancing up at her. "Your uncle certainly intends to give you to me."

She was out of options. She was going to be forced into marriage, sold like a milk cow. How was she to retain herself—her will, her pride, her vow to escape from her uncle—in this debacle? "I am not a *thing* to give."

He paused, still holding the decanter of wine, eyeing her thoughtfully. "No, you're not. *I* know that even if your uncle does not. Nevertheless, I'll still accept his offer. I'm too ruthless not to. But frankly I'd prefer a wife who consented to this union." He poured himself another glass of wine and set the decanter down. "So. Let us bargain, we two. What do you want?"

"I want my *life*." That was really all she wanted—that and Lucretia's safety. "My life to determine as I will."

He shook his head, not even bothering to look regretful. "You cannot have that. Name something else."

Oh, she wanted to do him violence. To run at him screaming. To hit him or stab him. To shoot him with a pistol if she had one. She would, too. She knew it in that moment. She'd kill this man if it would do her any good. She'd kill him and flee all the way to the American Colonies and she'd be free then.

Except that would leave Lucretia and her brothers, and while Julian could certainly take care of himself and probably Quintus could, too, even against Uncle Augustus, Lucretia could not.

Lucretia was a woman. And even an intelligent, crafty woman like Lucretia was no match against a man in England—particularly a man as powerful as the Duke of Windemere. He was bloody-minded enough to destroy both Lucretia and Messalina simply because he could.

Messalina took a deep breath and crossed to sit on a chair by the fireplace. The fire wasn't lit—probably Uncle Augustus's way of making her rooms less welcoming—but the night was warm. It was summer, after all.

She stared into the empty hearth and thought: What did she want? More importantly, what could she *have*?

At last she looked up and found Mr. Hawthorne had taken a seat kitty-corner to her. He lounged as complacently as a king and sipped from his wineglass as he waited.

She loathed him.

"I want to be free from my uncle and his machinations," she said. "But you can't give me that, can you? You're his servant, his *lackey*. How can you give me *anything* I need?"

"I think," he said softly, "if you use your imagination, you'll find many ways I can give you what you need."

His black eyes watched her over the rim of his wineglass as he took a sip, his gaze frankly heated.

Messalina recognized a double entendre when she heard one. It was quite obvious that the game he wanted to play was dangerous to her. But she'd moved in the most rarified London circles for over ten years.

She knew how to play dangerous games with men and emerge unscathed. She might never have taken a lover—unlike some sophisticated ladies—but she had overheard talk, had gossiped late at night with women already married, and had dabbled a bit with gentlemen who were safe.

She could do this—bargain with the devil and find *some* small benefit in this awful situation.

Messalina straightened.

It was past time she took control of the table. The single most important thing she needed was enough money to flee England with Lucretia. The question was, Could she get it from him?

"Can you?" she asked carelessly. "Give me what I need?" She let her gaze wander down his form, past broad shoulders and a narrow waist, pausing for just a second on the bulge in the placket of his black breeches, and then perused his long legs and booted feet. When she met his eyes again she wore a doubtful moue. "Perhaps. But can you give me what I *want*, Mr. Hawthorne?"

The corners of his devilish lips curled. "Ask me and see."

"Very well." She leaned back in her chair, mirroring his relaxed pose. Best to start small. "I want Lucretia to live with me."

He didn't hesitate. "Done. She'll live with *us*."

She swallowed, attempting to ignore the emphasis on the last word. "I want my pin money returned to me."

"Naturally," he drawled. "Though you'll need to wait until after we wed."

Her pin money wasn't enough to get her to safety anyway.

She lifted her chin, her pulse beating fast. She mustn't let him know how close to terror she was. How much was riding on her gamble. "I don't wish to couple with you."

"You hurt me." He placed his hand on his chest as if in jest, but his smile was hard. "I'm afraid you cannot remain untouched. I'll have no reason for you or any one of your family to try for an annulment. And besides"—he tilted his head mockingly—"I *do* want to fuck you."

The coarse word sent a visceral shock through her, making her imagine him naked. Hawthorne would be sleek, muscled, and dangerous, and she had no doubt at all that he knew how to make a woman moan. Her nipples peaked.

None of which was to the point.

She cast her eyes down as if disappointed. "We've come to an impasse then, haven't we?"

"I don't think so." He stared at her a minute, slowly tapping his fingers on the arm of his chair. "I find that I'm willing to bend—for you."

For her. Something flickered inside her chest at the words, even though she knew he was pretending sentiment.

She needed to concentrate on the matter at hand. She was backed into a corner, made to realize that she was going to be married against her will, and to *him* of all people.

To a rogue.

She raised her brows as if the entire discussion bored her. "Go on. How shall you bend?"

His smile this time was almost genuine. "I'll give you some small time before I bed you—say a week after we wed?"

"Three months," she snapped, clenching her hands to hide her trembling fingers. She couldn't believe they were debating when she would let him...

"A month," he drawled, his black eyes staring at her wickedly as he took another sip of his wine.

His throat worked as he swallowed, and she dragged her gaze to his face instead. "Two months."

He shook his head. "I won't wait that long. One month."

God. She'd woken this morning with her only worry a possible argument with her insane uncle, and now she was bargaining away her maidenhead.

She took a deep breath. If she had to do this, she'd best make it worth her while. "Very well. One month. But in return I want something from you."

He lifted his eyebrows in query.

"A portion of my dowry."

He nodded. "I'll give you a sum each quarter as pin money."

"No," she said, and this time her voice shook, but it was hardly from fear. She was angry. "It's *my* money. Money my father left me. Once we marry you'll have a fortune, and I'll not be content any longer with a pittance doled out at your whim. I want half."

One of his eyebrows rose. "You value your virginity very highly."

"Should I not?" she shot back. "It's what the men around me value. Should I turn shy maiden and ignore that *money* is what all this is really about? Pretend I don't know exactly how much I'm worth?"

"Maybe not." He pursed his lips. She would *not* look. "A tenth. At the end of a year of marriage."

She couldn't wait that long. "A quarter on the day of our wedding."

He narrowed his eyes. "You expect me to pay you before I receive my prize?"

She just refrained from snorting. "My *dowry* is your prize."

"Is it?" His eyes lingered on her mouth before meeting hers. "One-tenth in six months."

"One-tenth in a month." She let the disdain show on her face. "On the day after our marriage is consummated."

"Agreed." He eyed her contemplatively, then sat forward

with a businesslike air. "This will be a real marriage. You will be true to me—I won't abide you taking a lover."

The point was moot. Once she had her dowry portion she had no intention of remaining with him long enough to take a lover. "Certainly."

"You will live with me as my wife. You will sup with me every night. We will also move about society"—he waved a hand—"go to balls and the like."

"What?" she interjected. "Surely you know you'll not be welcomed in society."

His nostrils flared, and suddenly she was reminded that he'd killed tonight. "With your money and name I can and I *will*."

She simply stared at him.

He nodded as if the matter were decided and continued, "You can sneer at me as much as you like in private, but in public you will act like a devoted wife."

The man was a delusional ass. "*Devoted?*"

He sighed again. Evidently negotiating with her was quite trying. "A *content* wife, then. Does that meet with your approval, madam?"

No. None of this obscenity met with her approval. However, it was what must be done to win her and Lucretia's freedom. A tenth of her enormous dowry was more than enough to live on if they were careful. They could escape somewhere abroad.

Messalina studied Hawthorne. She didn't trust him. She didn't *like* him. And she had no other option. "If I agree to this—to pretending complacency—then you will fulfill the terms we've agreed to?"

He held her gaze. "Yes. You have my word."

The word of a paid tough. How charming.

"You'll regret this one day," she murmured, low, spitefully, and sincerely. "Regret forcing me to marry you."

"I don't think I will." He sounded entirely sure of himself. "Shall we marry?"

She reached over and took the glass of wine from his fingers and emptied it in one swallow. "Very well."

CHAPTER TWO

One day the tinker came upon an ancient wood. It was curiously untouched. Curiously still. Curiously shadowed. He journeyed deeper and deeper into the towering trees until he could no longer see the sky and the sun itself was blacked out....
—From *Bet and the Fox*

Julian Greycourt woke to the sound of someone banging on the cottage door. He was instantly alert.

No one was to disturb him here.

He rose, nude, ignoring the sparks of pain burning across his back, and threw on a banyan. Thank God his companion had left hours ago.

Julian glanced around. The croft was simple—one room, a fireplace, a cot, and a chair. Nothing else. Nothing to indicate what he did here.

Good.

He strode to the door, unbarred it, and threw it open.

Lucretia looked up at him, her fist still raised, as if she would knock upon his chest. "Oh, thank goodness! Quintus said you were staying at one of the cottages, but he must've given me the wrong directions. I've been looking for you for the better part of an hour."

"What are you doing here?" His words were perhaps too curt, but no one was supposed to know of this place.

Quinn had discovered the croft only because he'd followed Julian one night. Julian hadn't spoken to his brother for almost a week afterward. He'd thought he'd made it very clear to Quinn to keep his damned mouth shut about the cottage. And yet here was their little sister, wide-eyed and pink-cheeked on the step of—

Julian cleared his thoughts. "Where is Messalina?"

"With Mr. Hawthorne," Lucretia said, sounding exasperated that Julian didn't already know this. "He stopped our carriage on the return journey from the Lovejoy house party. You know their estate near the border of Scotland? I must say it was a most *unusual* party—"

"What did Hawthorne do, Lucretia?" Julian asked impatiently.

Lucretia pressed her lips together. "He told Messalina to get out of the carriage and come with him. She just had time to tell me to find you."

Julian frowned. "Why would Hawthorne do such a thing?"

"He said that Uncle Augustus wanted her—only her, not me." Lucretia twisted her fingers together. "That was over a week ago—nearly two now. I told my driver to head straight to Adders and you, but what with the horses and the road being so terribly rutted—"

"Just a minute," Julian said. "Stay here."

He shut the door in her face and ignored the resulting squawk of outrage. Julian hurriedly threw on his clothes, hissing beneath his breath as his linen shirt scraped across the wounds on his back. What the hell was Augustus planning? And what had their uncle been thinking to force Lucretia to travel so far by herself?

He shrugged on his coat and pulled his long hair from the collar, tying it back with a bit of ribbon.

Then he opened the door again.

"I can't believe Quintus is in his cups so early in the morning," Lucretia remarked crossly, as if there'd been no interruption in their conversation. "He *smelled*."

She wrinkled her small, straight nose as if assaulted by the odor of a cesspool.

"No doubt," Julian muttered. "Come. Let's go to Adders."

Her carriage was standing before the croft. The driver and a footman were half-asleep on the box while a second footman leaned against the carriage, nodding. The men came awake, though, on sight of him. The footman by the carriage scrambled to hand Lucretia in.

Julian glanced at the driver. "Back to Adders Hall."

"Sir!" the driver shouted, and the moment Julian was inside they were off.

He took the seat across from Lucretia and examined her. The early-morning sun made a nimbus of the fine strands of hair escaping the knot at the top of her head. "Where's your lady's maid?"

"I told Messalina to take Bartlett," Lucretia replied. "After all, she couldn't travel all the way back to London with just Mr. Hawthorne."

Julian raised an eyebrow at this logic, which left Lucretia traveling alone with just the coachman and the two footmen, but didn't bother replying.

Outside they passed more crofts—some occupied, some not. This had been a prosperous bit of land once, cottages full, fields teeming with sheep and cattle. But that had been before his mother's death.

Adders Hall was west of Oxford, nearly at the Welsh border, on land that should've been prosperous. When Julian had inherited Adders Hall and the small amount of property surrounding it from his mother, he'd had high hopes of being a competent landowner. One who would follow modern methods of agriculture and husbandry. One who would care for his tenants and their families.

He'd been but seventeen, very young, unaware that his father's will had left his parents' wealth in the hands of his uncle, Augustus Greycourt, the Duke of Windemere. The duke was to manage his inheritance until Julian came of age and could take over the accounts.

But when Julian turned one and twenty, Augustus had given him a paltry amount. His uncle had claimed that there had never been any wealth. That besides Messalina's and Lucretia's enormous dowries—set aside by his mother and now in the duke's control—nothing was left. Augustus had smiled when he'd told Julian that his father had run through his inheritance like a profligate.

The carriage bounced down a lane and into the Adders Hall drive. The beech allée to either side of the drive was in a shocking state—in need of trimming and re-planting in parts—and the drive itself was rutted and overgrown.

Adders Hall came into view, and Julian suppressed a wince. It once had been a modest but stately house, built in worn gray stone, but now the west wing was closed, the roof leaked, and many of the windows were boarded up. Weeds grew around the front steps like mice nibbling at a matron's hem.

A lone figure stood by the door, swaying slightly.

"Oh, good," Lucretia said. "Quintus came home." She glanced at Julian. "I found him in one of the cottages. I don't know why you both lurk around the tenants' cottages when you have a perfectly good house here."

Julian turned to look at the approaching ruin pointedly.

Lucretia frowned. "Well, a house in any case."

He snorted.

The carriage halted abruptly, nearly sending his sister into his lap.

Julian descended first, just in time to catch his brother, stumbling toward them. Quinn slumped heavily against him, making Julian brace himself. His younger brother was the same height as he, but Quinn was a good two stone heavier.

"Thought I saw Lu-Lu-Lu-*cre*-tia," Quinn mumbled, sending a puff of stale breath into Julian's face.

Good God. Quinn did indeed reek—a combination of alcohol, rancid sweat, and filthy clothes. He must've fallen in the mud at least once on his way home.

"You *did* see me," their sister said, having exited the carriage. She might be a head shorter than both of them, but her expression suggested the severity of a nanny about to scold an errant toddler. "Messalina needs your help."

Quinn blinked stupidly at her. How long had he been languishing in his cups?

Julian sighed. "A moment, Sister."

He jerked his chin at the footman on the carriage, and the man jumped down. Julian took one of his brother's arms, the footman took the other, and, with Lucretia trailing behind, they were able to drag Quinn into the house, down a dark hall, and to the kitchen, startling Vanderberg, Julian's valet, who looked to be in the midst of a good gossip with Mrs. McBride, the cook.

Vanderberg was a small man—barely five feet—dressed elegantly in dark blue to best show off his golden hair and pale complexion. The valet had been with Julian since both were teenagers—probably the only reason Vanderberg put up with a pittance in pay.

The valet leaped to his feet, assuming an expression of stoic servility, patently in contrast to his usual demeanor when alone with Julian. "Mr. Greycourt! I had no notion you had returned to the hall. And in dishabille."

His glance at Julian's hair was full of badly concealed horror.

"Quite," Julian said reprovingly. He hadn't time to smooth Vanderberg's ruffled sensibilities. "Fetch a bucket of water."

The valet opened his mouth, closed it, and turned. An earthenware cistern stood in the corner of the kitchen, and Vanderberg swiftly filled a bucket with water and brought it to Julian.

Julian jerked his chin at Quinn. "Douse him."

Vanderberg raised an eyebrow but obeyed, throwing the bucketful of water into Quinn's face.

Quinn straightened, sputtering. "What? Wha—?"

"Bathe him and make him presentable," Julian ordered the footman before glancing at Lucretia. "Have a cup of tea. I'll be ready in a half hour."

He didn't wait for her reply but strode from the room and back into the hall, Vanderberg trotting to keep up. Julian took the wooden stairs two at a time, careful not to use the banister—it had a tendency to fall off.

"Pack my things," he called to Vanderberg as they made his room.

Julian ignored the valet's mutter and stripped off his coat and shirt.

Behind him something clattered to the floor.

"Don't," he snapped, pouring water from a jug into a basin for washing.

"But, sir, your back," Vanderberg protested.

The valet was impertinent. Julian ignored him as he rubbed himself down with the cold water and a bit of cloth. He pulled a fresh lawn shirt over his head before dressing as quickly as he could in a silvery gray suit. He was relieved when he turned and saw that Vanderberg had finished packing several trunks.

"May I at least dress your hair?" the valet asked, his voice sounding injured.

Julian sat on a stool and submitted to having his hair tamed, the long wavy locks brushed and braided tightly. His hasty toilet was finished with a black ribbon wound around the end of the braid.

Vanderberg stepped back, surveying Julian. "As good as I can do in such a hurry."

"No matter," Julian replied. "Have the carriage driver help you with the trunks."

Downstairs he found Lucretia peering at a dusty shelf in the library, a cup of tea in one hand and a slice of seedcake in the other. "We leave in ten minutes. Get in the carriage."

She sighed. "I'm going to need another piece of cake in that case."

He didn't bother answering and left for the kitchen.

Quinn didn't appear any more sober, but at least he was clean. He looked up with bloodshot gray eyes when Julian entered. "Where're we goin'?"

"London," Julian replied curtly, taking one of his brother's arms while the footman took the other.

"Why?" Quinn slurred.

"Because," Julian said grimly as they staggered to the front door. "We have to put a stop to whatever Augustus has planned."

* * *

The sky wept on his wedding day although the bride did not, Gideon mused late the next morning.

The splatter of rain hitting the window was a drumbeat accompaniment to the bishop's droning voice. A *bishop*, and on less than a day's notice. Gideon eyed the cleric and wondered what spur the duke had used to obtain both him and the special license. Blackmail, judging by the way the bishop nervously eyed the old man. Gideon could almost feel sorry for the clergyman—if he ever wasted time or emotion on any aristocrat.

He put the bishop's distress out of his mind as he studied the duke. Windemere's expression was that of an indulgent uncle, but his eyes were filled with dark glee.

Last night the old man had been set on seeing them married at once. Gideon had argued for more than half an hour before the duke conceded and agreed to wait until the more civilized morning. As it was, they had only Messalina's maid and the Windemere House butler as witnesses. Well, and Keys, if one could count him as a witness. The young man lurked in the corner.

Gideon finally looked at his bride. Messalina wore a dark-gray gown that nearly matched the shadows under her eyes. Her complexion was sallow with fatigue, her mouth thinned into a stoic line, and her dark hair drawn into a tight, unbecoming knot.

And he still wanted her with a gut-deep pull.

She caught his eye and glared and he had the urge to laugh, but that wouldn't be wise—not only because it would provoke her but because it would reveal his mood to the duke.

This was a dangerous process, stealing Messalina away

from her uncle. Windemere was a man who liked control—one of the reasons Gideon had wanted to leave his employ.

Had the old man offered anything—any*one*—else, Gideon would be a free man right now.

But that was the point: Messalina was his weakness. There was no way he could've let her go.

The bishop pronounced them man and wife in a mumble, and the old man chuckled softly. "Congratulations, my dear. What an advantageous alliance you've made." He caught Gideon's gimlet stare and coughed, turning to the bishop. "Shall we celebrate with a wedding breakfast? I've instructed Cook to prepare a suitable repast."

The duke sauntered from the room, the butler trotting ahead to open the door for him and the bishop trailing behind. As Gideon turned to take Messalina's elbow, he caught Keys's eye. The man straightened and nodded.

Gideon bit back a smirk. Keys had been in his employ three years now, and despite the carelessness of his dress, he was meticulous in carrying out Gideon's orders. As Gideon guided Messalina from the room he glimpsed Keys waylaying the lady's maid—apparently to the woman's displeasure.

Then Gideon was out the door and into the hall, walking with his wife—his *wife*—behind the old man as they made their way to the breakfast room. The long ebony table was already laden with a feast that would easily feed a dozen hungry men.

The duke sat at the head of the table and snapped his fingers impatiently for a footman to bring him wine even as Gideon was pulling out a chair for Messalina.

The old man drank deeply as everyone else's wineglass was filled and then raised his own when it was refilled. "A toast to the happy couple!"

"Indeed. Indeed," the bishop murmured, and downed his entire glass.

Messalina merely pressed her lips together.

Despite the delicacies laid before them, his new bride hardly ate. Her uncle more than made up for it, greedily cracking a beef bone to scoop the marrow from it. Gideon watched both the old man and Messalina closely, and when the duke finally pushed back from the table Gideon was quick to rise.

He bowed to the duke and to the bishop. "My wife appears fatigued. I shall show her to our rooms to rest."

Predictably, this prompted a leer from the old man. "Naturally you'll want to get my niece alone as soon as possible, eh, Hawthorne? They do say the lower classes have stronger animal impulses." He switched his regard to Messalina. "I suppose you'll soon find out, won't you, my dear?"

Messalina didn't give any indication that she'd heard— or even noticed—her uncle, instead laying her hand on Gideon's proffered arm.

For a moment Gideon thought the duke would make Messalina acknowledge him, but it seemed that the heavy meal had mellowed him. The old man merely waved them away with a lazy hand.

Gideon strolled from the room, leisurely leading Messalina to the stairs and down to the hall.

She frowned. "This isn't the way to my rooms."

"Not your old rooms, no."

She looked around, then demanded, "Where are you taking me?"

He glanced at her and couldn't resist a wink. "To your *new* rooms."

Her brow was still knitted in concern, but she didn't protest.

They went out the back door and through an ill-tended garden and entered the mews behind the house by a gate.

His carriage was waiting, Keys standing by the door.

Gideon jerked his chin at him. "Did you get everything?"

Keys snorted. "Not 'alf of it, guv, but all the important bits, or so the maid tells me."

He opened the door to the carriage.

Messalina stared. "What—?"

"Oh, miss!" cried Bartlett from inside. The woman's face was red with what looked like indignation. "I didn't know what to do. That young scamp said as it was orders from Mr. Hawthorne, which—"

They hadn't time for this. Gideon placed a hand on Messalina's rump and leaned down. He could smell bergamot as he murmured in her ear, "Get in."

She shot him an irritated glare but obeyed, climbing into the carriage with his help. He took a seat next to her and then nodded to Keys.

The man slammed the carriage door shut, and in a moment they were moving.

Messalina said impatiently. "Well? What is this?"

He could still smell bergamot—faint and elusive in the air. He wanted to turn and bury his nose in her neck. Chase the scent and find its source.

That would probably make her scream.

No. Better to woo her with craft and cunning so that when she fell to his bed she'd think it *her* idea. "I promised you a house, remember?"

She turned to eye him mistrustfully. "Yes?"

This close he could see whorls of crystalline gray in her eyes. "I'm taking you there."

For a second her eyes widened, making her look bewildered and vulnerable.

He inhaled very carefully.

Then her sooty eyelashes swept down and she turned away, hiding her face and her expression. "My uncle expected us to spend the night in Windemere House."

"Yes, he did."

She stared at him thoughtfully. "My uncle will be furious when he discovers that you've spirited me away from under his nose."

He shrugged. "I can withstand your uncle's ire."

"But why do it in the first place?"

He turned slowly to her. "Because I can't bear the look in your eyes when you're under his roof."

Her lips parted. "I really don't understand you."

"Don't you?" His lips quirked. "Perhaps you should make a study of me."

"Perhaps I should," she said slowly.

He shook his head. "In any case I'm taking you to Whispers." He caught her puzzled look. "Our new home. Whispers House."

* * *

"Will there be anything else, ma'am," Bartlett asked in a weary voice that night.

Messalina simply blinked at her maid for a moment—she was that tired. They'd spent the afternoon settling in her room with the few trunks and boxes Bartlett had been able to hastily pack. Hawthorne had deposited them, the trunks, and two of his rather frightening men at Whispers House. The house had turned out to be a huge, moldering mansion in a not-very-fashionable part of London. Before Messalina could ask any questions, Hawthorne had returned to the carriage, off on some errand.

No doubt at the behest of Uncle Augustus.

Messalina shuddered. Truly, she'd never wanted to marry at all, let alone to marry a man who *enjoyed* violence.

She inhaled, pulling back her shoulders, standing up straighter. Now was not the time to give in to despair.

Now was the time to plan.

Messalina turned to her maid. "Did you pack my secretarie?"

"Yes, ma'am," Bartlett replied promptly, and she bustled over to one of Messalina's trunks resting against the wall.

There were few furnishings in the room: a massive bed hung with heavy red drapery, two chairs and a small table, and an old brass-bound casket—locked. Messalina wasn't sure if the lack of a wardrobe and a chest of drawers for her clothes had been a deliberate slight on Hawthorne's part or if he hadn't yet finished furnishing the room.

Bartlett returned with a flat wooden box in her hands. Messalina sat at the table before the fireplace and opened it. Paper, quill, and ink were all neatly stowed inside, for this was a traveling secretarie.

Messalina drew out a piece of paper, inked her pen, and paused, thinking of whom she might write to.

Hopefully Lucretia had already tracked Julian and Quintus down, so there was no point in writing them.

Messalina pursed her lips. Most of her friends were, like her, ladies and thus had very little real power.

There was one, however…

Freya de Moray had been Messalina's best friend when they'd both been girls. Until Aurelia had been killed and both their worlds had fallen apart.

Ran, Freya's elder brother, now the Duke of Ayr, had been accused of Aurelia's murder. Aurelia, the golden girl, whom everyone had loved. That same night he'd been beaten near to death by Uncle Augustus's men. Ever since, the Greycourts and the de Morays had been caught in a web of hatred and scandal.

They'd been estranged for many years, but recently Messalina had reconciled with Freya. That returned harmony had closed a wound Messalina hadn't even realized she bore.

She'd also learned what Freya had been doing all those years they'd been apart. For Freya had told her—in the strictest confidence—that she was one of the Wise Women. This ancient secret society was composed entirely of women and worked only to help other women.

And Messalina could certainly use some help now.

She dashed off a quick letter explaining briefly her dilemma, sanded the wet ink, and sealed the missive. Then with a small smile she addressed the letter care of the Duke of Harlowe—otherwise known as Kester—Freya's new husband.

She turned to Bartlett and handed her both the letter and several coins. "In the morning post this. You must be very careful that neither Mr. Hawthorne nor his men see you doing so. Can you do that?"

Bartlett looked affronted. "Course, ma'am. I'll find a way to leave the house on an errand. No one will find out."

"Thank you, Bartlett," Messalina said with relief. "You may retire for the night. That is, *do* you have a place to sleep tonight?"

"Yes, ma'am," Bartlett replied. "I asked that Keys person earlier and he assured me that there would be a bedroom ready in the servants' quarters."

Messalina frowned. The small amount of Whispers that she'd seen before retiring to her own room was appallingly uninhabitable—there was hardly a stick of furniture, and she wasn't even sure there were proper servants. "If you have any difficulty, please let me know."

Bartlett drew herself up to her full five feet. "Pardon me, ma'am, but I think I'll be *quite* able to deal with the situation myself."

For a brief moment Messalina felt a pang of pity for the absent Keys. Then she nodded to the maid. "As you wish. Good night, Bartlett."

"Ma'am." Bartlett curtsied and slipped out the door.

Messalina stood, smoothing down her chemise. Bartlett had brushed out her hair as she did every night, though tonight there was no dressing table or mirror in her bedroom. Messalina glanced around ruefully. Earlier she and Bartlett had shared supper—much to Bartlett's scandalized senses—at the tiny table. Both it and the bed looked to have seen better days, and Messalina suspected that her new husband had bought a house without the funds to furnish it. Or perhaps he simply didn't have the inclination.

She glanced around the barren room, suddenly aware that her life felt barren, too. Without friends or Lucretia, here alone, did she have any *purpose*?

She shook her head at her maudlin thoughts. It was late and she was tired. And this day...this day had been horrible.

Messalina walked to the bed. Tomorrow she'd explore the house, find out what her boundaries were, and consider her avenues of escape. Tonight she simply needed to sleep. She pulled back the counterpane on the bed, relieved to find the linens fresh and clean, and placed her knee on the mattress.

The door opened and Hawthorne strolled in.

Messalina was all at once wide awake, her heart beating fast. "*Get out.*"

"And a pleasant evening to you as well, madam wife." He closed the door behind him, his saturnine eyebrows arching as he slowly surveyed her form.

"I said *get out.*" She put her foot back on the floor and damned the fact that she wore only her chemise—made of the finest lawn and nearly sheer.

"You've nothing to fear," he said.

She snorted. "I'm not a half-witted *clam.*"

"Clam." He tilted his head slowly sideways.

She ignored his jesting. "I've been courted by the highest-ranked gentlemen in the kingdom—and I turned them down. Do you know why? Because those *gentlemen* were nothing more than worms, without intelligence or regard. I'm not about to submit to a bully boy like *you.*"

"I'm afraid you've disregarded two things," he replied coolly, his black eyes glinting. He looked the very devil and he could see her *nipples.* "One, that I'm no gentleman—"

"Indeed?" she interrupted sweetly.

"And two, this is my bedroom."

She blinked. "I'm not in the mood for games. Tell me why you're here or get out. Better yet, simply *leave* me."

"I'm here to sleep," he said, and took off his coat. He folded it neatly and placed it on a chair before spreading his arms. He actually had the—the *gall* to try to look contrite. "It truly is my bedroom."

Truly? She'd assumed that they wouldn't be sharing a bed.

Messalina felt her eyes widening in outrage. "*What?*"

"This. Is. My. Bedroom," he enunciated maddeningly as he began unbuttoning his waistcoat.

"Stop that!"

He suddenly stilled, his emotionless eyes pinning her. "Or what?"

Fear raced through her veins; she *knew* what this man was capable of. And yet she sneered at him. "I'll put an emetic in your beer or whatever you drink, see if I don't."

"That's..." He considered the threat. "Rather novel, actually. Not to mention effective. However"—the most untrustworthy smile she'd ever seen spread over his face— "You've spiked your own cannon by telling me your clever plan. Come. I'm weary and you must be, too."

She huffed. "I'll have you know that *most* married couples have separate bedrooms."

"No," he drawled, fastidiously setting the waistcoat on top of his coat. "*Most* people have but one chamber for their bed—and often only that."

That pulled her up short. For a moment she felt ashamed of her own class, imagining living in only one *room*.

Then she squared her shoulders. "But *I'm* not most people."

She pivoted to face him as he briskly moved around her to sit on the bed.

"You certainly aren't," he muttered under his breath.

Messalina rolled her eyes. "Surely there are enough rooms in this house—"

"Yes, there are," he said, cutting her off. He untied his neckcloth. "You can argue all you want, but you've forgotten something."

She set her hands on her hips. "What is that?"

"*I* don't want to make my bed in another room." He threw the neckcloth toward the chair. It missed. He shrugged, then glanced up through his ridiculous eyelashes at her, his black eyes glittering in the candlelight. "You'll just have to trust me."

If he was attempting to look trustworthy, he was failing badly.

An incredulous laugh burst from her lips. "You *must* be bamming me."

"I assure you I'm not. Despite any"—his gaze flickered to her barely covered bosom—"*desire* to consummate this marriage, I will not force you. That isn't part of my plans. We've made a truce with benefits to both of us. Why would I want to destroy this détente? I'd be a fool to wrong you now. And before you say it, I am no fool."

Messalina could feel the heat in her cheeks from that brief, searing glance. She bit her lip, undecided. What he said made sense, and his reasoning was oddly reassuring. Still... "Then tell me what you intend to do tonight."

"I intend to sleep," he said, flicking open the top button on his shirt. "I won't touch you until the agreed-upon month is over, but I *will* share your bed. I don't want this marriage contested."

For a second her gaze strayed to his throat, revealed by his open shirt. The tanned skin gleamed in the candlelight. She had an awful urge to *touch*.

Her eyes snapped up to find him watching her with a smile playing about those wicked lips. She stiffened.

"Messalina," he said, his voice a dark purr. "Come to bed."

She almost stomped to the door. But if she gave in to trepidation—or temper—now she'd have trouble regaining her footing with him.

Besides. There was her pride.

"Humph." Messalina went around to the other side of the bed and slowly got in, watching him all the while.

He ducked his head as if hiding one of his lopsided smiles, his fingers on the third button of his shirt.

She tried to look away, but really it was impossible to do so. Another inch of his corded throat was unveiled.

And then he stopped.

Messalina pursed her lips in irritation.

Hawthorne bent and removed his shoes and stockings. Something on a thin chain swung out from the top of his shirt.

"What is that?" she asked.

The object winked in the candlelight before he caught it in his hand and tucked it back inside his shirt.

"Nothing you need concern yourself about." He pulled the tie from his hair, letting his heavy, curling locks fall to his shoulders.

He stared at her, looking like some pagan god—the kind that demanded human sacrifice.

Messalina swallowed, aware that there was some part of her, inside and hopefully hidden, that found his physical form very, very alluring.

He stood and deliberately pulled back the coverlet. He held her gaze as he got in.

She looked away.

The mattress dipped and shook and then was still.

She tensed, staring up at the ceiling. The bed was wide enough that they didn't even touch. Still she was unnaturally aware of him, big and solid, only inches away. She'd never shared a bed before—at least not since she'd grown—and *certainly* not with a man.

He blew out the candle.

She could hear his breaths, even and deep, and she realized suddenly that she could *smell* him—not unpleasantly. He smelled like a man, she supposed. A man in her bed.

Her nipples tightened and she froze. She was afraid

he would *know* somehow. That he might take her sudden awareness of him as an invitation.

Tiredness finally conquered her vigilance. Her breaths became deeper, and she began to drift.

The whispered male voice in the darkness sounded almost like part of a dream. "Good night, Wife."

CHAPTER THREE

*Soon the tinker realized that he'd wandered from
the road and that he was hopelessly lost in the
dark wood.*
*"Oh!" he cried. "I'll never see my sweet wife and
darling children again."*
At that moment he saw a light shining up ahead....
—From *Bet and the Fox*

Gideon woke the next morning to the scent of bergamot and
a warm body flush against his side. For a lazy half second
he imagined that he was a boy again, crowded against his
brother on a thin pallet in some nameless room in St Giles.

Except the mattress was far too soft, and nothing had
smelled as nice as bergamot in St Giles.

Besides. Eddie had been dead nearly two decades now.

Gideon's eyes snapped open to the weak light of dawn
glowing in the bare windows.

He lay in his own bed. A bed acquired only a day before
he'd departed for the north of England to fetch Messalina.
He'd held Whispers for a matter of months and in that time
hadn't seen the need to furnish it with more than a few basic
pieces—he came home only to eat and sleep. But he could
hardly bring his wife to a house without an adequate bed.

His *wife*.

Gideon couldn't help the satisfied curve of his lips.

Against all odds he'd succeeded in marrying Messalina. She was his now.

He sat up and leaned over to contemplate her. She lay curled on her side, her cheeks flushed in sleep, her lips softly parted, vulnerable and sweet. Watching her made him want to lie back down, draw the coverlet up, and doze next to her. Perhaps wrap his arm around her.

Gideon frowned. And then she'd shriek and accuse him of assault.

He shook his head. He never slept in.

Gideon got up. Aristocrats lazed about. He hadn't dragged himself up from the muck of St Giles by lying abed contemplating what he already had. He'd clambered, clawed, and scrambled his way out of St Giles by keeping his eyes fixed on what he could gain next.

With that firmly in mind, he unlocked his old trunk. He pulled out a banyan, wrapped it about himself, and, refusing to look back at the bed, left the room.

His stride was brisk as he made his way down the hall to a room nearly at the end.

He threw open the door to half a dozen lit candles and Keys yawning widely as he sat at a desk.

"Mornin', guv," Keys muttered. The man's blue eyes were heavy lidded and his hair flattened to the side of his head. In all the time he'd worked for Gideon, Keys had not accustomed himself to rising early.

"Good morning," Gideon replied, tossing aside his banyan.

A bowl of hot water stood steaming on a dresser next to a cloth. Gideon splashed water on his face before reaching for soap and a wickedly sharp razor lying ready nearby.

"What news?" he asked as he began to lather his jaw.

Keys stifled another yawn. A teapot and teacup were at his right elbow, and he poured himself a cup as he consulted a small notebook. "Pea says as 'e still can't figure what the old man wants you to do in exchange for 'is niece. 'Is boys 'ave asked of the usual people, but if'n anyone knows they ain't talking."

Gideon raised his chin to scrape his throat free of soap and whiskers. "The old man's keeping it to himself, but I have no doubt that it'll be something filthy."

Keys grunted, whether in agreement or because he'd just taken a gulp of his hot tea it wasn't clear. "Shall I 'ave Pea continue investigatin'?"

"No. There's no point when I'm to see the old man today." Gideon grimaced. He disliked going into a meeting blind, but there was no help for it. The duke had refused to tell him his task before Gideon married Messalina.

"Maybe the duke just wants to keep you in 'is pay," Keys said diffidently. "You're the only one 'oo don't piss 'is pants when 'Is Grace gets in one of 'is rages."

"Oh, I don't doubt that he means to *try* to keep me," Gideon said sourly. "The old man doesn't like anything or any*one* slipping through his grasp—particularly anyone he hasn't first ground beneath his heel—but he's very pleased about our bargain. I have the feeling that he has something specific in mind for me to do."

Keys looked worried at his words, but he turned a page in his notebook without comment. "Staff reports that m'lord Bancroft played deep last night and just about lost 'is shirt. 'E borrowed from Staff to the tune of another two 'undred pounds. Staff wants to know if we keep 'im 'ooked or cut line."

"Keep him," Gideon decided at once. Viscount Bancroft was in a rather powerful cabal in the House of Lords. Gideon wasn't sure how he might use that now, but it was always good to have a member of Parliament quite literally in his debt.

Keys nodded and made a notation in his little book. "Mr. Blackwell says 'e wants to talk to you soon as you can."

Gideon had met William Blackwell years ago in a gambling den. Gideon had been there for two reasons. The first was to obtain information for the duke. The second was to attend to his own small business: collecting debts for moneylenders and pocketing a portion of the money.

The two jobs had fit rather nicely together.

But Blackwell had taken Gideon's business a step further. With Blackwell's help Gideon had bought a coal mine in the north of England. Coal was proving very profitable, and Gideon had recently bought another mine. Blackwell handled Gideon's accounts and his coal mines and was, for want of a better word, his business partner.

Gideon frowned. "Does Blackwell want to talk about the ledgers?"

Keys shrugged. "For your ears only."

"Oh, for God's sake." Gideon sighed. "He probably wants to argue about the coal mines again. He's like a dog with a bone he won't let go when he gets an idea in his head. Tell him I'm newly married and busy."

"As you say, guv."

"Anything else?"

"The rest is 'Is Grace's affairs. You've been gone nearly a fortnight and things 'ave been moving." Keys squinted. "*Are* we still interested in 'Is Grace's dealings? Thought you was out of that end of the business, now you're married to 'is niece."

Technically Gideon's pact with the old man encompassed only the one task for the duke. On the other hand, forewarned was forearmed.

"Best to still keep an eye on Windemere's affairs." Gideon splashed clean water on his face, rinsing any remaining soap away, then caught up the cloth to dry himself. "Let's visit Scratch's Coffeehouse to break our fast. You can tell me the details there."

"And Miss Greycourt?" Keys asked.

Gideon raised a pointed brow as he donned clean breeches. "*Mrs.* Hawthorne, you mean."

Keys winced. "As you say, guv. Mrs. 'Awthorne."

"What about her?"

"Erm…" Keys had an odd expression on his face. "Well, don't you want to stay until she wakes? That is"—he blushed wildly—"after your wedding night?"

Gideon paused, his arm thrust into a fresh shirt, to stare at his man. "Why, Keys, I never knew you had such a romantic soul."

Keys opened his mouth.

"No." Gideon quickly shook his head, forestalling him. "Mrs. Hawthorne will no doubt need a day of quiet. Be sure to tell Reggie to watch her like a pickpocket with a mark."

His tone was sharper than need be, and the realization made him pause.

For a moment he remembered Messalina's sweet, soft face as it had appeared this morning in his bed, and a part of him wondered if he *should* stay. *No.* He firmly thrust away the vision. Messalina wouldn't greet his presence with happiness. She'd made that more than clear last night.

He had work to do, a hard path to follow to reach the goals he'd set for himself. Not even Messalina was worth deviating from that path.

Decided, Gideon opened the door to find Pea's worried face. The lad stood holding the arm of a younger boy. "Guv, I've something to tell yer."

* * *

Messalina woke much too early, as evidenced by the absence of Bartlett and the fire being dead. She stretched her legs under the covers, pointing her toes and flexing them lazily.

Then she remembered.

She turned as quietly as possible, but there was no need. Hawthorne's side of the big bed was empty. She slid her palm over the sheets. Cold. The only reminder that he'd lain beside her all night was the slight indentation in his pillow.

Messalina huffed out a breath.

Naturally she was pleased not to have to face her husband. However, she would have liked to *tell* him that he wasn't wanted. His escape from her scorn was oddly disappointing.

Messalina glanced around the room, at a loss. She planned to leave as soon as she received her dowry portion, but what was she to do in the month until then? Make the house more livable? Write letters to various friends?

It all seemed so unsatisfying.

She sighed. She ought to go back to sleep, but she was awake now and not at all sleepy. What if Gideon returned to the room? The thought had her up and searching for her wrapper as protection.

The door opened and for a second Messalina's heart raced.

Bartlett stepped into the room, holding a tray with a teapot, sugar bowl, strainer, teacup, and one piece of buttered bread on it. "Oh, you're already awake, ma'am."

She closed the door with her hip and set the tea tray on the tiny table.

"You're a wonder, Bartlett," Messalina said thankfully as she sat.

She poured herself a cup and then couldn't help wrinkling her nose as she sipped the tea. Mostly twigs. Well. At least it was hot.

"Thank you, ma'am." Bartlett carefully knelt on the grate.

Messalina froze with the awful tea halfway to her lips. "Whatever are you doing?"

"Sweeping the hearth," Bartlett said sturdily.

"But that's not your job."

"It is today." Bartlett vigorously wielded a hand brush. "There's no upstairs maids."

"None at all?" Messalina frowned in concern.

Bartlett shook her head. "Only a young scullery maid in the kitchens, ma'am. She was too frightened to come to your room."

Good Lord. She needed to hire maids right away. Bartlett already had a job that kept her busy.

"But there's a cook?" Messalina waved the slice of bread.

"Aye, that we do have," Bartlett agreed. "But no butler nor housekeeper nor even footmen. I'm afraid the house has barely a skeleton staff."

"That *is* a problem." Messalina took another sip of her terrible tea and was nearly startled into dropping the teacup by a shout.

"God save us," Bartlett exclaimed, looking at Messalina. The voice was loud, but the words were incomprehensible.

Messalina slowly set the teacup on the table. "What—?"

Another shout, louder this time, accompanied by commotion.

Messalina rose and hurried to the door. The corridor was empty, but now she could hear crying coming from her right. She clutched her skirts and near ran in that direction. The weeping sounded like a *child*.

Near the end of the hall a door was open, and she rushed inside.

And then skidded to a stop.

Hawthorne stood glaring down at a small sobbing boy. The child couldn't be older than eight.

"What in God's name are you doing?" Messalina demanded.

Hawthorne looked up and met her eyes. His were narrowed and so furious she nearly took a step back. "None of your concern."

Messalina flinched, feeling as if she'd been slapped. She glanced at the boy. His face was red and tearstained, his thin shoulders hunched. Light-brown hair curled around his ears. He wore a ragged pair of breeches, shoes that looked too big for his feet, and a shirt that might once have been white.

He was pathetic.

Rage, hot and intemperate, raced through her. "I think it is my concern if you mean to bully *children.*"

"No, it isn't." Hawthorne turned his back on her as if the matter were settled. "Sam. Have you learned your lesson?"

Messalina realized for the first time that there were others in the room. Gideon's man, Keys, stood to the side, his eyes watchful. Another, older boy was leaning against the wall, looking almost bored, and Bartlett was at Messalina's elbow.

"Y-yes, guv," Sam whispered. He straightened his shoulders. "I won't never do it again."

"Do what?" Hawthorne demanded, his expression still stern.

Sam swallowed. "Steal from you, guv."

"*Just* from me?" Hawthorne growled. "Not good enough."

Messalina scowled. "*Hawthorne.*"

No one paid the least heed to her.

"From anyone," Sam said quickly, his high voice sounding panicked. "I won't steal nothing from anyone at all!"

"Swear," Gideon demanded.

"I swears!" Sam said. "On—on me *mam*, I do."

"Your mother's dead," the older boy drawled.

Sam sobbed. "On me mam's grave, I meant."

Messalina's heart turned over. How could anyone hear this and remain unmoved?

But Hawthorne stared down at the boy for a moment more, his face implacable—*frightening*—with that silver scar on his cheek. "Swear on your life. For if I ever catch you again stealing from me, your life won't be worth a halfpenny."

"I swears on me life," Sam whispered.

Messalina was speechless with horror. What sort of man threatened to kill a little *boy*?

Gideon looked at the other youth. "Get him out of my sight and out of my home, Pea."

"Aye, guv," Pea said, pushing away from the wall. "Come on, you."

He pulled the still-weeping Sam none too gently from the room.

Messalina burst out, "I've never seen such a revolting display."

Gideon paused and then jerked his chin at Keys. The man nodded and walked to the door, ushering Bartlett out ahead of him. The door shut behind them.

Leaving them alone.

"You, madam wife, are sheltered."

"What does that mean?" she demanded.

He turned and finally looked straight at her, the anger still blazing in his black eyes. "You're an aristocrat."

She was...*not* hurt. "You're a cur."

He stilled, his eyes blacker than sin, as he walked closer to her. "I've not let many men call me that—and live."

For a moment she was frozen under his gaze, like something small and vulnerable in the sight of a wolf.

She drew a shuddering breath. His mood turned so swiftly. So dangerously.

She would not fear him. "Then," she said, keeping the tremble from her voice with effort, "it's as well that I'm a woman."

A corner of his lips lifted before he turned to thumb through some papers on a desk.

He'd dismissed her without saying anything.

She wasn't some weak chit to be pushed aside.

She pursed her lips. "What did that boy steal from you?"

"A brass candlestick."

"And that was enough to threaten him with death and cast him from your household?" she asked incredulously.

"Sam committed a crime," he said through what looked like gritted teeth.

"He's a little boy!"

"You do not know what you are speaking about," he said so softly a chill ran through her blood. "And now the matter is over."

"No, it isn't," Messalina shot back. "I'll not live with a man who is so savage to a child."

"You'll not live with me?" Gideon looked up at that, his face dark. "You've given your word, madam. Do you truly wish to have this battle with me?"

Messalina inhaled, steadying herself. One month. That was all she had to endure before she could leave him.

"No. But your behavior—"

"Just because you cannot understand my actions doesn't give you the right to judge them—or me." He stepped closer to her, his animal heat radiating off him as he stared at her with narrowed black eyes. "Will you keep the terms of our bargain?"

She was breathing fast, her heart racing with hatred...or some other emotion. "You have no—"

"*Messalina.*" He caught her chin, his hands hard as he

leaned close in a parody of a kiss. "Will you keep your word?"

She did not fear him. She did *not*. "Yes."

She yanked her chin from his fingers.

For a moment they stood there, she still breathing too fast, he with banked heat in his obsidian eyes.

He reached out and tucked a lock of her hair behind her ear slowly. Almost tenderly. "Thank you."

Her lips parted as she stared at him.

His hand fell and he bowed abruptly. "I've an appointment. I'll return tonight to sup with you."

He gave her one last piercing look before walking out the door.

Messalina's shoulders slumped as the tension drained out of her. *Lord.* How was she to sit and eat with Hawthorne tonight? Converse as if nothing at all had happened?

And then it struck her: in one month's time she'd have to do more than converse with Gideon.

She'd have to lie with him.

* * *

Thirty minutes later Gideon climbed the front steps of Windemere House.

He'd spent the walk here remembering Messalina's face. The expression of shock and disgust. It shouldn't bother him. After all, he'd never wanted kind looks before. Never *needed* them. He didn't need anything other than his own wits and cunning.

Still. That expression bothered him.

He shook his head and rapped sharply at the door. A minute later it was pulled open by the butler, a man named Johnson and one of the witnesses to his marriage to Messalina. The man paused to give Gideon a long look. Gideon couldn't help a hard, bright smile. He knew what the butler was thinking—in all the years Gideon had worked for the duke, he'd always entered this house by the servants' entrance.

Johnson stepped aside, his manner once again that of a rigid upper-level servant.

Gideon gave his hat to a footman and followed the butler up the stairs and down a narrow hall.

Johnson tapped at a door and then opened it. "Mr. Hawthorne, Your Grace."

Windemere looked up from a plate piled with smoked fish, ham, and eggs, and gestured with his knife. "Leave us."

The butler silently shut the door.

Windemere sat back in his chair. "Think you pulled one over on me, do you? Stealing my niece away."

Gideon didn't let an eyelash flicker. "No, Your Grace. My wife was merely eager to inspect her new home." He added smoothly, "I'm sorry that in her excitement we forgot to bid you farewell."

The duke grunted ill-humoredly and attacked the fish with his knife and fork.

Gideon wondered how many times he'd stood like this in front of the duke, waiting for orders, watching him gobble a meal. A hundred times? Two hundred?

Past any man's endurance, in any case.

"Well?" the duke finally barked, as if Gideon were the one holding up the discussion.

"I wanted to discuss our pact."

"Eager for her dowry, are you?"

Of course he was. He needed that money to make his way into society. Gideon merely nodded.

The duke ate the rest of his fish.

Gideon made sure to show no impatience. That would only reward the old man.

Windemere finally rose and walked to a tall desk against the wall. He took a key from a chain on his watch and unlocked the desk to take out a legal paper. "I've caused half of the moneys to be placed in a separate account. When you've finished the job I'll put the remainder of the dowry in the account and hand it over. Until you do, all the money is still in my hands."

He slid the document across the table he'd eaten his breakfast on.

Gideon picked it up, not bothering to read it. This wasn't unexpected, but it still made him angry.

He looked from the document to the old man, his eyes narrowed. "What shall I live on until then? How shall I keep your niece?"

The duke reseated himself and folded his hands on his belly. "I know you've a nice bit of coin saved. You'll do quite well."

All true, though it didn't make Gideon any happier. The duke had implied that he'd turn over a portion of the dowry once they'd wed.

Gideon had promised Messalina her money in a month. He had to fulfill the duke's wishes before then.

Gideon took a calming breath. "What can I do for you, Your Grace?"

The grin that spread across the duke's face was unsettling. "I want you to kill my heir, Julian Greycourt."

CHAPTER FOUR

The tinker followed the light until he came to a small clearing carpeted in wild thyme. Sitting there was a cottage. The walls were made of honeysuckle and sweetbriar and the roof was a mass of violets and oxlips. Lounging before the cottage was a great red fox, smoking a clay pipe....
—From *Bet and the Fox*

Late that afternoon Messalina stood in Whispers' cavernous library and tried not to look as appalled as she felt.

Along the walls lovely oak shelves reached nearly to the ceiling—entirely empty. "How can a library *be* a library without *books*?"

Reggie, who was their guide to the house, shrugged. "The guv 'asn't much use for books."

"Of course he hasn't," Messalina said bitterly. "He's a Philistine as well as a bully to small children."

Reggie was an enormous man with a heavy brow and thick lips. Despite his rather alarming appearance he was remarkably cheerful. Now, though, he wrinkled his great forehead. "Ma'am?"

Bartlett glanced up from the small notebook where she was keeping a list of the things that needed attending to. "Mr. Hawthorne disciplined a boy this morning. He was named Sam, I think?"

Reggie's brow cleared. "Oh, aye. Sam is one of Pea's lot. What was the guv 'auling the lad over the coals for?"

"Thieving," Bartlett said.

Reggie winced. "The guv is right strict-like when it comes to anyone stealing 'is things."

"Of course he is."

She knew what Hawthorne was. Why was she so appalled by his cruelty? Had she really imagined that the man was anything other than a savage? She remembered his fingers brushing her face as he'd pushed her hair behind her ear. How could the same man have terrified a little boy only minutes before?

She kept seeing Sam straightening his shoulders. Trying to look tough when he was only a small boy. If she could but help him somehow.

No. She must stick with her plan of fleeing this house.

Which reminded her. She glanced at Bartlett. "Let me see your notes."

The lady's maid handed over the little book.

Messalina ran her eye over the precise handwriting without really seeing it. She nodded as if in approval.

"This is very good. Let me just note a few books I'd like to bring here." She took the pencil and wrote at the bottom of the list, "Were you able to send the letter?"

Smiling, she handed the notebook back to Bartlett.

The maid glanced at the notebook and nodded. "A very good suggestion, ma'am. Why, just this afternoon I sent a boy to inquire about one of your favorite books, *The Gloom of Harlowe Hall.*"

"Did you?" Messalina raised her eyebrow at the rather imaginative title.

"Yes, indeed," Bartlett said sturdily.

Messalina smiled. "I look forward to his return, then. But I'd like to finish touring the house first."

"Yes, ma'am," Reggie replied. "Erm. This way."

He led them out into the passage at the top of the staircase and down a hall to another room. Reggie opened the door and said proudly, "The music room."

Messalina entered and glanced around. The small room was pleasingly proportioned and painted a soothing lavender, but it held only a single chair, sitting in the center of the room.

She turned to Reggie and asked carefully, "Why is this called the music room?"

Reggie seemed stumped for a moment before he said, "'Cause this is where music is played."

"And yet..." Messalina waved to the instrument-less room and then sighed. "Tell me, how long has Mr. Hawthorne been living at Whispers House?"

Once again Reggie's brow folded into deep wrinkles as he consulted the ceiling for an answer. "Must be nigh on five months now? Aye, that's right, cause 'e took it in payment for Lord Spinnet's debt to 'im." He smiled happily at Messalina. "Spinnet wouldn't give th' house up until the guv threatened to break both 'is nose *and*..." Reggie suddenly seemed to become aware of what he was saying. "That is...the guv's been living 'ere 'bout five months. Ma'am."

Messalina wrinkled her nose distastefully. "Naturally he did. Does the guv frequently resort to violence to get his way?"

Reggie tilted his head and said gently, "Sometimes 'e does. When 'e works for th' duke or when 'e's collecting on the debts others owe 'im."

"He's a moneylender?" She asked in as neutral a voice as possible. Reggie was obviously loyal to Hawthorne.

"That's *some* of what th' guv does," the big man said, leading them down the stairs. "But not all."

"What else does he do?" she asked before she could contain her curiosity.

"'E 'as a *proper* business now," Reggie said with pride. "Lets others do the rough work if there's need."

"Indeed?" Somehow she was doubtful that Hawthorne no longer did the rough work. "What is his business?"

"Oh, it's somethin' way up north," Reggie replied vaguely. "I don't have any 'and in that."

"Then what *do* you do for my husband?"

Reggie smiled benevolently down at her. "Oh, anything the guv wants."

Messalina sighed. Obviously she'd get no straight answers from Reggie. "I'm afraid I've lost our subject: the state of the house. Have you shown me all the rooms?"

The big man screwed up his face, squinting. "There's the top floor—attics and servants' quarters—and the lower with the kitchens and storerooms, but I'm supposin' you're not that interested 'bout those?"

Messalina rather wished that were the case. She glanced at Bartlett.

The maid looked apologetic. "Best you see for yourself, ma'am."

"I suppose I should if we're ever to have a decent meal," Messalina muttered. Lunch had been more bread and butter and the regrettable tea. "Very well. Reggie, if you'd show us the way?"

They tramped along a corridor to the back of the house where the kitchens lay. Messalina frowned as she paused at a door she didn't remember seeing before. "Good Lord, this house is a maze. What room is this?"

She reached for the doorknob but was stopped by a male voice.

"Don't."

The word was growled from behind her, and Messalina turned to meet Hawthorne's demonic gaze.

Her pulse leaped nervously at the sight of him. How had he sneaked up behind them in the passageway?

"That room is mine," her husband said. "You do not have my permission to enter it."

She stiffened, hurt at his brusque tone. "If that is what you wish."

"It is." His glance at Reggie was unfriendly, and the big man shuffled his feet as if he'd been caught out in some wrong. "I'm surprised that Reggie brought you here—he's supposed to be guarding you, not serving as tour guide."

Reggie went a deep red. "Won't 'appen again, guv."

"No, it won't," Hawthorne replied. "Off with you." He nodded to Bartlett. "And you."

Bartlett bobbed a curtsy and handed her notebook over to Messalina before leaving.

Messalina waited, lips pursed, the notebook clenched in her hand, until both servants were out of earshot before saying, "Do you plan to keep me locked up forever?"

His wicked eyebrows winged up as he took her arm. "Locked up? What are you talking about?"

"You set Reggie to guard me," Messalina replied sweetly.

He shook his head as he guided her back down the hall. "Reggie isn't here to keep you from leaving Whispers. He's here to keep you from harm."

Messalina let him take her to the main staircase. "What sort of harm?"

"Your uncle, for one," he said as they mounted the stairs.

She glanced at him swiftly. His upper lip was curled in a sneer.

"My uncle has already married me off," she said slowly. "What else could he do to me?"

"I have no idea," Hawthorne said grimly. "That's what worries me. You're *my* wife now. I'll not let him set one finger on you."

She eyed him with surprise. "You don't like him."

"I've worked for him for over a decade." He slanted an ironic look at her. "Did you think I had any fondness for him?"

"Well, no," she said, thinking it over. "But you've *stayed* with him."

He halted on the upper hall, watching her almost with pity. "It's not easy to leave the employ of the rich and powerful."

She lifted her chin. "You don't consider yourself powerful?"

His grin was quick and dangerous as he stepped closer to her. "Oh, I can make a man piss himself with fright, have no doubt, but is that really the same as your uncle manipulating *Parliament*?"

She pursed her lips. "No. You're quite right."

His eyebrows winged up as if he were surprised she'd agreed. His black eyes were suddenly intent as he watched her.

"Never forget," he said softly. "No matter the duke's power, I will keep you safe. You are...*important* to me."

Her lips parted as her heart gave a silly jolt.

Then she came to her senses. "My *money* is important to you, you mean."

"No, I meant what I said. You..." He touched the bottom of her chin with his fingertips, a line between his wicked eyes almost as if he were puzzled. "I can't look away from you. Your bravery, your pride, the desire that sometimes whirls in your eyes." His nostrils flared as if he were *inhaling* her. "The way you laugh—from your belly, unrestrained. With all your heart. No matter how I try, my gaze returns to you. Always you."

She couldn't breathe. His words sounded as if they'd been drawn from the very depths of his being. All thought fled. He was dangerous. Dangerous and *evil*.

Yet she still felt his pull.

"You *must* be lying," she whispered desperately.

"I am not."

She closed her eyes so that she could no longer see his lips, his wicked eyebrows, and those damned black eyes.

But she couldn't shut out his voice, low and rasping. "*Messalina.*"

"No." She raised her eyelids. "We agreed on waiting for—"

"Bedplay," he interrupted. "I'm not talking about that." He sighed. "Come. Let's eat supper."

She nodded at once. Placing a table between him and her was a very good idea indeed.

He bowed, waving his hand toward what must be the dining room. Inside was a small table by the fireplace set with various dishes.

Messalina stopped short. "Where did this all come from?"

"A very mysterious place," he murmured as he pulled out a chair for her. "It's called the *kitchen.*"

Well, she supposed she deserved that.

Messalina sat in the chair, very conscious of Hawthorne standing behind her. For a moment she could've sworn she felt his breath on her neck.

She shivered.

But he was already seating himself to her left at the head of the table.

She carefully set the little notebook on the table. "You *do* have a cook."

"Mm." He cut into one of the pies. "Yes."

She scoffed. "A cook seems so *ordinary*."

"Does it?" His look was ironic. "I hired him for you."

"Oh." She flushed. "But when?"

"Before I went north to fetch you." He thumped a plate down in front of her. It was filled with a gently steaming savory pie. "Naturally I prepared for when you'd be my wife."

She shivered. That he'd done this when she was still at a house party, innocently unaware that he was laying the ground to marry her, was…disconcerting.

She swallowed and found a different subject. "I was beginning to wonder if your cook could bake."

"Why?" Hawthorne poured the wine.

"Because we've only had bread and butter all day."

"What?" Hawthorne looked up at that, frowning.

Was she about to get the cook in trouble? She certainly didn't want that.

She replied more carefully, "Bread, butter, and some tea."

"I'll talk to the cook," Hawthorne said, and then grudgingly, "He worked in a tavern before I hired him. I doubt he's ever made a breakfast or luncheon for a lady."

She knitted her brow. "Why not hire a properly trained cook? Surely that would be easier than trying to instruct a—a barkeep?"

He glanced at her as he passed her a glass of wine. "Easier, yes. But I think my barkeep cook will learn well enough, given time. Besides, hiring a society-approved cook would be more expensive."

"Even with my dowry?" she asked pointedly.

He hesitated a moment, then said, "I have better uses for your dowry than hiring an expensive cook."

Yet Hawthorne wanted to enter London society, she

mused. Did he not know that in order to receive invitations he also had to *invite* people to his house?

But why would he? Hawthorne might lurk on the fringes of the aristocracy, but he wasn't one of them. He'd never moved in their social circles. He was trying to enter a foreign land without learning the language. Strange to think that a man otherwise so capable—so arrogantly sure of himself— might have this one Achilles heel.

She watched Hawthorne as he pushed the side of his fork into the slice of pie on his plate. His hands were long-fingered, deft, and strong. And competent, as if he was experienced in everything he might want to do.

Would he be so *competent* when he took her to bed?

She inhaled and looked away.

No doubt Hawthorne was used to simply putting his mind to a thing and seeing it done. Messalina took a sip of the wine to hide a smirk. She almost wanted to be here when he realized his error.

Hawthorne swallowed a bite of pie and said, "I trust your day was pleasant?"

Were they playing a happy domestic scene? "Pleasant enough, if a bit boring." Should she mention the empty library? But if he wasn't interested in hiring a proper cook, he probably thought books even more frivolous. "And you? What did you do?"

"I met with your uncle," he said without inflection.

And with that she felt the facade of happy domesticity fall.

"Ah," she said, and was quite pleased that she hid the bitterness in her voice. "That mysterious task you're meant to do for him."

He sipped his own wine, watching her over the rim. "Yes."

She cocked her head. "Not a hint of what it is?"

His black eyes glittered like the very devil's in the candle-light as he whispered, "Curiosity can be dangerous."

* * *

Gideon watched as Messalina stiffened, her face closing down, and cursed himself. He was supposed to be seducing his wife, not alienating her with threats.

But the mere thought of Messalina discovering exactly what task he'd been given by the duke gave him chills. Somehow he doubted that she'd ever forgive him the murder of her brother. Though theirs wasn't a marriage of love—*obviously*—the prospect of Messalina actively hating him for the rest of their lives was terrible.

Which meant he had to be very careful that she *never* found out that he had already laid plans to kill her brother. He'd given Pea and his boys the names of several aristocrats and tasked Pea with finding out their haunts. Greycourt's name was buried among the list, the better to hide Gideon's true interest.

His lip lifted in distaste for what he intended to do. Gideon smashed a piece of crust. "I arranged for the rest of your possessions to be packed and brought here."

"Thank you," Messalina replied with suspicious sweetness. "Where do you expect me to put them?"

He lifted his eyebrows. What now? "I was thinking of our bedroom."

She sighed as if terribly burdened. "One usually has chest of drawers, wardrobes, and the like. For that matter I've noticed that the rooms in Whispers are very sparsely furnished." She glanced about the room, which of course held only the table and chairs. "Unless you mean for me to stack my clothes upon the floor?"

He was very tempted to tell her to do exactly that just to see her response, but a saner part of him ruled. "You know that most of London have only one set of clothes?"

"Yes, I know," she said, the color rising in her cheeks. "Do you think if I rend my clothes it would help those people?"

"Rending them, no," he said through gritted teeth. "I merely point out—"

"Besides," she said, "*you* are no longer poor like the vast majority of London."

He set down his wineglass and stared at her. "Your point?"

She lifted her chin. "Merely that you're no longer living in Whitechapel or wherever you were born—"

"St Giles," he cut in bitterly.

"St Giles? Then the rumors are true?" Her eyes were wide with interest, as if Seven Dials were someplace foreign. "Is it also true that you participated in competitive knife fighting?"

Competitive knife fighting sounded like a quite respectable name for a sweaty, bloody sport.

"Yes." His lips curled. "I fought bare chested. Sometimes women came to watch the matches."

"Humph." She sobered, her expression turning lofty.

He found her almost unbearably endearing. "You were about to explain your point?"

"I *know* that many people don't have clothes or shoes or even food," she said slowly. "And I'm sorry for them. But you've employment and have made enough money with my uncle to afford this"—she gestured to the dining room—"mansion, and now you've married me—or rather you married my *dowry*. You're rich." She said the last with the sort of relish that seemed to indicate that she'd scored a blow against him.

He didn't have her dowry, but she was quite correct on one thing.

He was rich.

Gideon leaned back in his chair, letting his eyelids droop lazily as he surveyed her from her neatly coiled black hair to the white expanse of her décolletage before flicking his gaze back up to her lovely gray eyes.

She tilted her head in inquiry.

"I might have your dowry"—or he would have it in any case—"but I married *you*, and it's you I shall bed, not your moneys."

The color rose in her cheeks again, and she caught her bottom lip between her teeth. She looked a little shy—*not* a word he'd normally use for Messalina—and at the same time completely alluring.

One month, he reminded himself, shifting discreetly to accommodate his swelling cock.

She let her poor abused lip go and said, "No, but you can spend it."

He tore his gaze away from her glistening mouth and tried to remember what they were talking about.

He frowned. "What?"

She sighed as if trying to find her patience. "Hawthorne, you may enjoy living in a house without furniture or books or enough servants, but I do not. My sister will be coming to live with us, and there isn't even a bed for her."

He sat forward, reining in his wandering attention. "Very well. You may furnish a room for Lucretia and purchase whatever you need to house your vast collection of clothing."

"And books for your empty library?"

He shook his head. "A waste of money."

"Of course *you'd* think so," she muttered under her breath.

He breathed in and out. "*Messalina.*"

Her eyes widened when she looked at his face.

"You do not want to bait me," he said softly. "I'm not one of your aristocrats. I don't play gently."

"I beg your pardon." She cleared her throat. "If you can assure me of how much I can spend, then I'll take the carriage tomorrow—"

"No," he said with rather more relish than was wise. "You aren't shopping alone tomorrow."

Her eyes narrowed. "Naturally Bartlett will accompany me..."

"If you must, but I think there's no need." He took a bite of the pie, watching her and trying not to smile. "I shall be going with you."

She said in a very level voice, "You're inflicting your presence on my shopping trip."

He tilted his head, considering. "Is 'inflicting' a word that a *devoted* wife would use about her husband?"

"I thought we had agreed on merely content," she snapped back.

He felt a corner of his mouth tilt up. "I shall be very happy to escort my *content* wife to the shops, then." His voice lowered. "And I expect you to adhere to our agreement while we are out."

She looked a bit as if she'd just bitten into a lime. "Naturally."

He helped himself to another slice of the pie. "And whilst we're on the subject, I've procured theater tickets for tomorrow night."

That caught her interest.

She leaned forward. "What is the play?"

"I've no idea."

Her lips parted as if she couldn't believe his words.

His gaze dropped to her mouth, glistening, warm, and *receptive*.

"You purchased tickets for the theater and didn't bother to discover what play you're seeing?" She interrupted his lusty thoughts.

"*We're* seeing," he said with emphasis.

She waved the point aside impatiently. "Yes, yes."

"The play doesn't matter," he said. "The point of attending the theater is to be seen by the aristocracy. Isn't that what your sort does, after all?"

My sort, she mouthed, and then said aloud, "I suppose that's what many people do." She pursed her lips. "This is how you want to enter society?"

"I want to do much more than simply enter *society*." He sneered on the last word. "I intend to be accepted as an equal, to become the confidant of dukes and princes, and of course to find rich aristocrats to invest in my business."

"But..." She stared at him as if he were a dog performing a trick.

He emptied his wineglass and set it down firmly. "*That* is why we'll go to the theater."

"Very well." She sat with her brows knitted for several seconds. Then she shook her head and abruptly rose from the table. "I'm tired. If you don't mind, I'd like to retire to bed."

He looked pointedly at his half-full plate. "I haven't finished my supper."

A small frown crimped those distracting lips. "I have."

He looked at her. "Humor me."

She scowled. "Why should I?"

He sighed. She was the most argumentative woman. "I wanted to surprise you, but you've forced my hand." He raised his voice and called to the shut door. "Sam!"

The door opened and Sam entered, carefully cradling a puppy in his arms.

Messalina sat abruptly.

"What is this?" She sounded confused as she glanced between the boy and the dog, her eyes wide.

Gideon stood and walked to her chair, beckoning Sam over.

"This," he said as he lifted the wriggling animal from the boy's arms and placed it in her lap, "is a puppy. For you."

* * *

Messalina looked at the puppy in her lap. It was small and sleek, an Italian greyhound, if she wasn't mistaken. It was gray all over except for a white line down the center of its nose and a white throat and stomach. But instead of an adult Italian greyhound's graceful demeanor and elegant lines, the puppy had triangle ears much too big for its head and the saddest button eyes she'd ever seen.

It whimpered.

Messalina hardened her heart and looked up into Hawthorne's assessing face. This was a scheme to soften her, she knew. "Are you trying to buy my affections with a puppy?"

"I merely thought you might like him." A corner of that far-too-sensuous mouth twitched. "Besides, I'm sure you're too intelligent to be won over by a puppy."

"Correct." Messalina ignored the silky fur, the pathetic whip tail, and the sad eyes and held out the puppy to Sam.

Sam looked at her with disappointment in his eyes. "Don't you want 'im, ma'am?"

Two pairs of sad brown eyes were staring at her now.

"No," Messalina said briskly and completely untruthfully.

"But ma'am—"

"You mustn't contradict Mrs. Hawthorne," Gideon drawled.

Sam looked crestfallen. "Will 'e 'ave to go away, then, guv?" he asked as he hugged the puppy.

"I'm afraid so," Hawthorne said gravely. "Once Mrs. Hawthorne makes up her mind she rarely changes it."

Messalina's heart contracted. It wasn't as if she didn't like dogs...or little boys.

"Erm..." She cleared her throat and said, "I suppose we might keep him—just for a bit, mind—to see if he will do."

Sam's smile was incandescent.

It made her feel so warm inside that Messalina couldn't help smiling back. "Do you think you can care for him for me, Sam? While I decide if I'll keep him, that is?"

"Yes, ma'am!" the little boy exclaimed before glancing at Hawthorne with wide eyes. "Can I, guv?"

"Yes. *If* you're diligent in your duties." Hawthorne waved the boy and puppy from the room.

Messalina immediately turned on Hawthorne. "Where did you get that puppy?"

His eyebrows rose. "The day of our wedding I asked Reg to find me a suitable puppy for you. Something a lady would like."

"I suppose that was thoughtful," she said gruffly.

"Is that a compliment, Mrs. Hawthorne?" He grinned outright at her.

It came to her that when he smiled naturally, he was devastating.

A good thing, then, that his smiles were rarely real.

"What do you think?" she asked impulsively.

He cocked his head, studying her. "Frankly, I don't trust compliments. When you fling your insults at me, you are honest. The rage lights your face, your cheeks redden, and your eyes glare. I find myself...*provoked*."

"Do you," she said just a tad breathlessly. "I assure you I have no urge to provoke you. But then I find that men are easily stirred to mindless excitement no matter a woman's intent."

"Mindless?" He touched his thumb to his bottom lip, pulling it slightly down. Messalina had trouble looking away. "No. My mind—and my imagination—are fully working."

"Then perhaps you should let both your mind and your imagination rest," she replied tartly. "They seem overfatigued."

The curl of his lips this time was secretive, and yet no less enticing. "I'm so glad that I didn't give you flowers or sweets or jewels. It would have been a terrible slight to your wit."

"But a *puppy* isn't?" she snapped. "I think you should add it to your list of useless gifts."

"No," he said softly. "Not when you looked at that puppy with joy in your eyes."

She bit her lip, knowing she was blushing. What was she to say to that? "I...I..."

He leaned forward across the table and said low, "I would travel to the depths of Siberia to bring that look to your eyes."

She stared at him, her blood thrumming in her ears. She knew he was playing with her, that he was not a truthful man, but those words.

How could any woman defend her heart against him?

"Messalina," he whispered, his voice rough.

She looked away from him, taking a steadying breath. "I—I should retire for the night."

She stood abruptly, nearly sending her chair crashing to the floor, and marched to the door.

Behind her she heard him murmur, "Coward."

Messalina made very sure she didn't react.

Maddening, cunning, awful man! She started up the staircase. The way he made her skin heat, the thoughts flee her head, truly was beginning to worry her. She *knew* he was interested only in her money, but when he said such romantic things to her, she couldn't remember. And when he smiled...when those charming, sensual, much too wicked lips curved and that dimple appeared, she trembled like a veritable ninny.

She had the awful urge to smile back at Hawthorne. To let herself go and laugh.

No. That way lay her total surrender. Her letter ought to reach Freya soon and then—

Messalina stopped with her foot on the top step. Her notebook! She'd left it on the dining room table—and with it the incriminating question she'd written to Bartlett. Hawthorne mustn't read it.

She turned and hurried down the staircase.

She walked swiftly across the hall and halted at the dining room's closed door. What if he'd already picked up the notebook? She exhaled and pushed open the door, her head held high, ready to face down Hawthorne and his terrible charm.

But the room was empty and the little book still on the table. Messalina let out a sigh of relief and crossed the room to pick it up. She turned to leave, but as she did so she heard Hawthorne's voice.

For a moment she thought she would be discovered. Except his voice didn't come from the landing outside, but rather from the servants' door nearly hidden on the other side of the hearth.

Messalina hesitated. She needed to go. Instead she tiptoed

to the door. It was not quite closed all the way, a thin gap showing. She put her eye to the gap.

Hawthorne knelt on one knee, the better to look Sam in the eye. The boy was standing ramrod straight before him. Between the two was the puppy, sniffing at the floor.

"—make sure he doesn't eat something nasty," Hawthorne said seriously to the boy. "You'll have to take him into the garden at least twice between the midday meal and supper. Do you understand?"

"Yes, guv," Sam said solemnly.

"Good," Hawthorne said, laying his hand on the lad's shoulder for a moment. "I'm relying on you, mind."

Sam nodded and bent to pick up the puppy, who immediately licked his chin. "I'll take good care of 'im."

"See that you do." Hawthorne stood. "Off you go, then."

Messalina jerked back, panic beating in her chest. She ran on tiptoes to the door, pushing it open and softly closing it.

She didn't wait to see if Hawthorne had come back into the dining room. She rushed up the stairs, not breaking stride until she was back in her bedroom.

There she leaned against the door, feeling her heart beat hard. Hawthorne was so confusing. She'd thought him a monster just this morning when he'd berated Sam. When she thought he'd sent the boy away. But he hadn't banished Sam. And tonight, he'd been almost fatherly with the boy. Which side of him was real? Or were they both?

She could withstand a violent rogue.

But Gideon's gentleness toward the boy was more devastating to her heart than any flower or jewel.

It might well destroy her.

CHAPTER FIVE

*"Sir Fox," said the tinker with great respect, for
he knew at once that this was no ordinary fox. "I
am most hopelessly lost. Can you guide me from
this wood?"*
*The fox took his pipe from his lips, blew a smoke
ring, and said, "Well, of course I can help you, my
lost tinker. The better question is: Why should I?"* …
—From *Bet and the Fox*

Messalina sat in the carriage the next afternoon surreptitiously studying her husband.

Hawthorne lounged recklessly on the squabs across from her, peeling an orange, his long, nimble fingers utterly distracting. Apparently he'd had no luncheon—or any breakfast, as far as she was aware. Once again he'd disappeared this morning before she'd risen, presumably on whatever mysterious business he did.

This time, however, he hadn't left before *she'd* woken. She'd been roused by movement under her arm. And as her muzzy brain cleared, she'd been mortified to find that she'd somehow come to wrap herself around Hawthorne during the night. She'd frozen at the realization and like a coward had feigned continued sleep.

And the worst thing was, it was so *nice*, lying there, snuggled up to Hawthorne. He was warm, and she felt an intriguing bit of hair beneath her fingers. With her eyes closed and immobile, she wondered if she was touching the hair on his arm or perhaps even hair that might be on his chest. And he smelled...Well, she couldn't describe it, but it was a nice scent. His scent made her feel *safe* and languid somehow.

She'd half expected Hawthorne to take advantage of the situation. To either caress her or mock her body's ill judgment in sleep.

He'd done neither.

Instead he'd quietly slipped from beneath her arm—and knee, good Lord!—and left their bedroom. Almost as if he hadn't wanted to wake her.

Almost as if he cared.

Messalina scoffed beneath her breath. Hawthorne was a bully for hire—cold, cynical, and emotionless. He didn't *care* about another soul in the world.

Except...did she really still believe that? He'd not been emotionless last night with Sam.

He'd not been heartless.

If Hawthorne *wasn't* an unfeeling villain, then her opinion of him had been wrong from the start. And that begged the question: What else had she gotten wrong about him?

Hawthorne glanced up as if aware of her thoughts, and the corner of his mouth quirked. "Orange?"

The segment he held out looked tempting—plump and juicy—but she pursed her lips and shook her head. "No, thank you."

"No?" Her refusal seemed to amuse him. He bit into the segment, the scent of orange bursting into the air. Juice ran down his fingers, and he sucked on a knuckle before popping the rest of the segment into his mouth. "It's quite good."

Her mouth was watering—whether for the orange or

something far darker, she didn't know—but she looked away from him pointedly.

He chuckled, the sound making her stomach tremble, and she couldn't help but glance back at him.

His black eyes met hers. "I don't taint the fruit simply by touching it."

She lifted her chin. "Are you sure?"

His smile this time was hard. "If food could be spoiled by common hands, all of London's aristocracy would be ill. Everything you eat and drink is made and served by the labor of commoners."

She frowned. That hadn't been what she'd meant. Her flippant reply had been a reference to *him*, not his rank in society.

Perhaps it didn't matter at the moment. She'd insulted him in a way that was simply wrong. Her antipathy for him was for his *actions*, not for who he was.

And she no longer was completely certain who he was.

She impulsively held out her hand. "Very well."

He stilled, his demonic eyebrows raised, before he slowly handed her a segment, brushing his fingers across her palm as he did so.

She had trouble keeping her breath even.

She bit into the fruit. He was right. The orange was sweet and acidic on her tongue, a single taste so acute to her senses that she closed her eyes in involuntary bliss. He made a small sound—a grunt or possibly a cut-off expletive—and she opened her eyes again.

He watched her with an expression that made her want to look away. Except she couldn't. His sinful lips were slightly parted and his black eyes were predatory.

She *ought* to be frightened of such explicit male regard.

She swallowed. "It's lovely."

His lips curved almost self-mockingly as he held her eyes. "Oh yes, it is."

Was he talking about her? They were such trite words, but the way he looked at her as he said them...

The carriage jerked to a sudden halt, and she was finally able to tear her gaze away. Outside the window, London bustled by. They were very near Bond Street if she wasn't mistaken.

"Shall we?" Hawthorne asked as he stood.

The carriage door opened, and he climbed down before turning to offer his hand to her.

It was only as Messalina placed her palm in his that she remembered. This would be the first time she'd been in public with Hawthorne as her new husband. Had the news spread yet?

Silly question. This was *London*. Such ripe gossip would've wafted through society like the stink of rotten fruit.

Messalina lifted her chin and took the elbow that Hawthorne offered her.

He turned and nodded to Reggie and a man she'd not seen before, short but muscled. "Stay within ten feet, but wait outside any shops we enter."

Reggie nodded for the both of them. "Guv."

Gideon turned to her. "You look as if you're going into battle," he said. "I had no idea that shopping was such grim business."

"Didn't you?" she replied lightly. "Well, then, you haven't done much shopping, I think."

The summer day was hot and sunny. The carriage was only steps away from Bond Street, and they had to enter the streaming throng in order to make their way. Ladies at the height of fashion strolled arm in arm, footmen or maids following discreetly behind. A gaggle of army officers swaggered by, their voices loud and crass. Young gentlemen in curling white wigs and pink and lavender suits walked along, preening as they caught a lady's eye. A flower girl bawled her wares, violets bundled in newspaper twists in a basket set upon her head. Liveried footmen hurried along on their employers' errands. A sailor, missing an arm and an eye, held out a tin cup in mute supplication.

And on every street corner a gang of small boys with ragged brooms stood in the way of those wishing to cross and demanded pennies to sweep the street clean.

As they neared a cluster of the boys, Hawthorne withdrew a handful of pennies from his pocket and gave one to each. The children scampered into the street, ignoring the shouted threats from a dray driver passing by. They swept with great vigor, though Messalina wasn't entirely sure that the street was any cleaner than before.

She leaned a little closer to Hawthorne. "I would've thought that you'd consider paying the street sweeper boys a waste of money."

She felt him stiffen fractionally. "It's just pennies."

"Mm," she murmured. "And yet it's rather kind of you."

She looked at him just in time to see him make a grimace of irritation. "Kindness has nothing to do with it. I was once a boy like that. The pennies they earn in a day might feed not just them but—"

"Miss Greycourt!"

Messalina stopped. It was either that or walk into the handsome gentleman before them.

Lord Coxson's gaze flicked from her face to Hawthorne's, and her heart dropped as a malicious smirk crossed his face. "Oh, but I beg your pardon. It's Mrs. Hawthorne now, isn't it?"

* * *

His knife slipped into his palm as naturally as breathing.

Gideon narrowed his eyes at the aristocrat blocking the walkway. The man wore a greasy grin beneath an overcurled wig and carried a long ebony cane as an affectation. Gideon couldn't remember his name, but the face was recognizable enough—the lordling had courted Messalina two years ago. His self-importance had set Gideon's teeth on edge. It had been all the more satisfying, then, when Messalina had turned him away.

He could feel Reg and Johnny behind him, and Gideon gave a hand signal meaning *stay back*.

He examined the fop blocking their way.

"Stand aside," Gideon said, and for some reason that made the ass's grin widen.

He'd wipe that grin right off—

Messalina laid her palm on Gideon's chest, surprising him into immobility. "Now, darling, you mustn't be so impatient with well-wishers." She turned to the man with a suspiciously placid smile. "Lord Coxcomb, isn't it?"

"*Coxson*," the man snapped. His grin had slipped.

"I do beg your pardon. Lord Coxson, of course," Messalina replied, waving aside his correction as if his name mattered little. "This is my dear husband, Gideon Hawthorne."

The adoring smile she turned on Gideon made something in his chest trip. *Fool!* She was obviously acting for the dandy.

"Hawthorne." Coxson tapped his forefinger against his chin, making a play out of pretending to think. "Why, don't you work for your wife's uncle? Please tell me if I misremember."

Gideon rolled his shoulder in preparation for—

"Oh dear," Messalina cried, looking concerned. "Forgetfulness at your age, my lord? Indeed, you must see a physician immediately. What if it's a symptom of some concerning—perhaps *fatal*—disease of the mind? I should *hate* to see you die at so callow an age." Coxson frowned, but before he could reply, Messalina pulled insistently at Gideon's arm. "We must be away, but I do thank you for your gracious felicitations on our marriage."

Gideon glanced at her.

Messalina widened her eyes pointedly.

He sighed and reluctantly slipped his knife back up his sleeve as they walked on.

They were several yards distant from Coxson when Messalina whispered, "Was that a *knife* in your hand?"

"Yes."

"You can't stab a man on Bond Street," she hissed.

He glanced at her pinkened cheeks and pulled her closer. "I assure you I can."

"That's not what I mean!"

"No?" He suppressed a smirk. "Then what is?"

She heaved a gusty sigh as if terribly burdened. "You must be on your guard."

"I rather thought I was."

"Oh, my Lord," she muttered under her breath. "Not *that* sort of guard."

"Then?" he demanded. "What are you trying to say?"

She was silent for several steps and he was surprised.

He didn't think her so easily silenced.

She said, slowly, "You need to watch for people like *him*, and you *can't* use your knife, no matter the mockery and sly glances. There'll be more of those, you know, especially if you truly want to somehow enter society. The aristocracy will close on you like wolves on an injured rabbit and tear you apart."

"That's quite a bloody image," he said mildly. Did she really think an aristocrat could ever touch *him*?

She made a sound almost like a growl under her breath.

An elderly gentleman passing them shied away.

Messalina didn't seem to notice. "Doesn't it bother you? The manner in which Lord Coxson looked at you?"

As if he were a worm beneath Coxson's shoe.

Gideon said grimly, "Oh, it bothers me. But unlike you, I'm used to that expression."

She was silent as they strolled up Bond Street.

Finally he said, "Perhaps you think that dirty looks are no more than I deserve."

She said pensively, "I'm not certain anymore what you deserve."

"Aren't you?" He watched her as she seemed to contemplate the matter.

"No," she said, turning to give him a searching glance. "You're so obviously a blackguard on the outside—you seem to revel in it, in fact. And yet I see these glimpses of another man sometimes."

"And what do you think of this other man?" he asked politely, even though he knew well that there was no other man. He was exactly what he appeared—a man who would do anything to get what he wanted.

"I don't know yet. I've only seen him once or twice." She hesitated, then said, "I saw him last night, I think. When you gave Sam the job of taking care of that puppy."

He grunted. "Don't mistake practicality for kindness."

"Practicality would have been dismissing a servant caught stealing."

He frowned at that thought. "Sam has no family. Pea said

that Sam stole the candlestick for a gang of older boys. I doubt they would still be friendly to him were he dismissed. He'd starve on the streets."

"Starve?" Messalina stopped suddenly.

He turned to look at her.

Messalina's eyes were wide in alarm. "But there must be places he could go?"

Gideon shrugged. "The poorhouse. But it's overcrowded and nasty. He might beg on the streets. He'd probably not make enough to feed himself. If he did, any coin he gathered would be stolen from him." Gideon didn't mention the less savory ways a small boy could make money on the streets. "He'd likely be dead within the year."

"That's awful," Messalina whispered. "I suppose I never thought of what happened when a servant is turned off."

"You never had to," he replied, urging her to continue walking.

"No, you're right," she said pensively. "But it makes your decision to keep Sam all the more laudable."

The look she gave him was a new one—one he'd never seen directed at him by her.

She looked approving.

And something within him sank. Because he wasn't a kind or gentle man. He was going to kill her brother.

That didn't matter. What he did for the duke and his marriage to Messalina were separate things. And if she never found out how her brother had died... Well, then it wouldn't affect him. He wouldn't *let* it affect either him or Messalina.

She must never know the price he paid for keeping her.

He stopped and pulled open a door beneath a huge, showy sign that read, *Harrison & Sons Fine Furnishings*.

"After you," he said, letting her precede him.

The room they entered was a wide space lined with all manner of furniture, from tiny ornate tables on spindly legs to massive bed frames with carved posts.

A young, bewigged clerk hurried forward and bowed. "May I be of service, sir, madam?"

Messalina smiled easily at the man. "Not at the moment, no. We would like to look at your wares first."

"Naturally. Naturally. Please let me know at once should you have any questions." The clerk bowed again and went to lurk near the door, most likely the better to pounce on any entering customers.

Messalina inhaled deeply as if tasting fresh ocean air. "Isn't this wonderful?"

Without waiting for his reply, she strolled deeper into the maze of ridiculous furniture. Gideon trailed her, watching her skirts swish as she flitted from piece to piece. She seemed to be in her own dream, delighted by the wealth of choices before her.

Gideon's lips twitched.

Messalina stopped to trace her fingers over the mother-of-pearl inlay on a small table. Both impractical and very, very expensive-looking. "So pretty."

Gideon felt his jaw clench.

As if aware of his silent criticism, she peered up at him through her eyelashes. "You look as if you've swallowed something disgusting."

"Such extravagance"—he gestured at the room—"makes me feel..."

"Miserly?" she cut in, and then, before he could answer, came back with, "Parsimonious? Closefisted? *Penurious?*" A smile was flickering about her lips.

Her smile could stop a man's heart.

"Your vocabulary is excellent, madam," he said drily. "All this makes me uneasy." He laced his hands behind his back as they continued their meander. "It isn't in my plans to furnish my house like a princeling. Why spend money on items made more for show than for function? One eats the same whether on rough boards or on an ebony table."

"That's true, but..." She was silent a moment, and then she said slowly, "You were born poor."

His eyes narrowed. Was she mocking his past? "Yes."

"Did you lack for food?" Her brows knitted; perhaps she was remembering their earlier discussion about Sam.

He laughed shortly, without amusement. "Every day. My mother was a charwoman, among other things." He glanced at her and decided not to mention the nights that Mam had walked the streets. The nights when there was no food to be had and all their coin was gone. Gideon had spent those nights huddled with Eddie under shop bulks or in doorways. Even a bed in St Giles was a penny or two.

"And your father?" Messalina asked softly.

He shook his head. "Never knew him."

"Yours must've been a lonely childhood," she said with far too much sympathy.

That he didn't like. He didn't need her pity. "I had a younger brother, Eddie."

Either she didn't see his distaste for the subject or she didn't care. "Where are your mother and brother now?"

"Both dead." He stopped and said bluntly, "Do you pity me? You needn't. I'm a man grown."

His tone was aggressive, but her voice remained gentle as she answered, "I'm so sorry."

He studied her face. He knew she hated him for forcing her into marriage, but the simple words seemed in earnest. "It was long ago. I hardly remember what they looked like."

Her eyes widened in what seemed like horror. "That only

makes it worse. At least I have miniatures of Mama and Papa and poor Aurelia to remind me of their faces. I don't suppose…"

He laughed, the sound sharp. "There were no miniaturists in St Giles."

She nodded. "I can understand, then, why you are careful with your money. Once you had none at all."

He eyed her, suspicious as to where her words were leading. "What do you mean to say?"

She shook her head as if irritated at herself, walking away. "I…No matter. I shouldn't interfere."

"Messalina."

His growl stopped her. She looked back at him, proud and aristocratic and unreadable.

But then her expression broke and she spoke as if unwillingly, her words urgent. "You aren't that boy in St Giles anymore. He might be inside you, and some aspects of him may never disappear, but you are a wealthy man now. What is more, you wish to enter society. If you are to do that you have to understand that furniture, carpets, draperies, and all the small items that decorate a great house are important not simply for their beauty or comfort, but because society will judge you on how your home is furnished." She stepped closer to him, her hand hovering near his chest as if she would touch him before she let it drop. "You aren't a penniless orphan anymore. Don't live like one."

He shouldn't trust her pretty pleas. She wanted the furniture, and her argument served her wishes. What did she understand of him and his goals?

But.

But Messalina's face was open and strangely vulnerable as she watched him. He shouldn't trust her. He shouldn't.

And yet he did.

"Very well." Gideon took the hand she'd let fall by her side and tucked it into his elbow. "Let us buy furniture, then."

* * *

Two hours later Messalina watched Hawthorne from under her eyelashes. They were in the carriage, returning home after an exhausting but fruitful shopping trip.

He was sprawled on the worn seat cushions across from her, watching her from under his eyelashes, his midnight eyes glittering. "Satisfied?"

"You know I'm not," she said crisply. "I told you that you'll need far more furniture for Whispers if you want to entertain the ton."

No emotion crossed his face. "I see no need to throw balls or useless parties for my entrance into society. It's a waste of both my money and my time."

He dismissed her by staring out the window, arms crossed against his chest, long legs taking up far too much room in the carriage.

His stubbornness shouldn't bother her. She would be gone from his house and his life in less than a month now. And yet she couldn't help replying, "But that's the way things are done in the aristocracy. There's an introduction, polite discussions over several social meetings, a sort of dance between the partners, studying each other before the subject of business is even broached."

He snorted. "The aristocracy are terrible at business—it takes them too long to come to the table."

She pressed her lips together. *This wasn't her problem.* "You are possibly the most obstinate man I know."

He turned to look at her, his wicked eyebrows slanting

devilishly. "And you are the most stubborn woman I've ever met."

She widened her eyes in mock innocence. "You've known so many women, then?"

"A few." His sinful lips curved at some memory.

Damn him.

She could feel the heat invading her cheeks, but she pressed on. "Were they women who were able to speak their minds freely to you?"

"What do you mean?"

"If they were beholden to you, they could hardly tell you what they thought of you," she pointed out. "Servants, shopkeepers, ladies who, er…"

She floundered a bit at that point.

"Whores, you mean." He was watching her still.

She nodded stiffly, refusing to look away from him. "Yes. Mistresses and streetwalkers. They are paid companions and thus are hardly likely to speak ill of you."

"No woman has ever had occasion to speak ill of me." His eyelids lowered, his face impossibly voluptuous.

She narrowed her eyes at him. "Except me."

"Except you." He cocked his head mockingly. "But then you haven't seen the best of me."

"No, I haven't," she replied, leaning forward as the carriage swayed around the corner. "If—*if*—there is a good side to you. If there is something redeeming within you, why haven't you shown it to me? Why did you hide your kindness to Sam?"

He shrugged, glancing away from her stare. "I don't hide anything. I'm surprised you're interested in the boy."

She inhaled. "You think I wouldn't care about the welfare of a small boy?"

His lips twisted. "A small *poor* boy."

She felt the insult like a blow to her stomach. "I assure you," she said, "that Sam's station in life doesn't matter to me."

"Doesn't it?" His expression was cynical.

"No."

"As you will."

She fumed silently as the carriage rattled through London. Why would he think so badly of her? Or did he have the same jaded view of everyone?

"I don't understand you," she burst out. "I can't tell if you are simply a villain or if you're something more."

His upper lip lifted as he drawled, "It's easier for you to think of me as a villain, isn't it?"

"It is." She stared at him. "I'm still not sure you're not the villain, frankly."

"Mm. Have you noticed that villains have no thoughts of their own?" He spread his hands and tilted them toward his own chest. "They are there only to be hated."

"Is that what you want to be?" she asked softly. "Hated?"

He thought and then shrugged. "It doesn't matter if I wish to be hated or not. I'm not the one who decides."

She bit her lip, glancing down at her lap. Had she wronged him in thinking him a villain? But his actions toward her *were* villainous. This might be only a ruse to confuse her—a more subtle form of persuasion than the puppy. She simply couldn't tell.

She looked back up at him. "What happens if I decide that you're not a villain?"

He blinked—a small sign, almost unnoticeable, but she caught it. "Nothing."

She cocked her head, feeling as if she'd scored a point in this obscure game. "Truly?"

He simply watched her, not answering, but his black eyes seemed puzzled.

Messalina smiled at him, suddenly feeling quite cheerful.

The carriage stopped, and she glanced out the window and saw they were back at Whispers.

Hawthorne helped her from the carriage and accompanied her into the house, where he hesitated a moment.

He seemed to come to a decision. "I want to show you something."

He held out his arm, and though she was a bit suspicious, her curiosity won out.

She placed her palm on his arm.

They walked back through the house, past the mysterious door she wasn't allowed to open, and to the kitchens.

As Hawthorne ushered her into the kitchens, a young redheaded man caught sight of them and jumped up from the stool where he'd been sitting.

"Guv!" the young man exclaimed. He was tall and thin and carried himself awkwardly, as if he didn't know what to do with all his long limbs.

Beside him was a girl who couldn't be more than twelve or thirteen. She simply gawked at them, her hands tangled in her apron.

"Stand down, Hicks," Hawthorne said.

But Messalina was distracted by what she saw near the fireplace. She walked over, Hawthorne following her.

Curled up there was Sam, asleep on a pallet with the puppy draped over his chest, the animal's small head nestled into the boy's neck.

Messalina turned to Hawthorne and whispered, "You are shameless."

Hawthorne cocked a brow.

She huffed, turning back to the sleeping boy and puppy. They were simply adorable.

"Shall I wake them?" he asked.

"No, let them be," she said. "I'd rather talk to your cook instead. Where is he?"

His lips twitched as if he knew a joke she did not.

"Actually, I was about to introduce you to him." He took her hand and turned her around so that she faced the redheaded youth. "This is Hicks, my cook."

"Ma'am," Hicks said, nervously fiddling with a wooden spoon and then dropping it.

He hastily bent and retrieved it, his cheeks now redder than his hair.

Messalina felt her eyes widen. Hicks couldn't be more than twenty or so. No wonder he had no idea how to make a proper breakfast—or indeed anything other than pies, it seemed. This morning she would've berated the cook and told him that his services were no longer needed.

But that was *before* her afternoon with Hawthorne. Before she'd found out how dire it might be for a person out of work in London.

And before she'd seen Hicks's wide blue eyes.

Messalina took a bracing breath and said to Hawthorne, "Would you excuse me, please? I'd like to discuss the meals with Hicks."

Hawthorne seemed to search her eyes for a moment, and then he leaned forward, murmuring in her ear, "Don't forget I'm taking you to the theater tonight."

He was out the door before Messalina had fully recovered from his hot breath against her cheek. She stared after him, absently touching her fingers to her cheek.

Hicks cleared his throat awkwardly. "'Ow can I be of service, ma'am?"

Messalina turned to him. "I thought we should discuss breakfast."

Hicks gulped, his prominent Adam's apple bobbing. "Yes, ma'am?"

She smiled. "Have you ever made shirred eggs?"

"Uh…"

"What about kippers?"

His eyes widened in what looked like alarm.

"Chocolate? Buttered kidneys? Porridge?"

Hicks shook his head at each item.

"Well." Messalina felt her smile slipping a bit, but she continued briskly, "Time enough for you to learn those dishes. Perhaps we should start with something more—"

She was interrupted by the patter of tiny paws. The puppy came gamboling over, his tail wagging so madly his entire rear end wriggled.

"Oh," Messalina said softly, and bent to catch him in her arms. His little body felt almost boneless, his puppy fur rippling beneath her fingers as she scratched his neck gently. "You are terribly beguiling."

The puppy licked her fingers and then tried to nibble.

"No biting," she said sternly, tapping him on the nose.

The puppy looked confused and then began squirming.

She put him down, and he raced back to his pallet, where Sam was sitting up sleepily.

Sam caught sight of her and his eyes widened. "Ma'am." He scrambled to stand, looking worried. "I'm sorry. I didn't mean to fall asleep."

"That's quite all right." Messalina made sure her voice was reassuring. "Has he been good today?"

Sam looked down uncertainly at the puppy, now wrestling one of his shoes. "'E's been doing 'is duty *mostly* in the garden." The boy looked at her earnestly. "'E's right clever and 'e's *trying* not to bite."

The puppy lost his grip and fell over before taking an interest in his own tail.

"He does seem very clever," Messalina said gravely. "I wonder what I should name him."

Sam opened his mouth and then shut it.

"Hmmm." Messalina tapped her finger against her lips, making a show of considering the matter. The boy stared at her urgently. "Sam, do you have any ideas?"

"Daisy!" Sam exclaimed, as if the name had been bottled up in his throat and he'd just uncorked it. "Cause 'e likes to sniff them in the garden."

Messalina blinked and looked at the puppy, who was now attempting to catch his own tail. The puppy toppled over again with a squeak.

Messalina's lips twitched. "Then Daisy it is."

Sam grinned happily up at her and Messalina felt warm. As if she'd single-handedly brought joy to the little boy.

At that moment Daisy began circling and sniffing the floor with purpose.

"Erm," Messalina began, alarmed.

"Daisy, come 'ere!" Sam ran for the door leading into the garden.

Thankfully the puppy chased him.

"Sorry, ma'am," Sam said at the open door, "'e's going to—"

"Yes, yes, go on." Messalina waved him out the door.

When she turned back, Hicks looked surprised but respectful. "Thought that dog would never learn to go outside for 'is...erm, duty."

"Then Sam must be doing a good job," she replied. "Now. Why don't we start with something simple? Have you ever boiled an egg?"

When Hicks's face fell, Messalina took a deep breath.

Good thing she'd watched her nursemaid make soft-boiled eggs almost every day in the nursery.

She set to work. Her smile was wide, her attention seemingly all on Hicks...or so she hoped. For inside, her mind had turned to the problem of Hawthorne. She was letting him in, finding herself too interested in how his mind worked, becoming sensitized to his nearness, his eyes, the wicked way he smiled at her. And all that?

Was dangerous.

* * *

Julian doffed his tricorne as he entered the small inn. Water spilled out from the curled brim and spattered into the puddle already on the flagstones.

He huffed and made his way to the tiny private room at the back of the inn.

"Well?" Lucretia immediately asked as he entered.

Quinn sat beside her with a tankard in his fist.

Julian shook his head and pulled a chair closer to the fireplace. "The road's a river. The coachman refused to drive on it, and there's no other road that will take a carriage."

"Oh, but we can't wait another day!" Lucretia looked near tears.

"I'm sorry." Julian took a moment to wipe his face with an already-sodden handkerchief. He hated the delay just as much as she, and were he alone he might try riding to London.

But he *wasn't* alone. He had Lucretia and Quinn with him, and while Julian *ought* to be able to leave his sister with his brother...Julian glanced at Quinn's nodding head. How many tankards had he drunk already?

Julian sighed. If only he could find out how Aurelia

had died that night fifteen years ago. How was the duke involved, had Ran truly killed her, and had it been murder or an accident? Perhaps if he discovered the truth, Quinn could have some peace.

He shook his head and glanced at Lucretia. "I've ordered dinner. We'll stay here the night and leave when the roads are drier in the morning." He caught Lucretia's disappointed look. "I'll save her from whatever nefarious plans the duke has. I promise."

CHAPTER SIX

*The tinker felt for his purse and spilled its meager
contents into his palm. "I've money."
The fox grinned. "What good is your money to me?"
The tinker spread out the bundle holding his tools and
wares: hammers, shears, nippers, a tin cup, two pie
pans, and various bits and pieces of solder and tin.
But the fox shook his head before the tinker could
speak. "I have no use for such."...*
—From *Bet and the Fox*

That night Messalina frowned at herself in the small mirror
on her new dressing table. She'd spent the rest of the afternoon with Hicks and the little scullery maid, whose name
turned out to be Grace. Fixing the problem of their meals
had turned out to be relatively easy. She'd shown Hicks how
to boil an egg and set about finding a more experienced cook
to teach him the craft.

Hawthorne and her feelings for him presented a bigger
dilemma.

Which was why she frowned now.

"Is the way I've dressed your hair not to your liking,
ma'am?" Bartlett asked from behind her.

Messalina met the maid's eye in the mirror and hastened to
smile. "It's quite lovely. I was thinking of something else."

Bartlett nodded and resumed placing two jeweled pins.

Messalina's smile slowly drooped. Ridiculous to spend the beginning of the afternoon *enjoying* her husband's company like some brainless ninny. She could not forget that Gideon Hawthorne was using her. He kept secrets. She still didn't know what was in that locked room by the kitchens. He hadn't told her what Uncle Augustus wanted of him.

Really, she knew very little about Hawthorne.

Except…he'd been kind to Sam. He'd hired Hicks to cook even though the boy had hardly any skills. And what was more, he'd *listened* to her as she presented her case for buying furniture—truly listened, as if her ideas and thoughts were as important as a man's.

As important as his own.

Men never did that. Oh, a gentleman at a social event might smile and nod as a lady babbled about frocks and gossip and the weather, but should she offer her opinion on something more serious—politics, philosophy, literature— his eyes would go blank. He'd gaze over her shoulder. He'd fidget. And—if he had nothing to gain from listening to her—he would simply walk away.

Men didn't value women for their *thoughts*.

How odd to realize that even her brothers rarely engaged her in serious discussion.

And yet Hawthorne—a man without education, from the streets of St Giles—had valued her enough not only to listen, but to be *swayed* by her argument.

Such consideration was seductive.

The thought made Messalina uneasy. She had to remember that her plan was to *leave* Hawthorne. To get as far away from both him and her uncle as she could. It was her only chance to live her life freely.

Wasn't it?

"There now." Bartlett stepped back from Messalina and examined her handiwork. "I think that's quite elegant, if you don't mind me saying so, ma'am."

Messalina turned her head from side to side to better examine herself in the mirror. Bartlett had pulled most of her hair into a simple knot at the back of her head, but the hair near her face had been curled into loose ringlets. The butterfly pins set with diamonds, garnets, and yellow gems were placed to highlight the curls.

Messalina touched one of the little pins. "You've done a superb job as always, Bartlett. I quite like how you've used Mama's jeweled butterflies."

"Thank you, ma'am," Bartlett replied briskly. "The pearl earrings?"

"Yes."

Bartlett went to the open jewel box and retrieved the earrings, then bent over Messalina to affix them. "Had I two more lady's maids, we would've dressed you within an hour or less."

"I know," Messalina replied, wincing. They'd been in the bedroom for two hours. "You've done a marvelous job on your own."

Hawthorne really needed to hire other servants. A large house simply could not be run without them. She made a mental note to try again to persuade him.

Except... she was *leaving*. What did it matter to her if his house collapsed from lack of servants?

She suddenly wondered if Bartlett would want to come with her and Lucretia. The lady's maid had never protested travel, but of course they always returned to London. If they journeyed abroad, would Bartlett be willing to leave England? Did she have family?

"Bartlett?"

"Ma'am?" The maid was busy positioning a curl.

"Where do you come from?"

The maid glanced up into the mirror, looking startled. "Why, I was born near Oxford, ma'am. My mother was a maid and my father a butcher."

"Do you still have family there?"

Bartlett smiled. "A sister. She writes me often and tells me of her children—a boy and a girl."

"Sisters are so important, aren't they?" Messalina said softly, thinking of both Lucretia and Aurelia, forever lost to them now.

"Yes, indeed," the maid replied.

Had Lucretia reached Julian yet? Or was she still trying to find him? Messalina sighed and rose. "We shouldn't be too late. A little after midnight, perhaps?"

"Aye, I'll be waiting, ma'am," Bartlett replied as she busily put away the toilet items.

Messalina paused by the door. "Thank you, Bartlett."

"Ma'am." Bartlett bobbed a curtsy.

Messalina started down the stairs, contemplating how many years she'd employed Bartlett without knowing she had family in Oxfordshire. How could she have been so unaware of Bartlett? It was as if she'd gone through life wearing a scarf wound round her eyes, and now that scarf had fallen.

Or rather, Hawthorne had pulled the scarf from her eyes.

She saw him then, waiting in the entryway of Whispers, and for a moment her breath caught as she was struck anew by how magnetic he was. Hawthorne stood there, his long legs braced apart, his arms crossed, his full mouth curving just slightly at the sight of her.

She *must* remember that she couldn't trust him. That if she did, all her hopes and dreams not only for herself, but for *Lucretia* would be lost.

She braced herself as she descended the last steps. She would *not* react to him.

Belatedly she noticed what he was wearing—the exact same suit he'd worn that afternoon. At least it looked the same. Black coat, waistcoat, and breeches without any ornamentation at all. Did he *have* any other suit? Whyever hadn't he changed for the theater?

He walked toward her, moving with a feline sort of grace that made her swallow.

He held out his hand. "You are beautiful, Mrs. Hawthorne."

Her silly, silly heart leaped at his words. She'd heard the same thing or similar from countless gentlemen, usually in much more flowery terms, but when Hawthorne said it with his black eyes glinting wickedly...

She swallowed and curtsied, taking his hand. "Thank you."

Had her voice shaken? Lord, she hoped not.

He led her to the door, and she glanced down at her hand on his plain black wool coat sleeve.

Should she tell him he ought to change his suit? But surely he must know that people of quality wore, if not their best, then certainly clothing to be seen in when they visited the theater?

She glanced sideways at him as he opened the door, gesturing for her to precede him. She hesitated. Was he so arrogant as to defy all convention? If he planned to move in aristocratic society, he needed to dress as someone who *belonged*.

He raised a slanting eyebrow. "Is there a problem?"

It was on the tip of her tongue to tell him. But then she remembered that he'd lived all his life without her advice.

He didn't need her.

Messalina shook her head and proceeded through the door.

* * *

Gideon watched Messalina's face as the carriage jolted over cobblestones. Since they'd left the house she'd grown quiet and was avoiding his gaze.

What else had he expected? One afternoon of something like a truce was not enough to make up for what had come before. Messalina was a proud, stubborn woman who knew her own mind. She wouldn't be swayed into accepting him as a husband so lightly.

He needed patience.

Still he found himself searching her eyes when he handed her down from the carriage some five minutes later. She smiled slightly and his chest flooded with warmth.

Fool.

Gideon nodded at Reg, sitting in the box beside the driver. Earlier he'd ordered Reg to stay with the carriage when they went into the theater. A brace of bodyguards was too conspicuous.

Gideon was very aware of Messalina's smaller body beside his as she shook out her skirts. The summer air was still warm from the day, and the night was alight with lanterns and torches. The classical facade of the theater was thrown into bright light and people crowded the steps.

Gideon held out his arm to her. "Ready?"

She glanced up at him as she laid her fingers on his forearm, her eyebrows arched pointedly. "Yes. Are you?"

He felt the corners of his mouth curl, the scent of bergamot teasing his nostrils. Within the theater before them lay his quarry. His pulse quickened at the thought, the coming hunt. But he had no need for nerves.

How could he fail with her on his arm? "We'll find out, won't we?"

Inside the theater the air was warm with the press of bodies and the heat of dozens of candles from three grand chandeliers. Gideon made for the stairs, aware as they moved that heads were turning to look at them. They left a trail of murmurs in their wake.

He glanced out of the corner of his eye at Messalina. She held her head high, a faint smile playing about her lips.

He bent to her, murmuring in her ear, "Very good."

Her breath caught, but she said only, "I'm so glad you approve of me."

"I do," he replied. "I approve of your grace, your intelligence, and your strength. I don't approve of your stubbornness, but I confess, I like it."

That got him an indignant sniff. "Where is your box?"

"Third level," he said, and added to provoke her, "Intimate and discreet. I inspected it myself when I bought the tickets."

"Hardly discreet, since it overlooks the theater," she replied tartly with her smile still in place.

"I assure you," he drawled lazily. "I can most certainly find a way to be intimate."

She glanced at him sharply. "The people across the way can certainly see us."

"Yes." His lips twitched. "But only above the waist."

For a second her face was perplexed, and then bright pink flooded her cheeks, making her look young and unbearably pretty and he wanted...

He looked away. He had a plan, a series of steps to get what he wanted. Finding himself enthralled by his wife was not one of them.

He had to keep his head.

He was still thinking over the matter when they reached

a landing on the stairs and a matron in a deep-orange gown and lavender-powdered hair cried out, "Messalina! I didn't know you had returned to town."

An outright lie, judging by the eager expression on her face as she stared at Gideon.

"Lady Gilbert," Messalina replied sedately. "May I introduce my husband, Gideon Hawthorne?"

"Hawthorne? Hawthorne?" Lady Gilbert's watery blue eyes turned sly as she held out her hand to him. "Why, I don't remember any Hawthornes. Tell me, who are your people, Mr. Hawthorne?"

Messalina stiffened beside him.

Gideon took Lady Gilbert's hand and bowed over it, not *quite* touching her knuckles. "My people are terribly scandalous, my lady." He straightened and let his lips spread into a dangerous smile. "I come from thieves, whores, and murderers."

"Oh my!" Lady Gilbert looked positively giddy with excitement.

Messalina's face was blank as she nodded to the woman. They moved past Lady Gilbert and mounted the stairs.

"She'll spread what you said," Messalina muttered. "Everyone in the theater will be talking by the end of the play."

"Let them."

He felt her glance at him. "You want *everyone* to know your past?"

"There seems very little point in trying to hide it, so I've decided not to bother." His lips twisted. "I won't apologize to anyone for my birth."

They would know exactly what he was—and why they should fear him.

She was silent a moment and then said softly, surprising him, "No. You're quite right."

They came to the third floor, and he stopped and looked at her.

Messalina met his gaze, and he saw that her clear gray eyes were defiant. "It's not your *birth* I object to."

"No?" He leaned closer to her, inhaling bergamot. "Perhaps you should detail my flaws in our box."

She scoffed. "That would take all night."

He snorted.

She was witty, his wife.

Too witty. He was in danger of forgetting his mission here.

The thought made him uneasy. He couldn't lose his drive, his pride, *himself* in her.

They'd reached the rented box, and he pulled back the curtain for her, letting her enter first.

The box was almost over the stage, and from it they could see not only the actors but the milling audience in the center of the house. Gideon seated Messalina before taking his own chair and glancing about. He'd had information from Pea and his gang that the Earl of Rookewoode, Sir Barnaby Bishop, and Viscount Hardly would be attending tonight, yet Gideon couldn't make out any of the men.

His gaze was drawn back to the stage. Several performers were dancing about, but no one appeared to be paying any attention to them.

Gideon frowned. "I thought the play had begun."

He felt Messalina glance at him. "It has. Or rather the entertainments before the main play have begun."

"Ah. Of course." He nodded curtly.

People were still entering the theater, and half the boxes were empty. In the occupied boxes, more than one pair of eyeglasses was aimed at him.

He showed his teeth.

"Have you not been to the theater before?" Messalina asked softly beside him.

He glanced at her.

She looked at him curiously, but without any sort of scorn.

"No," he said.

Her eyes raked his form, and she pressed her lips together as if repressing words.

Then she relaxed, her smile mocking. "You don't enjoy the entertainments?"

"I haven't the time for entertainments."

She cocked her head, drawing his eyes to the long, sweet line of her neck. The dress she wore tonight exposed the upper mounds of her breasts. Her skin was so white it seemed to glow in the theater's candlelight. "No entertainments at all?"

What was she probing for? "No."

She stared at him. "Music?"

He felt his mouth flatten. "No."

"Gambling games?"

He arched a brow. "Gambling—or rather *other* men gambling—is a business for me, nothing more." He glanced back to the audience. "Or it was. I'm moving into different endeavors now."

"What—?" She shook her head. "No, I shan't be diverted. What about books?"

He stiffened, turning to meet her eyes. "I can read, if that's what you're asking."

"I'm asking if you read *books*," she said gently.

He'd never reached that skill with his letters—how could he when he'd never had schooling? But he held her gaze. It was too humiliating to confess his weakness. "No."

She was silent a moment, and a great roar of laughter rose from the audience.

Gideon glanced at the stage. One of the players was bent, his coattails lifted to expose his buttocks to the audience. The player was swaying from side to side.

Gideon blinked. Was this really what the aristocracy enjoyed?

"Is there anything in your life you do simply for...amusement?" Messalina asked.

He turned to her, honestly confused by her questions. "Why? I work for my bread. You know that."

"Mm," she hummed. "I do know that. You've made it more than plain. But most people, even the absolute lowest among us, find ways of playing. I've seen ragged boys throwing knucklebones on the street. I've seen two old beggars singing together. I've seen a scullery maid use a month's pay to buy a book. Really, I'm not sure that working for your bread has anything to do with it."

He shook his head, glancing back at the stage, where a vigorous sword fight with wooden swords was under-way. Impossible to explain to her his drive to gain money and power. How could she understand—she who had never wanted for food or shelter?

He drew a breath. "I cannot let *play* distract me from my goals."

She was silent a moment, then said, "That sounds like a very dull life."

Gideon looked at her. Messalina's gray eyes were wide and sincere.

"What do you like?" He cleared his throat. "For enter-tainment?"

"Books." Her lips quirked, and she leaned a little closer to him, as if she were telling him a secret. He could see the swirling gray of her irises. "And not the instructive type. I like scandalous biographies and the tales travelers tell of strange foreign countries, and I *love* terrible tragedies with innocent heroines."

He could just imagine her curled in the corner of a

library, reading her books. Something about the image drew him, and he was puzzled. It was a picture of Messalina not under his sway, not helping him to achieve his goals, but simply *being*.

Simply content.

He shook the thought away and said gruffly, "I suppose a few books in the library at Whispers wouldn't be amiss."

Her smile was glorious. "Thank you."

He couldn't stop himself asking, "Are books your only pleasure?"

"Oh, of course not. I enjoy listening to music, though I have no talent myself, and my voice is quite atrocious, my sister assures me. I like the theater"—she nodded at the stage—"and opera and really most entertainments. Riding is a pleasure, as is strolling, especially if it involves shopping. I *adore* shopping, as I think you now know." Her mouth twisted wryly. "After all, unlike you, I don't need to earn *my* bread. My time is entirely free to do as I wish with. You must think me—my family and the aristocracy as a whole— such lazy beasts."

He pressed his lips together at that because the aristocracy *were* lazy beasts. He'd always known that.

But he didn't want to hurt her.

"I think," he said carefully, "that most of humanity is born to labor. A very few are born lucky and never know want. The latter often confuse luck with divine righteousness."

She said softly, "I'm not sure what you mean?"

He looked at her and saw that her head was tilted inquisitively.

He frowned. "Many of your peers think that they come by their birth—their *lucky birth*—because they are superior to the common man. That being born rich means they are more intelligent, better able to lead, and have a better sense of morality. That God or whatever divinity they believe in made them so and put them on the earth to rule over other, lesser people." His lip curled slowly. "They are wrong. God does not crown kings. Mankind does."

Her lips had parted during his diatribe, and she looked at him now almost in wonder. "You are a philosopher, sir."

His eyes narrowed in suspicion. "You mock me."

"No." She laid her hand over his on the arm of the chair. "No, I am not mocking you. You yourself said that no man is better than another by right of birth. It seems to me, then, that the reverse must be true as well. No man is *worse* than any other because of his birth. And that means that you, Gideon Hawthorne, my uncle's henchman, might be a philosopher every bit as intelligent as those who write learned books."

Her smile was teasing, but her words were serious.

And they moved him.

He turned his hand over so that he grasped her delicate fingers, raising them to brush his lips against her knuckles.

Her fingers trembled. He had a sudden wish that they were somewhere else—somewhere private—where they could spend the evening discussing the books she read and the differing thoughts they had. Where he might, at the end of the night, taste the rose red of her lips.

Instead of doing the work he needed to do tonight.

But that was impossible, so he said, "I'm lucky to have you as my wife, madam."

She raised a brow. "I think *luck* had very little to do with it."

He was about to retort when the curtain of the box opened behind them and two people entered.

The Duke of Windemere stood there, his smile disarmingly benevolent. "Ah, I was told I might find you here. The gossips are in full cry in the lobby." The old man's gaze speared Gideon. "I say, Hawthorne, didn't your loving wife tell you to dress for the theater?"

"I did not expect to see you this evening, Your Grace." Gideon pulled his hand from Messalina's grasp, curling his fingers into fists. He forced a smile to his lips. "And in my box. I'm honored, of course, but surprised you're out so late. At your *age*, I mean."

Windemere didn't like that at all. Any mention of his mortality reminded him of who would succeed him.

The duke's upper lip curled into a soundless snarl.

Gideon rose to bend over the duchess's hand. She was a meek little thing, the third of Windemere's wives, and, like the others, childless, despite three years of marriage. "Your Grace. I trust you are in good health?"

The duchess blushed. She couldn't be more than two and twenty. "Oh, erm...yes. Quite. Thank you."

She darted a nervous look at her husband.

The duke ignored her. He'd regained his aplomb and was smiling beatifically at Messalina. "My dear, I haven't seen Lucretia since you and she traveled to the north. I would hate to lose touch with her. It's my duty, as head of this family, to see she marries as well as you did."

Messalina sat still as stone at the clear threat.

Gideon gritted his teeth, fighting an urge to lay the old man flat for distressing her. If they'd not been in the theater—

Messalina stood suddenly and reached out to take the duchess's hands. "Have you enjoyed the play, Aunt?"

The duchess's eyes grew wide. "I don't know."

Messalina smiled. "Come sit by me."

She led the duchess to the far side of the box.

Windemere turned to Gideon and said lower, "I'm surprised that you've found the time for such frivolity as the theater, Hawthorne. I thought I'd set you a task to occupy you, but if you find yourself free, perhaps I should give you another as well."

Gideon raised an eyebrow. What game was the old man playing, discussing this matter in the open? In front of Messalina?

"The *subject* isn't in town yet," he murmured. "And when he is, I will move slowly and carefully. I'm sure"—his words dripped with irony—"Your Grace would hate for me to be caught."

"Oh, naturally," the duke said carelessly, his gaze drifting over Gideon's shoulder.

Gideon felt sweat start at the small of his back. He refused to look behind him to see if Messalina was paying attention to their discussion.

The duke frowned as if disappointed. "Just as long as the job gets done."

"It will," Gideon replied, staring the old man dead in the eye.

"Good." Windemere leaned close to him, washing Gideon's face with the sour odor of his breath. "Because if you don't, I shall destroy you so that you'll never be received in society, my niece for a wife or no."

Gideon didn't think his expression changed, but he must've made some sign.

The duke smiled. "Oh yes, I know of your fantasy of obtaining titled business partners." He cocked his head, watching Gideon. "You're quite insane. Men of your ilk may serve us, may even run our businesses, but that doesn't mean that they"—he gestured to the now-filled boxes—"would ever deign to sup with you. You ought to try being a secretary. With Messalina as your wife you may just be able to attain such a position. But not if I put a word in an ear or two. Do you understand?"

Gideon snarled, leaning into the other man's face. "This works both ways. I *know* you and I've proof. Do *you* understand?"

Windemere's nostrils flared as he whispered furiously, "How dare you. What proof do you have? I'll—"

"It's always lovely to chat with you." Messalina's voice interrupted whatever the old man had been about to say. The ladies had risen and were drawing closer.

Gideon merely smiled.

Windemere cleared his throat. "I'm glad to see that you haven't been distracted by marriage...and its delights."

Gideon lifted an eyebrow at this poor retort.

But before he could comment, Messalina, staring her uncle in the eye, said, "There's certainly more delight for some than others."

Windemere's face convulsed with rage. It was well known that the duke desperately wanted a son.

The duchess turned pale and moved to the old man's side.

He never acknowledged her, instead continuing to glare at Messalina. "I'm so glad you've found yourself satisfied in your marriage, Niece. Come, Ann."

The duchess started to babble a farewell, but he pulled her out of the box before she could finish.

Gideon stared after the old man. He'd assured the duke that he'd fulfill his task. He glanced at Messalina. She was smiling shyly at him.

Could he really kill her brother?

* * *

Messalina watched Gideon after they sat. He'd seemed unperturbed by her uncle's visit, but now his brows were drawn together.

She cleared her throat. "I shouldn't have said that about delight and marriage. Poor Ann. She's quite sweet, you know."

At her words his brow smoothed. "You're fond of her?"

Messalina shrugged, now feeling guilty. "We have little in common, I'm afraid. We tend to discuss fashion when we meet, which isn't often. I avoid my uncle, as you know, and as a result don't see Ann very often." She sighed. "I remember when they wed. Ann looked so young and happy. Their match was the wedding of the season. Now she's like a ghost of her former self."

She shook her head and then realized that Gideon was no longer paying attention to her. He was gazing at the theater, every once in a while scanning the boxes as if searching for someone. Was he working for her uncle now? Intent on finding a certain person and then...

She didn't want to imagine what he would do—what he *could* do.

Most of society—the ones who had not retired to the country for the summer months—were at the theater tonight. Besides Lady Gilbert she could see Mr. and Mrs. Evelyn, Viscount Norbourne, the elderly Henley sisters, and the Holland family accompanied by the Earl of Rookewoode, just sitting down.

Impulsively she asked, "Whom are you searching for?"

"I have information," he said absently, "that several aristocrats I'm interested in will be here tonight."

The curtain to the box parted again and a handsome young man stepped inside. "Hawthorne! I never thought to find you at the theater."

"My attendance is a wonder to all," Gideon replied with a bite to his voice. "Messalina, may I introduce my business partner, Mr. William Blackwell. Blackwell, my wife, Messalina Hawthorne."

Business partner? She'd had no idea Hawthorne had a business partner. Messalina extended her hand, being sure to keep the surprise out of her face. "How do you do?"

"It's a great pleasure to meet you, ma'am," Mr. Blackwell said, bowing elegantly over her hand.

He wore a simple but well-cut nut-brown suit several shades lighter than his hair, which was clubbed back neatly. His eyes seemed iridescent, changing from blue to gray to green.

He slid a sly glance at Gideon. "You could've struck me down with a feather when I heard the news that Hawthorne had wed. He seemed a confirmed bachelor."

"You're hardly one to talk," Gideon returned. "I can't count the number of feminine hearts you've led astray."

"You've painted me a cad," Mr. Blackwell said with mock hurt. "I don't know how I'll gain your wife's favor now."

"Your skills at flirting are quite adequate on their own," Gideon said drily as he stood. "You can practice them while I attend to some matters."

With that Gideon bowed and exited the box.

Messalina couldn't help staring after him with a sense of hurt. He'd not asked her opinion before abandoning her with a virtual stranger.

But what else did she expect? Gideon had made it more than plain that theirs was a union of practicality, not affection. Just because they'd been able to converse amicably this afternoon didn't mean that Gideon had thrown away everything he'd said before.

And that was *good.* Uncle Augustus had threatened Lucretia. Now more than ever it was imperative that they leave just as soon as she had enough money. Nothing could stand in the way of that vow.

"I hope my presence doesn't distress you, ma'am," Mr.

Blackwell said, drawing her wandering attention back to him. "But I couldn't help seeing for myself when I heard that Hawthorne was in attendance tonight. I can leave if it pleases you."

"Not at all," Messalina replied warmly. "Will you have a seat?"

He grinned, revealing charming dimples at the corners of his mouth. "Thank you."

Messalina nodded, thinking of how to phrase all the questions she had for him. "Forgive me my abstraction. I was just wondering how it was that you met my husband?"

"Ah, well, I'm afraid the tale doesn't show me in a flattering light," Mr. Blackwell said, sounding sheepish. "I was in a notorious gambling den some ten years ago when Hawthorne caused a commotion. He was collecting a debt owed to His Grace by a rather disreputable lord. Hawthorne couldn't have been over twenty years at the time, yet he strode into that house as if he were the devil himself, malevolent and sneering. He caught the attention of everyone there."

Messalina couldn't repress a shiver. It wasn't hard to imagine Gideon in that role. "What did he do?"

"He demanded payment from the younger son of a duke." Mr. Blackwell shook his head. "Such establishments don't like those sorts of disruptions, and they have bully boys to guard their houses. Hawthorne fought three of these bullies without turning a hair. By the time he got the money from his blubbering mark, everyone else had fled the table."

Across the way Messalina could see the Hollands and Lord Rookewoode in their box. It appeared to be quite crowded, but someone was trying to push their way to the earl. Surely it couldn't be...?

She realized suddenly that Mr. Blackwell had stopped in his story, apparently waiting for some comment from her.

She cleared her throat, trying to remember what he'd been saying. "And did you flee as well?"

"No." Mr. Blackwell smiled deprecatingly. "I'm afraid I wasn't there to game."

"Why were you there, then?" Messalina asked absently.

It *was* Gideon, and he seemed to be attempting to talk to the Earl of Rookewoode.

Without an introduction.

She watched with a sort of fatalistic horror.

Mr. Blackwell explained, "I'd come to collect on a debt as well, though not nearly as successfully as Hawthorne did. In fact, after observing him obtain his money so easily I approached him on the street afterward and made a rather daring proposition."

He stopped and looked at her expectantly.

Messalina had to tear her eyes away from the box across the way. Something in her chest had seized at the sight. Gideon was in plain clothing, while every other man in the box wore silk. Lord Rookewoode wasn't even looking at him.

She forced a smile for Mr. Blackwell. "What did you propose?"

Mr. Blackwell grinned. "I suggested that he collect my money, and in return I offered to invest some of that amount and a bit of his own money and split the earnings."

She raised her eyebrows in some astonishment. "And he agreed to this?"

She had to fight to keep her gaze on him rather than Lord Rookewoode's box.

"I did rather have to talk him into the partnership." Mr. Blackwell winced. "Which entailed spending *quite* a lot of time in his company."

He stopped speaking for a minute, and Messalina looked at him curiously.

Mr. Blackwell wore a troubled expression. "I don't know if you've noticed, but your husband is a rough man. And a rather...er"—he darted a worried look at her—"*dangerous* man. I hope I don't offend by saying such."

"Of course not," Messalina murmured. Gideon *was* dangerous. There was no point in denying it.

Mr. Blackwell pressed his lips together as if trying to contain himself before blurting, "Please, ma'am, be careful. Your husband has a prodigious temper, and the violence he's capable of is..."

He trailed away, shaking his head.

Messalina stiffened. "I do not need to be warned about my own husband."

He shrank back. "I beg your pardon, ma'am."

Messalina nodded coolly.

"In any case," Mr. Blackwell resumed after an awkward pause. "It took all of my courage to keep returning to Hawthorne until he at last gave in and went to collect my money. I think in the end he did it simply to make me go away."

"I doubt that," she said. "You must've been very persuasive."

She risked a glance at Lord Rookewoode's box, but Gideon was nowhere to be seen. Her heart sank. Why did he care so much that a *gentleman* invest in his business? Surely there were other investors?

"Fortunately, we made money from the start," Mr. Blackwell was continuing. "I doubt Hawthorne would've had the patience to wait for a return on our investment." He stopped abruptly and looked at her with a contrite expression. "But I'm boring you, Mrs. Hawthorne, with this talk of business."

Messalina blinked. She'd been occupied wondering what Hawthorne was doing. Was he going to come back to his box?

She forced a smile and asked lightly, "Do you still invest my husband's money, then?"

"*Our* money, for we're in business together, but yes, that is the majority of my work," Mr. Blackwell replied. "I manage coal mines now as well as keep track of the accounting and—"

Gideon stepped back into the box, holding a cup of what looked like punch. His lips were white and his expression grim. "Are you gossiping with my wife, Blackwell?"

Mr. Blackwell started, staring at Hawthorne's expression.

"Guilty as charged." Mr. Blackwell jumped nervously to his feet. "I'd hate to bore you further, Mrs. Hawthorne. I'll leave you both to enjoy the play."

"Good night," Gideon drawled as he took the chair absented by the other man.

Mr. Blackwell hesitated. "Shall I see you tomorrow?"

Gideon grimaced. "If I've the time."

"I'll look forward to it," Mr. Blackwell said drily. He bowed. "A good evening to you, Mrs. Hawthorne."

Messalina murmured a farewell.

Mr. Blackwell slipped out of the box.

Messalina turned back to Gideon, eyeing him. He still held the cup of punch and was glaring at the boxes across the way. She inhaled. "Is that for me?"

He turned to her, but his gaze was blind for a moment before he seemed to gather himself. "Yes. Here."

He shoved the glass into her hand.

Messalina took a sip and found the drink overwatered.

"I confess I've lost track of the play," she said lightly.

They both turned to look. On the stage a rotund man was chasing a very thin man around a settee, trying to strike him with a rose.

"Perhaps it doesn't matter," Gideon grunted. But as if

almost in spite of himself, he leaned a little forward, intent upon the action.

Messalina felt a wave of . . . fondness? No, that couldn't be. He was a brute, her uncle's henchman. A man comfortable with violence according to Mr. Blackwell, his own friend.

She inhaled, mentally shaking her head. "I noticed," she said carefully, "that you were in Lord Rookewoode's box."

She immediately regretted her words.

"What of it?" Hawthorne's eyes burned with an alien hatred, and his hands were clenched into fists.

For the first time since her marriage she felt . . . *fear* in his presence.

Perhaps she should've paid more attention to Mr. Blackwell's warning.

CHAPTER SEVEN

"This is all I have," said the tinker in despair. "What else can I possibly give you?"
"Hmm," said the fox, gazing contemplatively at the sky. "Well, I could do with a wife, and you, I hear, have a daughter."
"Yes," the tinker replied, trembling. "Her name is Bet."
The fox smiled a very foxy smile....
—From Bet and the Fox

Gideon couldn't keep the loathing from his voice, even as he watched Messalina's face shutter.

Damn Rookewoode and the rest of the bloody, smug aristocracy with him. The man hadn't looked once in Gideon's direction the entire time he'd stood in Rookewoode's box. And the more he'd stood there without acknowledgment, the more Gideon had felt his anger mount, until now he couldn't help but growl at his wife.

But Messalina was a woman who wasn't easily cowed. "Why did you go to Rookewoode's box?"

Gideon gritted his teeth as he stared at the stage. The play, so oddly distracting before, had lost his interest. There was no reason to confide in her. It wasn't as if Messalina would understand—or even care—about his business.

She *had* asked, though.

"The entire point of attending the theater tonight was to see the earl. Blackwell and I have coal mines in the north of England, on the east coast. I'd like to buy more." He inhaled, his nostrils flaring as he remembered his reception. "I went to discuss the possibility of investment with Rookewoode. He's known to be quite rich and looking for suitable investments. A business association between us would suit both our needs, and yet he ignored me." He sneered. "As if I were the dirt beneath his diamond-buckle shoes."

"Ah."

His head snapped to her.

Messalina's face was in profile, and she looked pensive. She opened her mouth as if she wanted to comment, and then closed it again.

He rocked his head to one side and then the other, trying to loosen his shoulders. He wanted to smash something . . . or better yet, slash the fucking smile off Rookewoode's face.

Determinedly he fixed his gaze upon the bloody stage.

Two minutes hadn't passed before he couldn't stand Messalina's silence anymore. "*What?*"

She started and raised her brows. "I beg your pardon?"

He breathed deeply before saying evenly, "What was that 'Ah' about?"

"Oh." She hesitated. "I doubt you'll like my answer."

His eyes narrowed. "Nevertheless."

"Well." She turned fully to him. "If you truly wish to converse with Lord Rookewoode—or really with any gentleman of quality—you'll need an introduction. And what is more, you'll have to *look* the part."

He frowned impatiently. "I have money and I have a business that will make *him* money. Why should I—?"

"Because that's the way it's done." She took a deep breath as if trying to calm herself. "I know you might find it silly and—and even offensive, but he's an *earl*. One can't simply walk up to him and ask for his money. Not, at least, if you want to truly do business with him."

Gideon grimaced. He knew she was right. He might work for a duke, might ghost around the edges of the aristocracy, but he had done so as a *servant*. Now what he wanted to do was actually mingle among them. To be recognized as their equal.

An entirely different thing indeed.

Christ. He was going to have to ask for her help.

He sighed and asked grudgingly, with near-physical pain, "What did you mean that I need to 'look the part'?"

Messalina's entire face lit up, and for a moment he was startled that such a joyful expression should be cast his way. Her gray eyes were soft, her plush lips wet and open in a smile.

She was beautiful.

Something twinged within his chest—not his heart. He hadn't much of a heart, and what he had was atrophied from long years of disuse. But it felt near enough, and the feeling filled him with something close to fear. He *couldn't* care for her. She was a means to an end. A stepping stone to his better future.

If he cared for her, he couldn't kill her brother. He couldn't fulfill his dreams.

Besides. An aristocrat such as she would never give her heart to a baseborn blackguard such as he.

Gideon was so caught up in his alarmed thoughts that he nearly missed his wife's words.

"You need to dress as if you were born to the aristocracy." Messalina gestured to the theater and its audience. "As if you're a man of means, a gentleman that other gentlemen can trust with their money."

Gideon snorted. "The majority of gentlemen have no idea whatsoever of how to make money. They scorn the making of money."

"Yes, you're quite right," Messalina said slowly, "but oddly, that doesn't matter. Gentlemen are more likely to talk to other gentlemen. I admit freely that their prejudice is ridiculous, but that's the way it is."

He scoffed. "Much of what the aristocracy does is ridiculous—and somehow set in stone."

"I suppose you think their—our—rules are awful." Her cheeks colored as she added, "They *are* awful."

He had a foolish urge to comfort her. "People in power tend to protect that power by excluding others. It's merely human nature."

"But in this case entirely wrongheaded." Her brows knitted. "You could attempt to contact Lord Rookewoode's secretary or man of business and make your appeal that way, but—"

"No." Gideon stiffened at the suggestion. Going through Rookewoode's lackeys would place him firmly at the level of a servant. He was Rookewoode's equal. He was *any* aristocrat's equal, and he'd damn well prove it to them. "I'll make the deal with Rookewoode himself or not at all."

"Then..." Messalina indicated the boxes across from them.

He turned in the direction she indicated, examining the gentlemen attending the theater. Several wore pink—a most fashionable color—and there were men in purple, green, yellow, and several shades of red, and one individual in blinding white silk. Nearly all wore white powdered wigs. Diamonds—or paste made to look like diamonds—sparkled on hands, buttons, cuffs, and, of course—though he could not see—shoe buckles. Every waistcoat was heavily and colorfully embroidered.

He scowled. "I don't want to wear such frivolous clothes. It's a waste of money."

She shrugged and turned back to the stage.

He looked as well, but he couldn't seem to see the players or what they were doing. Messalina had been *talking* to him. Without disagreement or hate. And she'd been interested in his problem.

"I'm not wearing yellow," he said tightly, still staring at the damned stage. "Or pink. And I'm not wearing a bloody wig."

"I think a wig would be quite becoming on you."

He turned to look at her in horror.

A slight smile was playing about her mouth.

Was she *joking* with him?

Messalina rolled her eyes. "Very well. But you'll certainly need several new suits."

"Ah." He tapped his fingers against the arm of his chair. "What would you recommend?"

She glanced speculatively at him. "Perhaps red or sapphire?"

Gideon winced.

She sighed. "Gray?"

"Fine." He spent a moment more scowling at the stage. A performer in a comically wide frock was dancing. He narrowed his eyes. A man, if he wasn't mistaken. Gideon cleared his throat. "Perhaps you might accompany me on a visit to my tailor."

She shook her head, and for a second his heart plummeted. "I think you need a new tailor altogether. One who is aware of the current fashions."

He blew out a breath in frustration. "And how am I supposed to find this wonderful tailor?"

"You could ask your wife."

He turned to meet her soft gray eyes, and for a moment couldn't think. He blinked. He'd never asked anyone for help, but he'd be a fool to toss aside this olive branch. "Will you help me?"

"Yes." She turned back to the play, but he could see her smile. "Of course, I'll want to help pick out the style and materials of your suits."

"Of course." His words were rote, but in truth he was rather amazed by her.

Messalina spoke as if no other thought but to help him had entered her mind. As if this was a joint venture, a goal they would achieve together.

Gideon watched her, his beautiful society lady, bred and raised in a world entirely alien to his, and for the first time realized that she could be not just his wife or a stepping stone to something greater, but his *ally*.

"Thank you," he said gruffly.

She looked surprised. "What for?"

He cleared his throat, waving a hand. "For this. For helping me."

"Oh. Of course." The smile she bestowed upon him was sardonic, but there were the beginnings of real humor. "I *am* your wife."

* * *

What have I done? Messalina wondered nervously as she and Hawthorne stepped from the theater several hours later. She'd agreed to help him. It was a small thing, really, finding a tailor for him. Picking out new suits. But it represented a softening in her thoughts toward him.

A possible weakness.

If all went well, she'd be gone shortly after she received the dowry portion he'd promised her. That was *her* goal. Her plan from the very start, and she meant to carry it out. She couldn't begin a—a *friendship* with Hawthorne *now*.

She meant to leave him. She wouldn't feel guilty for pursuing her own dreams.

She wouldn't.

She glanced at Hawthorne as he offered his arm to her. A smile was tilting his devilish lips.

Blast it, she felt guilty.

No! Messalina mentally shook herself and gazed up at the full ivory moon hanging just over the rooftops of London.

"What a lovely night," she murmured to distract herself.

"It is." Hawthorne guided her past the crowded front of the theater.

The street was too narrow and busy for carriages to pass. Messalina was glad that the night air was balmy, for they'd have to walk a bit to where Reggie had parked their carriage.

She glanced at Hawthorne. The bright torches and lanterns outside the theater dimmed as they strolled. Still a few shop lanterns glowed by themselves on the lane. In the moonlight her husband's profile was austere, nearly menacing.

And yet he no longer seemed as frightening to her.

Hawthorne cleared his throat. "I hope you enjoyed the play."

"It *was* quite funny," Messalina replied.

She felt him look at her. "You didn't find the humor too...coarse?"

"Oh, a little coarse." She shrugged. "But sometimes one needs a belly laugh instead of complex witticisms. Besides, I couldn't help noticing that you seemed to enjoy the jokes."

She'd caught her husband grinning more than once during the performance.

The sight had made something catch in her throat.

"I did enjoy the jokes," he replied, his voice sounding self-deprecating, "but then I'm a common sort of man."

"Hm," she hummed doubtfully. "I've noticed that most men—of whatever stature in life—seem to derive unreasonable amounts of pleasure from comedy involving buttocks, fornicating, and the breaking of wind."

He snorted.

She had to hide a smile.

"Perhaps we could attend again," he rumbled beside her. Why had she never noticed how smooth and deep his voice was?

"I'd like that," she replied truthfully.

He nodded, but he seemed distracted.

Their footsteps echoed in the lane.

Messalina glanced around, realizing for the first time that the street was no longer populated. They'd walked into a nearly deserted area of closed shops.

The carriage was still not in sight.

"What is it?" she whispered.

The muscles of his forearm tensing beneath her fingers was her only warning.

Hawthorne yanked her, all but flinging her against a shop. "Stay behind me!"

Messalina gasped at the painful impact.

She glanced up in time to see her husband turn his back to her and face three men—ugly, armed, and frighteningly big.

Footpads.

Except the strangers didn't demand their purses.

They simply attacked.

Messalina screamed as all three charged Hawthorne.

He crouched, his feet spread, and in a darting, snakelike movement lunged at the man on his right.

The man gave a cry, falling to the ground, a spray of blood spattering to the cobblestones.

How—?

The remaining two men skipped back warily. One had a club with a spike at the end. The other had either a long knife or a short sword.

"Thief! Thief!" Messalina shouted as loud as she could. She had no weapon nor anything to use as a weapon. Even with one footpad down, that left two against Hawthorne. Her heart was beating fast with fear. "Help!"

Moonlight glinted off something in Hawthorne's right hand. He held a thin blade almost delicately in his fingertips and waved it in front of himself idly.

The still-standing footpads parted, spreading to opposite sides of Hawthorne.

They were going to try to divide his attention. Make him turn his back on one of them.

The wounded man had regained his feet. Half of his face was painted with blood from the cheek down. He looked uncertainly at the other two men.

"What are you waiting for?" Hawthorne rasped, and the words made goosebumps come up on Messalina's skin. His voice was soft. Dark. Deep, with a tinge of *laughter* in it.

What sort of man laughed in the middle of a fight?

"My wife's lungs are strong," Hawthorne continued. "You'd best run or have another try at me. Help will be here soon."

At his words the man with the knife darted at him with a wild cry.

Hawthorne moved fluidly, his hand thrust out, almost too fast to follow.

His attacker wavered, his fingers clutching his side.

Hawthorne moved in, holding the man in what looked like an embrace as he stabbed the footpad. Again and again and again, too many times to count, his fist a blur.

Grinning all the while.

Messalina realized that she had covered her mouth with her palm.

The footpad slipped from Hawthorne's grasp and fell to the ground unmoving.

Hawthorne resumed his ready crouch in front of her almost lazily.

"*Jaysus*," one of the remaining men gasped.

Someone shouted from down the lane.

Both footpads' heads turned to the sound.

Then they were off, running away into the dark.

For a moment Hawthorne was still, as if making sure there was no other danger.

He turned to Messalina. "Are you hurt?"

"They didn't come near me." She stared at him. His knife was put away already, but his hand was wet with something. *Blood.* "You're hurt."

He followed her gaze and then grimaced, wiping his hand on a handkerchief. "It's not mine."

She glanced at the man on the ground. He was very still. Had Hawthorne—?

Pounding footsteps approached as Hawthorne caught her arm, turning her away from the body.

Reggie skidded to a stop before them, two other men that Messalina didn't know behind him. "All right, guv?"

"Yes," Hawthorne growled menacingly. "No thanks to

you and the bloody coachman taking the carriage so far away. My *wife* was nearly killed."

Reggie blanched. "I-I'm sorry, guv. Won't 'appen again. I swear it."

"It had better not," Hawthorne snapped. "Now I want to get my wife to safety."

Reggie nodded. "John Coachman is bringing the carriage."

"Good." He jerked his head to the body. "Take care of that."

"Right away, guv, right away."

Hawthorne hurried Messalina along, craning his head to look around, obviously watching for another attack.

Somehow she'd forgotten.

That he was used to fighting. That in her uncle's service he'd done much worse.

Hawthorne was deadly.

Her breath was coming fast in her breast. She ought to be scared, she knew. Horrified by what had just happened. But all she could think was that Hawthorne had kept her safe.

That she felt *safe* right now in the company of a man who had just killed.

The carriage rattled around the corner up ahead. Hawthorne barely waited for the coachman to bring the horses to a stop before hauling open the carriage door and shoving her inside roughly.

He jumped in behind her and knocked on the roof.

Then he was beside her and throwing an arm around her shoulders.

She looked up at him. His eyes glittered wildly, his body strung taut.

She couldn't look away.

Something inside her melted under his savage gaze.

"You didn't answer me back there," he panted. "Are you hurt?"

"No. No, not at all." She glared up at him. "You were the one fighting three men, not me."

He grinned suddenly. "Brave girl."

His head obliterated the light from outside the carriage as he bent to kiss her.

* * *

It was a strange thing that happened sometimes—the urge to fuck after a fight. The raging of a libido glad to be alive. Gideon hadn't experienced it in years. Perhaps it was because Messalina had been in danger.

Or perhaps it was simply Messalina—her courage, her intelligence, her *warmth*.

He gathered her close, pressing the lush expanse of her breasts against his chest. The low neckline of her dress had been driving him mad all night, and he wanted to tear the cloth from her body. To lick and press and suckle the delicate skin he knew lay underneath. He wanted more than this. More than simply her mouth and her arms. He wanted her belly and thighs, the sweet scent of her cunny.

He wanted to *bury* himself in her and never leave.

He angled his mouth over hers seeking the warm, wet depths between her lips. Wanting.

Wanting.

But he felt her go still in his arms. Stiffen and pull back. And he knew that if he didn't stop, he'd lose what ground he'd gained.

He broke away, feeling as if he tore the skin from his body as he did so. He could still feel the panting of her breath on his lips as the carriage bumped over something in the road, jostling them together. The scent of bergamot surrounded him, a siren's lure, and he nearly took her again.

Damn it. He'd survived winters without proper shoes or regular food as a boy. He could survive one carriage ride with Messalina.

"Have I frightened you?" he asked, his voice rasping even to his own ears.

"No. A kiss—even from you—is not enough to frighten me." Her voice caught and she whispered, her words ghosting over his cheek, "I thought they might kill you."

He closed his eyes, trying to calm himself. "They were common footpads—nothing I can't handle." Except they'd seemed more intent on murder than theft. More like paid—if unskilled—assassins.

"There were *three* of them." Her voice brought him back from his black thoughts.

A corner of his mouth kicked up. He supposed he should be insulted that she thought he might be taken down by footpads, but he found instead that her worry was charming. "I assure you I've taken on bigger and better-skilled men before."

"Still," she said worriedly.

He turned his head to see her face and discern her expression, but the carriage was too dark. All he could see was the shimmer of pale skin flashing in and out from the lanterns on the street. A cheek, the length of her neck, the slope of her pretty breasts.

Jesus. How was he to survive a month like this? But he had to if he wanted Messalina in his bed of her own accord.

And he did.

He inhaled and said quietly, "By the time I was fifteen my knife had become a part of me. I'd learned to attack without hesitation or quarter. To put aside fear and thought and simply live to best my opponent. I never lost a fight after that."

He felt her finger trace the scar on his cheek. "I'm glad," she said softly. "I'm glad you learned to be so ruthless if it saved your life tonight."

"And yours," he murmured near the delicate curve of her ear. Tempting. So tempting. He pulled away. "Especially yours."

The carriage rattled through London as Gideon closed his eyes, leaning his head on the cool windowpane. He was battling his baser instincts, trying not to alarm her, but when Messalina slipped her small hand into his, he could not make himself let go.

He held her hand all the way home.

Gideon raised his head when the carriage stopped.

Keys opened the door and met his eyes, giving a slight nod to indicate the way was safe.

Gideon helped Messalina out, alert despite Keys's assurance. He hurried her into the house and relaxed his shoulders only when the door shut behind them. Most likely it was him the assassins—if they *were* assassins—had been after, but he couldn't discount the fact that Messalina had been with him.

Was Windemere carrying out his threat to harm Messalina? It didn't make any sense to Gideon, but then the duke didn't always have logical reasons for his actions. Gideon hated the idea. If the old man—or any other person—thought they could hurt his *Messalina* they'd find out exactly how skilled he was with a blade.

Keys had followed them inside, leaving Reggie to take the carriage to the stable yard.

Keys glanced at Gideon with raised brows.

Gideon shook his head. "Tomorrow. We'll discuss business tomorrow."

Keys's eyes darted to Messalina, and he seemed to catch Gideon's meaning. Keys nodded and drifted into the shadows.

"Come," Gideon said to Messalina, trying to keep the darkness from his voice. "I think it time for bed. Unless you'd like some refreshment before you retire?"

Messalina shook her head, stifling a yawn. "I'm exhausted suddenly. I don't know why."

"The attack," Gideon murmured as they mounted the stairs, his hand on her waist. "The danger brings first a pounding alertness followed by weariness. I've felt it before."

"Have you?" He knew her curious gaze was on him. "Outside of your prizefights?"

He darted a glance at her. How much did she really want to know about him? What he'd done in the past? Surely she understood that his soul was blackened by his work? The thought made him uneasy. When he killed her brother his soul wouldn't be just blackened.

It would be devoured.

His tone was rough, then, when he answered her. "Why do you ask?"

She stopped on the landing. "I suppose I'm curious." She lifted her chin. "Have you?"

"Sometimes." He was going to stop there, but something inside him urged him on. To reveal the truth she already knew. To make her see the worst of him. "Often while in your uncle's service. Danger was what I did for him."

She licked her lips, drawing his eyes to her mouth. "What do you mean?"

He leaned into her, propping his hand on the wall above her head. "I mean when your uncle wanted to scare someone or teach someone a lesson, he sent me. I was the one that put fear into their hearts."

She swallowed, but her gaze remained fixed on his. "You hurt people for him."

He nodded slowly. "For years and years."

"Did you—?" She inhaled as if steadying herself. "Did you kill?"

The sound of their breaths was loud in his ear, and he wished suddenly that he'd never turned down this path.

But he had. "No. Tonight was the first."

"Tonight?" Her eyes widened. Obviously she hadn't expected that answer.

"Yes. I'm not an assassin." Or he *hadn't* been. Once he murdered her brother he would be.

If she knew, she'd never let him close again.

And he *needed* her—her money and her advice for maneuvering through the aristocracy. He couldn't give those things up.

Couldn't give *her* up.

He inhaled and straightened, holding out his arm. "Come."

She nodded, though a line was still etched between her eyes. Had he lost all the ground he'd covered? Did she hate him now?

His mood was foul as he escorted her to their bedroom. The maid was waiting up for them—or rather for Messalina. He hesitated, but really it was for the best. He needed to calm himself before he was near her again.

Gideon bowed to Messalina. "I'll be a few minutes before I retire."

She glanced at the maid and then him, and he thought there was apology in her eyes. But then that might've been wishful thinking. "I shan't be long."

He nodded again and closed the bedroom door behind him.

How the hell did aristocrats live like this—with servants all around them and underfoot? He wandered to the end of the hall, where a window looked out over the small garden in back of the town house. The garden had long been untended, and only a few overgrown trees remained, casting long shadows in the moonlight. Something moved, and Pea emerged from under one of the trees, his lanky form recognizable even in the near dark. He tilted his head up to the window and nodded.

Gideon returned the nod, glad that Pea was alert.

He watched the night for a few more minutes before a door opened in the hall behind him. He heard the patter of the maid's retreating footsteps.

Gideon waited a moment and then retraced his steps to the bedroom. Messalina was already abed, the covers pulled to her chin and her eyes closed.

He shut the door and paused for a moment. Dear God, he wanted to climb in beside her. Pull the covers from her body and rip aside that damned chemise.

Instead he snuffed out the candle and walked to one of the chairs before the fire.

"Aren't you coming to bed?" she whispered.

Had she any idea? Any idea at all of the restraint he was having to maintain?

"Not yet."

He heard rustling as she moved in the bed. He kept his gaze firmly on the glowing embers in the hearth. He waited.

But even after her breaths had evened and deepened into sleep, he didn't retire to bed. He was thinking. Tonight was the second time they'd been attacked by robbers inside a week.

And in both cases the attackers had been more interested in murder than money.

Which meant they were bent on killing either him or Messalina. He'd been defending himself since the age of thirteen. Gideon feared no one.

But if it was Messalina they were after...

He clenched his jaw. *No.* Not Messalina.

That couldn't be borne.

CHAPTER EIGHT

"Then I shall take Bet as my payment," the fox said.
The tinker wept and pleaded, but the fox stood firm.
In the end the tinker was forced to agree to give his
daughter in marriage to the fox. The only concession
the fox made was to wait until the tinker's baby
daughter should turn eighteen.
And then finally the fox showed the tinker the way
out of the wood....

—From *Bet and the Fox*

"What a good boy," Messalina crooned early the next morning.

The puppy sleeping in her arms didn't reply.

Daisy had his little head tucked into her neck, dozing blissfully, while Bartlett made the finishing touches to Messalina's toilet.

Messalina stroked the puppy's triangle ears, softer than her kid gloves.

There was a scrape at the door, and she glanced up to see Sam shyly looking in.

"You've come just in time," Messalina told the boy. "I'm afraid that Daisy will want to visit the gardens when he wakes. Can you take him?"

"Yes, ma'am."

Sam crossed the room to stand beside her.

Messalina carefully transferred the puppy to Sam's arms, but she needn't have worried. Daisy still slept, his small body warm and limp.

She smiled. "Hopefully he'll wake when you take him outside, but if he doesn't, you might as well stay in the gardens until he does."

Sam's face bloomed into a grin. "Aye, ma'am! Thank you, ma'am!"

She waved him out of the room.

"You'll spoil that boy," Bartlett said gruffly.

Messalina glanced at her in surprise. "Do you think so?"

Bartlett met her eyes in the mirror. "You've made him your pet, but he will grow into a man eventually. A man who will never find a mistress or master as kind as you."

Most ladies would not allow such impertinence in a servant. But Bartlett's homely face was creased in genuine concern.

And besides. It was Bartlett.

Messalina frowned. "Then what do you think I should do—treat him with scorn? Ignore him?"

Bartlett shrugged. "In the end it might be more merciful."

To be unkind so that he would expect unkindness for the rest of his life? Instinctively she hated the idea. Why should boys like Sam be taught that they were inferior simply because of the poverty they had been born in?

Sam should be educated. His clothes should be decent. And he should be able to discover some other life than joining a gang of thieves.

If only . . .

Her thoughts were interrupted by Bartlett. "Will that be all, ma'am?"

"Yes, of course."

Messalina stared at her reflection in the mirror. What

would Hawthorne say should she share her thoughts on little boys and their expectations in life?

Messalina cleared her throat, stopping Bartlett at the door. "Ma'am?"

"I was just wondering where Mr. Hawthorne might be," Messalina said as casually as she could.

Hawthorne hadn't slept in their bed at all last night, and as usual he was gone when she'd woken.

Bartlett gave her a far too knowing look.

Messalina hurried into speech. "Never mind. I'm quite scattered this morning."

The lady's maid said gently, "Actually, ma'am, I think if you go to the kitchens you'll find the master."

"The *kitchens*?"

Bartlett looked shifty. "*Near* the kitchens, ma'am. More than that I really ought not say. If that will be all, ma'am?"

At Messalina's nod the maid bustled from the room, a pile of linens in her arms.

Messalina stared after her. Whatever was Hawthorne doing in the kitchens—or rather *near* the kitchens?

Curious, she descended the stairs to the lowest level of the house. She was striding toward the kitchens when she saw Keys step into the corridor ahead of her and hurry away without seeing her.

Messalina stopped. The man had come from Hawthorne's room.

The room he'd forbidden her.

She approached the door and examined it, biting her lip. She glanced up and down the hallway and put her ear to the door. If someone found her doing such a childish thing she had no idea what she'd say.

There was no sound from inside.

Messalina wrinkled her nose at the door. Well, it was probably locked.

She tried the doorknob and it turned beneath her hand. Impulsively she pushed open the door and walked in.

A bathtub sat in the very middle of the room, the largest she'd ever seen. Copper gleamed in the candlelight, white bath sheets draped over the edges. The floor was tiled in white marble that extended to a pretty little mantel with a fire crackling merrily underneath.

All this she saw in a glance before her gaze was snagged by the man in the tub.

Hawthorne said nothing, his angry black eyes glinting in the candlelight.

Messalina felt her face heat as she stumbled back under Hawthorne's glare. His black hair curled damply on the smooth muscles of his shoulders. He rested his arms along the rim of the tub, a chain glinting through the curls on his chest. It held some sort of small pendant.

He looked arrogant and completely in control, though he was obviously naked.

Quite, quite naked.

She worked to keep the kiss in the carriage from her mind, but really it was impossible. Her gaze dropped to his bottom lip, and she bit her own. This man had had his tongue in her mouth last night.

"What the hell are you doing here?" he barked, making her jump.

"I…I'm sorry," Messalina stuttered. It had never occurred to her that Hawthorne's secret would be a *bathing* room. "I'll leave—"

"No." His sharp voice caught her as she was turning.

She looked back.

"I beg your pardon." He inhaled and let his breath out slowly. "Your entrance startled me."

"Well." Messalina cleared her throat. "Naturally it would. I *did* intrude on you."

"Yes, you did." He wiped his hand down his face. A small smile quirked the corner of his lips. "Curiosity, I presume?"

She felt her face heat. "I'm afraid so. I mean, a forbidden door..."

"Did you think I had the bodies of my previous wives in here?"

"No, of course not," she replied, a bit too loud.

He laughed.

She stared, for she couldn't remember seeing him laugh before. Hawthorne grinned slyly, smiled cynically, smirked and sneered. He did not laugh.

His obsidian eyes crinkled, his white teeth flashed, and a dimple appeared on his cheek. He was gorgeous. She caught her breath, a frisson of desire rippling down her center.

"Would you..." Messalina had to stop and clear her throat. "Would you like me to...to help you with your hair?"

He cocked his head, a smile still hovering around his sensuous lips. "You wish to act my valet?"

Was he mocking her? She raised her chin. "Yes, if you want."

"Oh, I want," he said softly.

The rasp in his voice made her hands tremble. What on earth was she thinking?

But...she wanted to stay. Wanted to touch that gleaming skin.

She shoved her doubts aside and crossed to the tub. Beside it was a stool holding cloths, soap, and a tin cup. There was also a tall tankard of what looked like coffee, but that she ignored. She looked around and saw a chair, which she dragged closer.

She sat at the head of the tub and took the cup, turning to him, but then nearly dropped it again at what she saw.

His body was covered in knife scars.

Thin white lines were hatched all over his chest, belly, and arms, but there were thicker scars as well. Angry pink skin in raised welts. The result of stab wounds? They must be. One high on his left chest, just below his collarbone, the chain glinting beside it. She could see now that a farthing, of all things, hung from the chain—how odd.

But she hadn't time to wonder about the thing, for she was still cataloguing his scars. Two more were over his ribs on his right side. And another just above his navel. Surely that should've been a killing blow? How had he survived so many wounds? She followed the trail of wet hair that disappeared into the water. His penis lay there between his thighs, quite a bit bigger than she'd imagined and not exactly quiescent.

Messalina jerked her eyes up and her gaze met his.

His head was canted to the side, his eyelids drooping over glittering black eyes watching as she examined him.

Her face nearly went up in flames.

"You are *very* curious, aren't you?" he said softly.

For a moment she couldn't think at all. She could feel her nipples, sensitive against her chemise, and something inside her clenched.

"I suppose I am." She stared at that scar barely above the water. The one that should've been fatal. "How . . . ?"

She glanced up at him again, and this time she looked at him through tears.

His face shuttered. "There's not much in the way of proper work in St Giles," Hawthorne said quietly. "Not for a boy without a living family. I nearly starved before I found the knife fights. But then I did find them, and I decided to be the best."

She shook her head. "You just *decided*?"

"Mm." He lifted his arm to push back his hair, revealing yet another scar on the underside of his upper arm. "Yes. I wasn't going to *stay* in St Giles, and to get out I needed money. I started planning the day I was in my first knife fight. By sixteen I had a nice little amount saved when I received this"—he gestured to the scar above his navel—"and was bedridden for several weeks." He grimaced. "All my savings were spent in those weeks—for the bed, for food, and for medicine."

She inhaled sharply. "That must've been devastating."

He shrugged, the light sliding over his slick shoulders as he did so. "When I was better, I went back to the fights. I figured it would take me another two years to make enough to abandon St Giles—assuming I wasn't wounded or killed first. But then your uncle discovered me and made me a better offer."

She frowned. "How is working for my uncle better?"

"Because working for your uncle paid well enough that I could escape St Giles at once. I would've worked for the devil himself if it meant leaving St Giles."

She swallowed. Such ruthless determination should've repelled her, but she was very much afraid that it did not.

"Do you understand?" he asked when she remained silent. His voice was gravelly. "I've plotted my entire life to escape my birth. I would've done *anything* to find a way to rise above where I was born, then and now."

She thought about what it would be like to be all alone in the world. To have to fight in order to eat. "I understand."

He still looked grim. "You're too good to be married to me."

A week ago she would've agreed immediately with that sentiment.

Now? She wasn't entirely sure. "Lean back."

He obeyed, his eyes closed.

She stared at him a moment, this complex, hardened man. A *naked* man. She'd never seen an entirely nude man before—not a live one, anyway. She'd seen male statues, of course, but she rather thought they weren't any more accurate than the female statues she'd seen—the ones without hair or natural feminine parts.

And she was right. Hawthorne had wet curls of hair on his chest and beneath his arms. He had nipples that were dark and furrowed.

And his penis was certainly larger than any Greek statue's, veins vining up the length, the hood pulling back from the tip. It was red and looked engorged.

Messalina swallowed and placed her hand hesitantly on his shoulder, shivering despite his heat at the feel of his smooth skin and the hard muscle beneath. She could feel ridged scars under her fingertips. "They don't hurt anymore, do they?"

He shook his head, not bothering to open his eyes. "Most aren't deep."

She frowned a little at that, moving her fingers to the bumpy scar beside his collarbone. "Not even this one?" She could see now that the wound had been crudely sewn together.

"It once hurt, but that was years ago," he murmured.

She was distracted by a dark shadow on his upper arm, twisting to see better. A bruise. "And this?"

"The footpads last night at the theater."

She looked at him. He was so close that she could see his individual eyelashes, dark and sooty. "You use your body like a weapon, without regard for how it might be hurt. I think you probably take better care of that knife you keep up your sleeve."

His lips quirked. "Perhaps. But there are other ways I can use my body. Will you let me show you?"

Her mouth went dry.

"I…" Did he mean something *other* than the act of consummating a marriage? She'd heard rumors that there was more that a man and a woman might do in bed.

Or, a voice whispered in her head, she could allow him to bed her *before* the month was up. She wanted that dowry money, didn't she? What better reason to let him run his hard hands over her body, to put that big cock in her body?

And then she could leave.

The thought made her go cold. *Could* she leave him after she'd let him into her body?

But she had to. Lucretia was not safe within reach of their uncle.

Messalina took a breath to steady herself and dipped her cup into the water to wet his hair. "I would not have taken you for a man who craved luxury."

"I'm not."

"But this bath…?" She poured the cup over his hair, careful to keep the water off his face.

He sighed, tilting his head into her hand, and she wondered if he was aware of the movement. "I stank when I lived in St Giles."

"What?" She stared down at him.

His beautiful mouth was twisted by some bitter memory. "When you are poor you stink. Lice crawl in your clothes. Grime is ground into the grooves of your hands. Your hair becomes greasy. And when someone sees you—someone who has water and soap and a ready fire—their eyes fill with disgust. That's how your uncle looked at me when we first met. As if I were shit stuck to his shoe."

"I..." She swallowed, another full cup hovering over his hair. "I'm sorry."

What an inadequate word.

She slowly poured the water over his head and then picked up the soap, lathering her hands.

"I have heard aristocrats bemoan the laziness of the poor," he said softly. A muscle tensed in his jaw. "They say that we *enjoy* wallowing in filth. I don't think any human likes being dirty."

"No," she agreed.

"To bathe." He took a deep breath as if to steady his voice. "To bathe in St Giles I'd have to haul water from the common pump. Up floor after floor of stairs because we lived like sheep penned together for slaughter. And then once I reached my shared room, I'd have to use my little bucketful of cold water not for drinking or cooking, but for the *luxury* of washing."

She winced at his repetition of the word she'd used. In the light of his memories, her careless use of the word *luxury* seemed thoughtless. Perhaps even stupid. Messalina knew that it was a great deal of work for the servants to heat and haul water for a bath, but she'd never considered how impossible it would be simply to *wash* if one were poor.

She whispered, "You must've wanted to bathe very much when you lived in St Giles."

"Always," he replied, lifting his head a bit so that she could scrub the hair at his nape.

His neck was hot beneath her fingers. She felt intimate touching him in such a vulnerable spot.

"That sounds terrible," she said as she rinsed his hair, causing it to lie flat and glistening against his skull. He might've been a selkie intent on seducing a mortal. "I can see why you would want a bathing room all to yourself."

He opened his eyes, watching her with black, fathomless eyes. "Can you?"

She nodded.

"Your sympathy is quite dangerous," he murmured thoughtfully. "You might very well be my downfall, madam."

Her eyebrows winged up. "*Me?*"

"Mmm." His sensuous lips twisted as if he were confused. "There is something about you that draws me, makes me lose my sense, my intelligence, my very *control*." He inhaled. "You are like an exotic poison in my blood—one that should kill me, but instead keeps me alive. I truly do not know if I can live without you."

Her lips parted in wonder. Did he know what he was saying?

She didn't think before she leaned down and kissed him.

His mouth was warm and sensuously soft, as if the hot water he soaked in had infused his flesh and relaxed all his muscles.

He let her lead.

She tilted her head, suddenly breathless. She'd kissed a man or two before, but she'd never initiated the embrace. The feeling of control made her giddy with possibilities.

Slowly she ran the very tip of her tongue over his bottom lip, feeling for herself the wicked curve. His lips parted passively as if he waited for something.

It took her a second, and then she was licking into his mouth, tasting the smoky coffee he'd drunk, dancing dangerously with his tongue.

She gasped, inhaling the breath in the thin space between them, and reluctantly pulled away.

His eyes were hooded, sleepy and gleaming wickedly, and his voice when he spoke was a dark rasp. "If you stay, I may break our pact to wait a full month before taking you to bed. The decision is yours."

She was tempted—so very tempted.

But something within her still hesitated. Did she truly know Gideon yet? Could she trust him?

It seemed somehow that she ought to trust him before letting him bed her.

Or perhaps she was simply making excuses for her trepidation.

"I'll leave then," Messalina said, shocked at how husky her voice was.

"How responsible," he mocked gently.

Already she was regretting her decision, but she rose from the chair, her knees only a bit wobbly as she walked to the door.

She couldn't help one last glance over her shoulder as she closed the door.

Hawthorne's head was tilted back, his eyes closed, and his right hand moved beneath the water.

* * *

It was early afternoon by the time Gideon rapped on Blackwell's door. His business partner lived in a modest house, one of a row in a solidly respectable part of London.

After a moment's wait, Blackwell's small maid opened the door.

She looked up at Gideon and bobbed a curtsy. "Will you come in, Mr. Hawthorne? Mr. Blackwell is in his study."

She didn't wait for Gideon's reply, but turned to lead him into the house.

Gideon followed her past a hall table and mirror and to the door of the study.

"Mr. Hawthorne to see you, sir," the maid announced as she opened the door.

Blackwell looked up from a desk covered in papers. He immediately put down his pen and took off his small square reading glasses. "Hawthorne! I was beginning to think you'd never come around to see me."

Gideon raised his eyebrows as he threw his tricorne on a small table near the door. "I just saw you at the theater last night."

"Indeed, but we couldn't discuss business *there*—even if you'd wanted to. Not with your lovely wife in attendance." Blackwell tilted his head. "How exactly did you manage to marry a duke's niece?"

Gideon sat in a chair in front of the desk. "Not a subject I'm prepared to discuss."

Blackwell threw up his hands in feigned disgust. "Of course not. You'll just continue to be a cypher, even to your poor, beleaguered partner."

Gideon snorted. "Why would I confess to such a gossip? You're no better than an old woman."

Blackwell turned to the little maid, who had reappeared with a tray of tea and cakes. "Molly, do you hear how your master is slandered?"

But Molly merely shook her head and set down the tea tray on the crowded desk before leaving again.

Blackwell picked up the teapot and began pouring. "Well, at least you now have a wife to keep you company in that big house of yours."

"Not only a wife," Gideon said, taking the teacup and pouring milk into it himself. He and Blackwell didn't stand on ceremony. "I plan to install Messalina's younger sister when she comes to town."

"Oh?" Blackwell sat back, munching on one of the small cakes. He swallowed. "Is she in the schoolroom?"

"Not at all," Gideon replied, amused he was now gossiping. "Lucretia is..." He squinted, trying to think. "...two and twenty? No. Three and twenty."

"Then she'll probably marry and move away soon," Blackwell mused. "Unless she's terribly plain."

"She's almost as lovely as her sister," Gideon said objectively. He'd paid far less attention to Lucretia than Messalina. "And she has just as large a dowry as her sister, too. It's not for lack of suitors that she's not married yet."

Blackwell leaned forward, sounding intrigued. "Then what is it?"

Gideon shrugged. "The Greycourt women are a stubborn—and choosy—lot. I think Lucretia simply hasn't seen the right gentleman yet."

"Oh dear. Mrs. Hawthorne's eyesight must be impaired," Blackwell said sadly.

Gideon looked at him suspiciously. "Why?"

His partner grinned at him. "Because out of all the men in London she chose *you*, my friend."

He chuckled along with Blackwell, but Gideon was aware that the opposite was true: Messalina *hadn't* chosen him. Had she the choice, she'd have rejected him. Would a gentleman such as Blackwell have felt guilt for forcing a lady to marry him? Yes. No doubt at all.

But Gideon couldn't bring himself to regret forcing Messalina to marry him. She was softening, day by day, hour by hour. If, in the end, she was truly content with their marriage, perhaps even happy, what did it matter that she hadn't started that way? It was merely a small quibble.

And her brother's murder? Just this morning Pea had presented Gideon with a short list of Julian Greycourt's London haunts. When the man finally arrived, Gideon would be more than ready to do the deed. A knife slipped between Greycourt's ribs and it would be all over.

He shifted at the thought, putting his teacup down. "What was it you needed to talk to me about?"

"Mmf." Blackwell had just taken a large bite, and he waved his hand to indicate *wait* before he swallowed. "The accounting." He started lifting papers, evidently searching for the ledger to their business. "Ah, here it is."

Blackwell hauled out an enormous leather-bound book. He bent his head, turning pages until he came to the section he wanted. Blackwell swiveled the volume toward Gideon, tapping a figure in one of the long columns. "See here."

Gideon pushed the ledger back. "You know I don't do numbers well." He felt an angry flush heat his cheeks. He didn't like admitting it, even to Blackwell, who already knew.

"All right." Blackwell took the book good-naturedly. "I'll tell you, then. The Nightingale mine is doing very, very well for us. Even better than Last Man's Hope mine—we've made back nearly double what we invested in the mine." Blackwell leaned forward as if there were listening ears in his house. "There are rumors—rumors, but ones I have reason to believe—that old man Marshall is going to sell all three of his mines. We need investors, Gideon!"

"Which is why I'm seeking rich men to sell shares to." Gideon sighed. "It's proving a more tedious job than I first thought."

Blackwell nodded sympathetically. "Rich men are loath to part with their moneys even if it is in service of making more money."

Gideon shook his head. "I still think you need to be in Newcastle to manage the mines—especially if it's now to be more than two. I dislike managers I do not know who are so far away. What's to stop them from pocketing our money and recording a smaller revenue?"

"Mathers and Barkley are good men. I picked them out myself, and I make the trip north to see them and the mines at least once a month. Besides, who would manage our accounts in London?" Blackwell raised his eyebrows. "You told me that your man Keys wasn't ready to take over the ledgers."

"No, but he will be soon," Gideon said. "Keys is studying hard with a tutor I found for him."

"Is he?" Blackwell sat back in his chair, smiling. "That sounds like an extravagance, hiring a private tutor for a boy off the streets. It doesn't seem like something you'd do."

Gideon glanced at him sharply. "It's an investment. When Keys can work the accounts for us, he'll be more valuable for the business and you can take over other duties."

"Of course." Blackwell held up his hands as if in surrender. "Your championing of the lad is very kind."

Gideon grunted. Kindness was a weakness. "Is that all the business you have to discuss?"

Blackwell seemed surprised. "Yes, it is. Are you leaving already?"

"I've other matters to attend to." Gideon rose and picked up his tricorne. "Thank you for the tea."

Blackwell had risen as well. "You're more than welcome." He hesitated. "You know we can meet for more than simply business. I like to think we are friends."

Blackwell held out his hand.

Gideon eyed the hand. Blackwell had always been more open—more congenial—than Gideon himself. Still..."As do I."

He shook Blackwell's offered hand and had turned to the

study door when he remembered something. "Did you have any trouble returning home from the theater last night?"

Blackwell's eyebrows winged up. "No. Why do you ask?"

"Because Messalina and I were attacked," Gideon said grimly.

"What?" Blackwell stared. "Good God. The Covent Garden footpads are getting more and more bold. Did they take anything off you?"

Gideon gave his partner a look. "Of course not. Nor did they ask."

"I don't understand."

"The footpads—if such they were—never demanded my purse or Mrs. Hawthorne's jewelry," Gideon replied.

"You think they weren't footpads at all." Blackwell frowned, dropping into his chair again.

Gideon nodded. "Have we stepped on any toes with our business?"

"Not that I can think of." Blackwell waved a dismissive hand. "Besides, most of our business is up north. Have you thought about your own affairs? After all, you've emptied many a gambler's pocket of his last penny. Many might blame you for that instead of their own ill luck."

Gideon grunted. "Maybe."

"In any case," Blackwell said, "I trust you will be more careful in the future. And for God's sake, put a guard on Mrs. Hawthorne. I would hate to see that lovely lady hurt."

"Already have," Gideon growled irritably. He didn't like the insinuation that he couldn't take care of Messalina.

"Well, good," Blackwell said mildly. "Shall I see you to the door?"

"No." Gideon nodded curtly and left.

Outside the London street was a-bustle with street traffic. An elegantly dressed gentleman argued from his open carriage with a dray driver blocking his way. The various people on foot paid them no mind, streaming around the two vehicles.

A dog barked, scampering next to a ragged band of boys, and Gideon was reminded of the puppy and Messalina. He had to put more guards on her.

She would hate that. Would probably think he was merely curtailing her freedom.

On that gloomy thought Gideon glanced up and realized that his musing had brought him all the way home. He was admitted into Whispers by Reggie, looking nearly respectable in a new suit.

"Where is Mrs. Hawthorne?" he asked the man as he handed him his hat.

"In the kitchens, guv," Reggie replied. "Went back there maybe 'alf an 'our ago."

Gideon nodded. "From now on, double the guard on her when she leaves the house."

Reggie frowned. "It's those footpads from last night, innit? They've got you spooked."

"I don't know about spooked," Gideon muttered. "But I certainly don't want last night to be repeated. And Reggie?"

"Aye, guv?"

"Make sure the boys you have guarding her can do so discreetly. She's not going to like it."

"Right you are, guv."

Gideon grunted and made his way back to the kitchens. Hopefully Messalina hadn't decided to dismiss Hicks, because the boy really didn't have anywhere else to go.

As he neared the kitchens, he heard Messalina's bright, feminine laughter. The mere sound had him hard in seconds. He closed his eyes, leaning against the passageway to the kitchens. Only yards away was his bathing room, where this morning she'd run her cool hands over his shoulders and back.

Where he'd taken his cock in hand only moments later, thinking of her.

He took a deep breath to steady himself. Then he silently entered the big room and saw Messalina crouching in the middle of the kitchen flagstones, Hicks and the scullery maid to one side, Sam on the other, and the puppy sprawled upside down in front of them. The animal was attempting to wrest a length of string from Messalina's hands.

Messalina glanced up and immediately hid both her hands behind her back like a guilty child. "Hawthorne! I didn't expect you home yet."

"No?" He strolled into the kitchens, suppressing a smile. She'd obviously grown fond of the puppy and just as obviously didn't want him to know. "I suppose you were discussing the menus with Hicks?"

"Well…" Messalina looked guiltily at the cook while the puppy attempted to scramble onto her lap. It slipped and fell back to the floor with a little yelp.

Sam gasped.

Hicks and the scullery maid looked worried.

And Messalina snatched up the puppy.

Gideon raised his eyebrows and waited patiently.

"Oh, fine!" Messalina muttered, looking as if Gideon were crowing in victory. "I've decided to keep Daisy."

Sam whooped.

Hicks and the scullery maid smiled.

And Gideon said faintly, "*Daisy?*"

* * *

"Daisy is a perfectly good name for a dog," Messalina said an hour later as she and Hawthorne strolled along a lane just off Bond Street. They'd been bickering about the name for almost the entirety of that time, and Messalina felt rather lighthearted.

"Daisy is a perfectly good name for a cat. A *female* cat," Hawthorne replied. "It's humiliating for a male dog. Even a male *lapdog*."

Messalina repressed a smile. "I'm not changing his name."

Hawthorne sighed heavily, as if Daisy's name personally offended him, but changed the subject. "What is wrong with the tailor I've always used?"

Messalina refrained with great effort from rolling her eyes. She should've known that convincing Hawthorne to see a proper tailor wouldn't be as easy as it had seemed last night at the theater.

She glanced at him. Her husband wore an irritable frown, which should've made his face quite ugly. Or at least unattractive.

Alas.

She looked quickly away as if doing so could erase the memory of those devilish furrowed brows, the scar, just visible in the sunlight, and his diabolical lips frowning at one corner. It occurred to her that most women would find it near impossible to deny him anything.

Well, she wasn't most women.

"Your *former* tailor," she replied, "was undoubtedly a competent man, but we need far more than mere competence."

"Hmm" was his only rejoinder.

Messalina pressed her lips together. They walked with her hand tucked into the crook of his arm, but other than that he seemed to be trying not to touch her, and she felt...

Well. Not disappointed, naturally. It wasn't as if she *wanted* him to touch her. Of course not.

Except...

She stole another glance at him.

Unfortunately, his lips remained ridiculously beautiful. She couldn't keep from remembering—over and over—his gleaming skin in the bath. The kiss they'd shared. She'd never been so overwhelmed, her body surrendering without her consent to his tongue, his taste, his *passion*.

And then there was the sight of his hand moving under the water as she'd left the room. She couldn't get the picture out of her mind. It haunted her—Gideon, his head tilted back, his strong neck limned by the candlelight, and that moving arm...

Had he been touching himself? Did he spend like that?

Did he imagine her?

Messalina felt the heat climb in her cheeks.

She had to stop thinking about Hawthorne. Had to somehow forget that too-short touch that had promised so much more. She was *leaving* him. Although—a small voice inside her head reminded her—she would *have* to lie with him before she could gain her moneys.

What would those long legs, those broad shoulders look like without the veil of soapy water?

Oh, good God.

"Here we are!" she chirped in a voice much too loud for the day.

Hawthorne shot her an odd glance as he opened the door for her.

She ignored his look, sailing beneath an extremely discreet sign reading merely *Underwood*. The shop was deceptively plain—only two chairs before a low table and a counter in the back. Bolts of jewel-colored cloth were displayed on the wall. Rumor had it that this shop filled the clothing needs of more than one royal gentleman.

"Good afternoon," the young man standing behind the counter said. He was dressed in a dull gray suit exquisitely fitted to his slender frame. "May I help you?"

His gaze moved discreetly between Messalina—dressed in the height of fashion in a cream day frock covered in yellow, blue, and red embroidered birds—to Hawthorne, who was of course in his black suit. The clerk was obviously of the highest sort, for he made no comment or assumptions. Messalina had a small moment of mirth when she realized he might think she was outfitting her lover. After all, she'd heard there were ladies who did such.

"I need a suit," Hawthorne replied without grace.

"*Several* suits," Messalina cut in. "My husband, Mr. Hawthorne, finds he needs something more..."—both she and the clerk assessed Hawthorne's attire, and she smiled brightly as the clerk gave her a look of understanding—"*appropriate.*"

"Naturally, madam," the clerk replied. "Please let me summon Mr. Underwood himself."

Mr. Underwood was revealed to be a tiny man, several inches below five feet tall. He seemed to know at once what was needed and began ordering down bolts of cloth in a rainbow of colors.

None of which Hawthorne liked.

Messalina reined in her impatience and said to him, "Will you trust me to pick out the style and color?"

His eyes narrowed, and for a moment she thought he would refuse. "If you wish."

"I do," she said firmly, nodding to Mr. Underwood.

The tailor bowed to Hawthorne and nodded at his assistant.

The young man gestured to the back room. "If you'll come this way, sir, we can note your measurements."

Hawthorne gave a rather desperate glance at Messalina before disappearing into the back room. The clerk followed closely, as if to make sure Hawthorne didn't escape.

"Now then, my dear madam, would you care for some tea?" Mr. Underwood asked.

"Yes, indeed." Messalina gratefully took a seat as the tailor rang for tea and another two assistants. "You see," she said to Mr. Underwood, "my husband is used to quite *simple* clothing, without adornment or even color. He would like several new suits, something that will be fashionable and show him to be a man of the world. I fear, though, that he will simply reject anything he considers *too* ornamental."

"Of course," Mr. Underwood replied with a confidential air. "Perhaps you will permit me some suggestions?"

"Oh yes," Messalina said, and sighed with pleasure as a hot cup of tea was handed to her by one of the assistants, with the remainder of the pot and the accessories placed on the low table before her. She couldn't help noting that a small plate of tiny cakes was also included.

Mr. Underwood contemplated the wall of silks, velvets, and brocades, muttering beneath his breath, and then clapped his hands for his assistants. The two younger men rushed to him and were given orders in a voice too low for Messalina to catch.

The clerks hurried away and in a moment were back again, their arms piled high with cloth.

Mr. Underwood selected a dark-gray velvet with just a hint of violet. He presented it to her. "Subtle, but elegant. I have a lovely pale-silver waistcoat embroidered in black, purple, and gold thread. It can be fitted to Mr. Hawthorne quite easily."

Hawthorne had said no purple, but really he couldn't go altogether without embroidery. "That sounds exactly right," Messalina decided happily.

Over the next hour she picked out three more suits—a blue so dark it was almost black, a striking emerald green, and finally a deep bloodred silk shot through with ruby and purple threads. The last was rather pushing the boundaries of Hawthorne's stated preferences, but Messalina simply couldn't resist. The iridescent bloodred silk would look so dashing on him.

Except, she suddenly realized, it was unlikely that she'd ever see Hawthorne in it. The suit would take weeks to finish. She might already be gone by the time he received it.

She frowned at her empty teacup. The thought was rather disappointing. Perhaps if she stayed a *little* longer than a month...

Hawthorne emerged from the back room, looking harassed. "I trust you are done?"

"Of course." Messalina rose and just had time to thank Mr. Underwood before she was hustled from the shop.

Outside Hawthorne inhaled deeply. "Thank God for fresh air."

Messalina eyed the horse droppings in the middle of the street and said, "If one can call it fresh."

Hawthorne gave her one of his quick, devastating grins. "To a Londoner born and raised even the stink of horse shit smells like home."

"Hm," Messalina hummed doubtfully as she took his offered arm. "I think I prefer the country air."

"That's because you are not a Londoner," Hawthorne said, turning off Bond Street.

"I am too!"

He glanced at her, his black eyes wicked and amused. "Where were you born?"

"At Greycourt," she answered.

"Which is so far north it nearly trips into Scotland." He looked irritatingly smug.

"Yes, but we spent the winters in London, when I was quite young. I might be..." She trailed away because he was no longer paying attention to her. Instead he was staring ahead. "What is it?"

"A hanging." His voice was almost a whisper.

And now she could see the crowd, coming closer, the sound of jeers and shouts growing louder. Above the milling heads was a man standing—or rather cowering—in the sledge. He must've been just condemned and on the way to Tyburn to be executed. For a great many people, such an awful event was as good as a fair.

Messalina looked curiously at Hawthorne. "It's a disgraceful sight, isn't it?"

He didn't answer, his face blank and staring at the parade to the gallows.

"Gideon?" she said softly.

Abruptly he turned, as if he'd had to physically tear himself away from the spectacle. "Come, let's go. We can walk to the carriage this way."

He strode briskly, almost as if he were running away from the clamor of the crowd. Messalina had to trot to keep up, glancing anxiously at Hawthorne. The carriage was on the other side of the hanging march. No matter which way they turned, eventually they would confront the madness.

Hawthorne led her down a tiny alley and then turned into an even smaller lane. His muscles were taut beneath her fingers, his face grim and set. The shouts grew louder.

Abruptly they met the parade at a crossroads.

Hawthorne recoiled as if shot, pushing Messalina behind him.

His broad back was heaving, and she saw sweat beading at the nape of his neck.

She peered around him.

Small, ragged boys were running alongside two dirty terriers, their faces nearly maniacal with glee.

Messalina glanced worriedly at Hawthorne. "The crowd is thinning. We only have to wait a moment or two and the way will be clear."

She could see his Adam's apple bob as he swallowed. His face was harsh, his features drawn, the silver scar standing out vividly on his cheek. His hands were balled into trembling fists as if he'd explode at any moment.

Anyone who didn't know him would mistake his expression for something else. Something violent. Would think him remote and ruthless and awful when he *wasn't*.

She would've thought that a week ago.

She laid her hand on his arm. "What is it?"

"Nothing." He swallowed, his eyes still fixed. "*Nothing*. I dislike hangings."

Didn't anyone with feelings? But this was more than simple dislike. She could see that clearly.

"Come." Hawthorne tugged on her hand, leading her across the now-cleared street, but Messalina hardly noticed, she was thinking so hard.

What could cause such...revulsion?

CHAPTER NINE

*The years passed and Bet grew into a fine young
woman with laughing green eyes and a smile so
bright it was like sunshine.
On her eighteenth birthday her family gathered after
their simple supper and her mother presented her
with a small cake. Bet had just cut into the cake when
there came a knock at the door....*
—From *Bet and the Fox*

Gideon felt a fool as they rode back to Whispers House. His
hands still trembled slightly, and he was...disconcerted. A
deep aversion churned in the pit of his gut, making him
nauseous.

He always had this—this *revolting* animal reaction—to
the sight of a hanging parade. The simultaneous urge both
to flee and to attack.

To tear the bloody glee off the faces in that parade.

He drew a calming breath and darted a glance at Messalina
beside him.

She was turned away, perhaps looking out the window.
But she still clasped his hand, her fingers white and smooth
against his darker, calloused fingertips. They shouldn't fit
together. Their skin was too different.

He scowled. Did she think he needed to be comforted like
a child? Because of a moment of anxiety?

Fucking hanging parade.

She said, not looking at him, "There was a stable hand at Greycourt where I grew up. He'd been in the war in the Colonies against the French. He was a big fellow, gentle with the horses. But when he heard a gunshot it was like all intelligence fled. He'd run to the back of the stables and stand there, just trembling. The fits might last an hour or more."

"I've not lost my intelligence," Gideon snarled. "I'm not a half-wit."

"No," Messalina said quietly. "Nor was the groom. He was—"

The nausea rose again, acid in the back of his throat. "Stop. I have no wish to discuss this."

Messalina's mouth snapped shut.

They rode in silence for several minutes, Gideon still clutching her hand.

He couldn't make himself let go.

Perhaps she'd never talk to him again. He'd barked at her, her feelings must be hurt.

"You ought to throw a soiree," Messalina said suddenly. "Or even a ball."

He blinked, his mind blank. "What?"

"Yes, a ball." She turned to him, her face alight with eager enthusiasm as the carriage came to a halt. "I've been thinking about this—your wish to enter society. If you want to show yourself equal to the gentlemen you wish to join your business—to *prove* to them that you are to be taken seriously—you need to invite them all to a proper ball. The ball of the *season*."

She was so excited, so certain, he didn't like to burst the bubble of her plans. "In Whispers House? With the few servants I have and my lack of furniture?" He shook his head. "I don't even know how to throw a ball."

"But *I* do," she said, and then paused, her eyes wide and startled as if she herself was surprised by her assertion. "*I* do," she repeated more slowly. "I can plan and throw a ball. I've done so for my uncle and my brother. And we've already ordered some furniture. We can buy more. We can furnish Whispers and hire servants."

"How long would all this take?" he asked, already calculating. "And how much money would I have to spend?"

She ignored the question of money entirely.

"Weeks," she said, biting her lip, hesitating. Then she looked up at him, her beautiful gray eyes meeting his determinedly. "More than a month, if we do it properly, and we *should*. But the season doesn't really start until late September. We have the time." She swallowed, her face paling, though he couldn't tell why, and said more slowly, "If we *want* to do it. If we want to take the time."

He searched her expression, trying to determine what had upset her. "Do you?" He lifted his hand to her cheek, not quite touching. "Do you want to take the time?"

"I..." Her voice died as he trailed his thumb across her cheekbone. "Yes," she said breathlessly. "Yes, I do."

He smiled at her—too wide, too savage—as something primitive rose inside him. "Beautiful girl. With you by my side I can do anything."

Messalina had never looked at him this way—soft and giving, her red lips parted.

Those lips shone in the light as if she'd just licked them, and he wanted—

The carriage door was wrenched open.

Gideon had his hand on his knife when a bright-blue whirlwind tumbled into the carriage and threw herself into Messalina's arms.

"I'm so sorry!" Lucretia Greycourt cried. Her face

was pressed against Messalina's neck, muffling her voice. "We've failed you. *I* failed you."

Gideon looked out of the carriage and into two sets of familiar gray eyes.

Quintus Greycourt frowned and glanced away, but the eldest brother held his gaze.

"Hawthorne," Julian Greycourt drawled, "what in hell have you done to my sister?"

* * *

Messalina wrapped her arms around Lucretia and hugged her tightly. She was shocked—startled—but so very glad that her sister had finally arrived. She hadn't seen Lucretia since Hawthorne had forced Messalina into his carriage over a fortnight ago. Since then...

Well, since then everything had changed.

"Greycourt," Gideon said. The sound of his voice— mocking and low—made her glance apprehensively at him. He was grinning in an entirely untrustworthy manner as he said to Julian, "Come to wish us felicitations on our marriage?"

"Sod you," Quintus growled, and had Julian not held him back, he would've stepped forward.

Julian's gray eyes were narrowed, and Messalina recognized the subtle signs of his temper rising. Julian might seem detached most of the time, but when his anger was engaged he could strike like a snake—fast and deadly.

Which was the reason she'd instructed Lucretia to find him when Gideon had kidnapped her.

Messalina hastily said, "Perhaps this is a discussion better had inside, where there aren't so many interested eyes."

"Of course," Gideon replied. He leaned out of the carriage

and jerked his chin at Reggie, standing near the steps to Whispers House.

The big man nodded and disappeared inside.

For a moment Messalina thought Julian would challenge Gideon. Her brothers stood in front of the carriage door, effectively blocking them from descending. But then Julian stepped back silently, and Quintus grunted and shadowed him.

Gideon ignored the moment, jumping down and then turning to help Lucretia from the carriage.

Lucretia, however, glared at him and hopped down herself.

Gideon met Messalina's eyes and raised his brows as if asking if she'd allow him to help her.

She took a breath and put her hand in his, aware all the time that Julian and Quintus were watching closely.

Her brothers and Lucretia fell into step behind Gideon and Messalina as they entered Whispers House. Messalina felt conflicted. Just days ago, she would've welcomed Julian's interference.

But now—?

Now she didn't know what she wanted.

She'd been on the cusp of kissing Gideon when Lucretia had interrupted them. Even now, Messalina couldn't look at Gideon for fear that heat would rise in her face and her cheeks' coloring would betray her. But she was aware of him all the same. Of his lean form prowling beside her. Of the muscles of his forearm shifting beneath her fingers.

Of the heat of his body.

They climbed the stairs to the second floor and the sitting room—such as it was. The only pieces of furniture in the room were a pale-blue settee with two gilt-armed chairs and a little table to the side. Messalina had bought all four pieces ready-made.

Thank goodness.

She led Lucretia to the settee, watching from the corner of her eye as her eldest brother stalked around the empty sitting room. He looked bored, but Messalina had no doubt that Julian was sizing Gideon up.

Waiting to strike.

Gideon, for his part, was standing to the side and just in front of Messalina in a none-too-subtle guarding position. His hands hovered near the pockets of his coat, and she wondered if he kept a knife there. And then she scoffed at herself and wondered *how many* knives he kept on his person.

The tension in the room from the men was thick. Awful. She wanted to shout at them. They were acting as if they were dogs about to fight over a bone—and really, she was so much more than a mere bone.

"I'm sorry I was so long in bringing Julian," Lucretia murmured. "When Mr. Hawthorne took you out of our carriage and into his, I only waited until you were out of sight before I told our driver to make haste to Adders Hall."

Messalina nodded, squeezing Lucretia's hand.

Quintus had gone to lounge by the fireplace as if he was unconcerned. But she noticed that the hand not on the mantel was balled at his side.

"It was ages traveling to Adders," Lucretia said. Her mouth was thin and unsmiling. Lucretia was usually sly and gleeful, not this sorrowful girl, her gray eyes filled with tears. "And then when I arrived I could find only Quintus, quite in his cups."

Quintus pressed his lips together, turning his face away from Lucretia's glare. His wildly curling shoulder-length hair swung forward, hiding his eyes. Had he even put a comb to it today? He wore a beautifully tailored bottle-green silk suit, the material fitted expertly over his broad shoulders, but she could see from here that there were stains at the hem.

Lucretia shook her head at Quintus and looked back at Messalina. "He was so drunk I couldn't get any intelligible words from him for an hour. When I finally found Julian, we set off at once, but then the roads were muddy and we became bogged down..." She inhaled. "Perhaps I should've forgotten Julian and Quintus and made my way to London by myself from the start. If I had I could've somehow *helped*—"

Messalina interrupted, "There was nothing you could've done. Uncle Augustus had already brought the bishop to Windemere House when we arrived. He had a special license." She pressed her lips together. On the day of her wedding she would've welcomed help with open arms. Now...She glanced at her husband's back. It was stiff and set. "I don't know if anyone could've prevented the marriage."

"Did you try?" Julian asked in his velvet-soft voice. Sometimes Messalina wondered if he had practiced in order to attain a tone both melodious and threatening at the same time.

How dare he?

She glared at her older brother. He flanked the other side of the fireplace now, his arm, clad in silver brocade silk, propped on the mantel. Unlike Quintus he was meticulously turned out. His black hair was severely pulled back into a long, tightly braided queue. The ever-present pearl drop hung in his left ear, the gem matching the color of his Greycourt-gray eyes. Julian was handsome, she supposed, but he was cold. *Ice* cold, even with his family.

Perhaps especially with his family.

"Why do you ask, darling brother?" Messalina smiled. "After all, you don't appear to *care* one way or the other."

Quintus straightened from the mantel even as Julian murmured, "Could you have not stalled for a time? Even a day or two? You seem to have arrived at Windemere House and without complaint married the day after. And now you're busy making a happy home in this near-empty house in an unfashionably dingy neighborhood."

In front of her Gideon growled, his fingers resting on his coat pocket.

Quintus was watching Gideon, his head lowered, his hands clenching and unclenching. "He's Uncle's paid bully, Messy. He's left men drenched in blood. There are rumors he's *killed*."

Messalina felt her face suffuse with heat. She rose. "Do you really think I had *any* choice once I was at Windemere House?"

She glanced anxiously at Gideon. He knew already how she had felt when they first wed, but after the kiss this morning and the almost-kiss in the carriage, it seemed a betrayal to discuss it in front of her brothers.

"I *think*," Julian enunciated with slow, cut-glass accents, "that I am disappointed in how easily you *submitted* to a—"

"Watch your words," Gideon snapped.

"You *ass*," Messalina said at the same time to Julian. "You pompous, selfish ass. *I* disappoint *you*? When have you done anything for me or Lucretia or even Quintus in the last decade? Have you thought to ask Lucretia if she has any suitors? Have you taken Quintus's bottles and bottles of wine away from him? Have you ever inquired of me how my life is? No," she said, dodging around Gideon and advancing on Julian. "All you've done is obsess over Uncle Augustus's doings."

Julian simply looked at her. "With good reason, it seems."

But Messalina wasn't done. She'd lived under the dictates of Greycourt *men* for years and years, had been forced into marriage against her will, and now was being *blamed* for it. She was sick of everything. "You failed Lucretia, you failed Quintus, you failed me, Brother, and before that you failed *Aurelia*."

Behind her Lucretia gasped.

Julian merely blinked. Slow as a lizard. Had he any heart at all? Or had years of living with their uncle as a youth frozen any emotions he once had?

In contrast Quintus went white and strode forward to grip her arm. "Don't say her name."

"Quinn," Julian murmured softly in warning.

Just as Gideon shoved Quintus away from Messalina. "Keep your hands off my wife."

And with that Quintus swung at Gideon.

* * *

Gideon braced himself as Quintus Greycourt swung a meaty fist at his head. Quintus was broader and taller than Gideon, but he was an aristocrat.

Not a fighter born.

Gideon swiveled aside, the blow landing on his shoulder instead of his cheek. Gideon continued his turn so that he was sideways to the other man's chest. Then he delivered a short, sharp elbow jab to the aristocrat's stomach.

Quintus *oof*ed, reflexively curling inward. The man was determined, however. He straightened almost immediately, his lips pulled back from his teeth, and stomped on Gideon's foot before driving his fist into Gideon's side.

Gideon swore, rage blooming in his chest. He shook his knife from his sleeve and swiped at the aristocrat, fast and dirty, catching Quintus's forearm. Droplets of blood spattered to the floor.

From the corner of his eye he saw Julian Greycourt advancing.

If the elder Greycourt joined the fight Gideon could end all of this now. A simple thrust to the gut. A twist upward. The excuse that Julian had attacked first.

In only seconds he could kill Greycourt and gain all the dowry money at once.

Messalina screamed, the sound cutting through Gideon's brain and jerking him from his thoughts. He couldn't kill her brother in front of her.

He couldn't hurt her.

Greycourt caught Gideon's left arm.

Gideon swiftly pressed the point of his blade against Quintus's belly with his right.

Both brothers froze.

Gideon smiled into Quintus's face and whispered so low no one could hear but the three of them, "Your waistcoat may be embroidered in gold, but I assure you it'll prove no more barrier to my knife than worn wool. Your belly will spill your entrails just as fast as any pauper's in St Giles."

Quintus hissed at him, his pale-gray eyes raging.

"Pax, Hawthorne," Julian Greycourt murmured. "I hardly think my sister would enjoy you spilling our brother's blood in her sitting room."

No, she wouldn't—which was why Gideon had no intention of injuring either brother further.

Not that he need tell either Greycourt or Quintus that.

"What makes you think he cares anything for Messalina?" Quintus muttered.

"What makes you think I don't?" Gideon arched a brow.

Quintus's eyes narrowed.

Gideon smiled mockingly and pressed his knife more firmly into the man's waistcoat, slicing the pretty embroidery.

"I'll stand down if you give me your word not to continue your attack."

For a moment it looked as if Quintus would decline the offer of a truce.

Then Julian placed his hand on his brother's shoulder, whispering, "Quinn."

Quintus flung himself away with a snarl.

Gideon waited a moment and then palmed his knife, sliding it smoothly up his sleeve and into the sheath strapped to his forearm. He raised his voice, keeping his gaze on the two men. "Darling wife, will you take your sister to perhaps find some refreshment?"

"Not unless both you and my brothers swear that you'll not start fighting again," Messalina replied, sounding angry.

Stubborn woman. Gideon sighed. "Certainly. I swear not to lay hand on either Quintus or Greycourt." Of course, he could *kill* both men without ever touching them...

Julian eyed him as if aware of Gideon's omission. "I swear not to fight as well."

Everyone looked at Quintus.

He scowled. "Fine. Yes, I swear to you, dear sister, not to murder your husband."

Messalina lifted her chin, but she couldn't quite seem to hide the hurt on her face at her brother's sarcastic tone.

Gideon felt a violent urge to force Quintus to apologize to his sister.

"Very well," Messalina murmured. "We'll retire to the dining room."

She escorted Lucretia from the room.

There was a moment of silence after the ladies left.

Then Gideon took a deep breath and gestured to the settee. "Please."

Quintus turned his face aside, but Greycourt sat and

glanced around the otherwise empty room. "Your house seems to lack a basic level of livability, Hawthorne."

Gideon shrugged. "Messalina is enjoying decorating and furnishing it."

That prompted a snort from Greycourt. "Cut line, Hawthorne. What is your game?"

Gideon examined him. Julian Greycourt was a nobleman, born to luxury and power, yet stymied by his uncle, who held the family purse strings. Most aristocrats in his position would've cozied up to the Duke of Windemere and made sure to ingratiate themselves with the man.

Not Greycourt.

When Gideon had first started service with the duke, Greycourt had lived with his uncle. He'd been a silent, watchful shadow in Windemere House. When he turned one and twenty, Greycourt had either received permission to escape or he'd gathered the nerve to flee. In either case, in the years since he'd been frigidly polite with his uncle—and at the same time had made no bones of the fact that he loathed the man. That took either bravery or recklessness.

In other circumstances Gideon might have liked the man. *Might.*

"I would think my game—as you call it—was obvious." Gideon spread his hands as if showing that he held no weapons—which was patently false, since his knife was still up his sleeve. "Riches and power."

His gaze moved between Greycourt, sitting still and watchful on the settee, and Quintus, prowling about the room. The latter's eyes were shadowed and puffy in his red face. Did Windemere want Greycourt dead so the title would go to Quintus instead? Perhaps he thought Quintus with his rage and drinking would be a more malleable heir?

But to what end?

"You're frank," Quintus growled.

Gideon arched an eyebrow at the younger man. "Would you prefer I lie?"

Quintus barked a laugh. "Perhaps, since we're talking about *my sister*."

Interesting. Did Quintus actually care for Messalina?

Gideon glanced at Greycourt. The elder brother certainly didn't seem to have any real affection for his family. *His* concern had always appeared to be more about besting his uncle in whatever obscure game they played.

But then Greycourt was an icy fish.

"You think I should tell you I married her for love," Gideon said, ignoring Greycourt's soft snort to address Quintus. "But since you know that's not the case, I think such protestations would only make you scorn me the more."

"I doubt we could scorn you any more than we already do," Greycourt replied, his thin lips stretched in a humorless smile.

Gideon returned the smile—*with teeth*. "Oh, Brother, you wound me."

Quintus's nostrils flared, and he started for Gideon, but Greycourt put his hand up, halting his brother in his tracks. Julian stared stonily at Gideon. "I will have this marriage annulled."

Gideon tutted, making very sure that his expression didn't change. "And how would you do that when we were married by a bishop and with the Duke of Windemere's blessing?" He shook his head gently. "We've been married nearly a week. I'm afraid the time is quite past when you could've interfered."

Quintus paled at his oblique reference to the marriage bed. Gideon was reluctantly impressed by his obvious worry for Messalina.

But Greycourt had gone silent, his snakelike eyes narrowed

and watchful, and Gideon felt a thrill of alarm. Did the other man suspect his lie? If he questioned Messalina, all Gideon's plans would crumple to ash like a paper house set alight.

Julian could have their marriage annulled if he realized it hadn't been consummated, and then? Gideon would lose everything. The money. The chance to prove himself equal to any aristocrat.

And Messalina. Sweet, stubborn, far-too-intelligent Messalina.

He couldn't let that happen.

Gideon had to bed Messalina tonight.

CHAPTER TEN

Before her father could warn her, Bet had run to the
door and opened it. There stood the fox, wearing a
fine plumed hat and leaning on an ebony stick.
"Good evening," said the fox, tipping his hat with a
foxy grin. "I believe you are my intended...."
—From *Bet and the Fox*

"I do hope the cook has made something besides meat
pies today," Messalina muttered to herself as she escorted
Lucretia into the dining room. There really wasn't anywhere
else to *sit* in the house, since the sitting room was occupied
by the men. Well. Besides the bedroom.

Lucretia looked alarmed at her statement. "Your cook
only makes meat pies?"

"Erm...yes."

"But...but what about sweet things?" Lucretia asked as
if she were on the point of starvation. "Cakes or pies or
jellies or tarts...?"

Oh dear. Lucretia had always loved her tarts.

"I'm afraid not. But he *is* learning," Messalina added
hastily. "Just yesterday he made shirred eggs. By himself.
I just need to find a tutor for him. Well, and hire more
servants."

Lucretia was muttering about "no scones for breakfast."

But she stopped at her sister's words and stared. "No *servants*?"

"I'm afraid not," Messalina replied.

"Not at *all*?"

"There's a scullery maid?" Messalina heard her own voice go up in an apologetic, questioning way. She cleared her throat. "Oh, and Gideon's men, of course."

Lucretia's eyes narrowed, and Messalina suddenly remembered how very cunning her sister had been with her revenges as a child. "Why are you suddenly calling that man by his Christian name? I thought you loathed Mr. Hawthorne. I brought our brothers here to *save* you."

"And I'm grateful," Messalina said sincerely. "You did exactly what I wanted you to do. But the marriage is done now." She added thoughtfully, "I'm not sure I can be saved from it."

"There must be a way," Lucretia replied stubbornly. "We've plotted so long to escape."

"Hush." Messalina glanced at the door warily. It would hardly do for the men to overhear them. She looked back at Lucretia's expectant face and sighed. "I've an idea, but we must wait a bit. I'll have a portion of my dowry soon, and then we can leave England."

The words brought a pang to her heart. Only this afternoon she'd promised to help Gideon.

Lucretia frowned. "Why would Hawthorne give you that much money?"

She wasn't about to tell her younger sister exactly *how* she would get her dowry. "Just leave it to me. Have I told you that I've been preparing a room for you?"

That successfully diverted Lucretia. She gasped. "A room? *My* room? Whatever do you mean?"

"I've a room here already furnished for you—well, mostly

furnished—but there's definitely a bed. Your room was one of the conditions I made with Hawthorne." Messalina smiled, glad both to deliver good news and that she'd bought Lucretia's bed already made. "Before I married him, I told Gideon that I wanted you to live here with me, and he agreed. You need never live with Uncle Augustus again."

Instead of looking happy, Lucretia looked even more concerned.

Messalina took her hand. "I thought you'd like the notion?"

"I do," Lucretia said, squeezing her hand. "Of course I do. You know I'd much rather live *anywhere* but with Uncle Augustus. But I hate that you had to marry that...that *man* in order to procure us a home."

"He's not quite as awful as I first thought him." Messalina felt guilty heat rise in her cheeks as she remembered his bath this morning and the passionate kiss. It wasn't loathing she'd felt when he'd smiled at her.

It was longing.

She swallowed, chasing the thought away, and watched Lucretia's expressive face.

Her sister was eyeing her oddly now. Lucretia leaned forward, peering suspiciously at her. "He's drugged you."

Messalina groaned. "Lucretia..."

"No, but you might not even know that you'd been drugged," her sister said with a perfectly straight face. "I've heard of concoctions that can sway a person's thoughts, muddy them, and make the person more susceptible to suggestions."

Messalina nearly gaped. "Where have you heard of such things?"

Lucretia looked shifty. "Here and there."

"I suppose at genteel afternoon teas."

"No need to be sarcastic!"

Messalina shook her head. "In any case, I assure you I haven't been drugged by my husband."

The suspicion didn't leave Lucretia's face. "But just a fortnight ago when he snatched you from our carriage you were afraid of him. I *know* you were, Messalina. How can your regard for him have changed in so little time?"

"I don't know. I don't know, but I think it truly has." She searched for the right words to explain. "At least I'm no longer *afraid* of him. Gideon is much more...complicated than I realized. He's been almost kind since we came to Whispers."

Lucretia squinted. "*Kind.*"

"He agreed to let you live here," Messalina defended Gideon—and perhaps herself as well. "He agreed to let me furnish the house and to invite whomever I please to visit."

A look of understanding suddenly dawned on Lucretia's face, and she said quite kindly, "Is it the bedchamber? Has he won you over with...erm...his talented bedsport?"

Talented bedsport? Messalina's eyes widened. "*What?*"

"Well, he *is* quite good-looking." Her sister shrugged and said thoughtfully, "I mean, those hands and his shoulders and that *mouth*. I've overheard matrons discussing gentlemen using their mouths to—"

"Lucretia!" Messalina felt heat suffuse her face as she imagined just what Gideon could do to her with his tongue and lips. She took a deep breath. "As it happens, Gideon agreed to postpone our wedding night."

Lucretia blinked. "You mean...?"

"I mean that although we share a room and a bed we haven't—"

The door to the dining room opened and the gentlemen strode in, none of them looking very happy.

Messalina had leaned close to Lucretia during their conversation, and she straightened almost guiltily.

Gideon raised a brow, looking amused.

Julian, as always, merely seemed bored, while Quintus leaned against the doorjamb. Sometime in the last fifteen minutes he had gone pale.

Julian spoke first. "It is growing late, and Quinn and I must find rooms at an inn for the night. Come, Lucretia. We'll take you to Windemere House."

"*No*," Messalina blurted.

Both of her brothers looked at her.

Lucretia lifted her chin. "I'm staying with Messalina."

Quintus groaned near the door. He was rubbing his temple as if it ached. "Not you, too."

Messalina bristled. "Not her too *what*?"

Quintus waved his hand at Gideon. "She's willing to sleep under the same roof with *that*."

Messalina opened her mouth, but Lucretia beat her to the reply: "I'm staying with my *sister* because I love her."

Quintus flushed blotchily, looking away.

Julian sighed. "I understand not wishing to stay with our uncle, but I must point out that this house hardly seems livable."

"There's a bedroom suitably fitted for her," Gideon replied. "Thank you for your concern."

Julian ignored him. "Lucretia?"

"I'm staying," Lucretia said firmly.

Messalina let out her breath in relief and took her hand.

For a long moment Julian was still, and Messalina wondered if he would argue the point. He *mustn't*. She had to tell him and Quintus—*alone*—that their uncle had threatened Lucretia.

She glanced at Lucretia's happy face from under her eyelashes. She didn't want to wipe that expression away.

Julian nodded. "Very well. I'll say goodbye to you both." With that he pivoted and walked from the room.

Quintus looked exasperated, then glared at Gideon. "We plan to stay in town. If you do *anything* to harm either of my sisters, we'll know about it—and you'll pay."

"I tremble in my boots." Gideon's lips curved mockingly, belying his words. "However, I have no intention of hurting either Messalina or Lucretia. They're under my protection."

Quintus scoffed at that, but he strode to where Messalina and Lucretia sat and pulled them up one after the other and swept them into a bear hug.

Messalina closed her eyes. Even with the sour scent of old liquor about his person, Quintus's broad shoulders had always been comforting.

"Tomorrow morn I'll send the direction of the inn we'll stay in," he murmured before drawing back so he could pin them with his glare. "If *anything*—anything at all—makes you uncomfortable here, I want you to come to us at once. Barring that, send a letter. Do you understand?"

Messalina nodded. She was certain now that she'd have no need of such help, but she might as well put Quintus's mind at ease.

"Yes," Lucretia answered him solemnly.

"Good." With one last piercing glance he strode after Julian.

"Well," Messalina said, and then she had nothing to add.

"I don't suppose you've anything to sup on," Lucretia asked gloomily.

"Actually, we do," Gideon answered her.

"We do?" Messalina asked in surprise.

"Hicks has been practicing." He shot her a devilish grin before going to the door and calling, "Reggie!"

After a second the big man appeared. "Aye, guv?"

"Tell Pea to bring in the supper."

"Right you are."

Five minutes later Pea and Reggie brought in a bowl of apples, some cheese, bread and butter, and a roast chicken—only slightly burned.

Messalina clapped her hands. "Oh, he *is* improved."

Lucretia glanced from her to the blackened bird. "This is improved?"

Gideon ignored her incredulity. "Good lad," he muttered to Pea as the youth filled a glass of wine and handed it to Gideon. "Make sure to compliment our cook."

A wide grin broke across Pea's face before he hastily brought his expression back under control.

Messalina tilted her head. Odd. She hadn't noticed before how Gideon's men seemed to almost worship him.

"The apples look nice at least," Lucretia murmured, distracting her. She was seated next to Messalina, with Gideon sitting across from them.

Pea and Reggie left as Gideon began carving the chicken.

"Thank you," Lucretia said, accepting her plate from Gideon. "I suppose you still do my uncle's dirty work?"

Messalina nearly choked on her wine.

Gideon, though, seemed unperturbed, continuing to carve the chicken. "Yes, I do."

He handed a plate to Messalina.

"Isn't that rather awkward?" Lucretia asked with feigned concern.

"No more than it ever has been," Gideon replied.

"Ah, I forget," Lucretia said sweetly. "You've worked for my uncle since you were a youth. He found you in St Giles, didn't he? Rather like a stray cur."

"*Lucretia,*" Messalina hissed, mortified. She tried to kick her sister under the table and missed when Lucretia deftly moved her leg.

"Oh, *exactly* like a stray cur," Gideon said very softly. "He found me in a back alley fighting a man twice my size with a knife." He sipped his wine before carefully replacing his glass on the table. "I won. No doubt that's why he decided to hire me at once—he wanted a savage. Someone without morals or remorse to do the things an aristocrat couldn't— or wouldn't—do."

Messalina stared. Was that how Gideon saw himself? As someone beyond the bounds of humanity?

There was a clatter of silverware from Lucretia. "Our uncle is a *beast*. He's the savage."

And Messalina remembered again why she loved her sister so much.

But Gideon looked thoughtful. "Perhaps we're both savages."

Lucretia stared at him as she slowly took a sip of her wine, her eyes narrowing. "For your sake I hope not."

* * *

Gideon studied Messalina from beneath his eyelashes as he sipped his wine. She looked embarrassed by Lucretia's veiled threat, but not displeased, which made sense.

They were closer than most sisters.

He'd watched them when he'd first come to Windemere's house. Seen how they sat together, so close they were almost on top of one another. Sometimes Lucretia laid her head on Messalina's shoulder.

He'd seen also how both girls would straighten when the duke entered a room. Draw apart, their expressions blanking until it was impossible to tell how they felt.

They'd been each other's shield and protection against Windemere.

He needed to win Lucretia's favor in order to win Messalina's.

Gideon turned to Lucretia. "Do you have everything you'll need to stay the night?"

Lucretia nodded as she buttered a piece of bread. "I think so, but I can borrow from Messalina if not." She looked up at her sister, her brow wrinkling. "Have you brought all your things from Windemere House?"

"Yes," Messalina said. "Tomorrow we can send for your clothes and such."

Lucretia raised her eyes. "Shouldn't I go to make sure everything is packed?"

"*No*," Messalina said overloudly. "That is, I think it best that you stay here, darling."

"I'll go," Gideon said.

Both women looked at him in surprise.

Gideon spread his hands. "Don't you trust me?"

"No," Lucretia promptly replied.

Messalina seemed conflicted. "Erm..."

Her hesitation shouldn't hurt. He'd hardly done much to make her trust him. More, he intended to betray her.

He intended to murder her brother.

The thought gave him pause. How would she look when the news that Julian Greycourt was dead reached her? Would she weep?

Would she suspect that it was he who was the assassin?

Lucretia interrupted his dark thoughts. "Why would you want to help me at all?"

Gideon raised his eyebrows. "You are my sister-in-law now."

Lucretia picked up an apple and for a moment looked as

if she wanted to throw it at Gideon's head. "That was hardly my choice—or my sister's."

"Perhaps I'm a nice man."

Lucretia snorted in a very unladylike way as she began to peel the apple. "No. You are not. You have some dark reason to offer, I know."

Gideon smiled with gritted teeth. "Perhaps my dark reason is a desire to enjoy your lovely company at every supper."

Messalina made a choking noise.

His gaze swung to her, and he saw her eyes were filled with mirth as if she were just barely holding back giggles. Strange. Her eyes were the same shade of gray as her brothers' and her sister's, but somehow they were completely different. For a moment he lost himself, contemplating their depths, their beauty. Messalina's eyes were ever changing, betraying her emotion while the rest of her face often remained stoic. He might spend the rest of his life studying them.

Messalina's cheeks were turning a deeper pink even as he watched her. "Perhaps you simply wish to be done with this conversation."

His voice when he replied was husky. "Perhaps I do it for you."

Those eyes widened, her rose-red lips parting in innocent invitation.

It was all Gideon could do to stifle a groan.

"Well!" Lucretia said loudly—Messalina actually started. "I don't suppose there's any dessert? An entire *week* with Julian and Quinn and not a tart or syllabub in sight. You would not *believe* the awful inn we stopped in last night. We were served a dinner of cabbage soup with bits of gristle and a wine which I swear had turned to vinegar. And the bed!" Lucretia shuddered. "I don't think the linens had been changed this year. I spent the night in a chair before the fire."

She ended this rant by biting aggressively into a slice of apple.

"I'm so sorry you had to endure such privations," Messalina said gravely. "And I'll be sure to have dessert for tomorrow's supper."

Lucretia sniffed. "See that you do."

Her tone was light and bantering, but her gaze was still suspicious when she glanced at Gideon.

He sighed. It would take more than one meal to win Lucretia to his side. He'd need many, *many* meals to make the little termagant stop glaring at him as if he enjoyed maiming kittens.

Then Messalina looked at him with dancing gray eyes, her mouth pursed sweetly to keep from laughing.

She was worth all the trouble in the world.

* * *

"That will be all, thank you, Bartlett," Messalina murmured later that night. She sat at her dressing table, stroking a sleeping Daisy as the maid moved around the room and Gideon sat before the fire. He fingered a glass of wine and seemed rather strained. Perhaps the fight with her brothers bothered him more than she had realized.

"Shall I summon Sam to take the dog?" Bartlett asked, straightening from the chest of drawers.

Messalina started and turned to look at the lady's maid.

Bartlett's return gaze was knowing.

Messalina cleared her throat and tried to seem properly sedate. "Yes. Please call Sam."

She glanced through her lashes at Gideon, only to find him

watching her. Lit by the flickering fire he looked particularly demonic tonight.

Which she didn't find seductive *at all*.

Bartlett peeked out of the room and called, "Sam!"

The boy must've been very close, for he was in the room in seconds. "Ma'am?"

Messalina smiled down at him. "I think Daisy is ready for bed. Mind you take him into the garden before you put him in his basket by the kitchen fire."

"Yes, ma'am!" Sam was entirely earnest. He obviously took his job seriously. He cradled the puppy carefully as he left.

Bartlett stood by the door. "I'll just see to Miss Lucretia, shall I?"

"If you please."

Bartlett nodded and quietly closed the door.

Which, of course, left Messalina alone with Gideon in the bedroom.

She took a breath. He'd not slept with her the past couple of nights. Perhaps he'd leave.

She glanced at him as she fiddled with the ties to her wrapper.

Gideon was taking off his waistcoat, his coat and neck-cloth already removed.

Perhaps not.

She stared as the waistcoat was tossed to a chair.

He wore only shirtsleeves and breeches now.

The white linen provided a contrast to the darker skin at the top of the parted shirt. As she watched he refilled his wineglass from the decanter on the table and took a sip, tipping his head back.

She saw his throat work and something within her heated.

She looked away and met her own reflection in the mirror

over the dressing table. Her cheeks were pink, her lips wet, and her eyes were a little wild.

She inhaled. "Thank you."

"For what?" Gideon asked from behind her. She met his eyes in the mirror as he strolled closer with two glasses of wine in his hands.

Her mouth twisted into a rueful smile. "For bearing with my brothers—and Lucretia's conversation during dinner."

Gideon's gaze slid away from hers. "They're family. You can't control what your family does or believes, and besides. They were right."

Messalina turned in her chair to face him. He was so close her knees bumped his legs. "You think so?"

"Yes." His lips quirked, drawing her eye. They were curved, one side drawn up in a wickedly sensuous smile. "Your brothers seek only to protect you, and your sister is rightfully wary of me."

He handed her the second glass of wine.

She absently took it and sipped. The fruity taste spreading warmth through her.

She asked, "You're not angry that I sent Lucretia to bring Julian and Quinn here?"

He snorted. "I would've been surprised if you hadn't found some way to send for reinforcements."

Messalina bit her lip, thinking almost guiltily about her letter to Freya. She still hadn't received a reply, which made her think that her letter had gone astray somehow. Or perhaps she was impatient and the reply just hadn't had time to arrive.

"Messalina?" His dark voice broke into her thoughts.

She looked up. Gideon had leaned his hip against her dressing table and was studying her with a slight line between his brows.

He stood nearly between her legs.

She whispered, "Yes?"

"I…" His expression was serious. "I'm not angry with you, you understand? I've always considered you a worthy opponent." He grimaced. "That's not quite the word I want, but I think you know what I mean. I admire your intelligence. Your stubbornness."

"Thank you," she said gravely, though a part of her was vastly amused by such an awkward compliment, however heartfelt it might be.

He shook his head. "You're mocking me now."

"Only a little," she replied, taking another sip of her wine for fortitude. "Perhaps we're past the point of being opponents?"

That devastating half smile played around his lips again. "Shall I press for a truce?"

Her nipples were tight and pointed, stabbing at the cloth covering them. Could he see? "On what terms?"

"Oh, I think the terms should come from you," he murmured, his voice deepening.

She took a breath and wondered when the air had left the room. "Then I ask that you refrain from killing my brothers and be very, *very* patient with my sister."

His smile seemed to drop for a moment, but perhaps that was her imagination, for in another blink it was as roguish as ever.

"You bargain hard, madam," he whispered roughly, "but I am sure I can abide by those stipulations."

"And if I have one more?" she asked, searching the depths of those black eyes.

"I suppose that depends on what it is," he replied softly, leaning closer.

She bit her lip and his gaze fell to her mouth. "You will take me to the theater at least twice a month."

Any other man in her experience, caught in a moment of flirtation, would've turned surly at her mild suggestion. But somehow Gideon's sharp black eyes softened. "Of course. If it would amuse you."

Actually, she wanted to return to the theater with him so that *he* might be amused.

Her smile was private.

"But," he continued as he knelt between her spread legs, "I find I have terms as well."

He was so close, his hard chest brushing against her soft breasts.

She swallowed.

"Do you?" She held his gaze, though her heart had begun to beat faster.

He nodded. "Just one."

She found herself leaning closer to him, his breath caressing her lips. "What?"

"A kiss."

He barely waited for her nod and then his mouth was on hers, commanding and wild. He groaned, deep and loud in the silence of the room, and took her face in his hands, thrusting his tongue into her mouth.

She could taste the wine, and she suckled him as if to appease him. She was trembling. How could he make her feel this way? As if she was no longer in control of her own body?

As if she needed something more.

She broke the kiss, gasping, leaning her forehead against his.

"Can you," she said, her voice shockingly raspy. "Can you take off your shirt?"

He stilled, and for a moment she thought she'd gone too far. That her desire to see his skin—his *naked* skin—was a bedroom faux pas of some sort.

She drew back and saw that he was staring at her with something like triumph.

He began to unbutton the placket of his shirt, and her gaze dropped to watch, her breath coming fast. He was so close that his knuckles brushed her breasts with every move.

She was wet there in that place between her thighs.

The neck of his shirt parted to reveal black, curling hairs. He came to the end of the buttons and reached behind his back to pull the shirt off.

The farthing on the chain around his neck swung forward. She caught it in her hand, momentarily distracted. The metal skin-warm. Britannia was so worn, her head had nearly disappeared. A hole had been carefully drilled at the upper edge for the chain.

She looked up. "Why do you wear this?"

He began unbuttoning his breeches, there before her. "No reason."

He must have a reason, surely? And if so, why wouldn't he tell her?

As she pondered, he pulled the coin from her hand. Then he shucked off breeches, stockings, and shoes.

She caught her breath.

Gideon was wearing only his white linen smalls now, standing proudly, almost arrogantly. His penis and bollocks hung heavy against the thin cloth.

As she helplessly watched, a tiny dot of moisture marked the cloth. She pulled her gaze from the spot and looked up at him.

He watched her as if challenging her.

She could end this now. Stop whatever was forming between them and simply go to sleep.

Or she could take her courage and plunge—into a real marriage—a *real* connection—with Gideon.

A part of her called *Too soon! Too soon*, but she ignored it. She *wanted* this.

Messalina rose slowly before him.

His eyes glinted as he watched her.

She took a deep breath and untied the bow at her throat. She felt as if she were revealing much more than her body.

The wrapper fell to the ground.

She stood trembling a moment in her sheer chemise before she licked her lips and turned to the bed. "Are you coming?"

He caught her wrist as she reached the bed, spinning her around. His mouth claimed hers as if he could no longer hold himself back. As if he'd held on to his restraint by the tips of his fingers.

He angled his head, opening his mouth over hers, almost desperately thrusting his tongue past her lips, his fingers splayed against her cheek all the while.

He held her tenderly even as his mouth ravaged hers.

Warmth shot straight down her body to settle between her legs, throbbing. She moaned, lifting her hands to clutch his head. She wanted more. Wanted something that she wasn't sure he could give her.

Wanted the freedom to come undone.

She turned her face from his, trying to thread her fingers through his hair even as he ran his mouth down her neck. She was breathless, almost giddy from trepidation, anticipation, and *need*.

The tie in his hair frustrated her efforts. She yanked it free, making his black hair fall about his cheeks. She smiled at the sight, gathering his curls into her hands. She felt almost privileged. Gideon didn't let down his guard for many.

In an abrupt movement, he lifted her to the bed and followed her, settling by her side.

She looked up at him, gasping for breath.

He was formidable like this—his hair wild and untamed, his hairy chest no longer kept hidden.

And his eyes. They were so possessive, so focused on her, that she felt a shiver run down her back.

The ache in her quim grew, pounding with her heartbeat.

He levered himself up, leaning over her. He took the ribbon that gathered her chemise at the neckline and pulled, untying it.

She stilled like a cat caught by a far larger beast.

She felt him spread the neck of her chemise before he slowly drew it down. Until the fine material caught on her nipples.

For a moment he simply stared at her. Then—when she was about to demand he do *something*—he moved, tracing her areola through the lawn chemise with one finger.

She swallowed hard. It was so odd—such a tiny touch—it felt almost like pinpricks, except it was pleasurable.

Unbearably pleasurable.

Her whole body felt alight.

One finger. That was the only part of him touching her, and she feverishly wondered what would happen when he used his entire body. She arched at the thought.

He placed his palm flat on her upper chest, holding her still, and then he bent to lick her nipple through the chemise.

She had to close her eyes.

Oh Lord, this was wonderful.

He suddenly drew that bit of flesh into his mouth and suckled, sending streaks of pleasure throughout her body. It was so sweet, so intolerable she wanted to scream.

He lifted his head and she opened her eyes. Just in time to see him transfer to her other nipple, sucking strongly until the material was damp. He drew back, his eyes frankly on her breasts, looking very satisfied.

She felt the chill of the damp material and she wanted to squirm.

He glanced at her face and flashed her a roguish smile before impatiently pushing down her chemise.

When he took her naked breast into his mouth the heat made her cry out.

She panted as he drew at her breasts one after the other, pulling pleasure from her center through those taut peaks.

She *ached*.

He sat up, taking all that sensation with him, and she couldn't help but grasp for him.

He growled, pulling her chemise over her head.

And then she was naked for the first time with a man. She froze, controlling the impulse to cover herself while at the same time feeling as if she might explode.

He was watching her, though, and the hunger, the *want*, in his gaze made her relax.

He still wore his smalls.

"Take those off," she ordered, her voice low and throaty.

He stood and unbuttoned his smalls, letting them fall to the ground. She just had time to glimpse his angry red cock and then he was back in the bed, crawling over her, gently nudging apart her thighs and settling atop her, the chain and farthing pooling between her breasts.

His hard penis pressed into her thigh.

She thought that he might immediately mount her, but instead he kissed her.

Slowly.

His lips parting hers, his tongue lazily sweeping into her mouth.

She gasped, arching under him, feeling the hardness of

his thighs against her own, the slight scrape of his hair on the tender skin between her legs. She drew on his tongue, suckling it. Suckling him.

Her hands stroked over his shoulders, feeling the muscles of his back, the long indentation of his spine, and his taut buttocks. She drew up her legs, driving her toes into the mattress, opening herself to him.

She *yearned*.

Until finally he raised himself a little and reached between their bodies. She felt his knuckles on her belly and then lower, brushing against her wet folds.

He positioned himself.

She inhaled, glancing up, meeting his gaze.

He did not look kind.

He stared down into her eyes as he *pushed*.

She swallowed, feeling him invade her. He was large, foreign, *male* where she was most female.

"All right?" he murmured, breathless, his voice dark.

She nodded.

"Sure?"

She lifted her chin as something pinched. "Yes."

He began to retreat, the drag of his flesh against hers making sparks light within her. Just when she was about to complain, to clutch him and call him back, he thrust into her again.

Solid.

Hard.

Wonderful.

Her eyelids half closed against her will. Why had no one told her how sweet this was? Animal, crude, but sweet as well?

She spread her fingers along his throat and demanded, "Again."

He stretched his lips in what might've been a grin and complied, his strong body thumping into her, his cock even deeper somehow.

"Like that?" he whispered.

"Yes." She twisted, reveling in the feeling.

No wonder this was forbidden to women unwed. If young ladies knew about it, they'd never wait for marriage. They'd throw aside convention and social mores and bed any man who pleased them.

All of society would be turned upside down.

The thought made her slide her palms down his back, over the indentation at the small of his back and onto his pumping buttocks. *She* was allowed this. She was allowed *him*.

He was pounding into her now, his voice reduced to grunts in time to his thrusts. As if he'd lost the veneer of civilization.

And then, as she was watching, as she clutched the muscles of his bottom, she felt him tense.

As if he were having a seizure.

As if he were dying.

His head was thrown back, the cords of his neck shining with sweat and strain, beautiful and savage in the candlelight.

She watched him, rapt, as he stilled and shuddered.

He slumped onto her, unexpectedly heavy. Slowly he rolled off her.

She couldn't help a pang of disappointment. Her body was still strung taut. Was it over? She'd somehow thought there was more. That the feeling that had been building within her would have some outlet.

Instead everything had simply stopped. Perhaps later, when he fell asleep, she could—

He leaned over her again and placed his hand on her feminine triangle.

"What—?" she began.

He stroked a finger into her folds, watching her, his half-lidded eyes lazy, satiated, and then he touched that bit of flesh.

She squeaked.

"Like that?" he murmured.

"*Yes.*" She clutched at his arm, but not to stop him. To hold him there.

He smiled slowly and bent to kiss her, relentlessly stroking her all the while. She could hear the sound of him working her—wet and explicit—and it filled her with needy heat. Should she be embarrassed? Perhaps, but she couldn't care right now. All of her being was focused on that one finger.

She moaned.

She was so close.

So close.

And then he thrust his tongue into her mouth and she clenched her thighs around his wrist, whimpering as she shook apart.

CHAPTER ELEVEN

*Well the tinker wept and Bet's mother shouted, saying
that Bet need not honor a promise her father had
made years ago.
But Bet looked at the fox and shook her head slowly.
"Father gave his word and the fox saved him from
the wood." She held out her hand to the beast. "I will
marry you."....*
—From *Bet and the Fox*

Gideon woke the next morning to the feel of Messalina's
soft lips brushing against his shoulder.

He opened his eyes and met her beautiful gray gaze.

Her eyes crinkled at the corners as she smiled. "Good
morning."

He cleared his throat, but his voice still sounded like
knives scraping when he said, "Good morning."

He had a moment to think that something was wrong.
That he should feel guilty for something. But then she
leaned down.

"We didn't wait the full month." She blushed.

"Is that all right?" he asked slowly, trying to understand
her mood.

"Yes." A corner of her mouth quirked up. "And it means
I'll have my moneys sooner."

Little schemer.

She kissed him, her pretty breasts crushed against his chest, and he tried to push away the apprehension. The guilt.

This could not last.

For the moment she was his—fully and in every way. No one could take her away from him because now their marriage was real.

But Julian Greycourt had come to London. No doubt the duke already knew and would be demanding Gideon's part of the bargain.

He was going to have to murder Greycourt within days.

And when Messalina discovered that he'd killed her brother—and she would discover, he knew it now—all this would evaporate. She would look at him with horror and loathing.

She would leave him.

His time with her was fleeting. Soon—too soon—it would be over.

Best he use it well, then.

He rolled to his back and pulled her over him in a sprawl, catching her giggle in his mouth.

This, *this* was what he'd wanted all his life.

He ran his hand down her naked back to her arse, palming one plump buttock with possession. She was soft and warm from sleep, pliable in the way her limbs slumped over him, and he could feel his cock, hard and throbbing, pressed into her belly. He shifted her hips, bringing her velvety cunny over his erection.

She moaned into his mouth as he spread her legs to either side of his hips. She might be sore this morning and he didn't want to hurt her. He ground against her slick folds instead, gently, letting her get used to the notion.

She wriggled, nearly making him lose control of their movements. He had the animal urge to *thrust* and *penetrate*, but he beat it down.

Easy.

Slow.

There was no rush, after all. Not this morning, anyway. This was his wife, his bed. He twisted his head, seeking the depths of her mouth, chasing the quiet whimpers she made. He could feel her wetness now, that plush feminine softness, and it was taking all he had to keep this languid.

He heard her gasp. She pulled back her head, her hair brushing against his face and throat.

She swallowed, her lips parted and shining wet from their kiss.

He grasped her hips and arched against her, rubbing his penis into her cunt, his balls drawn up tight, his blood beginning to boil.

Her brows drew together as if she were choosing the trim on a new frock. If he'd had the breath he might've laughed at the thought.

But then she bit her bottom lip and he was jealous of the movement.

He caught her mouth, licking that bottom lip, soothing it before he claimed it for himself, biting and teasing.

She groaned and stiffened, her hands clutching his shoulders, her fingers scrabbling against his perspiring skin. She shuddered and he felt the heat of her orgasm.

He thrust into her sweet, soft mouth, taking advantage of her limp relaxation.

His.

His.

His.

He came on the thought. On her sweet, wet softness. On her lips, open in submission to him.

She was *his*.

For now.

* * *

Late that morning, Julian Greycourt stood on the steps of Windemere House and stared down the butler. Johnson was his name, and he'd been in service to the duke since before Julian and his siblings had come to live at Windemere House.

The butler was an imposing man of middle age with a great sloping belly and a perfect, snowy wig on his head. He'd been one of the most eager of Augustus's spies and informants.

Johnson attempted to block his way. "Shall I see if His Grace is in to receive you?"

"No need." Julian placed the flat of his hand against the man's chest and pushed.

The butler stumbled back with a yelp.

Julian strode inside the house.

Two burly footmen converged on him.

Julian raised one eyebrow and drawled, "Really?"

The footmen halted.

Julian didn't bother acknowledging them further, but simply climbed the stairs to Augustus's study.

The duke looked up when Julian opened the door and then glanced to the clock atop his desk. "You're late. I expected you days ago."

"Did you?" Julian took a chair before the desk, because there was no point in waiting for one to be offered. Augustus enjoyed making people stand before him like criminals about to be judged. "Is that why you've done this obscene thing?"

"You mean arrange lovely Messalina's marriage?" A slow smile crossed the duke's face, revealing a dent in his left cheek.

Julian made himself continue looking at his uncle. The dent—indeed everything physical about Augustus—reminded Julian of his father. The brothers had been so similar, some had mistaken them for twins.

It was hard to stare into the face of the man he hated most in the world and see his father's ghost.

Julian made sure his voice was calm, even, nearly bored when he answered. "Yes, my sister's marriage." He examined his nails. "You could have found a much more advantageous match—both for her and you—which makes me wonder how you've benefited from marrying Messalina to your guard dog."

He flicked his eyes up on the last, watching for any tell, any revealing change of expression on his uncle's face.

Naturally there was none.

"Bravo, Nephew," the duke said. "You've learned well from my tutelage."

Julian took a careful breath before he spoke. "I learned nothing from you."

Augustus shrugged. "You certainly didn't learn to look for your enemy's motives from your father." His upper lip curled ever so slightly. "Claudius never saw anything beneath the surface his entire life. I vow he died thinking I loved him."

Julian cocked his head and said gently, "Instead of realizing what a monster of a brother you were."

That hit Augustus. His face reddened as he leaned forward and hissed, "Your father was a thorn in my side all his life. I can still see his milksop face looking at me so sorrowfully, as if he pitied me." He sat back panting. "But I won, didn't I, dear boy? Your father died falling on his face, while I still *live*."

The look Augustus sent him was wildly triumphant.

Julian would not remember Papa when he died. Would not remember the hideous apoplectic attack that had sent his father to his knees, half his face sagging before he'd indeed fallen and died.

Instead Julian yawned. "My father might be dead, but he was able to ensure his line. A line"—he stood leisurely—"which it seems will soon continue the Dukedom of Windemere."

Strangely, Augustus smiled at this. Usually his temper rose at any mention of Julian's being his heir. Instead he seemed to have calmed. "Well," the duke drawled. "I suppose that might be so. Unless…" He trailed away as if a thought had struck him. "Oh, unless you prove to have as poor a constitution as your father."

Julian's eyes narrowed. "My father died at eight and thirty. I'm only two and thirty and far more likely to outlive you, dear uncle."

"Are you?" Augustus shrugged as if it mattered little at all.

A chill went through Julian. The duke's words were a clear threat on his life.

"Well, this has been a pleasant chat," Julian said dryly, "but I fear I must be off on other errands."

"A pleasure as always, Nephew," Augustus replied lazily. "I do hope, though, that you'll be attending the ball Her Grace has arranged to celebrate Messalina's marriage? It's in a week's time."

"Naturally," Julian drawled. If nothing else, attending the ball might give him an idea of what Augustus was up to with Messalina.

The duke grunted. "Lucretia needs to return to Windemere House to help Ann plan. Where is the girl, anyway?"

"She's at Whispers House with Messalina," Julian replied carelessly. "Where she'll remain."

Augustus leaned forward, his face slowly reddening. His words, though, were calm when he spoke. "I have interested gentlemen I wish her to meet. Do make sure she attends the ball or I shall have to talk to her in private."

Julian stared at the duke. Augustus was waiting for his reaction, nearly slavering for it.

He bowed. "Good day, Uncle."

With that he strolled out of the room, making sure to keep his pace leisurely as he descended the staircase and strode out the door.

Outside he flipped a coin to the small boy holding his horse before mounting and setting off at a trot.

He still didn't know what Augustus was planning with Messalina's marriage to his lackey, but Julian did know one thing.

He had to make certain Lucretia didn't suffer the same fate.

* * *

"Purple?" Lucretia wrinkled her nose doubtfully later that day.

"Purple," Messalina said firmly. She smiled fondly at the swatch of fabric laid over the sturdy armchair, then nodded at the clerk standing hopefully beside her. "Four, please. All upholstered in the purple. Now." She glanced around the cavernous furniture shop. "A dressing table for you," she said to Lucretia.

"Guest rooms?" her sister asked, trailing behind.

"Well, naturally that as well." Messalina pursed her lips. "At *least* four, then."

"I can't believe Mr. Hawthorne's just letting you spend whatever you like on the house," Lucretia muttered.

"Well, why shouldn't he?" Messalina inquired, a bit

hypocritically considering all the arguing she'd had to do on her *first* trip to this shop. She paused by a side table with a red marble top and fanciful gilt legs that might work for the library. "It's my money, after all."

"But it's not," Lucretia replied. "Not legally, anyway. It's all his."

"I already told you I have plans to regain some of it." Messalina stopped and turned toward her younger sister curiously. "Do you *want* Gideon to keep me from my money until then?"

"No, of course not." Lucretia scowled at the side table. "I'm just suspicious about his motives."

"You're *always* suspicious. But I do understand why you're worried over this in particular." Messalina sighed, strolling past the side table. It *was* very garish. "All I can say is that we've made the best of this marriage, Gideon and I. He's ambitious and has a terrible past, it's true, but he's very clever, and I find his conversation quite stimulating."

"Stimulating," Lucretia said flatly.

Messalina felt heat invade her cheeks. "Yes, stimulating."

Lucretia stopped, and Messalina took several steps before she realized she'd left her sister behind. She turned.

Lucretia's mouth had fallen open. "You bedded him!"

The clerk who had begun to discreetly shadow them did an about-face and appeared to remember an urgent matter on the opposite side of the showroom.

Messalina glared at Lucretia. "Must you announce my affairs to the *entire* shop?"

Lucretia hurried to her side and hissed, "You *did*."

At least her voice was a little lower. "I don't—"

"Last night," Lucretia continued, pursing her lips and inspecting Messalina all over as if looking for a sign proclaiming that Messalina was no longer virginal. "Because you said just yesterday that you *hadn't*. What was it like?"

"*Lucretia.*" Her face felt as if it were *pulsing* with heat.

But her sister had an intent *thinking* expression on her face. This was exactly why no one who knew Lucretia would play charades with her anymore. "You must've enjoyed it because you called him *stimulating*. And this morning at breakfast you had a silly smile on your face—"

"I did not!"

"I think you enjoyed it very much indeed."

"Oh my Lord," Messalina sighed.

Lucretia narrowed her eyes. "Was there blood?"

"What," Messalina muttered, looking around for something to distract her sister.

A blond young woman was standing by the door to the shop, her bearing oddly familiar. For a second Messalina stared. She almost looked like—

"Because," Lucretia continued relentlessly, drawing Messalina's attention back to her, "they always go on and on about blood. If one is to believe the tales, it's a wonder that all newly married women don't bleed to death on their wedding night."

For a moment Messalina could only gape in horror at her sister. She glanced back at the doorway, but the woman was gone.

Messalina shook her head and pointed blindly at a dressing table. "What about this one for your room?"

They both contemplated the table. It had a yellow marble top, and the legs were made entirely of gilt curlicues and...cupids. Naked gold babies with hardened middle-aged man faces.

Lucretia tilted her head, staring at the abominable dressing table. "Truly?"

"Dear goodness, no."

"Hm," Lucretia mused. "You know..."

Messalina looked at Lucretia when her words trailed away. Lucretia hardly ever hesitated to say exactly what she thought. "What?"

Lucretia frowned horribly and said in a rush, "I only want you to be happy. *Truly* happy, not just content. You used to loathe Mr. Hawthorne—we both did, the way he spied and lurked. I just don't understand how you can have changed your mind so quickly."

"Well, part of it is I didn't truly know the man," Messalina said dryly.

"And you do now?" Lucretia's gray eyes—the same shade as her own—searched her face.

"Not completely," Messalina admitted. "I've only been married to him less than a fortnight. But in that time he's talked to me. He's *listened* to me. Perhaps...perhaps I'll find out something to his detriment in the future, but right now I have hope." She half smiled. "I think even in the best of marriages that may be the only important thing."

"But"—Lucretia turned to face Messalina, her expression grave—"have you thought about what will happen when we leave?"

Messalina blinked. She'd rather been avoiding the thought of leaving Gideon. She traced the inlay on a cabinet. "I don't—"

"Because you might be with child."

Messalina stilled at the stark words. Of course she knew that. Of course she'd considered that lying with her husband might result in a child.

Except she really hadn't—not explicitly, anyway. The only thing she'd been thinking about last night was the pleasure Gideon was giving her.

She inhaled and looked at her sister. "If I'm with child, then...then we'll deal with it. I certainly wouldn't be the first woman pretending to be a widow to settle in a small town."

"Very well," Lucretia said, though she still looked worried.

Messalina glanced around the shop. "Which dressing table do you like?"

"I was thinking of that one." She pointed to a darling rosewood dressing table inlaid on the top with various colored woods to form a basket of roses.

"That *is* lovely," Messalina said. "Naturally we'll buy it for your room."

Lucretia looked doubtful, but thankfully didn't pursue the matter. Instead they spent the remainder of their shopping trip picking out odds and ends and arguing pleasantly over a fire screen.

When Lucretia collapsed dramatically on the carriage squabs, she moaned, "It's tragic that your cook can't make cakes. Or tartlets. Those tiny lemon curd ones that you can pop whole into your mouth."

Messalina snorted. "Only if you want to demonstrate your lack of manners."

Lucretia waved a dismissive hand. "Should we worry about manners when we're only with family?"

"Yes," Messalina said firmly as the carriage made them both sway. "As for my cook, well, there's something you should know about him."

She proceeded to explain Hicks's circumstances.

"Oh," Lucretia said when Messalina came to the end. "Now I feel wretched for maligning him." She stared at the ceiling of the carriage for a contemplative moment. "Do you know, I've never truly thought about how cooks are trained." She turned to Messalina. "Have you?"

"Well, *now* I have," Messalina said. "But you're right. I enjoyed the meals but didn't think about who made them.

After all, the cooks in the houses we've lived in or visited have always been just *there*."

"And yet," Lucretia mused, "I can see that it would be hard to learn the art of cookery if one hadn't a position in a big house."

It would, Messalina thought. Unless he cooked for one of the big inns in London, there weren't many places a young man could learn to cook. Hicks had apparently worked at a tavern where the food was quite simple.

She mused on the thought for the rest of the carriage ride home.

When they arrived back at Whispers some half hour later, Lucretia was rather wilted.

Messalina eyed the four big men descending from their carriage. All four had trailed them through Bond Street, only steps behind.

Gideon had doubled her guard.

Lucretia had noticed their shadows, pressing questions on her. Messalina rather thought her sister didn't believe the excuse that Gideon liked showing off his retinue.

"I don't understand," Lucretia said as she slumped up the stairs to the house, "why I should be so terribly exhausted. After all, we spent the day merely pointing to things and buying them. I feel as if I've run thrice around London Town."

"Shopping is always tiring," Messalina replied. She spotted Reggie inside the entryway.

The big man shuffled his feet. "Two ladies waiting for you in th' sitting room, ma'am."

Messalina stared. And then she grabbed Lucretia's hand and squeezed it. "Could you please ask Cook for some tea and refreshments?"

"Aye, ma'am," Reggie replied. "Though I don't know that 'Icks is familiar with ladies' refreshments."

"Maybe not," Messalina murmured. "If he doesn't know what to send, tell him bread and butter with some jam will do."

Reggie nodded and retreated in the direction of the kitchens.

Messalina tried to keep calm as she led the way upstairs.

Lucretia hissed as they walked along the upper hall, "What is it? Do you know who your guests are?"

But Messalina couldn't speak, the anticipation was too strong.

She hurried through the open sitting room doors. Inside a woman with flaming red hair stood by the settee where another lady was sitting.

"Freya!" Messalina ran to the red-haired lady's arms.

Freya Renshaw, the Duchess of Harlowe, hugged her for several long seconds before stepping back. "Darling, you must explain everything."

"You got my letter, then?" Messalina asked.

"Letter?" Freya said slowly. "No. But then Kester and I have been on the road to London for the past week."

"You must've crossed paths with it," Messalina sighed.

"Are *all* London rooms so bare?" asked a husky voice behind them.

Messalina started and only then remembered Lucretia and the second woman sitting on the settee.

She turned to look.

Lucretia was still standing, watching her and Freya raptly.

The other lady, however, was perusing the room, her head thrown back to look at the mural of bathing nymphs on the ceiling. She was plump, her cheeks rosy, and her hair was a cloud of red and gold, rather messily pinned up.

"Male painters are quite fascinated by buttocks, aren't they?" the woman said in a surprisingly throaty voice. "And quite pink ones at that."

Her eyes dropped and she glanced at the other ladies in the room. "Have I missed anything?"

Freya rolled her eyes. "Do you remember my sister Elspeth?"

"Elspeth?" Lucretia looked suspicious. "The same Elspeth who used to steal the strawberry jam when she visited our nursery for tea?"

"I do love strawberry jam," Elspeth said dreamily.

Lucretia narrowed her eyes.

"How wonderful to see you again." Messalina smiled, crossing to give the younger woman a hug. She stood back to examine Elspeth's face. "Though I'm not sure I'd recognize you without Freya's prompting. You were only five, I think."

"I was six," Elspeth said, and she fixed her light-blue eyes on Messalina. "And I remember *you* because you read to me once."

"I did?"

Elspeth nodded solemnly. "Poems. Elizabethan poems. I don't believe I understood a word, but I liked the sound of your voice. That summer before it all happened."

It was long ago—fifteen years—but they all knew the date. It was when Aurelia Greycourt had died and Ran de Moray had been maimed.

For a moment no one spoke.

And then Lucretia said, "*And* you stole my top."

She was glaring at Elspeth.

"Did not," Elspeth replied far too quickly. "You *gave* it to me."

Lucretia placed her hands on her hips. "I didn't. I left it by that awful bust of some Roman emperor in the library. And when I came back it was gone."

"Hmm," Elspeth murmured thoughtfully. "No, I remember

you gave it to me when we were having tea in *your* nursery."

Lucretia's face looked like a thundercloud.

Fortunately, at that moment Pea came in with the tea.

"Oh, bread and jam," Elspeth said. "Is it strawberry, do you suppose?"

She smiled at Lucretia.

Messalina blinked and glanced upward at the painted ladies on the ceiling. When Elspeth smiled she looked rather like an old master's beauty.

Lucretia sat next to Elspeth—apparently to guard the jam.

Messalina sighed heavily as she gestured for Freya to take one of the chairs while she sat on the other.

She poured the tea. "I'm so glad you're here."

Freya took a cup. "Tell me."

Messalina explained what had happened when she and Gideon reached London and how she'd been forced into marriage.

When she finished, Freya said, "I wish I could have been here." She shook her head and glanced at Elspeth. "But Kester and I had gone to fetch Elspeth from the Wise Women compound. My sister was in training to be the Wise Women's next Bibliothacar—the keeper of our history and books."

Lucretia looked between Freya and Messalina. "Wise Women?"

And Messalina realized with a guilty start that she hadn't told Lucretia about them.

But it was Elspeth who replied to Lucretia. "We are an ancient society of women, descended some believe from priestesses who guided these isles before the Romans came." Her eyes lit. "Our history is really quite fascinating, for instance—"

Freya cleared her throat. "Perhaps it's our *modern* history that's most pertinent at the moment."

"I think I disagree there, Sister," Elspeth said gently.

"Ancient priestesses?" Lucretia burst out. "Is this a jest?"

"Oh no," Elspeth said earnestly. "We've a compound in—"

Freya loudly cleared her throat.

"—the north," Elspeth said without missing a beat. "We have—*had*—nearly two thousand people there, including children and men—"

"Wait," Lucretia interrupted, looking intent. "How can there be children if this society is made up of priestesses?"

Elspeth smiled a little condescendingly at Lucretia. "Priestesses who aren't from a *male*-led religion. We have never been celibate. But in any case, we no longer call ourselves priestesses. We're Wise Women. Although," she continued with an academic air, "you do bring up an interesting aspect of our society, namely sex with men. There are quite a few differing opinions—"

Freya coughed. "Perhaps we should return to the main point."

"Yes." Messalina's brows knitted. Did she truly want to leave Gideon anymore? "I'd thought perhaps..."

"That the Wise Women could help you?" Freya exchanged a grim glance with Elspeth. "No, I'm afraid they can't."

"Not since the closing," Elspeth said sadly.

"What closing?" Messalina asked.

Freya pursed her lips. "The leaders who have come to power in the Wise Women have decided to isolate the compound." She met Messalina's gaze. "They intend to close the Wise Women to all outside influences. The Women who didn't agree with that ruling left."

"And went out into the wide, wide world," Elspeth

murmured, watching Lucretia pile jam on her bread. "Like a fairy tale."

Messalina felt a guilty wave of relief. She'd have to wait, then, until Gideon handed her the money.

She glanced at Freya. "And Caitriona? Did she stay behind?"

Caitriona was the middle de Moray sister.

Freya frowned in what looked like frustration. "Caitriona had already left when Kester and I got there. I don't know where she is. We even stopped by Ayr Castle, but Lachlan swore he hadn't seen her."

Lachlan was the second brother in the de Moray family. Messalina vaguely remembered that he managed his brother's estates.

"Caitriona makes her own way," Elspeth said calmly. "There's no point in chasing after her."

The door to the sitting room opened. Sam came in, carefully holding a tray. Daisy was trotting by his side, his eyes firmly fixed on the tray. "'Icks said as 'e thought you might want more 'freshments, ma'am."

Lucretia gasped, "Why didn't you tell me there was a puppy in the house?"

She made kissing noises at Daisy, who happily gamboled over. Lucretia scooped him up, and the puppy responded by attempting to lick her face. "Oh, what's his name?"

Sam said shyly, "'Is name is Daisy."

"What a lovely name." Freya smiled at the boy. "Is he yours?"

"No, ma'am," Sam said as he set the tea tray on the table.

"He's mine," Messalina cut in. "But Sam is Daisy's keeper and takes care of him for me."

"Is he?" Elspeth fed the puppy a piece of her bread. "What a smart boy."

"He is indeed," Messalina replied, thoughtfully.

Sam *was* smart. He ought to have an education.

She realized suddenly that the boy was looking at her expectantly. She smiled. "Would you like to go to the kitchens for tea and some bread and butter while we watch Daisy?"

"Yes, ma'am," Sam said at once, and spun on his heel to hurry out.

"Where did you get him?" Freya asked when the door had shut.

Messalina arched an eyebrow. "The boy or the dog?"

Freya shook her head at her jest. "*Daisy* of course."

The puppy scrambled over Lucretia's arm to get to Elspeth and her bread.

"Gideon gave him to me."

Messalina suddenly found herself at the target of three sets of eyes.

"Did he?" Freya asked thoughtfully.

"I think I should do anything for a puppy," Elspeth remarked, letting Daisy down.

And Lucretia said with alarming approval, "How Machiavellian."

The puppy had wandered over to sniff at Messalina's skirts.

She bent and lifted him to her lap, where he greeted her with a wet nose.

"I don't know why everyone should find that so surprising," Messalina said in what even to her sounded like a defensive voice.

Freya was still eyeing her. "Perhaps you should tell me what has happened *since* your marriage?"

"You really, really should," Lucretia muttered.

Traitor.

Elspeth put down her tea and reached into the pocket of

her gown. She produced a small notebook and a tiny pencil, then looked earnestly at Freya. "Might I take notes?"

Oh, Good Lord.

* * *

By the time Gideon returned to Whispers House that night he was dead tired.

Exhausted in both body and something deeper. Perhaps his soul. He'd realized as he'd set out that morning that he'd never cold-bloodedly planned to murder a man. He didn't like Greycourt—far from it. Had anyone asked him a month ago if Gideon would hesitate to kill Greycourt, he would've laughed in their face.

It was *thinking* about the man and how to murder him that made the deed so ghastly.

He'd spent the day shadowing Julian Greycourt—or attempting to. It had taken him until well after noon to find Greycourt drinking coffee in a crowded coffeehouse. Greycourt had been all alone; not even the younger brother was about, which seemed...odd.

After that Gideon had followed the man to his tailor, to a dueling club, and finally back to the inn where Julian was staying with his brother.

It was as Gideon had been lounging across the street from the dueling club, waiting for Greycourt to emerge again, that he asked himself what exactly he was doing. He already had a list of Greycourt's usual places from Pea. If he wanted to kill Greycourt, why didn't Gideon simply choose a place and wait until the man arrived? Come to that, couldn't he have shot the man in the London crowd? Or if that was too loud, he could get close enough and stab him.

In the back.

Aristocrats considered stabbing a man in the back ungentlemanly. And while Gideon made a point of hating nearly everything the toffs did, he reluctantly had to agree with them in this case. He wasn't sure he could sneak up on a man—on *Greycourt*—and kill him without giving the man a chance to defend himself.

Had he grown weak? It was so simple a thing—a quick jab and everything he'd ever wanted would fall into his hands.

Everything except Messalina. He would lose Messalina.

He was tense, his fingers clenching, as he entered the dining room in preparation for supper. But something happened when he caught sight of his wife, busily gossiping with her sister.

His heart lightened.

What a strange feeling. It made him uneasy somehow—to have his very mood changed by another person. Gideon had always needed only himself.

He paused for a moment inside the doorway to draw himself together and then noticed the third person in the room, sitting across from Messalina and Lucretia.

"Hawthorne!" Will Blackwell exclaimed, turning around. "I'd begun to fear that you'd abandoned your wife and her lovely sister." He darted an uncharacteristically shy glance at Lucretia as he said the last part.

Lucretia's color rose.

As did Gideon's eyebrows. Was Blackwell interested in his sister-in-law? Normally he wouldn't stand a chance of courting Lucretia. But then, normally Gideon wouldn't be married to Messalina.

"Good evening," his wife said with a smile.

His pulse leaped at her expression.

All three were looking at him expectantly, so he bowed.

"A good evening to you all. I'm sorry for my tardiness. I wasn't aware we were to have a guest."

He took his seat across from the ladies.

"That's my fault, I'm afraid," Blackwell said rather sheepishly. "I came to call on you and somehow stayed for supper."

"That's because we *invited* you to supper," Messalina replied. "After all, you're my husband's business partner and friend. Naturally you're quite welcome at our house."

"That's very kind of you," Blackwell said.

Lucretia tilted her head as Reggie brought in a platter of charred-looking roast beef. She murmured, "You may not think that once you've tried the food here."

Pea followed with a bottle of wine and a bowl of gray cooked...stuff.

"I'll be taking my supper down at the tavern, guv," Reggie muttered as he thumped the roast beef on the table.

To Gideon's surprise, Messalina said, "Oh, Reggie, couldn't you stay? I know Hicks is trying his best."

"No doubt about it, ma'am," Reggie readily agreed. "But..." He glanced at the blackened beef and winced. "I suppose I can eat my dinner here."

"Thank you." The smile Messalina bestowed on Reggie made the big man blink.

Both Reggie and Pea exited the room.

Blackwell turned to Messalina. "Your concern for the cook does you credit, ma'am."

Gideon grunted, feeling the dullard for not having complimented her first. "You'll have all my men turned to tame lambs soon."

He reached for Messalina's glass and poured the wine.

"How dreadful," Lucretia murmured. "Who would you have to do your nefarious deeds then?"

Blackwell choked.

Gideon raised a brow at Lucretia, who looked very far from repentant.

Messalina cleared her throat loudly. "Do you often attend the theater, Mr. Blackwell?" She turned to Lucretia. "That is where we met."

The phrase sounded so intimate. It wasn't, though. Gideon stared at his wineglass, refusing to be jealous.

"I'm afraid not." Blackwell looked rueful. "Business takes up the majority of my time. I do, however, like to read when I'm able."

"Do you?" Lucretia sat up a little straighter. "I'm reading *The Adventures of David Simple in Search of a Faithful Friend* right now."

"Ah," Blackwell said. "A favorite of mine. What do you think of the author's sentiments on morality?"

Lucretia appeared to hesitate, then said slowly, "They are very noble, but they seem to me a bit idealized."

"Exactly," Blackwell replied. "For instance, David Simple is appalled by London and its people, while I find them most congenial."

Messalina looked interested. "I must read the book after you've finished it, darling." She glanced doubtfully at Gideon, hesitating.

"No, I haven't read it," he said gruffly.

"Gideon dislikes literature of all kinds," Blackwell said cheerfully. "He is a very busy man."

Gideon narrowed his eyes at his partner. Blackwell made him seem a clod.

Messalina hastily asked, "How was your day, Gideon? I haven't seen you since well before luncheon."

He'd left her, warm and limp with pleasure, that morning. He cleared his throat. "Very good." Considering he'd spent most of it contemplating how to murder her brother. Gideon glanced down. The slice of beef on his plate suddenly seemed much too greasy. He strove to think of something light to say. "And your day, madam?"

"We shopped on Bond Street." She hesitated and then squared her shoulders. "Then we came back to Whispers and found the Duchess of Harlowe and her sister Lady Elspeth waiting for us in the sitting room."

"We had tea and a lovely chat with them," Lucretia said defiantly.

Gideon raised his brows. Did they think he'd disapprove of having tea with other ladies? He'd never forbidden Messalina her friends.

"My mother always finds a day shopping to be invigorating," Blackwell said. He turned to Lucretia. "What did you buy, Miss Greycourt?"

"I'm afraid I came away with only a pair of kid gloves," Lucretia replied. "Does your mother live in London, Mr. Blackwell?"

"Alas, no. She's in a little town south of London. But I visit her whenever possible."

"One wonders," Gideon said dryly, "how you have time for business at all after attending the theater, reading books, and visiting your mother."

Messalina shot him a look of exasperation.

But Blackwell laughed. "Indeed. And on that note, I confess that I must leave you all early."

"Oh, must you?" cried Lucretia.

While at the same time, Messalina said, "But you haven't finished your meal."

Blackwell stood and bowed to them. "I'm afraid I have an engagement later this evening. I do hope you'll forgive me?"

The ladies were profuse in their assurances of forgiveness.

Gideon nodded with a half smile as Blackwell made his farewells. He couldn't help but wonder what sort of engagement Blackwell was going to. When Gideon had first met him, Blackwell had been fond of gambling—and he hadn't been an especially lucky player.

He turned to Messalina. "And what did you buy on your shopping trip, madam wife?"

Messalina brightened and told him about her day and though he listened to her, most of his attention was on her face.

Her happy face.

He felt a pang. He wanted Messalina to always be this happy. To never experience sorrow or disappointment.

Gideon dropped his eyes to his plate. *He* would bring her sorrow. *He* was the monster that would bring tears to those merry gray eyes.

Was there any way he could live with himself afterward?

"Shall we retire to the sitting room for tea?" Messalina asked, interrupting his thoughts.

Gideon snorted. "If you wish. Although you'll have to explain to Reggie why we have to move to the sitting room to drink tea."

"Of course." Messalina sighed.

Lucretia looked blank. "Why?"

"Because"—Gideon rose and helped Messalina to her feet—"your sister is bound and determined to improve my house and servants."

"Well, *someone* has to," Messalina muttered. She laid her hand on his arm. "That reminds me. I'll be interviewing new servants in a couple of days. I hope I have your approval to hire as many as we need?"

"I don't know about *approval*," Gideon mused as they

strolled out of the dining room with Lucretia trailing, "but you have my consent to do so."

"Then that will have to do," Messalina said briskly. Reggie was just outside the dining room, and she turned to him. "We'll be taking tea in the sitting room."

Reggie's broad forehead wrinkled. "Yes, ma'am?"

"Thank you, Reggie," she said.

The big man nodded and hurried to the kitchens.

Gideon continued to escort Messalina and Lucretia to the sitting room.

Messalina sank into the settee. "Actually, I'm not sure why we take tea after supper."

"Because"—Lucretia took a chair opposite the settee—"it's an excuse to have cake."

Gideon sat next to Messalina, almost but not quite touching.

The sitting room door opened again, and Reggie entered and held the door for Pea, who had an enormous tray of tea.

"Oh, lovely," Lucretia said, clapping her hands. "Are those sweets?"

The tray held an assortment of sugared plums and tiny cakes.

"They are," Messalina said slowly, eyeing the sweets as Pea placed the tray carefully on a table. "But I never thought that Hicks would be able to make these." She glanced at Gideon suspiciously. "Do you know anything about this?"

Gideon shrugged carelessly. He was pleased by both Messalina's and Lucretia's reaction to his surprise. "I sent Pea to buy them this morning. I thought you might like them."

He winked at Pea, who grinned in return before scampering from the room.

Messalina's eyes narrowed. "Are you trying to bribe my sister?"

He leaned close to her ear and whispered, "Yes."

"It's working," Lucretia said happily. She was already munching on a pink cake with tiny white flowers.

Messalina laughed and began pouring the tea.

Gideon took his cup and said, "I saw you had mail when I came in."

Lucretia groaned.

Messalina winced as she poured a cup for Lucretia. "We received an invitation to a ball that Aunt Ann is having in a week at Windemere House. It's rather late notice, but Lucretia and I think we can find something to wear. And I've sent a note round to your tailor to hurry one of the suits we ordered for you."

"I am relieved," he replied dryly. "But you don't sound very enthusiastic."

"Well, Uncle Augustus." Lucretia helped herself to another cake as she shared a glance with Messalina.

Did she know of the old man's threats?

"Why go at all?" Gideon asked.

"It seems Aunt Ann has decided that the ball is to honor our marriage," Messalina answered.

Gideon had raised his teacup to his lips but hadn't taken a sip yet. He paused, looking over the rim at Messalina to assess her emotions on the matter.

Messalina gave a small smile back at him. "The theme is probably Uncle Augustus's idea. Poor Ann simply does as he says. She's quite frightened of him."

She frowned at her teacup.

He hated to see her upset.

"Her Grace is a very wealthy woman married to one of the most powerful men in England," he said gently.

"She can't enjoy her wealth if she's dead," Lucretia said simply. She chose another four delicacies.

Gideon raised his eyebrows, watching his sister-in-law. He'd never seen a woman eat so many sweets in such a decorous manner.

"Lucretia!" Messalina glanced nervously at the dining room door.

There were whispers about the duke's first two wives and their early deaths. One had been thrown from a horse, while the other had somehow fallen down a flight of stairs.

"You've heard the rumors as much as I have," Lucretia said.

"Yes, but I don't want Uncle Augustus to learn that we're whispering them," Messalina said.

Lucretia tilted her chin. "I'm not afraid of him."

Messalina's lips firmed. "Perhaps you should be."

"Neither of you need be afraid," Gideon cut in.

The sisters both looked at him as if they'd forgotten he was there.

He nodded. "You live with me now. I've men like Reggie in the house, and outside as well."

"I don't know if I feel any safer knowing I'm in an elaborate cage," Lucretia said sweetly. "The men following us down Bond Street today were quite conspicuous."

"As they should be," Gideon said. "Deterrence is the best protection I know. I will never let anyone hurt you." He looked into Messalina's clear gray eyes and said softly, "Either of you."

Messalina smiled at him, and for a moment he could see nothing else.

Lucretia cleared her throat. Something had softened in her face at his words.

"Thank you," she said gruffly.

He nodded. He would've protected Lucretia regardless.

She mattered to Messalina.

Lucretia said to her sister, "Didn't you say you were going to interview servants?"

Messalina immediately turned to her sister, and in seconds they were discussing...lady's maids versus housemaids?

Gideon sipped his tea, watching the sisters with amusement.

Inside, though, he was thinking about Windemere and the possibility that he'd helped with his wives' deaths. Gideon had been young when he first entered the duke's employ, so he hadn't paid much attention to the rumors surrounding the second duchess's death. But now...

Now he knew that the old man was capable of hiring an assassin to murder his nephew. If he could do that without blinking, then was it so far-fetched to think he'd kill a woman?

He frowned as he placed his teacup down. Did Windemere's murderous loathing of Greycourt extend to the rest of the family? The duke had certainly never shown any kindness or affection to Messalina or Lucretia.

He glanced at Messalina, who was engaged in a whispered argument with her sister. Her glossy hair caught the light, and the turn of her head made the long line of her neck glow in the candlelight. But it was the way her pink lips pursed before reluctantly relaxing into a small smile that caught his eye.

Gideon dropped his eyes to the dwindling supply of sweets. How much longer would he have her smiles to enjoy?

Chapter Twelve

That very night Bet and the Fox were wed and he
took her away. He drove a small wicker cart drawn
by four roe deer, and when he cracked his whip,
the cart near flew through the countryside. When
dawn broke, they pulled up in the clearing with the
honeysuckle-and-sweetbriar cottage....
—From *Bet and the Fox*

Several hours later, Messalina watched as Lucretia yawned so widely she couldn't hide it behind her palm.

"Oh my," Lucretia sighed, slumped against the settee cushions.

Gideon had long since retired to his study.

Messalina swallowed the last of the milky-sweet tea in her cup and regarded the beautiful piece of luxury in her hand. The tea set had a pink hatch pattern around the rim, and each cup had a different bird on the side. Messalina had fallen in love on sight.

Staring at it she asked, "Have you ever considered how much we spend on—on *things*?"

Lucretia glanced down at her own cup, which depicted a goldfinch. "No? Why should I? I don't understand."

"It's just..." Messalina frowned at her lovely tea set. "Well, for instance, Sam would be on the streets, without shelter or food, if Gideon hadn't employed him." She nodded at the set. "The price I paid for this could keep him in comfort for years. It doesn't seem fair somehow."

"But Gideon *has* employed Sam," Lucretia pointed out. "He seems healthy enough."

"Yes, but there are other boys," Messalina said. "And girls as well. I just... wish I could do something."

"Such as?" Lucretia asked.

Messalina knitted her brows. "I don't quite know..."

She felt something brewing inside her, though. A vague idea of ragged boys and all they needed to start life properly.

A purpose.

Lucretia yawned again.

Messalina looked at her. "You need to retire to bed."

"I'm not sleepy," Lucretia said petulantly.

Messalina smiled at her fondly. "You sound like a five-year-old."

"Humph." Lucretia played with her cup. "Messalina..."

"Yes, darling?"

Lucretia frowned a little at her teacup. "Do you think it wise for me to attend the dance at Windemere House?" She glanced up, and Messalina saw that her sister's face was unusually grave. "It's just that... what if Uncle Augustus makes me *stay*?"

A frisson of horror went down Messalina's back.

Their uncle *had* made that threat against Lucretia. But if they didn't attend, Uncle Augustus would be enraged.

And he might take that rage out on someone closer to him than they.

Suddenly the tea was bitter on her tongue. She set down her cup. "Remember that Gideon will be there. He will keep you safe."

"Even so..." Lucretia bit her lip. "Perhaps I should cry off with a headache or some such."

Messalina shook her head. "That will only draw attention to you. Better that we seem to do as he bids like docile little sheep."

Her sister wrinkled her nose. "Ew."

"Quite." Messalina grimaced in sympathy. "What if Julian and Quintus come as well? I'm sure they've been invited—or rather ordered—to the event. Then you'll have three protectors."

"Very well." Lucretia knit her brows and then blurted, "The thing is, what if Uncle Augustus plans to arrange a marriage for me as well? He sprang yours on us without any warning. It would make sense that he has some awful man lined up for me as well."

Messalina's breath stopped in her chest. Should she tell Lucretia of the duke's threat? But to what end? Lucretia was already nervous and on edge.

Would telling her do anything besides make her *more* fearful?

"I doubt he'd do it at Aunt Ann's ball," she said slowly. "There would be too many witnesses who might intervene. But you're right. We need to get you away from Uncle Augustus."

Which meant she needed her portion of the dowry.

Lucretia sighed. "I haven't even heard from Julian or Quintus. Did they send word to you?"

"Blast," Messalina muttered, rummaging in the pocket of her dress. "Yes, they did, and I meant to tell you. They've taken rooms. Here."

She held out a note with the Greycourt seal.

Lucretia took it and opened the paper to reveal Julian's elegant scrawl. She scanned the short note and handed it back. "I confess that I'm surprised they haven't called on us today. After last night's row I was sure they would storm the door and drag us both away."

Messalina pursed her lips at the nymphs above them. "Perhaps Julian has lost interest."

"And Quintus is probably in his cups."

"They didn't used to be this way, you know," Messalina said quietly. "Before Aurelia."

"I seem to remember Julian laughing," Lucretia said musingly.

"He *did* laugh," Messalina said, feeling a sharp pain in her breast. "They all did—Jules, Ran, and Kester."

They'd seemed like young gods to her girlish eyes. It was difficult to remember that they'd been only seventeen.

Not men at all.

But Freya had made her peace, both with Messalina and with Kester, enough to fall in love with Kester and marry him.

"I don't remember much before Aurelia died," Lucretia said sadly.

"Well, you were only eight. It's hard to explain." Messalina thought a moment. "Aurelia was so *bright*. So golden. She seemed to glow with laughter and impishness and kindness. When she died, I think something in our family was lost."

Lucretia sighed wistfully.

"Before she died I remember all three boys being the best of friends," Messalina continued. "They ran wild in the country, were closer than brothers. At the time I never would've imagined them apart." She smiled sadly. "But then I never would've imagined Julian so grim, either."

"I wish I could remember more about that time," Lucretia said softly. "More about Mama and Papa and Aurelia. More about what it was like before."

Messalina didn't say anything, but her shoulder bumped Lucretia's. Papa had died when Messalina was eleven and

Lucretia seven. And the next year Aurelia had died in mysterious circumstances, followed very quickly by Mama. They'd lived in Greycourt their entire short lives and it was a shock—a terrible shock—to lose not only Mama on the heels of Aurelia's death but their *home* as well.

For the last thing Mama had done before she'd died was make sure that Messalina and Lucretia would be sent to her cousin. That cousin had been a bachelor gentleman, elderly and not interested in the sudden acquisition of girl children. They'd been comfortable enough, fed, clothed, and housed, but it hadn't been *home*.

And when their cousin died, they were forced to live with Uncle Augustus. Their cousin had been indifferent, but the duke was malicious, and that was far worse. He'd never harmed them physically, but he enjoyed berating them nightly for the smallest of things—a torn hem, laughing too loudly, not finishing their porridge. His punishments had been petty and cruel.

In the end they'd learned to avoid their uncle at all costs. And, if they caught his notice, to show no reaction to his vicious moods.

That was why Messalina had always wanted a home of their own for her and Lucretia—always until very recently. Because of Gideon, she'd found her determination wavering. Guilt swept her at the thought. She needed to think about Lucretia and her safety.

She couldn't give up their plan to run away—not with the duke plotting to marry her sister off.

She couldn't.

Lucretia yawned again and put her teacup down. "Oh, I suppose I really ought to go to bed," she said reluctantly. "Do you know when I was little I used to wish I was an owl?"

Messalina blinked, startled. "Why?"

"All the most interesting things happen in the dark of night," Lucretia replied sleepily,

Messalina laughed. "I'm afraid even owls need sleep."

She rose with Lucretia, and they made their way companionably up the stairs before saying their good nights at Lucretia's door.

Messalina turned to go to her own bedroom. Gideon had said that he had work to do after dinner, but perhaps he would be done and waiting for her.

She remembered how he'd held her the night before and quickened her steps.

But when she arrived at their bedroom she saw that he wasn't there. Instead Bartlett stood ready to undress her.

Messalina was forced to hide her disappointment.

Her evening toilet was quick tonight—Messalina wanted to brood by herself. Only minutes later she dismissed Bartlett and wandered to the fire. She wasn't at all sleepy, and she wished she'd bought a book during the shopping trip with Lucretia.

She turned to the bed and for the first time noticed a folded piece of paper on her pillow.

Messalina bit her lip, quelling the smile that threatened to take over her face, and opened the letter.

I AM BATHING

That was the entire note, but Messalina knew an invitation when she received one.

* * *

When the door to the bathing chamber opened, Gideon didn't raise his head from the rim of the tub. He knew who it was, and he knew, beyond a shadow of a doubt and on the eternal damnation of his blackened soul, that to seduce Messalina now was immoral. Unethical. *Sinful.*

He couldn't make himself stop.

His hunger for Messalina had grown beyond his control.

Every step of his every day had always been meticulously mapped out to eventually lead him to his ultimate goal: power and money. Yet since he'd married Messalina there had been a worrying amount of deviation from his plots and plans.

He was spending too much time with his wife. Spending too much time *thinking* about the day he'd lose her.

He'd never been so conflicted over a decision that should have been simple: kill Julian, receive his money.

But there was Messalina, haunting him with her kindness. With her tenderness.

He'd never flinched from a knife fight, no matter how big the opponent. He'd lived and worked in St Giles without any trepidation. Had looked a duke in the eye and made pacts with the man. But now?

Now he was afraid to his very depths—afraid of losing her.

Afraid of betraying her.

He opened his eyes and saw Messalina standing just inside the door. She wore her white wrapper, her black hair down about her shoulders in a glorious wave, and he *longed* for her.

She closed the door and leaned against it. "You owe me my dowry portion."

"I do," he said. "And you shall have it."

"When?"

He calculated how soon he could get the moneys from his bank. It would nearly beggar him, but the only other way meant the death of her brother. He couldn't make that move quite yet. "In four days' time."

She looked momentarily conflicted. Then she raised her chin. "Very well."

"Let's not talk money now." He held out a hand to her.

She sauntered to the tub. "I thought you might want company?"

Her words were bold, but her fingers trembled as she laid them in his palm.

"I do," he said, pulling her closer.

"Do you?" she asked, breathless, as she bent to him.

He slid his hand into her hair, leaving behind a wet trail on her skin. As if he'd marked her as his. The thought made his cock pulse with need.

"Take this off," he rasped, his voice gravel-rough, tugging at the ribbon that held the wrapper closed.

She let the garment fall to the floor before she pulled her nightgown over her head. And then she stood before him, nude.

Beautiful, nude, and, in this moment, *his*.

He let himself look. From sweetly curved breasts to the indent of her belly to the long, smooth lines of her hips. To the black bush between her thighs, red lips peeking out from the curls.

When he glanced up at her, her cheeks were almost as red.

"Join me," he whispered.

She looked doubtfully at the bathtub. "It's too full. The water will spill out if I get in."

He pulled her closer. "I don't care."

She braced her hand on his shoulder and stepped into the water, her legs straddling his. She hesitated, standing there as if uncertain how to proceed.

"Like this," he murmured, tugging her closer. "Sit down facing me."

She folded her legs, the splash of water on the tiles loud

as she lowered herself. It was a tight fit, but in a moment she was on his lap and he was too busy gathering her plump breasts into his hands to care. Her soft arse was nestled right against his cock and balls, torturing him with temptation.

She lifted the farthing on the chain about his neck. "Do you never take this off?"

He pushed the thought of his dead brother away. "Never."

"It must be important to you if you hold it so dear." Her gray eyes searched his.

He shook his head, refusing to answer, and watched her eyes grow a little sad.

Then she leaned toward him, offering her lips, and he took them. Her mouth was sweet and hot and she suckled on his tongue as he flicked her nipples with his thumbs. Her hands were braced on his shoulders, and he felt her nails digging into his skin and didn't care.

He didn't care about anything save her at the moment.

He lifted his head to draw breath, to try to still the beating of his heart, to slow down, but he'd lost all reason, it seemed. He dipped his right hand into the water, feeling her maiden hair curl about his fingers, delicate and fine.

"Gideon," she moaned. "Oh, Gideon."

His name, whispered on her rose-pink lips, was the most erotic thing he'd ever heard.

He trailed his fingers into her valley, finding that little pearl sitting at the top of her slit. He caught it and rolled the nub between his fingers, bracing her back with his arm as she arched. She tried to widen her legs, but the tub was confining.

He stroked into her depths with his middle finger, feeling her heated velvet flesh catch and hold him.

God, he wanted his cock there instead.

But he was a canny man. A man who could wait and

bide his time for the perfect moment. He thrust into her with one hand—slowly, gently—as he pinched her pearl with the other.

She moaned, loud in the quiet room, and it came to him that the door was not locked. That Keys or Reggie or one of his other men might come at any moment to see if he wanted more hot water.

He should quit and bundle her together. Take her away to hide her nakedness.

But he couldn't. His prick was rampant between them, hard and demanding. The ruddy thing seemed to pound with need.

He turned his head to kiss her jaw. "Come for me, darling."

She bit her lip as if in agony, and he pressed down on her clitoris, rubbing in a gentle circle.

"Oh," she said. "Please."

He felt a spike of desire and had to steady himself. Not yet.

She gripped his shoulders hard, her eyes closed tightly, her lips parted, her head thrown back.

Wanton.

As seductive as a siren.

"Come," he whispered.

He wanted to rub his cock against her.

But this wasn't for him.

Her hips arched up, shaking, splashing more water onto the marble floor in a wave.

She froze for a moment like that, moaning softly as he worked her through her bliss.

Then she sagged against him, limp and sated, her lips bitten red.

He lifted her, urgent, a bit clumsy. He was in danger of spending before he could breach her. He'd outsmarted himself by waiting so long as she twisted sensuously against him.

But she raised her head, lifting her hips for him as she looked him in the eye. He held his cock in one hand until he found her wet, hot, welcoming softness.

And then he thrust.

She moaned as he entered her, parting those folds, sinking into her, but not far enough. Only the head of his prick penetrated her.

Jesus.

He needed more. It was agonizingly frustrating.

He wanted to claim her, bury himself in her and make her his.

She rode him carefully, sheathing him and unsheathing his head, again and again, far too slowly.

Driving him mad.

Every muscle in his body shook as he held himself still.

"Gideon," she slurred, teasing him with her cunt. "Oh God, Gideon."

He *wanted* . . .

"Deeper," he gasped. "Take me deeper."

She shook her head.

He thought he might die.

She opened her mouth over his, hot and wet, as she ground herself against him. Her nipples brushed his chest and he wasn't sure he could take any more.

Then slowly, almost lazily, she took his prick inch by inch inside her.

God. Her heat. Her tightness.

His tilted his head back and groaned, his cock pulsing. His come was pulled from him in almost painful ecstasy as he filled her.

As he marked her as his.

But he knew even then in his extremity: it was *she* who had claimed him.

* * *

Three days later Messalina placed her hand in Gideon's broad palm and stepped down from their carriage. She shook out her skirts as Gideon turned to help Lucretia. Then she looked up.

Windemere House was alight with torches and lanterns as carriages delivered the cream of society to its front steps.

Messalina assessed the attendance. There would be more people in town in another month. She'd have to prepare for a larger assembly when she threw a ball for Gideon.

She realized suddenly that she was planning to stay with Gideon.

The thought made her smile tremulously.

"How do I look?" Lucretia asked, drawing her attention.

Messalina turned to contemplate her sister. Lucretia wore a shimmering ice-blue frock with white lace spilling from the elbow-length sleeves. Her bodice was embroidered with yellow and red flowers, and the edges of the dress were trimmed in silver lace all along the front. Lucretia's glossy black hair was pulled back from her face and knotted at her crown, with pearls threaded through the locks.

If not for the fear in her eyes, she'd be perfect.

"You're lovely," Messalina said with sincerity. "Every gentleman at the ball will fall at your feet, and every lady will turn green with envy."

"Oh, good," Lucretia replied with a nervous pat to her hair. "That *was* what I was aiming for."

Gideon snorted and held out his arms. "If you're ready, ladies."

Messalina caught her breath at his smile, feeling herself blush. The last few days had been full of lovemaking— *tender* lovemaking—and she was both more comfortable with her husband and shyer. Which really didn't make sense, but there it was. Gideon had held her all last night, his nude skin against hers in their bed, and it had felt so warm and cozy and *right*. As if they were married in more than just name.

Maybe they were.

But if she stayed... Her gaze went to Lucretia as she took Gideon's arm.

If she remained with Gideon and had a *real* marriage with him, Lucretia would be in danger. Unless Julian could somehow take her away?

Then Messalina could enjoy a life she'd never expected to be granted.

Her heart squeezed at the thought of living far away from Lucretia. Perhaps Gideon and his men could be protection enough for her sister. Perhaps they could live together in London, happy and content. And if Messalina *didn't* use her dowry portion to escape, then...

She had a vision of Sam's eager face. Of other boys like Sam.

Her future held exciting new possibilities, precious and fragile like the skin of a newborn.

Right now, though, they had to run Uncle Augustus's gauntlet. Messalina squared her shoulders and made sure her smile was in place. Gideon wore one of his new suits—hastily put together at a truly exorbitant price by Mr. Underwood and his tailors—and he looked as fine as any gentleman.

Tonight she planned to introduce Gideon into society.

She took a shaky breath.

Gideon caught her eye and winked, and she felt something perilously close to hope flutter in her chest. *He* was the reason she was doing this.

They mounted the stairs to Windemere House, and Messalina couldn't help reflecting on how much happier she was tonight than the last time she'd entered her uncle's residence. Their awful marriage seemed so long ago now, though of course it wasn't.

Gideon led them inside. The entryway was refreshingly clear, a single footman taking their gloves and shawls. If this had been a ball thrown during the height of the season there would be bodies packed from wall to wall.

Gideon guided them up the snaking grand staircase to the upper-floor ballroom.

There they came face-to-face with Uncle Augustus and poor Ann.

The duke was ruddy with good humor—never a good sign. "My darling nieces! How lovely to see you *both.*"

She wouldn't look at Lucretia.

He leaned close to kiss first Lucretia and then Messalina. Messalina held very still—as if a spider were crawling up her arm.

Uncle Augustus turned to Gideon, his smile twisting. "And Hawthorne." He looked Gideon up and down. "A new suit? Why, one would hardly know that you were born to a whore in St Giles."

Messalina felt Gideon stiffen beside her. *Had* his mother been a prostitute? Even if she had, for the duke to call her such to Gideon's face...

She tightened her grip on her husband's arm and glanced at him from under her eyelashes.

His face was perfectly composed. As if Uncle Augustus had merely exchanged pleasantries with him.

Messalina felt unease trickle down her spine. She knew that Gideon wasn't cold or uncaring, but he hid his emotions so well. *Did* he see her as more than a means to money?

Had he succumbed to their union as she had?

Messalina pressed her lips together.

Other attendees were crowding behind them, making their greetings blessedly brief. Messalina just had time to murmur something to Ann, dressed in an unfortunate purple frock, and then they were past both duke and duchess.

Messalina glanced around, noting the faces that pointedly turned away. Well. She'd known this would be a challenge, but she rather thought she—and Gideon—were prepared.

She smiled up at him. "Shall we perambulate?"

Gideon glanced down at her, the cold still lingering in his eyes making her shiver. "As you wish."

They'd taken only a few steps when Lucretia exclaimed beneath her breath, "There's Julian."

Messalina looked and saw their brother, dressed in silver, lounging by the wall. His head was tipped back as if he were about to fall asleep, a young lady and what looked like her mother attempting to engage him in conversation. He ignored both females to stare impassively across the ballroom.

At their uncle.

Lucretia leaned across Gideon to murmur, "I'd begun to think that they had left the city. I don't see Quintus, do you?"

"No." Messalina sighed, knowing that Quintus was most likely sequestered with other gentlemen at the gaming tables, where the drinks were much more potent than the watery punch in the ballroom. "I suppose we ought to greet Julian."

Lucretia laid her hand on Messalina's arm with a wry little smile. "Let me. If his mood is better than it looks, I'll come to you."

"Thank you," Messalina replied. She had no great desire to talk to Julian—not after the fight between Quintus and Gideon and Julian's hurtful words.

She frowned as she watched Lucretia make her way to

Julian. It would have been easier if her brothers *had* retired back to Adders Hall.

Then of course she felt guilty for such an unsisterly sentiment. But the truth was that she didn't want what was happening between her and Gideon interrupted. She felt as if she were about to open a present—or a new book. That a whole world was unveiling itself before her.

That maybe she was falling in love.

She darted a glance at Gideon. And maybe he was, too?

She had to hide a silly grin at the thought, working to compose her features as she continued strolling with Gideon. They hadn't taken but two steps before she spotted a familiar face.

"There's Lord Rookewoode," she murmured.

"So it is." Gideon was looking at the earl rather as a wolf did at a bunny.

"Shall I introduce you properly?" Messalina asked, moving in the direction of the earl. He was holding court with several gentlemen and a few ladies. One turned, and Messalina smiled. "Oh, and there's Arabella Holland. She and her sister and mother were also guests at the house party Lucretia and I attended." She leaned a little closer to Gideon, inhaling the scent of cloves. "In fact, there were rumors that she and Lord Rookewoode had come to an understanding."

"Messalina!" cried Lady Holland, holding out her hands. "What is this I hear of you marrying?"

Messalina smiled, catching the other lady's hands with her own. "May I introduce my husband, Mr. Gideon Hawthorne? Gideon, this is Lady Holland and her daughters, Regina and Arabella."

The girls curtsied at their names. Both girls had their mother's wheat-colored hair and pure blue eyes, but while they might be similar in looks, their personalities were completely opposite. The elder, Arabella, was reserved and grave, while Regina was merry and vivacious.

"Then it's true," Regina chimed in. "You have married. But why in a secret ceremony?"

Lady Holland hastily cut into Regina's guileless comments. "I'm sure we need not inquire into such a private matter."

Regina looked rebellious.

Messalina felt her lips twitch.

"Do you know Freya has eloped with the Duke of Harlowe?" Regina broke in excitedly. "And no wonder—they spent so much time together at the house party."

Messalina opened her mouth.

"Regina!" Arabella murmured.

"We do not talk scandal." Lady Holland looked sternly at her younger daughter and then amended, "At least not in public."

"I can't think why anyone would run away to have a slapdash wedding," Regina said, completely uncowed by her mother. "Oh!" she exclaimed, looking at Messalina with wide eyes. "I didn't mean—"

"That's quite all right," Messalina assured her. "I wanted a small wedding."

Regina looked relieved. "Mama has said that I may have a grand wedding with as many guests as I wish when Mr. Trentworth and I marry. I do hope you'll come with Mr. Hawthorne, Mrs. Hawthorne, though of course I shan't be marrying until *after* Arabella's wedding."

"We shall be delighted to do so," Messalina said quite sincerely, and she turned to Arabella with a bright smile. "I hadn't heard that you've become engaged. My felicitations."

"Thank you," Arabella replied, blushing. She glanced at her fiancé.

Lord Rookewoode appeared to be discussing something

quite important with another gentleman, but as if sensing Arabella's gaze he looked over and smiled. He turned back to the gentleman he'd been talking to, said a few more words, and then strolled to Arabella's side.

He held out his arm for her to take and then turned his sardonic eyes on Messalina. "Miss Greycourt. I trust you've recovered from our sojourn in the country?"

"I have, my lord," Messalina replied with a curtsy and a mischievous smile. "But I fear you've mistaken my name. It's Mrs. Hawthorne now."

"Is it indeed?" The earl's return smile was dashing, but then he was a very handsome man—and he knew it. "Congratulations. To you and your husband."

"Thank you," Messalina said. "My lord, may I introduce my husband, Mr. Gideon Hawthorne. Gideon, this is Leander Ashley, the Earl of Rookewoode."

"Hawthorne," Lord Rookewoode mused. He was still smiling, but something had hardened in his eyes. "I believe I saw you at the theater the other night. Don't you work for our host?"

Gideon bowed, his expression composed. "Yes, my lord."

Messalina looked between the two men, confused. "You've met my husband before?"

Lord Rookewoode turned to her. "Oh no. I've simply... heard of him."

"What an honor," Gideon drawled, which made Messalina want to step on his toes. Why was he antagonizing the earl if he wanted to lure the man into business?

She hastily said, "I understand that we must congratulate you, my lord."

The earl's smile returned at once as he looked to Arabella. "Indeed. I am most fortunate that Miss Holland accepted my suit."

It was a pretty sentiment, but not exactly true. Arabella's lineage was respectable enough and her dowry adequate, but in the normal course of events she'd never have caught an earl's eye. More than one unmarried lady at the ball was looking at her with open envy.

Arabella didn't seem to notice. She looked up with frank adoration at Lord Rookewoode, blushing at his gallant speech.

"Leander has made me the happiest woman in London," she said with what sounded like complete sincerity.

For a moment the earl looked disconcerted.

Then his easy smile was back. "Your happiness means everything to me."

Lady Holland cleared her throat, glancing at Gideon. "Do you still work for His Grace, Mr. Hawthorne?"

Her eyes darted curiously to Messalina, for of course most people knew she had a substantial dowry, and presumably her husband would never have to work unless he wanted to.

"I do, my lady," Gideon said easily. "But I also have my own businesses—coal mines in the north of England."

"Oh?" Lady Holland sounded politely uninterested at the mention of business.

Lord Rookewoode was already glancing at the gentleman he'd been in conversation with previously, and Messalina judged it time to move on.

She subtly nudged Gideon's side with her elbow.

He glanced at her, and she tilted her head toward the doors leading to the garden.

His eyes narrowed, and for a perilous moment she thought he'd balk at the command.

Then he bowed. "I hope you'll excuse us, my lord. Ladies." He glanced at Messalina, a wicked glint in his ebony eyes. "I'd like to take my wife for a turn in the garden."

She nodded to the Hollands and Lord Rookewoode, and then they strolled away.

He waited a half dozen steps before leaning toward her, his lips near the curls at her ears, making her shiver. "Why leave so soon?"

"This is simply an opening volley," she murmured, her gaze straight ahead so that she could survey the guests around them. "If you tried to talk business with Lord Rookewoode now, on the first introduction and in the middle of the ball, he'd likely cut you dead. He needs to become accustomed to you before you can propose your ideas."

He snorted softly, and she glanced up at him quickly.

His wide lips were quirked at her. "I had no idea that you were so devious, Mrs. Hawthorne."

"I *have* moved in society for almost a decade," she said dryly. "If you think those waters are not infested with monsters from the deep, you're sorely mistaken."

He laughed under his breath and she counted it as a victory, making Gideon laugh. She smiled privately to herself.

They reached the set of double doors in a corner of the ballroom, which were thrown open to let in the balmy night air.

"Where are we going?" she asked, confused.

"To the garden," he said.

Gideon drew her out onto a terrace that ran along the back of the house. The garden was a formal affair with hedges and graveled paths, all laid out in strict geometry, but it also had ornamental trees, severely trimmed to keep them compact. Small paper lanterns had been strung from the trees to make a fairyland.

She'd seen this garden a thousand times and had always thought it remote and chilly. But standing in it with Gideon was a different matter.

"It's lovely," Messalina whispered.

"It is." His voice was deep.

They strolled along, the gravel crunching beneath their shoes, until Gideon came to an intersection and stopped, turning to her.

Messalina looked up at him. His black eyes seemed to burn in the night air, and she reached up to stroke along his knife scar.

He bent his head and caught her mouth.

She shuddered, stepping into his embrace. His mouth was so hot, and the hand he cradled her head with was broad and strong.

Her heart bloomed as he licked along the seam of her lips. She wanted him. Wanted—

"Hawthorne!"

Gideon broke the kiss and swung her behind him as he faced Quintus.

Messalina put her hand on his arm, peering around him. Her brother's face was white with rage. Behind him was Lucretia, her eyes reddened, her cheeks wet, and with her was Julian, standing mute and watchful.

Messalina's lips parted, but it was Gideon who spoke. "What is this?"

Quintus lifted his upper lip, took two steps forward, and punched Gideon in the chin.

He staggered back against Messalina, and she felt him palm his knife.

"No!" She clutched his right hand between both of her own and addressed Quintus. "You're drunk!"

Quintus never took his eyes from Gideon. "I am, but that's not the reason your husband needs to be beaten."

Messalina looked at Julian. "Stop him. Please."

"I think not." Julian turned his merciless gray eyes on her. "Did you know that on the night we arrived, your husband told us that your marriage could not be annulled because you'd already lain together?"

"What?" Messalina stared stupidly at Julian, trying to understand his words. The night her brothers arrived . . . ?

Her heart suddenly tripled in rhythm as she felt something inside her break and fall. Far, far down, into an endless black hole without end.

The night her brothers had arrived was the night Gideon had first made love to her. There . . . there must be another explanation. Something so simple and easy that she'd laugh about this later.

But even as her brain scrambled to excuse him, she knew.

Gideon had *told* her he'd married her for her money. He might be physically drawn to her, but he'd never mentioned love.

Why hadn't she realized it sooner?

Lucretia sobbed, loud and ugly in the quiet night.

Slowly Messalina turned to Gideon. "Is it true what my brother says?"

Someday she might be proud that her voice didn't shake. That no tears filled her eyes.

But then she was well past tears.

Gideon merely looked at her, and she could tell he was calculating. What to tell her. How to bamboozle her. What lie would bring her back into his arms and his control.

If her heart had been a flower blooming only moments before, it was frozen now. Brittle and dead.

He'd never loved her, never even cared for her. It had all been a trap, set and sprung by her own silly *emotions*.

Messalina lifted her head proudly, facing Gideon, her lips still throbbing from his kiss. "*Tell me.*"

"Yes," he ground out. "But you must listen—"

"No. I will not." She turned and left the garden and the fairy-tale lights behind.

CHAPTER THIRTEEN

"This is your home," said the fox, opening the crooked door to the little cottage. Inside was a bed made of thistledown and moss with beside it a bark table and two chairs. "Keep it neat and clean. You may eat whatever grows within this clearing, but never ever venture into the wild wood." . . .
—From *Bet and the Fox*

Julian watched as Messalina stormed away with Hawthorne following.

Lucretia trailed behind without a word.

"It will be the talk of the town for months," Quinn muttered. "When she leaves him."

Julian glanced at him. Not so drunk, then. "Yes, it will."

He, too, followed Messalina. She wouldn't want to talk to him tonight—she was obviously devastated—but soon she must. Both she and Lucretia had to leave Hawthorne's home.

He and Quinn would see to it.

After that perhaps Hawthorne would meet with an untimely accident.

Not that Messalina would ever thank him for it.

But then he'd been protecting his family without any thanks for more than a decade.

By the time Julian reached the garden doors with Quintus

beside him, Messalina was storming across the ballroom, people parting before her.

Augustus was watching, his eyes flicking from Lucretia to Messalina to Hawthorne.

He smiled.

Julian almost stopped short, he was so startled. What was Augustus's game? The man ought to be displeased with his niece's very public anger at her husband—the man Augustus had arranged to marry her. Yet he looked almost gleeful.

Was it simple pleasure at Messalina and Lucretia's tears?

A murmuring rose in the ballroom as Messalina made her way farther into the room. Heads canted together, fans rose to cover whispering mouths. Hawthorne actually shoved aside a dandy too slow to move out of his path. The dandy squawked like a chicken pursued by a cock.

Julian strolled leisurely across the ballroom, following in his sisters' wake. He ignored those who tried to stop him. Those who actually tried to *talk* to him, their eyes alight with malicious glee.

He ignored them all. They didn't matter.

Only his family mattered.

As he passed his uncle, Augustus winked and raised his glass in mocking salute.

* * *

Gideon stared out his carriage window, unseeing. The night had started so well. The ball. The introduction to Rookewoode. The way Messalina had smiled up at him so…so trustingly.

So lovingly.

Something caught in his eye, and for a moment his vision blurred.

No. He could fix this. He was canny and cunning and

he'd never yet lost a battle of wits. That was all this was in the end. A war of words. He only had to find the right ones and he'd win her back again.

And then he would have her smiles again. Her *care* for him. Everything would be as it should.

He watched Messalina from beneath his eyelashes. She sat with her sister across from him, her head up, her gaze fixed on the seat beside him, dry eyed.

She wouldn't even look at him.

Something strange, something that might be *panic*—an emotion he never felt—battered the cage of his chest.

Damn Greycourt. Damn Quintus. Damn Lucretia. Damn every meddling Greycourt, every aristocrat intent on maintaining the sanctity of the aristocracy, every man, woman, and child who stood between him and Messalina.

He'd *had* her—her beauty, her wealth and position, her willing help with his ambitions.

Her tenderness.

He'd had her and he was suddenly afraid, not only that he'd never have her again, but that he might not survive without her.

The carriage shuddered to a stop and he glanced up, surprised to find that they were already at Whispers House.

Messalina moved to rise, and he had to scramble to get to the door before her. In the end he offered his hand to Lucretia first.

She slapped it away and leaped from the carriage like an Amazon bent on battle, scowling at him all the while with reddened, puffy eyes.

It was hard not to admire her.

But it was the woman behind her who had all his attention. Messalina tried to avoid his hand, but he was done with her sulking.

He grasped her wrist firmly. She yanked once in retaliation and then submitted to his help, descending from the carriage quietly.

Almost listlessly.

He jerked his hand away again as if her very passivity had burned him. Messalina never submitted to *anyone*, let alone him, and he didn't like it.

His fear made him bend and murmur in her ear roughly, "I will talk to you and you will listen." He *couldn't* show weakness.

The scent of bergamot seemed to hang heavy in the air.

She turned her head and looked at him for the first time since that damned, bloody, godforsaken garden.

Her gray eyes were blank. All emotion hidden.

He wanted to hit something.

"Very well." She glanced at Lucretia, her expression softening. "Good night, darling."

Lucretia looked mutinous. "But—"

Messalina placed her hand on her sister's arm. "I can handle this alone. I *have* to handle this alone. Try not to worry."

The way she spoke, he might not have been there at all. He had the wild urge to throw Messalina over his shoulder. *Make* her pay attention to him.

Lucretia bit her lip, and tears welled in her eyes again. "Are you sure?"

Messalina lifted her chin, proud and tortured. "Yes."

It made him angry that she should look like that—as if he'd torn something important inside her.

As if he'd hurt her irreparably.

He waited until Lucretia gave him one last threatening look and stalked into the house before pulling Messalina inside. He dared not let go of her wrist, because a part of him wondered if she'd flee. He would talk to her, use all his persuasive abilities.

He could set this right.

But there was no sense of reassurance or relief as he dragged her into the echoing library and shut the door behind them.

She freed herself from him then, pacing across the room to gaze stoically at the empty shelves. "Say what you wish to say to me and be done. I want my bed."

He inhaled and said carefully, "I'm sorry. I did not mean to hurt you."

"No?" She still addressed the bookshelves, as if even looking at him was too painful. "I can't believe you imagined any other outcome to seducing me merely so my brothers couldn't start a suit for annulment."

"I..." His voice died away, and, unbelievably, he couldn't think of what to say next. His pulse was pounding in a way that never happened during a knife fight. He'd faced death and not been the least bit perturbed.

But now...

He was afraid to his core.

"Well?" she asked.

She sounded *bored.*

That brought his anger to the fore and he fell back on it almost gratefully. "What difference does it make *when* I bed you?" He stalked to her, coming to stand so close she couldn't help but look him in the face. "We both made a bargain—that this would be a marriage in truth. That hasn't changed just because the timing of the bedding did."

"Doesn't it?" she asked softly. "Don't play the innocent to me, Gideon. When you took me to bed I thought that the connection between us had grown. That we might become..."

She broke off, shaking her head.

"What?" He desperately wanted her to finish that sentence. If she did—if she admitted her affection for him—then all would be right, surely.

Her chin jerked up, and he'd never seen her gray eyes so pained—or so angry. "*Love.* I thought we might be falling in love. That you might have found some way to care for me."

He stared, relieved. "You admit you feel something for me?"

"Yes, I *had* feelings for you," she said, turning away. "Unlike you. I doubt you feel anything besides greed for money and privilege."

He was desperate. He could feel her slipping through his fingers. "You *know* where I came from. You *know* what I wanted. Why do you act as if my desires are suddenly a surprise?"

"I shouldn't, should I?" she murmured, as if talking only to herself. "You made plain enough that you had no heart. No soul. I was a fool to ever doubt that, even for a minute."

Her lips were trembling, but she met his gaze with determination. "I've fulfilled my half of our marital bargain—more than once. I want my dowry portion tomorrow."

If he gave her the money, she'd leave him.

She'd leave him.

He shook his head. "I can't."

Her lip curled. "You can't or *won't* give me my money?"

He gritted his teeth. "Won't."

"Fine, then." She turned away. "When you give me my money—and you will give me my *own* money—then Lucretia and I will quit this house. Enjoy your bounty, Gideon, but do not try and trick me again. Leave me in peace."

He felt as if he'd been stabbed in the gut as she marched to the door. This was a nightmare.

He was *losing* her.

"*Wait*." He strode after her, meaning to grasp her arm.

But in a swift movement she wrenched away. "Don't touch me."

"Messalina," he said, his chest swelling. Breaking.

Shattering.

"No." Her voice was stern. "You may own this house, my money, and my name, but you do not own *me*."

And she left him.

* * *

She felt as if her limbs were lead. Messalina carried herself very carefully as she made her way to the staircase. It wouldn't do to show how mortally she was hurt.

How Gideon had so nearly broken her.

Just a few more steps, just a little bit more, and then she could rest, but in the meantime she held her head high.

She was a Greycourt, and she did not bow before disaster or humiliation.

Bartlett was in the hallway outside the room she'd shared with Gideon. "Ma'am? Are you well?"

"Yes." Messalina nodded jerkily. "You may retire for the night."

"But—"

Messalina ignored the lady's maid's bewildered protest. She continued down the hallway. She wished to never see the inside of Gideon's bedroom again.

She had her hand raised to knock on Lucretia's door when it was flung open. Her younger sister dragged her into the room and wrapped her arms around Messalina.

"I'm so sorry," Lucretia gulped. Her voice was rasping as if she'd started crying again. "I had no right to discuss your marriage with Julian. He was speaking so ill of Gideon and I blurted that you and he had consummated your marriage now, so you must be more at peace with him. Julian leaped on my words, demanding to know what I meant and..."

Lucretia pulled back, wiping her eyes with the back of her hand like a little girl. "I'm sorry, Messalina. I should've never spoken at all. Please forgive me?"

"There's nothing to forgive." Messalina shook her head wearily as they sat side by side on Lucretia's bed. "Really, it's best that I know. I was a fool living a pantomime."

"But you were so happy," Lucretia whispered, crystalline tears caught in her eyes.

"Yes, but it was a false happiness, wasn't it?" Messalina tried to smile and found she could not. "He doesn't care for me. Not in the way I cared for him. Perhaps not at all. He was pretending all along, I think. Sooner or later he would've revealed the truth: our marriage was a sham."

The tears so long kept in check suddenly overwhelmed her defenses. Her eyes blurred as she caught her breath on a sob.

She felt Lucretia's arms wrap around her again in a tight hug.

"I wish I could call Gideon out," Lucretia exclaimed fiercely. "I'd drive a sword right through his shriveled, black heart!"

Messalina snorted. "What a bloodthirsty thing you are. I do believe you'd do it if you could."

"Of course I would," Lucretia replied indignantly.

"Calm yourself, Mistress Tigress. I'd be quite alone were you to be imprisoned for illegal dueling."

"Oh, very well," Lucretia said with mock disappointment.

Her sister was trying to cheer her, she knew, but Messalina couldn't produce a smile, let alone stop her steadily falling tears.

Lucretia's voice was soft and gentle when she next spoke. "Let me help you with your bodice, Lina." For some reason the childhood nickname, one Lucretia had invented when she was still in leading strings, made Messalina sob aloud. Lucretia unpinned her, drawing off both stomacher and bodice. "There. Now stand and I'll untie your skirts. Careful."

Messalina wobbled to her feet. "I shouldn't have dismissed Bartlett," she said, gulping. "And you ought to have a lady's maid of your own."

"Oh, don't be silly," Lucretia replied, her voice unbearably gentle. Her clever fingers were working at Messalina's waist. "I've always been quite happy sharing Bartlett."

"If you say so," Messalina murmured. She was so weary! She felt as if she were wading through mud, her skirts dragging her down, down into black depths where she'd inevitably stop struggling at some point.

"I do say so," Lucretia replied briskly. Messalina's skirts fell about her feet. "Step out now. See, I can even act the lady's maid with you. We don't need anyone else at all."

"Except that neither you nor I know how to cook."

"Tush! I'm quite fond of lemon curd pies. I'm sure we could live on those alone."

A weak laugh burst from Messalina's throat. "As long as I have you and you have me, we'll always get along."

But in her heart she knew. She wanted Gideon as well. A man to hold her at night. To smile at her tenderly. To argue with her over the dinner table. A man who would love her for herself.

But that would never be, would it? She'd been a fool to ever forget that Gideon had married her for her name and money. Nothing else.

And now? She sighed wearily as Lucretia pulled off her

panniers. Now she had to make plans to flee the country, hoping that Gideon would not renege on their bargain and would give her the dowry money.

She didn't know if she could trust him even in that.

Lucretia pulled a fresh chemise over Messalina's head, the crisp folds settling around her body. She'd been dressed like a doll by her sister.

Messalina turned to Lucretia and took her hands. "Thank you."

Lucretia kissed her cheek and pulled her to the bed. "It's just like when we were girls, isn't it?"

"I suppose it is," Messalina said, trying to force a cheerful note into her voice. She very much feared that she failed utterly.

She climbed into the big bed and pulled the coverlet to her chin. She stared up at the ceiling as Lucretia blew out the candle. There was a rustling and the bed shook once or twice and then Lucretia lay still.

"Good night," Messalina said.

"G'night," Lucretia whispered.

Lucretia started making that purring sound, almost like but not *quite* a snore, only minutes later.

But it took hours for Messalina to sleep.

CHAPTER FOURTEEN

*That night the fox brought home a freshly caught
hare. Bet cooked it over an open fire in the clearing
and they dined on roasted hare, blackberries, and
hazelnuts. Then the fox stood on his hind legs,
yawned, and turned into a long, lean, red-haired
man....*
—From *Bet and the Fox*

Nearly a week later, Gideon met his wife coming up the
Whispers House staircase while he was descending it.

They both paused, he on the higher step.

"Good afternoon," she murmured, her gaze averted
from his.

Gideon wished he could reply as stonily. That he didn't
yearn for her acknowledgment. He should simply walk past
her without a word.

Except he couldn't. "How are you?"

Her glossy hair was neatly and elegantly dressed, her
frock a becoming shade of forest green, but there were
shadows beneath the eyes that wouldn't meet his. If only
she'd consent to *talk* with him. There must be words that
would stop this freezing alienation. That would make her
smile at him again.

He hadn't found the words before, a small, mocking
voice reminded him, but he shoved it aside. He wasn't

giving up. She was his wife, his lover, *his woman*—even if she denied it now.

"I am well," she replied coldly.

He took a breath. "I'll see you at supper."

There was desperation in his voice, and he couldn't hide it.

"Of course," she said, then nodded as if he were an acquaintance on the street—an acquaintance she didn't particularly like—and continued up the stairs.

Bloody, bloody *hell*.

Gideon ran the rest of the way down the stairs as if fleeing all his troubles. Perhaps at supper she would talk to him. If not, it would be his last chance of the day. She hadn't returned to his bedroom since the night of the ball.

"Guv," Keys greeted him warily as Gideon reached the entryway.

"What have you got?" Gideon asked as he strode to the door.

He'd set Keys to shadowing Julian Greycourt to find out as much as he could about the man's movements and habits. Knowledge was, after all, power, and Gideon intended to be in a position of power the next time he met Greycourt.

Keys hurried to catch up, reporting breathlessly as they descended the front steps. "I caught wind of some information. Greycourt might be meeting a gentleman."

"Where?" Gideon growled.

"Opal's."

Gideon's eyebrows shot up as they strode down the street. Opal's was a notorious coffeehouse frequented by the dregs of the aristocracy—ruined clergymen, shady bankers, and the odd thief. "Never thought Greycourt would patronize such a place."

"Aye, well, that's probably the point, isn't it?" Keys replied with damnable cheeriness. "Wouldn't nobody think to find 'im there. 'E can meet 'ooever 'e pleases without anyone the wiser."

Gideon shot a sharp glance at the man. "And you're sure of this?"

Keys tapped the side of his nose. "The brother talks when 'e's in his cups."

Gideon merely grunted in reply to this.

The day was stupidly lovely, the sun blazing in the sky. Around them London surged and whirled, delirious in the good weather. A gap-toothed pieman bawled his wares in a particularly grating voice. Chairmen jogged past, their burden a ruddy gentleman with an enormous bobbed wig. A gaggle of urchins played knucklebones in a doorway while a wagon driver cursed his enormous draft horses.

The entire scene was enough to make a man spew. Or possibly that was just Gideon's reaction.

They walked in silence for some twenty minutes before turning into a narrow lane, the space above their heads filled with shop signs.

Keys darted Gideon a nervous glance. "It's just past here."

"I know," Gideon snapped, then winced. "Sorry."

Another corner, and then Opal's was suddenly on their right. In contrast to the other businesses crowded into the narrow lane, Opal's bore no sign. In fact, the only clue to its presence was the rich aroma of coffee.

Gideon ducked as he entered the low doorway.

Inside, tall booths enclosed cramped little tables. The patrons of Opal's, unlike those of almost every other coffeehouse, had no urge to be seen. Long, blackened beams crossed the ceiling, and the only light was from a row of small, smudged windows facing the lane. At one end of the room was an elderly woman presiding over her tankards, coffee beans, and fire like an ancient priestess of some particularly malignant god.

"There." Gideon indicated with a jerk of his chin a booth set within the shadows of the far side of the room. "That'll give us a view of the door so we won't miss Greycourt."

Keys nodded, and they claimed their table.

Immediately a small, grubby boy slid two steaming tankards of coffee onto the table and accepted a handful of pennies in return without saying a word.

Gideon took a sip of his coffee, nearly singeing his tongue, and felt a loosening in his chest. Coffee was one of the seven wonders of the world, and those who favored tea were daft.

Well...except for Messalina. She used to close her eyes in bliss at the first sip of her tea.

The thought made him scowl at his tankard.

"'Ave you considered pretty talk?" Keys interrupted his sulk.

"What?" Gideon barked.

Keys's sky-colored eyes widened. "I just meant you seem, erm...down in the mouth, guv. And it's no secret there's been a bit of a dustup between you and the missus."

Gideon felt his upper lip rise. "And I suppose my domestic life has set Reggie, you, Pea, and his boys all atwitter. Bunch of gossiping old women, you lot."

Keys pursed his lips, screwing up his face as if judging the matter soberly. "That we are, fair enough. But, see, what 'appens to you, guv, it's sort of our business, too. If'n you're in a glum mood, why, that's 'ow our day goes. And mind, if'n you're thinking on the missus and what's not 'appening in your bedroom instead of work, some might take advantage, like. It's when the old tomcat is thinking on something else that all the other cats attack."

Gideon's lips twitched. "An authority on cats, are you, then?"

"Awful lot of them in the courtyard where I grew up," Keys said with great dignity.

Gideon nodded, fighting down the curl of his lips, for he had no wish to hurt the younger man's feelings. "You're a wise man, Keys."

Keys flushed with evident happiness at the praise. "Kind o' you to say, guv."

Gideon tilted his mug to Keys in salute before drinking. "What would you suggest, then, to win back my wife, since you're such a philosopher? God knows I've tried everything. I even bought her a bunch of flowers. She gave them to the scullery maid."

"Well, and I'm sure that most ladies do love flowers." Keys cleared his throat. "But I'm wondering if'n Mistress 'Awthorne might like something else."

"Like what?" Gideon asked impatiently. He hated being ignorant at any time, but with this—how to woo Messalina— he felt a right fool. He glared at Keys. "Bonbons?"

Keys cocked his head. "Are bonbons what she really wants?"

Gideon frowned as he kept his eye on the entrance to the coffeehouse. It was true that he hadn't much experience with wooing women. His infrequent trysts in the past had mostly been of the one-time variety: enjoyable to both parties, but also, by silent agreement, not taken seriously.

But now he was very serious.

What did Messalina truly want? What would win her over?

Because Keys was right: his mind was divided, constantly thinking of her and their strife even as he went about his daily tasks. It was like a sore on his soul, the...the *aching* distress it caused him that she no longer smiled at him.

That she *avoided* him.

He wanted her back in his bed, but it was more than that.

He wanted to watch her sip her tea again. Wanted to take her walking in the park. Wanted to ask her opinions on business and food and the theater.

Wanted to simply hold her in his arms as she slept.

Just thinking of her absence made him feel hollow—as if something crucial were missing from inside him.

The door to the coffeehouse opened and Greycourt entered.

"Hsst!" Keys warned him.

"I see." Gideon propped his head on one hand, partially concealing his face.

He watched out of the corner of his eye as Greycourt said something to the old woman supplying the coffee, making her grin so wide that it was clear she had an entirely toothless mouth. Greycourt strode to a table under one of the windows and accepted a tall tankard of coffee.

"I thought you said he was meeting someone," Gideon muttered.

As if in answer, a man with his hat pulled low over his face entered. The newcomer went directly to Greycourt's table and doffed his hat as he sat.

Gideon sucked in a breath.

It was the Earl of Rookewoode.

* * *

"A slice of seedcake?" Messalina asked Lady Gilbert that afternoon.

"Oh, thank you," the older woman replied, passing her plate.

It was entirely Lucretia's fault that they were holding an afternoon tea. Had Messalina her druthers, she would be facedown on the bed she shared with Lucretia, wallowing in her own misery. But yesterday Lucretia had bullied her into going shopping on Bond Street, where they'd run into Lady Gilbert.

Messalina well remembered the older woman's gleeful urge to gossip on the stairs at the theater. She thought surely Lady Gilbert would have relished the scandalous scene at Uncle Augustus's ball.

But Lady Gilbert had looked rather more lonely than mean. Before Messalina knew what Lucretia was about, her sister had invited the lady to tea. And then Lucretia had somehow persuaded Messalina to invite the Hollands and Freya and Elspeth.

Only Lady Gilbert was in attendance at the moment. Messalina was a bit amused, despite her own troubles. Lady Gilbert's cheeks were pink beneath her lavender hair and it was quite evident she was enjoying herself.

Perhaps Lucretia was right to have insisted on this tea.

"...and the lady never did find her garters," Lady Gilbert said, concluding some scandalous tale Messalina had lost track of.

"Really?" Lucretia was on the edge of her seat and leaning so far forward toward Lady Gilbert that Messalina was worried she'd tumble to the floor. "I had no idea."

Lady Gilbert nodded knowingly.

"But..." Lucretia's brows drew together. "Whatever happened to the pet parrot?"

"Weeell," Lady Gilbert began on a deep breath.

The door opened and their new butler, Crusher, intoned, "Her Grace the Duchess of Harlowe, Lady Elspeth de Moray, Lady Holland, and the Misses Holland."

All five ladies crowded into the room.

Elspeth was staring after the retreating butler.

Lady Holland smiled at Messalina. "How lovely to have tea with you and Lucretia and of course Lady Gilbert."

There was a flurry of introductions and curtsies.

Messalina sat on the settee, patting the space beside her for Freya. Her old friend was wearing a beautiful turquoise-and-white-striped gown, the crisp colors showing off her red hair, piled elegantly on her head. But Freya's green eyes were concerned.

Blast. She'd always been perceptive.

"How are you, darling?" Freya murmured.

Messalina shook her head. If she spoke, she might burst into tears.

Lucretia had already rung for more water and was handing out seedcake on little plates.

"Are you enjoying matrimony?" Lady Holland asked Freya archly.

Freya smiled crookedly, glancing worriedly at Messalina. "Perhaps more than I should."

Regina and Arabella giggled.

Messalina made herself hold Freya's gaze. It wasn't her friend's fault that Messalina's own marriage had failed so miserably. Freya should be able to celebrate her union with Kester. After all, they had married for love. Theirs would be a marriage of mutual love and genuine affection. Messalina had come so very close to that. So very close.

Except it had all been a lie.

Still she held out her hand for a slice of seedcake, a determined smile on her face. She ignored the worried look in both Lucretia's and Freya's eyes.

Messalina picked up her cooling tea, letting the talk of engagements and weddings wash over her. She ought to dump the tea and take a fresh cup.

All at once her longing for Gideon overwhelmed her. She *missed* him.

Damn him.

The man had betrayed her, and his only worry was finding a way to lure her back into his bed. As if his lies and deceit could be simply forgotten. Even his gifts were insulting. She loathed cut flowers. They died and left a cloyingly sweet scent in the air.

If only his regard had been true. If only she could trust that his feelings were real when he looked at her with those wicked black eyes.

"We had a small wedding," Freya said, interrupting her brooding thoughts. "In the village church near his country house. It was lovely."

"But were any of your family there?" Lady Holland asked with interest.

"I'm afraid it was just us and the witnesses," Freya said apologetically.

"Fancy if your brother the duke had come," Regina exclaimed. "There would have been two dukes under one roof." She squinted as if seeing the scene. "I wonder which duke would take precedence?"

"I don't know." Freya met Messalina's gaze and said lightly, "But I'm afraid Ran doesn't like to leave Edinburgh."

Messalina gave Freya a sympathetic look. Ranulf de Moray, the Duke of Ayr, didn't even leave his town house in Edinburgh, as she understood it. He'd lost his right hand to infection after the terrible events of the night Aurelia died. The tragedy had changed him forever—much as it had Julian and Quintus.

And her.

The conversation ebbed and flowed around Messalina. She tried to take part, remembering every once in a while to paste the smile back on her face, but mostly she simply sat.

That is, until Lucretia's voice rose, drawing her attention. "Lemon curd is much better than apple tarts."

Elspeth raised her eyebrows placidly. "Is it?"

Lucretia all but sputtered.

Messalina caught Elspeth's eye at that moment, and the younger woman winked quickly.

Messalina's lips quirked. The minx! Sweet, calm Elspeth was deliberately teasing Lucretia, and Lucretia hadn't yet caught on.

One had to have respect for anyone who could bamboozle Lucretia.

The door to the sitting room opened, and Sam came in with Daisy.

"Oh, good, Daisy's here." Elspeth smiled at the boy. "And Sam."

Messalina beckoned him to her.

Sam came to stand at attention, his eyes wide.

Meanwhile Daisy had trotted over to the Hollands.

"What an adorable puppy!" Arabella exclaimed, picking him up, and Daisy was passed around to be admired.

Lady Gilbert said, "I once knew a viscountess who had a three-legged pug."

Elspeth turned with interest. "*Did* you?"

"Oh yes." Lady Gilbert went off on a long, convoluted story that only Elspeth seemed to follow.

Messalina reached over and absently gave a slice of seedcake to Sam.

He was such a sweet lad. She'd begun to plan for perhaps opening a free grammar school for St Giles boys.

She'd have to leave behind both that dream and Sam himself.

Messalina bit her lip.

She'd had her courses this morning. The thought that they would never have children that Gideon could hold over her should make her glad. It should be a relief.

It *was* a relief.

Except she would like children. Gideon's children, despite his betrayal. She could see in her mind's eye a little girl, her black curls bouncing as she ran. Or a boy, solemn and serious, with black eyes under slanting eyebrows.

Her breast ached at the vision.

"We ought to gather more often." Lucretia glanced at Messalina and assumed a very determined look—an expression that Messalina was familiar with. That expression had once led to a live piglet in the nursery and the abrupt departure of the governess.

The governess had been the third that year, if Messalina recalled correctly.

"I propose we have a monthly salon," Lucretia said gravely. "To discuss matters of great importance."

"Such as three-legged dogs?" Regina asked confusedly.

"Three-legged dogs," Elspeth mused, "lemon curd versus apple tarts, and books. Books are very important." She thought a second and then amended, "Oh, and butlers."

"Butlers?" Freya asked.

Elspeth looked at her earnestly. "They're quite mysterious. Haven't you noticed?"

"I think it a very good idea." Arabella suddenly spoke up. "I'd like a place to discuss things other than fashion."

She glanced around the room to nodding faces.

Lucretia beamed.

Messalina was unsure if this idea was viable. After all, if she left with Lucretia, they would never have a chance to participate in this new salon.

But Lucretia obviously wasn't thinking of that. She clapped her hands. "Wonderful! Then we'll meet next month?"

All of the ladies nodded and began discussing topics they might explore at their next salon.

Beside Messalina, Sam had slowly slumped to the floor and was now asleep against the settee.

She smiled down at the boy as the others talked around her. She was fond of Sam. The thought of him alone on the dangerous streets of St Giles, without friend or comfort, made her heart ache. How many other boys like Sam were still in St Giles?

If only she could found her school...

Lady Holland rose and began politely taking her leave with her daughters. Lady Gilbert followed suit, and after dismissing Sam and Daisy, Messalina walked with her guests to the front door of Whispers.

"I'd like to stay a bit longer," Freya said casually. "It's been such a while since I've had an intimate chat with Messalina."

"Then we'll say our goodbyes," Lady Holland said.

Lucretia, Freya, Elspeth, and Messalina watched the ladies enter two carriages, and one of the new footmen closed the door.

Freya turned at once to Messalina. "Where can we talk?"

"The sitting room again." Messalina led the way back, conscious that Lucretia was looking curious.

Freya waited until they four were in the sitting room alone before turning to Messalina. "Out with it. Why are you so sad?"

Messalina closed her eyes, and the whole wretched story came tumbling out—how she had disastrously succumbed to Gideon's wiles, the revelation of his lies, and the frozen politeness of their marriage now.

When she had finished some minutes later, Freya was silent.

Lucretia bent forward and poured a cup of tea and handed it to Messalina. It was barely lukewarm, of course, but Messalina drank it anyway, willing her fingers to stop trembling.

Elspeth said in a very serious voice, "Shall I kill him for you?"

Lucretia stared at her. "Have you killed a man before?"

Elspeth shrugged. "No, but I don't think it would be very hard."

Lucretia looked respectful.

At last Freya inhaled and looked frankly at Messalina. "What do you want now?"

"I..." Messalina frowned. "What do you mean? Lucretia and I will leave when I get the money."

"That's one choice."

"What are the others?" Lucretia asked.

"You could stay with Hawthorne," Freya said, keeping her gaze steady on Messalina. "This is where your family is, where your friends are. Do you really wish to never see them again?"

"He's a lying rogue," Lucretia said with quiet venom. "A *manipulative*, lying rogue."

Freya inclined her head. "Yes, he is. But you see, I'm not the one married to him." Her voice lowered. "I'm not the one who welcomed him into my bed by all appearances quite happily. Am I wrong?"

Elspeth's eyes widened.

Lucretia started to object, but Freya held up her hand.

"No, you're not wrong." Messalina pressed her lips together. "But I don't see what you're getting at."

"I think you must've had some feeling for your husband. I think you may still have feelings for him." Freya sighed and sank back on the settee. "The question is, is that enough to stay?"

"I..." Messalina swallowed. "I can't stay." She looked

across at Lucretia. "*We* can't stay. Our uncle plans to force Lucretia into marriage as well."

Her sister went white, but she lifted her chin bravely. "I knew it. Nasty old man."

Elspeth scooted a little closer to her.

But Freya nodded. "Then it's settled." She rose. "Remember, though, we don't choose whom we love, none of us. You're angry now and with good reason. He's been despicable to you. But that doesn't stop love. No matter how much we wish it would." She looked at Messalina. "Do you love a lying, manipulative rogue, who likes to fight with knives?"

Messalina's brain was awhirl with doubts and fears, base longings and feelings. "I...have feelings for Gideon, but I don't know if I love him. And I can't tell if all his talk was lies or the truth, perhaps hidden even from himself."

"You need to find out." Freya nodded. "I suggest you stay until you're certain—one way or the other."

* * *

Gideon's tankard was empty. He'd long since finished his second round of coffee while Keys was gamely still sipping—and wincing over—his first. Across the room, Greycourt was sitting with Sir Samuel Peabody, Lord Hardly, and Rookewoode. Three of the men bent low over the table, their heads close together as they discussed whatever business they had. Greycourt of course was too proud to bend his head. He merely leaned a little forward, his long braid of black hair over his shoulder, that foppish pearl dangling from his ear.

Ass.

Gideon had never been particularly fond of Julian

Greycourt, but after the man had set Messalina against Gideon, he positively loathed him.

Really, it ought to be easy to kill the man.

Instead he was wasting his time *watching* him.

Gideon's eyes narrowed. Greycourt was clever, wasn't he? And he moved in the highest aristocratic circles.

Why did the old man want him dead?

"Do they mean to stay all day?" groaned Keys. "I 'ave to piss like a bloody 'orse."

Gideon snorted into his empty tankard. "Drank too much?"

Keys looked at his tankard. "S'pose I could use this to hold my piss. Wouldn't change the taste that much."

"I'll be sure to tell the proprietress," Gideon replied absently. Rookewoode had leaned back, and the others were making movements preparatory to rising.

"Oh, thank God," Keys moaned as the group left the coffeehouse. "I'm for the bog."

Gideon frowned as he stood. "I can't wait for you. I'm following Greycourt to see if he's off to meet anyone else."

Keys nodded and limped toward the back of the building.

Gideon clapped his tricorne on and strode to the door, ducking his head as he opened it in case any of the cabal were lingering outside. But none of Greycourt's group were in the lane. Gideon looked both ways. To the right, Hastings and Peabody were strolling away. To the left, Rookewoode and Greycourt were disappearing around the corner.

Gideon jogged left.

He came to the intersection of the lane and a wider street and checked before turning. Greycourt and Rookewoode were half a dozen paces away, mingling with the London crowd.

Gideon ducked around a porter carrying a brace of chickens hanging from the pole balanced on his back and hurried after his quarry. Another few steps and Greycourt and Rookewoode suddenly turned to cross the busy street. Gideon turned as well, only to find a cart filled with turnips directly in his path. The horses plodded past, blocking his view of both men.

Gideon ran back a few steps and crossed behind the cart.

Greycourt had disappeared.

Rookewoode was still striding up ahead, but Greycourt was nowhere in sight.

Damn it!

Gideon hated that he had no idea which way Greycourt had gone—to lose sight of an enemy made him uneasy.

But Rookewoode was still moving.

Should he return for Keys or continue following the man?

Gideon shook his head and half ran after Rookewoode, swerving around a group of sailors and pushing past a large butcher, standing in his bloody apron.

Behind him someone swore.

Rookewoode turned into a tobacconist's.

Gideon slowed his progress, coming to a stop just before the shop. He lingered, pretending an interest in the display of pocketknives on the table outside the shop adjacent to the tobacconist's.

He could see that the tobacco shop was a small one. If he entered, Rookewoode would be sure to notice him. That wouldn't necessarily be a problem, except that Gideon wanted more information about Rookewoode's ties to Greycourt before he took his offer of investment to the earl.

He lurked outside.

On the other hand, Gideon considered ten minutes later, he didn't want to lose the man altogether.

He went inside the tobacconist's.

The shop was, as he'd thought, small and gloomy and

redolent of tobacco. Large twists of the dried leaves were arrayed on the walls, and a small, plump gentleman was pointing to one as a clerk attended him.

No one else seemed to be in the shop.

Gideon turned, but the shop was one room; the wares were displayed on the walls with nothing to obstruct them.

There was a door behind the counter.

Gideon vaulted the counter.

"Oi!" the clerk cried, lapsing into an East End London accent in his shock. "You can't—"

But Gideon was already though the door.

He entered a room stuffed with barrels and crates of tobacco, the smell near overwhelming. At the back was another door.

Gideon threw it open and found himself in a small alley lined with tall, rickety buildings of the type that housed several families at once.

He turned in a circle, but caught no glimpse of Rookewoode.

He'd lost him.

Bloody, bloody *hell*!

Had Rookewoode known he was being followed? But then why not simply confront Gideon?

What was the earl hiding—and how was Greycourt involved?

He wouldn't have those questions answered today.

Gideon trudged down the alley, trying to decide whether to return to Opal's to find Keys or to go to Whispers House and leave Keys to return on his own. The buildings lining the alley were close here. Each story aboveground jutted out farther into the lane in an inverted stepped pyramid until the roofs nearly met overhead, giving the looming feeling that at any minute a building could fall on one's head.

Gideon shivered. This place reminded him too much of the wretched neighborhood he'd lived in when he was a boy. He passed a pair of girls hanging wash, and then the alley ended abruptly in a small courtyard. A dead end.

An old man smoking a pipe before a door turned and went in the house.

The hairs on the back of Gideon's neck rose. The courtyard was deserted. He was alone, with only one way back.

He straightened his arm and shook down his knife from the sheath strapped to his forearm, holding it ready between his fingertips.

A cat ran across the yard and disappeared into a crack between the houses.

Behind him a boot scraped against a cobblestone.

CHAPTER FIFTEEN

Bet stared at the red-haired man. "Who are you?"
He smiled a foxy smile at her and said, "Your
husband, of course. Sometimes I'm a fox and
sometimes I am not."
Then Bet knew that this wasn't a man at all. Men did
not turn into foxes at will. No, she'd married a fae,
powerful and strange, and she shivered in fear....
— From *Bet and the Fox*

Gideon ducked and turned, raising his knife at the same time in the little courtyard.

The knife meant for his ribs sailed past, slicing a line into his coat.

His assailant hardly took time to recover before slashing out again.

Gideon shuffled back, balanced on his toes.

The man attacking him was experienced.

And deadly.

Gideon's arm shot out as he went for the gut, but the man swiveled aside, a smile curving his lips. He wore a simple brown suit, but it was in good condition.

"Do you want my purse?" Gideon asked.

Not that he'd give it away, but he wanted to know what this man was about.

The man—hardly more than a boy, really—cocked his head. "I don't mind taking it off your body."

He ran forward, as swift as a scurrying rat, and made a pass at Gideon's ribs again, missing. The suit Gideon wore would never be the same again.

Gideon darted, slashing in a quick, tight zigzag motion.

The attacker raised his arm and Gideon's blade sliced.

He slid back, expecting blood spray.

There wasn't any. His attacker must have wrapped his arm with leather.

The man grinned, slipping forward, going for Gideon's left side, but then at the last minute slashing his right.

Gideon only just got his arm out of the way.

Or not.

He could feel warmth seeping through his sleeve.

There was no time to look.

His attacker was charging, slashing swiftly again and again, his knife a blur. Gideon spun aside once and then again, rallying to flick his blade at the man.

This time blood sprayed.

Gideon stood his ground, his knife thrust at waist height before him, grinning. He wove a dangerous figure eight with the knife.

Slash.

Slide.

Weave.

And dart.

He was elegant. He was swift. And he should've prevailed.

He was, after all, the champion knife fighter of St Giles. Had once brought down Grinning Jack and his infamous black dagger.

But alas.

He'd just made another slash when a cudgel hit Gideon

on the right shoulder. He felt it at once, the agonizing pain of the arm going out of joint.

His knife clattered to the cobblestones.

Too late he realized that he'd not kept an eye on the entrance to the courtyard.

The next blow got him in the ribs.

And the one after.

Gideon staggered, raising his left arm to shield his head.

He heard a shout, the familiar sound of Keys's voice, and had two final thoughts:

How disappointed Keys would be that he'd been too late to save him.

And how he wished he could've seen Messalina once more before he died.

* * *

"Do you truly want to stay with him?" Lucretia asked hesitantly after Freya and Elspeth had departed.

They'd returned to the sitting room, where Lucretia had draped herself over the settee rather like a languid cat and Messalina slumped in her chair.

"I don't know. I don't know anything anymore." She looked at her sister. "I had plans for you and me. We'd leave England, sail to the Americas, buy a little cottage—small, but big enough for a maid and a cook. I'd present myself as a widow and you could be an eligible young lady."

"That sounds lovely," Lucretia said. "But you'd never see Freya again if we did that."

The thought gave Messalina a pang. She'd only recently made up with Freya. To lose her so soon...

"Hopefully we'd never see Uncle Augustus ever again,

either," she felt compelled to point out. "He wouldn't have any control over you."

"Mmm," Lucretia replied rather indistinctly. The maids hadn't taken away the tea things yet, and she was eating the rest of the seedcake.

Messalina stared at her doubtfully. "You do know that we'll be having supper in another couple of hours, don't you?"

Lucretia nodded enthusiastically. "Yes, and Cook is making a leg of lamb." For a moment she stopped, and her gaze became unfocused, as if she was imagining the juicy meat in front of her. Then she sighed and smiled at Messalina. "I do love a good leg of lamb. I hope Hicks doesn't burn it."

The door opened as she was speaking, and Crusher entered. He waited respectfully to be noticed and then cleared his throat. "A Mr. Blackwell to see you, ma'am. Shall I show him in, or are you not receiving?"

He must've come to see Gideon. Messalina had no idea where Gideon was at the moment—or when he might return—but she quite liked Mr. Blackwell.

"Please show him in," Messalina replied, and then turned back to Lucretia. "Perhaps you should sit up to meet visitors."

Lucretia sighed heavily but obeyed.

A moment later Will Blackwell came in, and Messalina was startled anew by how handsome the man was. He was wearing a robin's egg–blue suit today—the same blue as his eyes.

"Good afternoon, Mrs. Hawthorne," he said, crossing the room to take her hand and bow over it. He smiled charmingly. "I do apologize for interrupting your afternoon tea."

Messalina indicated the tea table in disarray and the one remaining piece of seedcake, which Lucretia was eyeing forlornly. "As you can see, we've nearly finished. I do hope you'll join us, though."

"Thank you." Mr. Blackwell turned to bow over Lucretia's hand with a roguish twinkle. "I trust I find you well, Miss Greycourt."

"Mr. Blackwell." Lucretia nodded.

Messalina looked for signs of Lucretia's interest in the man but couldn't discern any. Messalina sighed. It would be very convenient if Lucretia found a man to love—marriage would help to shield her from their uncle.

Messalina rang for the maids to clear the dishes and bring fresh tea.

That done, she indicated a chair across the low table from her and Lucretia. "Please be seated, Mr. Blackwell. I'm afraid that Gideon is not at home."

"So your butler informs me," Mr. Blackwell said. "Do you know when he'll return?"

"I'm afraid not." Messalina tried to make her reply as casual as she could, but the fact was that she and Gideon had hardly spoken in the last few days. His schedule and work, which had always been obscure, were now entirely closed to her.

The thought was depressing. She had a marriage in name only, a union of two people yoked together for the rest of their lives. She could imagine becoming old and bitter. Such marriages were not uncommon in society. *This* was why she'd always been wary of marriage. Had always wanted her autonomy.

She'd thought she'd had *both* with Gideon.

She was a fool. She wished she could turn back time and never have married Gideon.

But then she'd never have seen the laughter in his black eyes. Never discussed boys in St Giles and the importance of a good tailor.

She would not have felt his hard hands on her body. Would never have seen his face softened in sleep.

Her heart was sore.

Mr. Blackwell tutted, interrupting her thoughts. "Odd. Gideon sent round a note to meet him here today to discuss some matters. Perhaps I have the date or time wrong. Hawthorne is usually punctual."

"I'm sorry to be of no help," Messalina replied as the maids arrived with the tea.

"Please," Mr. Blackwell said. "It is I who should apologize for thrusting my company upon you and your sister."

Messalina smiled as she leaned forward to pour the tea. Hicks had included more seedcake as well as Lucretia's favorite lemon tarts, which he must've sent out for.

Hicks's attempt at piecrust yesterday had been an unfortunate failure.

Lucretia seemed to perk up at the sight of the lemon curd tarts. "What sort of business do you and my brother-in-law deal in, Mr. Blackwell? Surely not the same business Mr. Hawthorne does for the Duke of Windemere?"

"Indeed, no." Mr. Black laughed, accepted a dish of tea from Messalina. "The business I engage in is much more civilized. Mining, mainly. I've a plan to—"

He was interrupted by a commotion from outside the sitting room.

One of the maids ran in. "Oh, come quickly, ma'am!"

Messalina jumped to her feet, dread in her stomach. She hurried to the stairs, vaguely aware that Lucretia and Mr. Blackwell were behind her.

Halfway down the steps the entry hall came into sight and she stopped, suddenly light-headed.

Reggie and the new footmen were bringing Gideon in on an improvised litter.

His face was entirely covered in blood, and he was still.

For a second she feared the very worst.

Then Keys glanced up and saw her. "I've sent for the doctor, ma'am."

Messalina sagged against the banister, nodding faintly. Lucretia put an arm around her shoulders.

Mr. Blackwell ran past them down the rest of the stairs. "What happened?"

"Set upon in Whitechapel," Keys said grimly. "We was followin'...." Oddly, he glanced up at Messalina again and pressed his lips together before continuing, "Doesn't matter. Got separated, and by the time I found the guv 'e was goin' down with two men upon 'im. Shot the bigger one and the smaller ran for it."

"Christ," Mr. Blackwell said, looking appalled. "Where's that bloody doctor?"

He reached to touch Gideon's right shoulder just as Keys shouted, "Don't!"

At the touch Gideon arched with a pained cry.

"What's wrong with him?" Messalina asked frantically.

"'Is shoulder's out of joint, ma'am," Keys replied, and then said to the men carrying the litter, "Up the stairs, careful-like."

Reggie grunted and began backing up the stairs, his massive arms bulging with the strain.

Messalina turned and with Lucretia hurried back up. She ran to Gideon's room and entered for the first time since the night of the ball.

The bedroom looked the same as when she'd last seen it only days ago. For a moment grief reached up to take her in an overwhelming wave.

Then Lucretia began to pull back the covers on the bed. "We need a fire in here right away."

"Yes." Messalina went back out into the hallway, moving aside to let the men carrying the litter by. She glanced at Gideon's face, but his eyes were closed. Was he insensate?

She caught the eye of the same maid who'd run into the sitting room. "Please bring another blanket." She turned to a second maid, "Go to the kitchens and tell Hicks that the doctor will no doubt need hot water."

"Yes, ma'am!" Both maids took off at a run.

Below, Messalina could hear the doctor arriving, and in a moment a middle-aged man with a bobbed wig puffed up the stairs.

The doctor caught sight of Messalina. "The lady of the house, I presume?"

"Quite." Messalina pointed to the bedroom. "My husband is in there." And as the man trundled slowly down the hallway, she couldn't help adding, "Please hurry."

The doctor nodded, saying soothingly in a voice that made Messalina want to kick him, "All in good time, ma'am. All in good time."

He was at the bedroom door now, and as he went in Messalina followed close behind.

She halted, though, when she heard Gideon's rasping voice from the bed. "Get her out."

Messalina glanced around, wondering which maid had irritated her husband so much he wanted her thrown from the room.

But then she realized: he meant *her*.

"I don't want her here," Gideon was saying, even as he groaned at the doctor's touch. "Get her out, I say!"

Keys was in front of Messalina, his expression apologetic. "Sorry, ma'am."

"But—"

The door shut in her face.

* * *

Julian Greycourt deliberately let the door slam as he entered the inn room he and his brother shared.

"Where have you been?" Quinn asked with his arm over his eyes. He lay in one of the two narrow beds in the room.

"Out on business," Julian replied, tossing his hat onto the table. He prowled to the window, peering out. The inn courtyard was nearly deserted. "And being followed by Hawthorne."

"What?" Quinn withdrew his arm, revealing bloodshot eyes. "What do you mean?"

"I mean that Hawthorne followed me from Opal's," Julian said absently. Was the boy lurking by the stables watching their room?

"Why the hell should he do that?" Quinn demanded.

"I presume he's doing it on our dear uncle's orders." The boy went inside the stables, and Julian turned to look at his brother.

Quinn was staring at him. "He means to kill you."

"Perhaps." Julian had of course already considered this possibility after his uncle's sinister hints. "Augustus certainly hates me enough to order my death."

"Bloody hell!"

Julian glanced at his brother, his lips twitching. Quinn could be nearly as dramatic as their sisters. "But that's not the only reason Augustus might order me followed."

Quinn groaned, rolling to stand from the bed. He wore only his shirt and breeches, the shirt untucked and hanging about his hips. His hair was a wild tangle. "Then tell me what Augustus is up to."

Julian shrugged. "Remember, I went to meet with Rooke-woode and his friends."

Quinn paused in the act of pouring a glass of wine, his eyes narrowed. "You think he knows of our plans?"

"It's one concern." Julian sauntered to the table, taking the wineglass from his brother's hand. "Augustus has certainly spiked our plans before."

He swallowed some of the wine and winced. Cheap swill.

Quinn poured himself another glass. He looked at Julian, and for a second Julian caught a glimpse of the laughing, quick-witted boy his brother had once been.

Then Quinn tipped the wine down his throat, emptying the glass. "What's the other concern?"

Julian pressed his lips together. He hated to speak of it. That he, the scion of generations of aristocrats, should have this... *humiliating* weakness.

Quinn must've been in better control of his senses than Julian thought, for he said softly, "Blackmail."

Julian nodded. He was a Greycourt. He had to face this. "If Hawthorne finds out..."

"Augustus will destroy you," Quinn finished. He poured more wine into Julian's glass and his own. "So the most pleasant reason for Hawthorne to follow you is our financial ruin."

"Yes." Julian clenched his stomach and swallowed some of the blasted wine. "The other options are worse: social annihilation or my own assassination."

"Well, then," Quintus said, his words hardly slurring. "It seems to me that we have no choice."

Julian met his brother's eyes and saw his determination mirrored there.

Quinn nodded. "We kill Hawthorne."

* * *

It seemed like hours later that Messalina found herself in the sitting room again, with Lucretia pressing a hot dish of tea on her.

Messalina glanced up to find her sister gazing at her anxiously.

"He'll be all right," Lucretia was saying. "Quite all right, I'm sure. Anybody shouting like that can't be too badly injured. And you know how men get when they're hurt. Remember when Quintus fell from his horse when he was seventeen because he was in his cups and he made such a fuss but then wouldn't let anyone near to help him and locked himself in his bedroom? And then it turned out he only had a twisted ankle, but he insisted on resting it on a pillow in the most annoying fashion for weeks and weeks?"

Lucretia stopped, possibly to draw breath.

Messalina looked down at her tea. It was growing cold, but she was afraid that she might very well cast up her accounts should she drink it.

There had been so much blood on Gideon's face, and she thought the hair on the side of his head had gleamed with more blood. What if he lost consciousness? What if he was dying at this very moment from the loss of blood?

Why hadn't he wanted her in his room? Had he come to loathe her so much because of their discord?

She must've made a noise—maybe a sob—for Lucretia suddenly took the dish of tea from her hands and pulled her into a tight hug.

"It's all right," Lucretia whispered. "He'll be all right, I promise, Messalina. I promise."

"I thought you didn't like him," Messalina gasped.

"I don't," Lucretia murmured. "But *you* do."

It was usually Messalina, as the older sister, who gave comfort. Messalina buried her face in her sister's shoulder and inhaled the scent of violets—wild and free, a perfume that perfectly matched Lucretia's spirit and exuberantly loving nature.

The door to the sitting room opened, and Mr. Blackwell came in quietly.

Messalina hastily sat up, blotting her face with a handkerchief. "How is he?"

"Better." He gestured to a chair by them. "With your permission?"

Messalina nodded. "Please."

He sat, his face grave. "The shoulder was dislocated, but the doctor has been able to set it again." He winced. "A rather painful process, I'm afraid."

Messalina gulped. She'd once seen a groom's arm dislocated. They'd been with a picnic party, several miles from home, and the decision had been made to set the arm there and then.

The groom had screamed as if he were being tortured. She grew faint thinking of the shouts they'd heard earlier from above.

"Is he awake?" She felt helpless, having to beg the information from another when it was her own husband hurt.

Were they really husband and wife in anything but name anymore?

"When I left him, he was," Mr. Blackwell replied. "But I believe the doctor wanted to dose him with something to make him sleep. Gideon didn't like the idea."

Lucretia muttered something about males, sickrooms, and bad patients.

Messalina ignored her. "Did . . . did he ask about me?"

The pitying expression on Mr. Blackwell's face made her immediately regret the question. "No. I'm sorry, Mrs. Hawthorne. He was in a great deal of pain, you understand.

The doctor thought he might have broken ribs, and there was a cut upon his head that needed to be sewn shut."

"I see." Messalina looked down at her clasped hands.

The gilded clock on the mantel chimed the hour, and Messalina was surprised to find it wasn't yet dinnertime.

Only an hour had elapsed since Gideon had been brought home.

She rallied her hostess skills. "We'd be very pleased to have you stay for supper, Mr. Blackwell. You've been such a help."

Mr. Blackwell's gaze strayed to Lucretia, but then he shook his head. "I regret I must decline, Mrs. Hawthorne. I'm engaged to dine with a business acquaintance already."

Messalina raised her chin, pulling the tatters of her pride about her. "Then we shouldn't keep you any longer from your appointments."

Mr. Blackwell hesitated.

Abruptly he said, "Gideon and I have been partners for many years. In all that time I've never known him to form a connection with a female that lasted for more than a night. Beg your pardon."

Messalina stiffened. "I'm sure I don't need to know this information."

"I'm not explaining myself very well," Mr. Blackwell said earnestly. "I only mean that Gideon has been alone for a very long time, perhaps his entire life. His family is dead, did you know?"

"He told me that he had a mother and brother," Messalina said slowly. It felt almost treasonous to be talking about Gideon's personal life with someone else. "I didn't think he had any other family beyond that."

"Then you are one of the very few he's told even that much," Mr. Blackwell said. "I only learned about his mother and brother after two years of partnership—and then because Gideon once got drunk with me. He doesn't drink to drunkenness as a rule. He spoke without any emotion at all of his mother's death and even of his brother's. He might have been reading a newspaper. It made me realize something about him."

He paused, and Messalina could see that he wanted the question from her. Reluctantly she asked, "What is that?"

"You must not be cast down by his insistence that you leave the bedroom. In some fundamental way Gideon is..." He wrinkled his brow as if searching for the right word, then nodded as if he'd found it. "He is wrong. He does not feel the emotions the rest of us feel."

Messalina stared at him. "You're saying Gideon doesn't know how to love."

Beside her Lucretia made an aborted movement as if to forestall Mr. Blackwell from answering.

But he looked at Messalina steadily. "I'm saying that Gideon doesn't even *know* what love is. Not for people, in any case." His mouth twisted wryly. "He certainly has an affection for money."

Messalina took a deep breath. "I thank you for your thoughts on the matter. I will consider them."

She rose, and Mr. Blackwell stood as well.

"Please," he said. "If there is any way that I may help you at this difficult time, I hope you will send word." He felt inside the pocket of his blue coat and withdrew a pencil and notebook, bending to scribble an address on it before tearing the paper out and handing it to Messalina. "This is where I can be found. Please don't hesitate to send a messenger at any time. I'm at your disposal." He paused to glance at Lucretia, standing quietly beside Messalina. "At both of your disposals, ladies."

He bowed and departed.

Lucretia sat abruptly on the settee. "Well. I don't know what exactly to say to that."

"I do," Messalina said softly. "Mr. Blackwell only stated what I already knew: there is no hope for me and Gideon." She glanced up at Lucretia. "Freya urged me to find out Gideon's feelings, but what if he has none? If the emotion is only on my side, then it's my soul that is in peril, not just my pride." She took a deep breath. "We leave as soon as I attain the money."

CHAPTER SIXTEEN

"What is your name?" Bet asked the red-haired man bravely.
But he shook his head. "My name can be used against me, and I have many enemies."
"Then you don't trust me."
He tilted his head. "No, my dear. I neither trust nor love you, but our marriage will be pleasant nonetheless. Now come to bed." ...
—From *Bet and the Fox*

That evening Gideon gritted his teeth against the pain from his ribs as he turned onto his side. The ribs on his right were wrapped. His arm was bound to his chest on top of the bandages so that the joint might heal in place. Altogether he felt like a trussed bird, ready for the oven.

He hated this, hated being injured, in pain, and vulnerable to attack. His men surrounded him—he knew this. There was no danger, no way an enemy could get to him. Even so, something primitive and animal made him want to find a hiding hole, back himself in, and growl at any who dared disturb him.

So of course Messalina walked in the bedroom without so much as a knock at the door.

"Get out," he said at once.

His sharp words had driven her away earlier, but now she simply drew up a chair next to the bed. He saw she had a bowl of soup in her hands.

"I've brought you your supper," she said, as composed as if she had sat down to luncheon with a bevy of ladies.

"Leave it here and go," he ordered.

She set the bowl on the bedside table. "Can I help you to sit?"

"No." He tried to push himself upright with his left hand and bit back a groan as his ribs protested.

"You're ridiculous," Messalina said quietly, and put her arms around him to help him up.

It was an undignified and painful process, but in the end he was sitting, even if he was panting.

He frowned at her. "You're stronger than you look."

She raised an eyebrow. "You're only now understanding that?"

"Humph." A spoonful of steaming beef soup was suddenly held before him. "I can feed my—"

She shoved the spoon in his mouth.

He glared as he chewed what was, he had to admit, a very good bit of tender beef. When he'd swallowed, he opened his mouth to say—

And she did it again.

The smirk on her face was almost worth the indignity. She'd not smiled at him since that night at the ball, and he secretly basked in it even as he retained his glare. *God.* He'd turn somersaults like a trained monkey if it would keep that smile on her face.

"I think I like this game," she said as she held out another spoonful of soup.

This time he didn't bother trying to talk. He wasn't enthusiastic about the prospect of choking on that spoon.

For several minutes he simply ate as Messalina patiently fed him. It was almost companionable, and he felt a great longing rise up within him.

Gideon turned aside from the next offering of soup. "No more," he said gruffly. "I've had a sufficiency."

He expected her to depart then, but she simply put aside the bowl and spoon.

"Who attacked you?" she asked.

He shook his head. "Two men, one quite good with a knife. I didn't recognize them."

But he had suspicions. He'd been following Julian Greycourt, after all.

Her brows knitted. "Were they intent on robbery?"

"I don't think so," he replied dryly, "since they never asked for my purse."

She paled a little. "Then they wanted to hurt you."

They'd wanted to kill him, he knew, but he wasn't about to tell Messalina that.

He shrugged. "Perhaps."

Her glance was sharp. "Why?"

Gideon should send her away. He couldn't tell her that he suspected her brother. Or perhaps the duke—though Gideon couldn't figure why the old man would kill him before he'd completed his task. Windemere would be bad enough, but for all their conflict, Messalina cared for Greycourt.

Messalina cared for so many people.

Perhaps even him.

He wanted Messalina's company. She was finally talking to him, even if it was only to ask unwelcome questions.

He'd waited too long to answer. She sat back and eyed him suspiciously. "It hasn't escaped my notice that you've been especially prone to footpads attacking you in the last several weeks."

He blinked.

She rolled her eyes. "You're surprised I noticed."

Gideon cleared his throat. "It's true that I don't usually attract footpads."

She cocked her eyebrow. "Who wants you dead?"

He simply couldn't tell her. "I don't know."

"You mean you have no enemies—or that you have too many?"

"I have a few," he said cautiously. "Your uncle has many more. And since I am his man, there are some who might want to hit at him by...removing me from his service."

She frowned, looking toward the fire. "Have you done that mysterious job for him, Gideon? The one that you promised him for my hand in marriage?"

Jesus, he had to get her away from this subject. "Not yet."

She turned back to him, her gray eyes solemn and clear. "Why?"

Because he couldn't hurt her. Now or ever. Promise to the dangerous Duke of Windemere or not. It was suddenly very clear in his mind that he had no intention of killing Greycourt.

Even if the man wanted *him* dead. "It's complicated."

"You won't tell me."

Sweat dotted his forehead. "No."

Her expression turned resigned. *Disappointed.* "You don't trust me."

He felt as if he'd been punched in the belly, the pain sharper than any hit he'd taken in St Giles.

"Messalina, please," he said urgently as she stood. "It's not that."

She paused and looked back at him, and he could see that her humor was hot as well. "I'm *married* to you, Gideon, through no fault of my own. If it's *not* that you don't trust me, then why won't you talk to me?" She shook her head as he remained silent. "*You* were the one who placed us in this position. If you didn't want a wife who cared, then perhaps you should've studied me better before you made your devil's bargain with my uncle."

And with that she swept from the room.

* * *

Messalina was just finishing her toilet the next morning when she paused to take a deep breath. She'd hardly slept last night, turning over and over Gideon's betrayal, how she felt about him, and whether he felt anything at all for her. Fortunately, she'd spent the night in one of the guest rooms, sparing Lucretia her restlessness.

When she woke there had been a moment—a tiny moment—when she thought Gideon lay beside her.

She swallowed. Her heart ached.

But no. She'd vowed to put the matter of Gideon's perfidy aside for the nonce. He was injured. Keys had even admitted—after intense questioning that Messalina wasn't at all sorry for—that Gideon had come close to being murdered. Had Keys not arrived in time…

She shuddered. The fact was, even angry with Gideon for his *many* wrongs and wrongheadedness, she still felt a pull toward him.

Someone knocked at her bedroom door.

"Come," she called as Bartlett started putting away the brush and hairpins.

A maid peeped in. "You've a visitor, ma'am. Mr. Julian Greycourt. The butler has put him in the sitting room."

Messalina felt a cowardly urge to tell the maid to inform her brother that she wasn't home. Julian had brought her only pain since his arrival in London, and he'd shown no remorse for it.

She stared at herself in the mirror and remembered a time when she was very young and had fallen on a wooden floor. A great splinter had embedded itself in her palm. She'd known that the splinter had to be removed, but even at so young an age, she anticipated the pain it would cause her. She'd shied away from the tweezers her nanny had held. It wasn't until Julian had been called to the nursery and talked to her quietly for ten minutes or more that she was able to let the nanny pull the splinter.

He'd been so kind then, so gentle, and she'd looked up to him as her perfect older brother.

But she wasn't a little girl now, and Julian had long ago lost the ability to comfort her.

"Are you all right, ma'am?" the maid asked.

Messalina glanced up. "Of course. Please let my brother know that I'll attend him shortly, and tell Hicks to send tea."

She walked down the hallways and stairs mulling on Julian and how far he'd wandered from the laughing boy of his youth. When she looked up, she found herself in front of the sitting room doors. She squared her shoulders, bracing herself to meet her brother before she opened the door.

Julian was standing by the fireplace, gazing into the small fire there, his long braid of hair thrown over his shoulder, his face pensive.

Sometimes she wondered if her brother posed as the romantic poet on purpose. But then he'd been all alone when she'd entered the sitting room.

Perhaps he was truly as lonely as he seemed.

He looked up belatedly as she crossed the room.

"I've ordered tea," she said. "I hope this will be a pleasant visit."

"I suppose that depends on your definition of *pleasant*," he drawled.

She sat on the settee. "Does it? Well, then, I define a pleasant visit as conversation that doesn't leave me in fear for my new furniture."

He raised an eyebrow. "I'd hardly attack you."

"No?" She placed her arm on the back of the settee, eyeing him soberly. "Not physically, of course, but I think you have no compunction about attacking my mental state."

He pressed his lips together. "Would you have preferred to never know about your husband's deception?"

"No," she replied calmly but with bite. "But I don't think *my* preferences came into your decision at all. You wanted to score a point against Gideon, and if you had to go through my heart to do it, you saw no problem."

He stared at her with gray eyes identical to hers—save for the fact that she'd never seen that cold expression in her own mirror.

She turned as the door opened. Two maids entered, bearing an enormous tray between them of tea and tiny cakes.

They were followed immediately by Lucretia. "Why didn't you tell me we were having tea?" she asked, eyeing the cakes.

"Good morning, Lucretia," Julian said dryly.

Lucretia waved a hand at him, probably because she'd snatched a cake before the maids had even laid down their tray and her mouth was full.

The maids finished arranging the tea and asked if there was anything else before leaving the room.

Lucretia plopped down on the settee next to Messalina and poured herself a dish of tea, adding half the pot of cream before leaning back and sipping. "What are you doing here, Jules?"

Julian winced at the nickname and took the seat opposite. "As it happens, I came to talk with Messalina, not you, urchin."

"Really." Lucretia took another cake, although this time she at least put it on a plate. She showed no signs of leaving the sitting room despite the heavy hint.

Messalina sighed and poured tea for Julian and then herself. "Why *are* you here, Julian?"

"Your husband has been following me," he replied, hesitating over the sugar bowl before sitting back with his tea.

Messalina busied herself selecting a cake as she thought furiously. "Oh? When was this?"

"Yesterday."

Damn Gideon for his secrets. He certainly hadn't mentioned that he'd been following her brother when attacked. Messalina paused for just a beat, her gaze sliding to Lucretia's. Her sister had stopped eating. "Where?"

"In Whitechapel."

Messalina looked at her brother.

Julian was a Greycourt—cold and ruthless when it served him, which in the last decade or so had been all the time.

She held out a plate with one of the cakes. "Two men attacked Gideon yesterday in Whitechapel. His shoulder was dislocated and he was badly beaten. He's in bed upstairs now."

Julian waved away the plate and crossed his legs, looking bored. "Is that so?"

Messalina narrowed her eyes. "Did you try to kill my husband, Julian?"

Beside her Lucretia carefully set down her plate.

Julian's thin lips curved into a cold smile. "Had I wanted your husband dead, he would be."

Messalina abandoned her dish of tea and leaned back,

examining him. Impossible to tell if he was lying or telling the truth. "Oddly, I don't find that reassuring."

"Actually"—Julian carefully set down his untouched teacup—"I came here to ask your husband if he wanted *me* dead."

"What?" Messalina stared at him, her heart beginning to beat in double time. She wanted to say that Gideon would never hurt a member of her family. That he wouldn't betray her so.

But she couldn't.

"I can think of no other reason for Hawthorne to follow me but the most nefarious," Julian said quietly.

Messalina tilted her chin and said desperately, "There could be any number of reasons he was in the same place as you."

"Indeed," Julian replied calmly, still holding her gaze.

She could only hold his gaze, knowing she was on the losing side. Gideon might have any number of reasons to follow Julian, but none of them were good.

Julian looked away for a moment and then back to her. "I don't trust your husband."

"Do you trust me?" she asked softly.

He stared at her, handsome and as chill as a marble statue. When they'd been children he used to bring her sweets when he returned on the holidays from school.

She sighed.

He stood. "Why are you taking his part, Messalina? The bastard forced you into marriage. He's the duke's man. He'll hurt you far more than I in the end."

With that pretty comment he bowed and swept from the room.

Lucretia sat up and poured herself a dish of tea. "Do you truly think Julian was behind the attack on Gideon?"

Messalina shook her head. "What else am I to believe—despite Julian's protests?"

"Jules is very hard to read," Lucretia said musingly, "but I don't know that he'd have Gideon killed."

"He's an ass."

Lucretia looked at her. "Jules or your husband?"

"Jules." Messalina waved her hand irritably. "Both."

"Jules may be an ass," Lucretia said softly. "But that doesn't mean he was wrong when he said Gideon would hurt you."

Yes, she'd thought about that. She was prepared for whatever mental and emotional pain he might give her.

But she wasn't prepared for Gideon attacking her brother.

* * *

By afternoon Messalina had calmed herself—mostly. She'd taken a very long walk in Hyde Park and poured herself a medicinal glass of brandy afterward. All of which made her serene enough to visit Gideon.

The problem was she'd begun falling under his spell again. Seeing him bleeding, laid out on that litter, had terrified her. She couldn't imagine a world without his savage grin or knowing gaze. She didn't even want to think about it.

But now...

Was he trying to hurt Julian? Could she believe him if he denied it?

And was there any point in asking him?

Well, she certainly wouldn't know until she tried it.

Messalina straightened determinedly and tapped on the bedroom door before opening it.

Instead of resting in the big bed like any *sane* man who'd

been recently assaulted, her husband was swearing foully as he attempted to don a shirt. He had the thing over his neck and one arm, but of course his right arm was still strapped to his side.

"Whatever are you doing?" Messalina demanded.

She set the book she was carrying down on his bedside table and crossed the room.

He looked up, his face reddened with his efforts. "I'm dressing."

"*Why?*"

"I've work to do." His words ended on a gasp.

His face twisted in pain and she wanted to—to *shake* him. Instead she pulled the shirt off over his head.

He actually growled at that, but she was too distracted by the sight of his torso. His ribs had been securely wrapped, but blue-black bruises peeped both above and below the tape, making her wonder with horror how bad he looked *beneath* the bandages.

She glanced up into his scowling face. He'd not shaved, and the black bristles on his chin made him look like a brigand. A battered brigand.

A man without a moral code, who thought he could accomplish anything as long as he willed it.

Her husband.

"Are you insane?" she demanded. "You've broken ribs, a wrenched shoulder, and ugly stitches in your scalp. Whatever work you have can wait *one* day. One day, Gideon." Sudden salt tears flooded her eyes, blinding her. "Please get back in bed."

She blinked and saw him staring at her with something close to horror. "Messalina?"

"*Gideon.*"

His mouth flattened, his slanted eyebrows drawn down,

making him look even more like a reckless pirate. "Fine. I'll get in the bed."

He hesitated a moment before scowling ferociously. "Don't weep."

He turned to the bed as if he couldn't bear the sight of her tears.

Was he one of those men who disdained a woman's emotions?

"Here." She swiped at her eyes, regaining control. "You can't rest properly in those breeches."

She stepped closer to unbutton the placket of his breeches, and she was so concerned for him that it was a moment before she realized what she was doing. Her fingers froze. Her hands hovered right over the swell of his manhood. She daren't look up, but he seemed to have ceased breathing.

She had to leave him. Now more than ever after Julian's revelations.

Determinedly she concentrated on his buttons and only his buttons. She eased the opened breeches off his hips, ignoring the sight of his smallclothes and what lay beneath. She nudged him to sit on the bed before pulling the breeches off.

She took a deep breath and glanced up at him. Despite his stubborn wish to rise, Gideon's face was lined with exhaustion.

Which didn't stop the tenting of his smallclothes.

She cleared her throat and looked away, fluffing up his pillows and helping him to sit back against the headboard.

Then she pulled the coverlet primly to his waist.

"There," she said far too loudly.

His wide mouth twisted wryly. "Thank you."

"You're welcome," she said, drawing a chair up to the

side of the bed and sitting. "I came to ask you if you intend to hurt my brother Julian."

He looked at her a moment, his expression blank.

Then he raised a sardonic eyebrow. "No, I'm not going to hurt your brother. Either of them."

The relief was overwhelming. Julian was wrong, but then he saw plots in every corner.

"Thank you." Messalina smiled.

She reached for the small book she'd set down when she'd first come in the room.

He eyed the book with distaste. "What are you doing?"

She didn't let his sour tone dissuade her. "I'm going to read to you."

For the first time that morning his lips curved up. "Don't I get a say in the title?"

"No." She opened the book and found the first page and cleared her throat before reading. "*The Life, Adventures, and Piracies of the Famous Captain Singleton*, chapter one."

As she began to read one of Daniel Defoe's lesser-known works, she was very aware of Gideon's eyes on her. Aurelia used to read like this to her whenever Messalina had been sick as a child, which had given her the idea for Gideon. But of course being read to by one's sister was very different than reading to one's . . . well, lover.

She tripped on a word and had to begin the sentence again.

Gideon was her lover. *Had* been her lover. Despite his betrayal and machinations, he had been, for a brief time, *hers*. Strange, but she'd never really thought about him in such a way.

He'd been hers and now he was not. She would leave him and travel far, far across the world from him. She'd never see him again, her erstwhile lover.

And she would never take another lover.

She knew that suddenly and completely—Gideon was the only man for her.

And yet it changed nothing.

She looked up on the thought and found that Gideon had fallen asleep.

Messalina marked the page with a hairpin and gently closed the book.

He was so rarely still. Gideon seemed constantly in motion, planning and plotting, but now his thick, black eyelashes lay quiescent against his tanned cheeks.

She could examine him to her heart's content.

The right side of his forehead was mottled with green and blue bruises. Beneath, his eyebrows still reminded her of a demon, dark and manipulative, but she had a certain... fondness for that demon now. He was *her* demon, after all.

Then there was his mouth.

Dear God, the mere sight of that sinful mouth made something warm within her.

But his appeal was more than his outer surface. He was intent and driven. Proud and unstoppable. Funny sometimes, harsh other times.

A man who kept secrets and lied without blush.

A violent man.

A man she could love.

If only...

If only he knew how to love—how to love *her*. Everything would change then. She might forgive him his machinations—hard as that was—and remain married to him. They could lie in bed together, lazy and content. Argue over the dinner table. Visit the theater and discuss the oddities of acting and the audience. She could spend her life with him, this devious man, this St Giles fighter, and never be bored.

Never dissatisfied.

But that was not to be.

Messalina sighed and bent to brush a kiss over Gideon's forehead. And if a tear fell there, too, she would not admit it.

Chapter Seventeen

*So Bet lay with the redheaded man, and in the
morning neither he nor the fox was there. She spent
the day tidying the little cottage, wandering the
clearing, picking berries, and peering nervously
into the wood. When the light began to die, the fox
emerged from the trees and joined her for the
evening meal.
And then he changed into a man and took
her to bed....*
— From *Bet and the Fox*

It was a full two days later before Gideon could rise from
bed without incurring Messalina's disapproving brow.

Or worse—her tears.

The sight of her eyes shimmering with unshed tears had
twisted something inside him. He simply couldn't stand it.

Gideon pushed aside the thought and stepped into his
entry hall.

Only a footman stood by the front door. Some new man.
Gideon didn't know the footman's name.

He turned to look up the stairs. Where was she? He'd sent
word to Messalina to meet him here at half past one and it
was exactly that.

Perhaps she wasn't coming.

Despite their unsteady truce, despite her willingness to

read him adventure tales, she still hadn't forgiven him. Maybe she was only doing what she felt was right for an injured man.

Oddly she hadn't demanded her money yet and he wasn't about to bring up the subject.

He was just about to go to her rooms to find her when he heard the tap of her heels on the stairs.

Gideon turned.

Messalina was wearing her favorite color, a sort of deep pink that complemented her glossy black hair. She lifted an eyebrow. "I've come to your summons. What is it about?"

Despite her demand, her eyes were alight with curiosity.

He shook his head as he held out his good arm. A lot rode on this—more, perhaps, than he could even acknowledge. He said gruffly, "We mustn't be late."

She cocked an eyebrow at him. "Now you're simply being maddeningly mysterious."

"Come." He led her outside to the carriage, which was already waiting. He helped her inside, settling on the squabs across from her.

She pursed her lips and looked him over. "Are you quite sure you feel up to a journey today?"

"I'm fine—as I told you yesterday and the day before," he replied irritably and then took a deep breath, forcibly moderating his tone. "Besides, we aren't going all that far."

That only piqued her curiosity, and she started questioning him as the carriage drew away.

He watched her sparkling eyes, the curve of her lips, the animated way she spoke. What was he to do if this didn't work? Before he'd married her, he would've been setting spies on Greycourt, repaying an attack with a greater one. He'd never been slow in his revenge and he never let his enemies win.

Messalina made him weak. He *knew* she made him weak—and he didn't care.

If she only smiled at him again, he'd become as docile as a lamb.

It was not until an hour later, as the carriage drew up before a rather dingy warehouse in Southwark, that he had a twinge of doubt about their destination.

He glanced at Messalina as he handed her out. "I hope you're not disappointed. I thought you might like this, but if you don't, we can certainly go elsewhere. In fact—"

His words were brought to a halt by her finger on his lips.

"I think I need to see what's inside before I decide if I like it or not, don't you?" she asked softly.

He nodded stiffly. "Of course."

She laid her hand on his arm and something inside him stretched in satisfaction. He escorted her up the steps and into the building.

They entered a vast room with a high ceiling and worn wooden floor. The place was nearly packed with gentlemen—and a few ladies—all wandering the room and examining the items on display.

Messalina glanced around. "What is this place?"

"An auction house," Gideon replied, watching her face closely.

He realized he was *nervous*. The emotion was alien to him. He'd never felt nervous when he'd stepped into the fighting ring with bigger, older men. But here with Messalina with what felt like his *life* on the line...

He inhaled and said, "The late Earl of Milton was an avid collector—to excess. He near bankrupted the earldom. His nephew, the new earl, put up for auction everything that was not entailed or an heirloom of the family." Gideon indicated the room. "What you see here is that auction."

Messalina's eyebrows rose as she looked again at the room curiously. "But there aren't that many things here. Although"—she nodded to what looked like a Greek statue of a stag—"what I see is quite lovely."

"These are only a few of the items to be auctioned," Gideon replied, drawing her closer to the statue. He pulled a pamphlet from his coat pocket. "The rest are described in here."

"Oh." Messalina took the pamphlet just as a bell was rung.

The attendees turned to the front of the room.

Gideon drummed his fingers on his knee. He'd spent days in his bed planning this. He didn't know what he'd do if it didn't work.

A tall, thin man in a gray wig mounted a small platform and in a surprisingly loud voice announced the first item to be auctioned. Four men emerged from a side room carrying an ugly table topped with purple marble.

The auctioneer gave a brief description of the table, and the bidding began.

Messalina wore a careful expression. "Erm…were you interested in that?"

"No." He raised incredulous eyebrows. "Try examining page five in there." He tapped the pamphlet in her hand.

She bent her head to turn the pages and then began reading the listings. He watched and knew at once when she'd come to the pertinent one.

She grew very still.

He'd meant to be composed and silent. Not say a thing until she decided on her own. But he simply couldn't wait.

He leaned over her. "Do you want it?"

She glanced up at him, her gray eyes shining like silver. "You know I do."

Gideon felt his entire body lighten. She *liked* his surprise—

his gift to her. He was close enough that were he to bend only a little farther—mere inches—he could kiss her.

He murmured in her ear, "I thought you might want the earl's library, but I didn't know for certain."

"But you brought me here anyway." She smiled.

He basked in that smile like a man seeing the sun after decades underground.

Messalina bent her head to the catalogue again. "The library is over a thousand books and includes an illuminated Irish psalter, a bound quarto of Shakespeare's plays, and the complete works of Euripides in custom red leather worked in gold." She took a deep, ecstatic breath. "Oh, Gideon, I want *everything* in this library."

He nodded. "Then we'll buy the entire library."

"But your idea." She looked at him curiously. "I've never seen you read a book."

"I don't. Books have never been..." He shook his head. "I may not need them, but I know you do. And I like when you read to me."

Messalina was silent as the auctioneer declared the winning bidder of the ugly table and the crowd seemed to all start gossiping together. There was a feeling of excitement and anticipation growing in the room.

He turned back to Messalina to find an expression on her face he could not interpret.

She opened her mouth, hesitated, then said, "I'm happy to read to you. I rather enjoy it, in fact."

"As do I," he replied, perhaps too intently. "You have a lovely voice."

He watched a small smile curl her lips before he returned his gaze to the auctioneer.

* * *

Messalina reverently cradled the illuminated Irish psalter in her hands as their carriage started forward an hour later. Gideon had arranged to have the crates of books delivered to Whispers, but she couldn't help but claim an illustrated atlas and the psalter at once.

The psalter was a tiny thing, barely as wide as her palm, but inside, the pages glowed in jewel colors. Tiny, meticulous illustrations, many picked out in gold, headed every book within. She'd never seen anything so beautiful.

And Gideon had bought it for her.

She looked up at him in wonder. He sat across from her, watching her with a faint smile curling his lips. Usually his smiles were cynical, but this one was entirely forthright. How had Gideon known she would want—would *love*—this little book? He'd tried to win her with flowers only days ago—a ridiculous misstep—and now he gave her something utterly perfect.

An entire library.

The gesture made her feel shaky somehow. As if she were uncertainly balanced between hope and despair. Because if he knew that the library was the perfect gift for her, did that mean he might actually *care* about what she wanted?

That he might care for *her*?

It frightened her—the possibility of hope—because it also brought the possibility of pain again. She'd yearned so helplessly these last few days since the ball and his betrayal of her trust. If she once again believed him, if she gave in to the tiptoeing return of desire, she would be devastated if he betrayed her again.

She wasn't sure she could believe her own senses.

She realized that he was watching her now with a little wrinkle between his winged brows.

She cleared her throat. "Thank you."

"I'm glad you liked my gift," he said carefully.

She tilted her head, trying to read him and failing. "Are you?"

"Yes." His jaw tightened, but he replied evenly enough. "I did it for you, after all."

"Why?" she asked, and held her breath.

He tilted his head back against the seat, those clever eyes pinning her. "I want you to be happy, Messalina. Simply that."

The words lit a small flame within her breast, flickering uncertainly.

He looked weary all of a sudden, his eyes closing as she stared at him, and she worried that the trip had been too much too soon.

The carriage jolted to a halt, nearly sending her to the floor.

"Damn," Gideon exclaimed, reaching across the carriage to catch her arm and steady her. "Are you all right?"

"Yes," she said breathlessly. "And more importantly, the psalter is as well."

He cocked an eyebrow pointedly. "It's not the psalter I worry about."

She bit back a delighted curl of her lips at his words, like a veritable ninny right out of the schoolroom. Her heart seemed unable to remain indifferent to his pull, no matter what her mind told her.

He leaned forward and wrenched open the window, muttering, "What's the delay?"

As soon as he opened the window, Messalina could hear the shouts and the sound of tramping feet, and she felt a shiver go down her spine. "What is it?"

The voice of their driver rose above the clamor. "'Anging, guv. Can't get around the crowd. We'll 'ave to wait them out."

Gideon made a small sound.

Messalina's gaze darted to his face.

He was white.

She remembered the last time they'd come across a hanging march. "Gideon?"

He sat again heavily, his fists clenched in his lap, his eyes closed. He didn't seem to have heard her.

"Gideon?" she asked again tentatively.

He shook his head. "I can't…"

She was alarmed now and rose to cross the carriage and sit beside him, her psalter forgotten. "Are you well?"

He made a noise that was not at all a laugh. "No."

"It's the hanging, isn't it?" she said softly. "Can I help?"

He shook his head and opened his eyes, his expression bleak. "You must think me mad."

"Not at all," she murmured, laying her hand on his shoulder. "Will you tell me why it hurts you so much?"

He stared at his fists. "Eddie."

Who—? For a moment her mind was blank as she tried to remember where she'd heard the name before.

And then she recalled. Eddie had been Gideon's younger brother. "What about him?"

Gideon said stonily, as if he didn't feel at all, "They hanged him."

"What?" She simply couldn't comprehend. "Who hanged him? *Why?*"

He finally looked at her, and she was shocked to see his black eyes dulled. "Eddie was hanged for theft. He was eleven."

"But…" That couldn't be, surely? She'd never heard of a child so young being hanged, let alone for *theft*. "I don't understand."

He sighed. "Eddie picked pockets. I didn't like it—far too dangerous—but when we were hungry I looked the other way. And we were very hungry that winter when Eddie was eleven and I thirteen."

She didn't like this story—she already knew the ending, and it was horrific. But she couldn't let him suffer alone. "What happened?"

Gideon's face twisted and he bared his teeth. "It was an *aristocrat*, an old doddering man in St Giles looking for a whore most like. Why else would he be walking the streets there? Eddie took his watch—his *gold* watch, silly fool. The lord's footman caught my brother. Eddie was hauled before the court, tried, and hanged."

Messalina gasped, appalled. That a *boy* should be executed for a man's crime was disgusting. She only vaguely knew the law, but this didn't seem at all right.

She whispered, "I thought that the magistrates would commute the sentence if the condemned was so young?"

"Oh, they would in the normal way of things." Gideon's voice was low and hateful. Had she once thought he had no feelings? "I found that out later. But the lord—a man named Cross—insisted on the sentence. He said that it was an affront to his dignity as a peer for his watch to be stolen. That Eddie must pay the price of his crime. It was only *proper*."

He snarled the last word, his expression transfigured into a sneering mask.

What could she say in the face of such injustice? Of Gideon's rage and grief? "I'm—I'm sorry." The words felt like a dainty handkerchief pressed to the bloody stump of a severed limb. Inadequate. Trite.

Useless.

Gideon didn't seem to hear her anyway. "I never saw him while he was imprisoned. I hadn't the coin to bribe the guards. He was in there alone and afraid, without food or blanket, and I could do nothing. *Nothing*."

His hands clenched and then opened, empty.

The horror washed over her. She couldn't comprehend. For a little boy... To be completely helpless... She shook her head, grasping for some light. *Anything.* "Your mother?"

The look he gave her was bleak. "Mam was soused much of the time by then. She was dead drunk, unable to form words even, when he was hanged." He glanced at the window and murmured, almost as if to himself, "When he was hanged..."

She couldn't ask. Didn't want to know or imagine. But she couldn't help running her hand from his shoulder down to his fingers. Taking his warm palm in hers and squeezing.

He inhaled, his hand tightening around hers. "I went, of course. I couldn't do else. I didn't want him to die—" He choked on the word and she knew he meant *alone*.

A child dying alone.

He closed his eyes. "I followed the procession. By the time we came to Tyburn there were too many for me to make my way to the front. I stood on a barrel to see my brother hanged."

He stopped again and swallowed.

Messalina felt tears pricking her eyes. She couldn't imagine. A boy watching his only brother hanged.

"I think he saw me. Maybe." He shook his head. "I might've been wrong, he was so far away. But I could see him. His face was pale. So very white..."

Gideon looked at her, and she saw that his eyes were damp, though no tears had fallen. His face was harsh, his features drawn, the silver scar standing out on his cheek, and she realized that anyone who didn't know him would mistake his grief for something else. Would think him remote and ruthless and awful when he *wasn't*.

She would've thought that a week ago.

"Eddie was younger than me," he said softly, his voice so low she could hardly make out the words. "It was my fault he was hanged. I should've protected my brother. I should've taught him not to steal."

The carriage lurched into motion. The procession must've moved on.

But Messalina hardly noticed, she was so stunned. It was as if a blinding light had shone into her mind. She remembered Gideon shouting at a weeping Sam that first day of their marriage. What had seemed like barbaric savagery was now flipped over, the other side entirely different. Gideon had been making sure Sam—a young boy like his brother—would never steal again. Because it was a hanging offense.

He hadn't been cruel for cruelty's sake.

He'd been protecting the boy as he hadn't been able to protect Eddie.

"Oh, Gideon," she said, feeling sad. "It was never your fault that they hanged Eddie."

"Wasn't it?" He looked at her fiercely. "I was the only one to watch over him. I was the only one he turned to." He fumbled suddenly with his neckcloth, jerking it so hard she thought he would strangle himself. "Do you know what he did, the last time I saw him? Before he went out pickpocketing and was caught?"

He yanked open his shirt, wrenching a couple of buttons off, sending them pinging to the floor.

He ignored the buttons to hold up the worn farthing he wore always around his neck. "He gave me *this*—to buy a bit of bread for our supper. I had a half dozen pennies but I took his farthing anyway—and when he went to prison he had *nothing*."

The helpless rage, the overwhelming grief she saw in his

eyes staggered her. Made her wonder how she'd ever thought him without emotion.

Messalina wrapped her arms around him. "You did your best. You watched over Eddie as well as you could." He shook his head violently, but she insisted because she knew now. "You loved your brother, and that farthing is the proof."

CHAPTER EIGHTEEN

*The days passed one after another with very little
difference until one evening the fox returned home
with a limp and a pair of red shoes in his paws.
"For you," he said to Bet.
She took the shoes and tried them on, finding that
they fit perfectly. "Why have you given me these?"
"To remember me by," he replied mockingly....*
—From *Bet and the Fox*

Messalina lounged in the sitting room late that night after
dinner, clad in a comfortable wrap in preparation for bed.
Lucretia was beside her, nibbling on a lemon tart. Her sister
appeared to have Hicks entirely in her thrall. Gideon had
disappeared as soon as dinner was done.

Messalina had meant to examine the new psalter on her
lap, but she kept remembering that afternoon instead. How
Gideon had been so hesitant when he'd taken her to the auction. His satisfaction when he realized she loved his gift.

And the rage and grief he'd let spill afterward when he
told her about Eddie. He'd never have spoken so frankly,
without scheme or guile, when they'd first married. She
knew that.

She felt honored that he'd revealed his hurt to her.

Tiny, sharp teeth nibbled at her fingers, dangling from

the side of the settee. Messalina glanced down and saw that Daisy had decided that her fingers were a late-night snack.

"Ow," she said in a scolding tone of voice. "No biting, please."

"I'm sorry, ma'am." Sam had been lying on his stomach by the fireplace, carefully turning the pages of the illustrated atlas she'd brought back. He jumped up and ran to the settee.

"You needn't worry, Sam," Messalina said. "Even the most well-behaved puppies like to nibble." She set the psalter down on the settee beside her and lifted Daisy onto her lap. She glanced at Sam. "That is, I hope Daisy has been well-behaved?"

The boy suddenly looked guilty. "'E may've found one of Mr. 'Icks's shoes."

Lucretia glanced up. "Did Daisy eat the shoe?"

"Oh no, not *eat*." Sam stared down at his toes. "Although he did chew them up a bit."

Lucretia widened her eyes with what seemed like alarm. "We must get Mr. Hicks new shoes at once. He's been coming along so nicely with his roasts."

The boy looked worried.

"It's all right," Messalina reassured him. "I'm sure it wasn't your fault Daisy found the shoes."

"Yes, ma'am." Sam didn't seem nearly as convinced of his own innocence.

Messalina suppressed a smile and petted Daisy, who had curled up on her lap. She watched as Sam returned to the atlas, and a sudden thought struck. "Sam?"

The boy lifted his head from the book. "Ma'am?"

"If you could do any work in the world when you grow up, what would you like to be?"

Lucretia raised her eyebrows. "What—?"

"Shh," Messalina murmured.

Sam gave the question serious thought, a heavy frown wrinkling his forehead, and then his brow cleared and he said, "A schoolmaster."

Messalina blinked, surprised. "Really? Why is that?"

"Well," the boy replied. "Schoolmasters don't live in St Giles. An' they're clever-like. Real clever. They read books."

It seemed a little unlikely that there were *no* schoolmasters living in St Giles, but Messalina could concede the other points. "I see."

Sam nodded and returned to the atlas.

Daisy stood at that point and yawned, and Messalina was reminded of how tiny a puppy's bladder truly was. "Can you take Daisy to the garden, Sam?"

"Yes, ma'am." The boy scurried over with an important air and scooped the dog up.

After the boy and dog left the room, Messalina turned back to Lucretia and saw that she was bent over the psalter.

"What is this, do you suppose?" Lucretia murmured, pointing to a drawing on the vellum page.

Messalina peered down at the tiny purple monster. "It's a whale, I think."

Lucretia seemed doubtful. "Is that what a whale looks like? I didn't know they had whiskers."

"I'm not entirely sure," Messalina said, taking the book to study the creature. Could it be a cat with a fish tail?

"Hmm," Lucretia murmured, and reached for another tart. "I never would have guessed that Gideon would be so generous. Your library must've cost a pretty penny."

"There's much about Gideon I certainly would never have guessed," Messalina said slowly. She remembered her husband's face as he'd talked about his dead brother. When she'd arrived in London she'd thought him a wicked man without feelings.

She'd been wrong.

"Certainly he doesn't seem the literary type," Lucretia mused.

"He's not. But he knows *I* am." Messalina turned to her with enthusiasm. "You should've seen the auction house, Lucretia! Filled with all sorts of things, many quite, quite ugly, but so fascinating. And the bidding—I had no idea how ruthless it could be. It was rather exciting toward the end. I was on the edge of my seat, hoping if Gideon could outbid..." She trailed away as she noticed Lucretia's thoughtful face. "What?"

"Oh, nothing," her sister replied, clearly lying. "It's just that you seem so happy."

"I am," Messalina said, feeling a tad defensive.

"Yet I thought we still plan to leave?" Lucretia questioned softly.

Messalina bit her lip, looking down at the psalter, remembering Gideon's face as he'd watched her open it for the first time.

Did she really want to leave anymore?

Because if Gideon was capable of love—even brotherly love—wasn't there a chance for happiness?

"I don't know," Messalina whispered.

Lucretia nodded, dusting crumbs from the tarts off her hands. "That's what I thought. I'll have to find someplace to hide, I think. Somewhere Uncle Augustus can't find me. Perhaps at Kester's northern manor? No"—she held up a hand to halt Messalina speaking—"I'm not berating you. I want your happiness. I just believe you ought to really think on it. Do you truly wish to leave Gideon?" Lucretia gave her a lopsided smile as she stood. "Good night, Sister dear."

Messalina watched her go and then slumped back on the settee. She knew what she wanted to do—she wanted to stay here with Gideon. She just wasn't sure if it was the morally correct move. After all, she was thinking only of her happiness. What if Julian continued to hate Gideon? What if her brother *hurt* him? And what if Lucretia had to be sent away to be hidden? It wasn't fair to Lucretia, for her to sacrifice her own happiness for Messalina's.

Besides. Messalina wasn't entirely sure she could live without her sister.

She was still deep in thought when Gideon entered the sitting room with a bottle of wine and two small glasses. "I hope you don't mind."

"Not at all," she replied, sitting upright hastily.

"Would you like a glass?" He indicated the bottle.

"Please."

He poured and silently handed her the glass of wine, their fingers brushing.

She shivered, sipping the wine to cover. It was delightfully fruity. She set the glass on a table and cleared her throat. "Have you come to discuss the library?"

"No." He abruptly set down his wine untasted. "Messalina. I'm not good with words where you're concerned. But I want you to know that…" His beautiful mouth twisted. "Stay. Please stay with me. If you'll let me—"

"Yes." She held out her hands for him, not waiting for him to finish. "*Yes.*"

And strangely—perfectly—she knew it was the right thing to do.

He took her hands, sinking down to the settee beside her, his eyes closed. "Thank you."

He lifted her hands palm-upward to his lips, brushing his lips over each one, sending shivers through her body, the touch light, almost reverent.

She caught her breath, tears pricking at her eyes.

He wrapped his arm about her waist and pulled her close, handling her as she had the psalter.

As if she were something infinitely precious and rare.

Something he didn't want to lose.

He pressed kisses to the corners of her mouth. To her upper lip and then to her bottom lip. Slow and sensual. His head bent to hers as he wandered to her throat, making her skin pebble beneath his tongue.

The psalter dropped to the floor.

She tugged the tie from his hair, threading her fingers through the wild curls and breathing, "Make love to me."

"Messalina," he whispered, his voice sounding desperate, his lips moving to the base of her throat.

She was trembling—with need. With hope and *love*.

She cradled his face between her hands, making him raise his head, and looked at him. His lips were reddened, his black eyes wild. "Gideon. *Please*."

"Yes."

His hands actually shook as he pulled at the tie to her wrapper.

But then he dipped his head, catching her nipple through the thin lawn of her chemise.

All thought fled her mind.

He suckled and all she could do was *feel*.

She arched beneath him, whimpering, and he switched to her other nipple. The first, covered by the wet lawn, immediately peaked further in the chill.

She shivered, but not from cold. She knew how sensitive her nipples were now and could therefore anticipate the pleasure he would give her. Her entire being seemed to be focused on those points of aching, tight skin as he sucked and licked and bit.

She moved restlessly, her center hot and melting. "Gideon," she whispered. "*Please.*"

He pulled her until she lay on her back on the settee and she looked up into his black glittering eyes.

He rose again, hovering over her in the dimly lit room, a strange creature conjured by her basest longings in the night.

"Pull up your chemise," he whispered. "Show me your body."

A hot thrill swept through her, so strong she pressed her thighs together. She gathered the voluminous skirts of her chemise and raised them, pulling until she had them bunched at her waist.

"Higher," he growled, his eyes on her naked body.

With trembling hands she drew the thin material up, revealing her peaked breasts.

He simply looked at her.

She felt her nipples contract even more, becoming almost painful she was so aroused.

At last he met her eyes. "Messalina."

And though it was only her name, in his voice she could hear all he meant to say.

He knelt over her, tearing at the falls to his breeches.

She held up her heavy arms. "Come to me."

He looked at her as if she were the key to staying alive. As if he might die if he didn't have her in the next minute.

He finally freed his cock, big and engorged. But when he began lowering himself onto her he suddenly stopped with a bitten-off exclamation.

Her eyes widened. "Your shoulder! Perhaps we should—"

"No. If you help me..." He shifted his weight to his left hand and looked at her.

Oh. She reached between them, taking his hard penis

into her hands. For a moment she simply ran her fingers up his shaft, feeling the shocking heat, the soft skin. Then she reached the top and she ran her thumb over the pearl of liquid weeping from his slit.

His penis jerked in her hands and he inhaled sharply. "Messalina..."

She smiled secretly to herself for making his voice so gravelly. Then she wrapped her legs over his hips. The fabric of his breeches felt strange against her inner thighs. She guided his manhood to her entrance, looked into his eyes as his flesh touched hers.

He returned her gaze, watching her as he nudged inside her. He seemed to be telling her something with his eyes, and her heart pounded as she wondered what it meant.

She moaned as he stretched her, slowly, slowly invading her body, making pleasure streak through her. She fought to keep her eyes open, her gaze locked with his. This act was different from the ones before. It felt nearly sacred, a joining of minds as well as bodies.

She could tell he thought the same because he stared at her with an intensity she'd never seen from him before. He flexed his hips and withdrew from her, slow and controlled.

She immediately felt the loss.

"Messalina," he said, his voice rasping and deep as he drove into her again.

He was blunt and implacable.

She gasped, her hand to his face tracing the arch of his devilish brows.

He looked driven as he made love to her, his eyes black and glittering, lines deepening around his mouth and nostrils. And his silver scar was like a brand on his darkened face.

He might've been a demon come for her soul.

But he wasn't.

He wasn't.

She arched beneath him, mindlessly turning liquid. Heating from her center as she clutched at his shoulders. She was so close, her peak just out of her reach.

She whimpered in frustration.

He slammed into her, shaking the settee, sweat beading his brow. "Touch yourself for me," he gritted out, sounding as if he tore the words from his lungs. "Please, darling."

The idea scandalized her. Made a thrill throb in her quim.

She burrowed her hand between them, feeling the flex of his stomach muscles, the scratch of the hair above his penis.

Biting her lips, staring into his black eyes, knowing that she could never do this for another man, she touched herself. Her skin was wet and slick, nearly too sensitive, and she clenched around him at how good it felt.

Her finger ground down on her pearl, firm and right, as he continued to...to...

He was *watching* her.

She bit her lip, unable to meet his black gaze. What they did was so *wicked*.

He relentlessly stroked bliss into her, the pleasure spiraling higher and higher, her fingers slick with her own excitement, until she bowed beneath him, unable to contain the ecstasy, blind with her own crisis.

She shuddered again and again as sparks spread through her, to her heart, to her mind, to her very fingertips.

And all the while he continued to pound into her.

When she could open her eyes, she looked up and saw a beautiful devil in torment. His eyes screwed shut, his lips pulled back from clenched teeth, his entire body sheened with sweat.

As if he were falling to hell.

As if he were ascending to heaven.

She held him as he shook and buried his penis deep within her. He froze in her arms, trembling, his head falling forward to hang heavy from his shoulders as he panted harshly. She closed her eyes, feeling sated and peaceful.

At last, moving slowly, he withdrew from her and stood up.

Messalina threw down the skirts of her chemise and wrap, self-conscious now that she was no longer in the throes of lovemaking.

Gideon held out his hand to her. "Will you come to bed with me now, Mrs. Hawthorne?"

"Yes."

She felt light as he pulled her to her feet, as if happiness were so close she could touch it. She leaned against him as they mounted the stairs. Reggie and the rest of Gideon's men must be nearby, but they'd discreetly disappeared into the shadows.

When they came to Gideon's room she pulled him inside and shut the door. Only then stopping and turning to look. "Do you want a true marriage?"

"Yes," he said, his black eyes boring into hers.

She nodded. "Then I need to know one thing. What is the task that my uncle set for you?"

* * *

His blood seemed to freeze in his veins.

He couldn't lose everything when he'd had it so nearly in his grasp.

Messalina squared her shoulders as if bracing herself. "I think if we are truly to start anew that there mustn't be any secrets. For instance, I've kept from you what I intended to do with my dowry money." She licked her lips. "I had planned to—to leave the country, leave everything and every*one* to start a new life somewhere else. I did not mean to stay with you once I had the money."

She took a deep breath and sighed as if a burden had fallen from her shoulders.

Then she looked at him with hopeful eyes.

He had to lie.

He *had* to.

She would not forgive him this. She would not live with him if she knew this. And she'd already made plans to leave him—leave the *country*.

She frowned. "Gideon?"

He stared at her, his mind spinning, scrabbling for the words to fix this. To make it better so that she'd smile again at him. To make things as they had been only *minutes* before.

"Gideon."

"Messalina," he whispered, crucified.

The fading hope in her beautiful eyes near killed him.

He reached for her hand.

She stepped away from him. "Tell me, please."

"I…"

The hope was almost entirely gone. Replaced with something fierce. "*Tell me.*"

He clenched his jaw. Hating this. Wanting to stop time. To push back the inevitable disaster.

But he could not.

And somehow he could no longer lie to her, either. "Your uncle ordered me to kill Julian."

She took another step away from him, shaking her head. "*What?*"

"I considered it," he said, putting all his soul into the truth. "At the beginning. But that was before. I would never do it now."

She closed her eyes as if she couldn't bear to see him. "Then why didn't you tell me?"

Because he'd wanted her never to know.

Because he was a coward.

Messalina opened her eyes, pinning him with her stark stare. "You were planning how to do it without me finding out."

"Yes," he breathed, knowing he was killing both her hope and his. "At first. But not anymore."

She turned to the door. "I'll have to wake Lucretia."

"Please," Gideon said, and was astonished. He'd never begged in his life. Not to the duke. Not to the men he'd lost knife fights to.

Not to anyone.

He'd beg Messalina, though, if it would but make her look at him for a second.

A fraction of a second. "*Please* listen."

She paused at the door, her back to him. "What can you possibly say to me?"

Panic rose in Gideon's breast. This couldn't be happening. "Goddamn it, Messalina, I didn't even know what the task was before I married you. I'm telling the *truth*. Please. You have to believe me."

"But I can't," she said, finally, *finally* turning to him. He saw to his horror that there were tears in her eyes. "You deceived me before for your own gain. I won't let you do it again. I wish that I could believe that you care enough for me to refuse to kill my brother. But I can't." She drew a shuddering breath. "I simply can't."

He felt as if his chest were cracking open. As if everything inside and all that he was—his hopes, his dreams, his very purpose in life—was leaking out.

As if he were dying.

And the truth burst from his bleeding chest. "*I love you.*"

Even as he said it, he knew it was too late.

She laughed—a terrible cawing sound. "No. No. *No.* That won't work. No more manipulation." She swiped across her eyes with a shaking hand. "I think I love you, Gideon. But that's not enough. Not anymore." She raised her head and looked him in the eye. "Goodbye."

He watched dumbly as she walked out.

Leaving him alone.

CHAPTER NINETEEN

*Autumn came, and one day the fox returned home
with a torn ear and a fine blue dress and
gave it to Bet.
She pulled on the dress and it fit perfectly. "Why have
you given me this?"
"To remember me by," the fox said mockingly....*
—From *Bet and the Fox*

Messalina couldn't leave that night, of course.

If nothing else, she needed a carriage.

It was morning, well past sunrise, when she stepped out of
Whispers House for the last time with Lucretia by her side.

"Oof." Lucretia was carrying the enormous wicker basket
Hicks had made for them. The cook had told them that it
contained Lucretia's favorite cakes.

Which was probably why her sister refused to let anyone
else carry the thing.

Reggie stood by her carriage—borrowed from Freya and
Kester—his large frame shuffling awkwardly from foot to
foot. He called as they neared, "At least let Pea go with
you, ma'am. 'E's small but 'e's a terror when 'e wants." He
glanced up at Whispers. "The guv is that worried."

Lucretia widened her eyes in mute appeal to Messalina.

Messalina shook her head. She wanted nothing to do
with her husband. "I'm sorry, Reggie, but I've the Duke of

Harlowe's men to protect us. I think that's quite enough. Besides"—she tried to smile and didn't quite make it—"We aren't going far."

The last was a flat-out lie. She intended to flee to Kester's country home to lick her wounds. After that she'd make her plans with Lucretia.

As dismal a prospect as that was.

Perhaps she could ask Kester for monetary help, for she hadn't even gotten her portion of her dowry from Gideon, fool that she was. He seemed to be avoiding her this morning, and that hurt more than anything else.

"I think I'll miss this place," Lucretia murmured, glancing back at Whispers. She sighed and let a footman help her into the carriage.

Messalina nodded to Reggie and turned to step into the carriage.

"Ma'am!"

She looked back.

Sam was running to her, Daisy clutched in his arms. "You forgot Daisy, ma'am!"

She'd had such lofty plans to help Sam and boys like him. Now that was gone. Everything was gone.

Sam stood before her now, his eyes wide and pleading, and held out a limp Daisy. "Take 'im or 'e'll be that 'urt. 'E'll think you don't like 'im."

Her eyes blurred. "I like both Daisy and you, Sam, but I don't know if he'd want a carriage ride. Can you"—she wiped at her eyes—"can you take care of him, please?"

Both puppy and boy stared at her bewildered. "Yes, ma'am. If you like." Sam's bottom lip trembled. "You're really going away?"

"I'm afraid so."

She entered the carriage before she started bawling in

the street. How had she come to care for Gideon's men and
boys? How had she let herself love him?

The carriage jolted, and she looked out the window as the
carriage rolled forward. Reggie was standing with his hand
on Sam's shoulder, Daisy still in the boy's arms.

She turned away from the sight and screwed her eyes shut.

She would never be whole again.

* * *

Gideon watched the carriage pull away from Whispers
House, taking with it Messalina and his heart.

He bowed his head, leaning his forehead against the
cold glass.

He needed her.

Like air. Like water. Like bread. She was essential to
his survival.

And he'd never see her again. The thought made his chest
freeze for a painfully long minute.

He straightened, turning away from the window. He had
business to attend to. Things that must be done.

He wouldn't think of Messalina. He *couldn't* think of
Messalina now. Better instead to attend to business. That
way he might never notice his mortal wound.

Gideon blew out a breath and left the room, running
down the stairs.

Outside, the sun was hidden by clouds, giving the day a
grayish tinge. Gideon began walking rapidly, making plans
in his head, trying to expect any eventuality. Though of
course that was impossible.

By the time he made the nondescript inn, his palms were
sweating, but he knew this was the only way.

The only way left to him.

He opened the door to a taproom being swept by a yawning maid. She gave him the direction easily enough, and he climbed to the upstairs rooms.

The barmaid had said the third door on the right. He rapped.

There was no answer, though the room was supposed to be occupied.

Gideon shook his knife down his sleeve and into his hand. If he'd come too late... Well.

He knocked again, louder this time.

He wrenched at the door, yanking it violently open.

Julian Greycourt stood there, in shirtsleeves and breeches, barefoot and with his long, black hair loose down his back.

He held two pistols, and they were both pointed at Gideon's chest.

* * *

Sometime past noon Messalina leaned against the window of the carriage, aware that Lucretia was staring at her.

"Are you sure this is what you want?" her sister asked hesitantly.

Which was ridiculous. Lucretia was never hesitant.

Messalina's head felt too heavy to move. "He was planning to murder our brother. I think that's quite unforgivable, don't you?"

"Well, it certainly would be if Gideon intended to go through with it." Lucretia paused, obviously trying to hold her opinion in, but then blurted, "But he *said* he wasn't."

Messalina could argue the point, but what was the use? Lucretia *knew* the reasons she'd made her decision.

It was all so useless.

"At least *think* about it again," Lucretia urged anxiously.

"We don't have to make any decisions right away. Goodness, it'll probably take *weeks* to arrive at Kester's country estate. Always assuming we aren't caught by Uncle Augustus first."

Messalina simply closed her eyes instead of replying. She didn't want to think about her uncle, and she wasn't going to change her mind about Gideon. It had been hard enough to leave him—it had felt like tearing parts of her flesh off. She wasn't going to go through that again.

There was a rummaging sound, then Lucretia muttered, "Hicks said he'd packed us some lemon curd tarts. Do you think he was lying to make me feel better? Because thinking there *are* tarts and then finding there *aren't* is far worse than having none at all. What's this?"

Messalina opened her eyes and saw that Lucretia was holding a leather envelope. She shrugged. "Keys handed it to me before I met you in the hall."

"And you didn't open it?" Lucretia gave her a sharp look.

Messalina closed her eyes again. "I didn't see the point."

"Humph." Lucretia unfolded the envelope's flap. "Papers, papers, this handwriting is nearly illegible..."

She fell silent.

Messalina wondered if she'd bother to get out of the carriage when they stopped for luncheon. She seemed to have lost all appetite for food.

Lucretia exclaimed, "Good God."

"What?" Messalina asked listlessly.

"He's given you over half your dowry with a promissory note for the other half when he obtains it."

Messalina raised her head. "What?"

Lucretia was staring at her. "I thought Gideon married you for your money?"

"He did," Messalina said dumbly.

Lucretia snorted. "He doesn't seem particularly interested in it if so."

"Let me see." Messalina snatched the document from Lucretia's hand, swiftly reading it. But it was merely a dry legal statement of what Lucretia had already said. "I don't understand."

Across from her Lucretia said, "That's odd."

"What is?" Messalina asked absently.

"There's a necklace in here."

Messalina looked up.

Gideon's farthing pendant swung from Lucretia's fingers.

"What a strange little thing," her sister was saying. "Whyever would one string a farthing for a necklace?"

"Love," Messalina whispered.

"What?"

"It means he loves me," she said louder, and her heart seemed to jolt into life. "We have to turn the carriage around!"

CHAPTER TWENTY

*Winter came, and one day the fox returned home
with a bloody head and a pair of golden earrings. He
gave them to Bet and she put them in her ears.
"Why have you given me these?" she whispered.
"To remember me by," the fox said, and he wasn't
mocking at all.
That night the red-haired man took Bet into his arms
and made love to her.
The next day the fox did not return home....*
                                    —From *Bet and the Fox*

Late that afternoon Gideon was staring at the crates of
books in the library when he became aware that Keys was
talking.

"...good news at any rate, don't you think?"

Gideon blinked, glancing at the other man. How long had
Keys been there? He honestly didn't know.

"What good news?" he asked, because Keys had a worried
line between his brows.

His gaze returned to the crates. Messalina's books nearly
filled the floor space. He'd been looking forward to seeing
her face as she unpacked the rest of them.

"...Guv?"

"Sorry?" Gideon asked absently.

Keys took a deep breath, obviously trying to find patience

as he began again. "Will Blackwell says as 'e's ready to turn over the ledgers to me. 'E wants to meet with you before 'e does, and then 'e'll travel to Newcastle. The business is doing well."

Gideon stared at Keys. His business. His money. He'd thought of little else for years and years. Plotted and schemed to get right here, on the cusp of a fortune.

And now?

He gasped and bent over at the waist.

"Guv?" Keys sounded alarmed.

Gideon couldn't reassure him because he was too busy choking on his own bitter laughter. Had he thought himself clever? More intelligent than anyone else? What a fool he was.

He'd gotten everything he'd ever wanted and lost the one person he needed to survive.

Oh God.

The thought sobered him abruptly, and Gideon dropped into the settee Messalina had picked out.

"Guv?"

Gideon shook his head, eyes closed. "I've lost her, Keys."

"Then get 'er back."

Gideon opened his eyes, if only to shoot Keys a weary look. "I can't. I tried and failed."

Keys wore the stubborn expression he normally had only when debating politics with Reggie. "You don't give up, guv. Not on this. Beggin' your pardon, but you *need* that woman."

That at least was true.

"But it seems she doesn't need me," Gideon replied tiredly.

"Don't know about that," Keys said loyally. "The missus watched you a fair bit when you weren't lookin'. Course," he continued, "you'll have to settle this business with the duke first."

Gideon glanced at the clock. "He's supposed to already be here. You did send that note, didn't you?"

"Of course." Keys gave him a wounded look and then furrowed his brow. "What if th' duke tries to kill you?"

Gideon met his eyes and shrugged. "I'll do what I have to."

Keys nodded but looked worried. "Killing a duke, now that's a rendezvous with the 'angman if ever I heard one."

Gideon nodded. "I suppose, then, that I should do my best not to kill him."

Keys shook his head. "I still say it could've been Greycourt who set those footpads on you."

"Greycourt wouldn't have endangered Messalina," Gideon said with conviction.

Keys's expressive eyebrows shot up nearly to his hairline. "So it must be the duke? Even though he wanted you to kill Greycourt? Seems a barmy plan to me."

"Why not?" Gideon said bitterly. "The man's insane. He's finally decided I'm too dangerous to him."

"But what about the highwaymen? The duke wouldn't 'ave wanted you dead before you wed the missus," Keys pointed out.

Gideon frowned. "I'm sure there are plenty who would not cry at my funeral—"

"Aye, you've a lot of enemies," Keys muttered.

"But to actually pay hired assassins, not once, not twice, but *thrice* bespeaks not only hatred but planning and the means to carry it out..." Gideon shook his head. "This is someone who knows me."

Keys threw his hands in the air. "It isn't me nor Reggie or Pea, guv, swear on my ma's grave."

Gideon glanced at him irritably. "I *know* that."

The door to the library opened. Reggie glanced nervously over his shoulder and intoned, "'Is Grace the Duke of—"

Windemere shoved him aside. "Yes, yes. Hawthorne! Where is he?"

Gideon stood slowly. "My money first."

The duke glanced at Keys and then Reggie.

Gideon nodded at the big man. "You can go."

"And that one?" Windemere jerked his chin at Keys.

"He's loyal to me," Gideon said firmly. "He stays."

"Very well." Windemere scowled at him. "I dislike being summoned to your hovel like a common tinker."

Gideon raised his brows. "I told you I couldn't risk moving him."

"Show me the proof."

Keys looked nervous.

"As promised." Gideon led the duke out of the library with Keys trailing uncertainly behind.

They made their way downstairs and to the hall that led to the kitchens.

"Your servants?" Windemere asked sharply.

"I've given them the night off," Gideon said levelly.

He should be on his toes, alert to any danger, but he found it impossible to care.

He led the way through the kitchens and to the low entrance to the cellars, stopped, and jerked his head to the door. "Down there."

Windemere looked between him and the door. "Show me."

Gideon gritted his teeth and lit a candle. "Mind the steps."

The stairs were shallow and wound around a central pillar, the way confined and slippery. Gideon kept his light high, and shadows loomed on the old stone walls of the cellar.

At the bottom the space was divided by crude wooden shelves, all but fallen down.

Gideon walked to the first shelf and halted.

The duke continued just past him, peering into the small space.

Gideon raised his candle so he could see.

Julian Greycourt lay crumpled facedown, the entire back of his head shining with blood. The sight was enough to turn a normal man's stomach.

Not Windemere's.

He began laughing.

Gideon stared in disgust for a moment before he motioned to Keys. "We've already drawn up the papers with an amendment to your earlier promissory note. We but need your signature."

"Of course." The duke continued to chortle to himself.

Keys had brought a flat wooden travel desk, and he held it steady as the duke signed the papers.

Windemere handed the papers to Gideon, a hideously triumphant gleam in his eyes. "Here's your money, and cheap at that for a man's blood."

"Well," drawled Greycourt as he turned over. "A pig's blood, anyway."

For a second the duke merely goggled at his nephew as the younger man stood and began brushing dust from his coat.

Then Windemere whirled on Gideon, his teeth bared. "You lying thief! You'll not see a farthing of that dowry because—"

"Because you want this murder plot spread far and wide throughout London?" Gideon asked, head cocked.

Windemere's eyes narrowed. "No one will believe you! No one."

"Oh, but I've witnesses," Gideon said as Quintus and Lord Rookewoode emerged from the dark farther back in the cellar.

Rookewoode brushed a cobweb from the shoulder of his exquisitely tailored coat. "I say, Greycourt. This is better than the pantomime."

Windemere was staring at the earl, the color draining from his face. One thing to accuse a member of his family of lying.

Quite another to question the word of an earl.

"Are you really going to risk it?" Gideon asked.

The duke stood glaring. He slowly turned his head to Greycourt, staring at him almost hungrily. "I'll have you. One of these days find your soft spot and then I'll have you."

Greycourt cocked his head and drawled, "But not today."

Windemere had little else to do but leave the cellar after that, his face reddened with rage.

"Is that it, do you think?" Quintus asked.

"No," Greycourt said. "Not at all. But for now he's had his cannons spiked." He looked at Rookewoode. "Thank you for coming on very short notice, my lord."

Rookewoode smiled. "Anything for a friend."

Greycourt nodded and turned to Gideon. "I think I owe you, brother-in-law, for warning me of my uncle's plans."

Gideon shrugged tiredly. "You helped me secure Messalina's dowry. I think we're even."

Footsteps came running down the cellar stairs, and Gideon braced himself. Far too easy for Windemere to simply walk away. If the duke had come back to—

But it was Lucretia who appeared, panting.

"Where's Messalina?" Gideon barked before she could speak.

Lucretia inhaled. "In the carriage. Out front. We were coming back to you and—" She shook her head, interrupting herself. "Never mind that. Mr. Blackwell has gone insane.

He shoved his way into our carriage and sent me to say that he wants to speak to you."

Gideon frowned. "What—?"

But Lucretia wasn't done. She took a desperate gulp of air and blurted, "He has Messalina at gunpoint."

* * *

Messalina stared at Will Blackwell across the carriage. Beside him was a hulking man Messalina remembered from the attack outside the theater. Mr. Blackwell held two pistols—carelessly, but she wasn't so foolish as to think that he wouldn't use them.

He'd already killed the driver of Freya's carriage.

Thank God he hadn't been interested in Lucretia. Thank God her sister had been sent outside to safety.

Messalina licked her lips and said with a firm voice, "Gideon won't come out."

Mr. Blackwell's face shone with sweat, and a muscle under one eye was twitching.

Messalina no longer thought him handsome or urbane or charming. He was a mad fiend.

"He'll come." Mr. Blackwell lifted one of the pistols.

Messalina froze, but he was only changing position.

She was very much afraid Gideon would come out. "What will you do to him?"

"What do you think?" Mr. Blackwell said absently, parting the curtain at the carriage window to peer out. "I'm going to kill him—or have him killed."

Her gaze met the hulking man's dull eyes, and her heart seemed to freeze.

"Why?" she asked desperately.

Mr. Blackwell glanced at her irritably. "Because he's

about to give the business ledgers to his man. Keys would be bound to realize that I've embezzled from the mines."

He meant to kill her. Why else tell her his motive so carelessly?

This was sheer madness. Did he really think he could kill either Gideon or her in broad daylight and get away with it? He'd be captured before he stepped from the carriage.

Of course, that might not save her or Gideon.

She swallowed and said with a semblance of outrage, "You've been stealing from Gideon?"

He shrugged, letting the curtain fall with a smirk. "For years."

The carriage door abruptly opened, and Messalina's heart near stopped when she saw Gideon climb in.

He started for her as the big man tensed, but Mr. Blackwell waved a pistol.

"No." He nodded to the carriage's floorboards. "Sit there, your legs crossed and with your hands in front of you."

Gideon looked at him without moving.

Mr. Blackwell swung one of his pistols to Messalina's head without taking his eyes off Gideon. "Unless you'd like me to shoot your wife right now?"

Gideon's nostrils flared, but otherwise he remained impassive as he dropped to the carriage floor.

"Keep your eyes on him," Mr. Blackwell instructed his bully, and then knocked on the roof with one of the pistols.

The carriage lurched into motion.

"I don't know what your plan is, Will, but I doubt it will work," Gideon said calmly.

He hadn't looked at Messalina again since he'd been ordered to the floor. She found herself desperately longing for his gaze. If they weren't somehow rescued...

Well. She wasn't going to think about that.

"My plan," Mr. Blackwell said, "is to kill both you and your lovely wife and then drain the business bank account before buying a ticket abroad." He shook his head with mock regret. "Simple. Easily done. This is your own fault, Gideon. We could've made so much more money if you'd hadn't been so stubborn about using the boys in the mines."

Boys? Messalina stared at Gideon. This was the first she'd heard of such a thing. How long had Gideon and Mr. Blackwell been arguing over how the business was run?

"You wanted boys under the age of *fifteen* to work those mines," Gideon growled. "They'd come out crippled or worse. I'll not have it."

"They'd work for half the amount of a grown man." Mr. Blackwell leaned forward, a sneer on his face. "Do you care so much for children you've never met?"

Gideon stared at him steadily. "Yes."

"You can care about them in hell," Mr. Blackwell hissed. "You and your wife."

The carriage swung wide around a corner, jostling everyone inside.

In that moment Gideon sprang toward Mr. Blackwell. He caught both of the man's wrists, swinging the pistol's aim away from Messalina.

There was a terrible *BANG* followed immediately by a second report.

Smoke hung heavy in the carriage.

Both Mr. Blackwell and the huge man were wrestling Gideon now, and Gideon was favoring his right arm.

Messalina looked wildly around the carriage for something to use as a weapon. When she couldn't find anything, she lifted her skirts and kicked as hard as she could at the huge man's leg.

To her surprise the man recoiled with a roar. He lunged across the carriage toward Messalina.

She prepared for another kick, but Gideon wrested one of the pistols away from Mr. Blackwell. With a twist he hit the big man on the back of the head with the butt of the gun.

The man fell like a stone, narrowly missing Messalina's feet.

The carriage jerked to a halt.

Mr. Blackwell swung at Gideon's head with the other pistol. Gideon ducked aside. His hand shot out, connecting high on Mr. Blackwell's left side.

The men froze for a moment.

Mr. Blackwell looked down and then up, his face twisted in shock.

Gideon drew back his hand, and Messalina saw that he held a bloody knife.

"You've stabbed me," Mr. Blackwell said, his face white.

"I've killed you," Gideon replied with grim satisfaction.

Mr. Blackwell slowly leaned against the side of the carriage, his eyes fixed.

And then he just stayed there.

Messalina sobbed in a breath.

Gideon turned to her. "Are you all right?"

"Yes, of course..." Her voice faded as she looked at him.

There was a hole in the shoulder of his coat, and something wet gleamed on the black cloth.

She touched it with her fingertips.

Her hand came away stained red with blood.

The carriage door was flung open. Julian of all people stood there, panting. "Are you all right, Messalina? Hawthorne?"

Gideon nodded, completely calm. "Fine. If you'll just—"

"*No*," Messalina said. "He's been shot."

Julian looked mildly interested. "Yes?"

Gideon grimaced. "It's just a—"

"Don't you dare say it's just a flesh wound," Messalina said furiously. She turned to her brother. "Get this carriage back to the house and send for a doctor."

Jules actually blinked. "Very well."

He turned to shout at someone outside.

Reggie's head appeared in the doorway.

"Reg," Gideon said. "Clear the carriage, please."

Messalina held back a scream as Gideon's men removed Mr. Blackwell and his bully boy.

Gideon watched her warily.

Messalina found her handkerchief—a pitifully small scrap of lawn—and pressed it to his shoulder.

He grunted, and her handkerchief turned red.

"If you die, I shall never forgive you," she said fiercely.

His expression was odd. "I thought you'd never forgive me anyway."

"Well, I won't," she said nonsensically.

"I love you," he said.

She peered at her pitiful bandage. "I know."

"I do love you," he said as if he hadn't heard her. "I know you won't believe me, but I do. I do."

"Hush," she said. Tears were gathering in her eyes. "I believe you."

"Messalina." He gently took her hand and drew it away from his shoulder. "The wound isn't so very bad. Listen. I love you and if you want to leave me"—his gruff voice broke—"go away to some foreign land, I don't know if I'll survive, but I'll help you go. I want you to be happy."

"Gideon..." Her eyes were filled with tears.

"But," he said softly, "if you have any pity at all for me, stay. Please stay with me, Messalina."

She choked and just refrained from hitting him. "Of course I'm staying, you awful man! I love you. I love you. I love—"

But her words were cut off as he gathered her in his arms and kissed her.

EPILOGUE

Bet sat in the thyme-covered clearing all the night long, waiting for her fox husband to return. In the morning she was still alone, and she stared into the trees, remembering what he'd told her: never ever to enter the wood.

Bet stood and briskly brushed off her skirts. Then she walked into the wood.

Now the wood was dark and eerie and Bet was afraid. But she remembered the red-haired man and the fox as well, and she bravely ventured on.

By and by she came to a squirrel busily running about gathering walnuts. "Dear me, dear me, how my feet do ache," muttered the squirrel to herself as she worked. "If only I had a pair of shoes!"

Without a thought Bet took her red shoes off her feet. "Pardon me, Mistress Squirrel, but you may have my shoes if you wish."

"Oh!" said the squirrel, seizing the red shoes eagerly, "how very kind you are." She put on the shoes at once, and though her squirrel feet were much smaller than Bet's own feet, the red shoes fit the squirrel perfectly.

"Thank you!" cried the squirrel. "Is there any favor I might do you in return for such a fine gift?"

"I'm looking for my husband, a fae fox. Have you seen him?"

"Indeed I have," said the squirrel. "The fox is well known hereabouts—though not always liked, for he has a sly nature. You should ask the bear where your husband has gone. But be careful. Mistress Bear has a temper and quite long claws." And the squirrel pointed the way.

Bet thanked Mistress Squirrel and continued on her search. But without her shoes her feet soon became sore, and she started limping. She wanted to rest but she remembered her fox husband and continued.

Mistress Bear was sitting discontentedly on a log, and when she saw Bet, she growled, a low, ominous sound. "Why do you disturb me, mortal? This is my natal day and no one has given me a present. Flee from me or I shall rip your limbs from you!"

"I wanted to wish you a happy natal day," Bet said hurriedly. "And I've a present for you—this dress."

So saying, Bet drew off her blue dress and gave it to the bear.

Mistress Bear put on the dress at once and twirled happily, for of course the dress fit her perfectly. "Oh, thank you, mortal, for my gift. May I ask why you are tramping through the wood without any shoes?"

"*I'm searching for my husband, the fox,*" *said* Bet. "*Mistress Squirrel said you might have word of him.*"

Mistress Bear snorted. "*Long have I told the fox that his tricky ways would someday land him in trouble, and I was quite right. The Wolf holds your husband captive and threatens to kill him ere long. He lives not far from here.*" *The bear pointed the way.*

"*Thank you!*" *cried Bet.*

She wore only her thin chemise now, and soon she was shivering, wrapping her arms around herself. How nice a fire would be! But Bet remembered the fox's face and continued. Miles and miles she walked until at last she came to a clearing in the wood.

There stood a small, neat cottage made of stone. An enormous wolf paced back and forth in the clearing, and in front of the cottage was an iron cage.

The fox was inside.

The wolf snarled when he saw Bet. "*Who are you, and why have you trespassed on my land?*"

Bet dipped a shivering curtsy. "*I am Bet, Sir Wolf, and I have come for my husband the fox.*"

"*This rogue?*" *the wolf sneered, waving at the fox trapped in the iron cage.* "*You've come in vain, then, for though you've found him, you'll not have him long. The fox has been my enemy for years, playing tricks and mocking me. I shall cut off his head with an iron knife once the sun sets.*"

Bet fell to her knees. "*Please, Sir Wolf, stay your hand and show mercy to my husband.*"

"*Why should I?*" *growled the wolf.*

"*Because I love him,*" *Bet said.*

"*You love a creature like that?*" *demanded the wolf*

*as he pointed at the fox. "But he's sly and secretive
and thinks too much of himself!"*

*Bet smiled despite her shivers and her aching feet.
"Love is a wild thing—it goes where it will."*

*"Humph," said the wolf. "Well, I don't know if I
can let him go, no matter your pretty plea. He whispered in my wife's ear, simply for mischief's sake, and
told her that if I truly loved her I'd give her the gold I
was hiding." He threw up his arms. "I don't have any
hidden gold!"*

*"That is easily mended." Bet took her gold ear-
rings from her ears and handed them to the wolf.
"Give these to your wife and tell her that you had
merely hidden them so as to surprise her."*

*The wolf brightened. "You are as clever as your
husband, but kinder. For your sake I will let him go."*

*He waved his hand, and suddenly the iron cage
was gone and the fox stood before Bet.*

*The fox took her hand and ran with her into the
wood. They had only gone a little way before he
stopped and turned into the redheaded man.*

*Then he frowned at her. "I told you never ever to
go into the wood."*

Bet nodded. "Indeed you did."

*He looked at her chemise. "You've given away
your blue dress."*

"Yes, I have."

*He frowned at her bleeding feet. "And your red
shoes as well."*

*She smiled and kissed him. "You are most
observant."*

*He sighed. "Not at all, for I never knew how much
I loved you."*

"Didn't you, Husband?" Bet laughed.

"I fear you are much wiser than me, my Bet." He shook his head and bent to her to whisper in her ear. "And my name is Tom."

—From *Bet and the Fox*

ONE MONTH LATER

Messalina looked around the crowded ballroom. People were squashed together in their colorful best, the punch was perilously close to running out, and if she wasn't mistaken, a married viscountess had just disappeared into the garden with a baronet.

In other words, her ball was a smashing success.

"Did you see Lady Hadley-Fields go out into the garden with Sir Simpson?" Lucretia muttered beside her.

"I think everyone saw it," Messalina returned in a near whisper.

"Well, hopefully not *Lord* Hadley-Fields," Lucretia replied. She took a sip of her punch. "I believe Quintus sneaked out while you were in conversation with Lord Chester."

Messalina sighed. She'd been discussing funding a small boys' grammar school in St Giles with Lord Chester, who owned suitable property. She wanted Sam to start as soon as possible so he could realize his dream of being a schoolmaster. It was just like Quintus to duck out when her back was turned.

"At least Julian is still here." She nodded toward the far wall, where their brother leaned against a pillar, ignoring the ladies whispering nearby.

She scanned the ballroom again. Where—?

"Messalina!" Freya called, struggling through the crowd with Elspeth behind her. "Have you really bought a library?"

"Yes." Messalina laughed. "My library is still mostly in packing crates, though."

Freya smiled. "I thought Elspeth might help you sort and catalogue the books."

"Thank you," Messalina said with real appreciation. "I'd much rather have my library on shelves so I can enjoy the books."

"Mmm," Elspeth murmured, and then cocked her head. "Is that man putting dust up his nose on purpose?"

Freya coughed. "It's *snuff*. I told you about tobacco before."

Elspeth looked perplexed. "But you said tobacco was burned."

Freya rolled her eyes and muttered to Messalina, "She spent nearly her whole life in the Wise Women's compound. She still finds the oddest things curious." She turned to her sister. "Come. I'll show you the buffet. Just wait until you've seen a jelly."

Lucretia perked up. "Oh, I'll come with you."

They disappeared into the crush, and Messalina began slowly making her way to the garden doors, stopped every step or two by her guests.

Finally she found the doors and slipped out. The night was clear, the moon a crescent hanging high above the city. She tipped her head back, trying to see the stars, but the light from the ballroom interfered.

Messalina walked farther into the garden until she could see each star winking at her in the blackness.

Firm hands closed around her shoulders, and Gideon whispered in her ear, "I thought you'd never leave that ballroom."

She turned in his arms to face him. The garden might be too dark to see clearly, but she knew he wore one of the suits she'd picked out for him, the dark gray that had just a hint of violet. The suit fitted his wide shoulders perfectly, and she loved the embroidered waistcoat—not least because Gideon wore it for her.

She placed her palms on his chest. "Were you looking for me, Mr. Hawthorne?"

"I was, Mrs. Hawthorne." He bent so close his lips brushed against hers as he said, "I always will."

He kissed her and she opened for him, a thrill going through her at his touch. She had a feeling she'd still have that same thrill decades in the future.

She stopped thinking, though, as he drew his teeth down her neck, scraping gently.

A giggle sounded nearby.

Gideon straightened and glared at the bushes in disgust. "I should be able to make love to my wife in my own garden."

Messalina linked her arm with his. "Yes, but not during a ball." She pulled him toward the house and the lights. "I saw you talking with Lord Rookewoode."

He grunted, his good humor not quite restored. "That man says the most frivolous things."

She leaned her head against his shoulder. "And yet he's smart enough to invest in your business."

"Yes, he is," Gideon replied, sounding satisfied. He darted a look at her. "Don't worry. I haven't been talking business at a social event."

"Good," she murmured, pulling him to a stop just before they entered the pool of light from the ballroom. She stood on tiptoe and kissed him again.

He grasped her arms, deepening the kiss, before he murmured against her lips, "What is that for?"

She pulled back. "Because I love you."

She saw the faint puzzlement in his eyes. He was still getting used to hearing the words—and returning them.

"I love you as well," he said as he touched her cheek. "I don't know how I lived before you, my world was so dark and empty. You give me joy."

Oh, but he was improving.

Smiling, Messalina linked arms with Gideon again and led him into the light.

Don't miss Elizabeth Hoyt's next book in
the breathtaking Greycourt series!

No Ordinary Duchess
Available Late 2021

ABOUT THE AUTHOR

Elizabeth Hoyt is the *New York Times* bestselling author of twenty-six lush historical romances, including the Maiden Lane series. *Publishers Weekly* has called her writing "mesmerizing," and in 2018 she received the *RT Book Reviews* Career Achievement Award for Historical Romance. She also pens deliciously fun contemporary romances under the name Julia Harper. Elizabeth lives in Minneapolis, Minnesota, with three untrained dogs, a garden in constant need of weeding, and the long-suffering Mr. Hoyt.

The winters in Minnesota have been known to be long and cold, and Elizabeth is always thrilled to receive reader mail. You can write to her at PO Box 19495, Minneapolis, MN 55419 or email her at Elizabeth@ElizabethHoyt.com.

You can learn more at:

ElizabethHoyt.com
Twitter @ElizabethHoyt
Facebook.com/ElizabethHoytBooks

For a bonus story from another author that you'll love, please turn the page to read *Night of the Scoundrel* by Kelly Bowen.

He is ruthless, dangerous, and known simply as King—no one knows his true name or where he came from. And when he learns that the man who betrayed him has returned to London, King has only one goal: vengeance. But he requires an unlikely ally—one who is as mysterious as she is beautiful. Exiled after the French Revolution, Adeline Archambault is determined to deliver the justice that is owed her. King's offer of help, in exchange for her assistance, is a bargain she can't refuse. But will this deal with a devil lead to a future she never dared hope for?

FOREVER

CHAPTER 1

King had seen the beginning of the fight.

He'd been standing too far away to keep it from starting but close enough to know how it would end. The three men who had slunk up the darkened alley had been arrogant mongrels, sure of their position as the superior predator. King knew their type—malice, avarice, or a combination of both snuffing any glimmer of intelligence.

He wondered if, even for a second, the men had questioned how an ebony-haired angel, dressed in dark breeches and a midnight coat, had appeared in such a filthy place and yet remained untouched and unscathed. Her cold demeanor and her utter lack of alarm should have given them at least a moment's pause, but it appeared as though uncommon beauty and uncommon opportunity had stirred the men's blood and rendered them oblivious to their peril.

By the time King reached the mouth of the alley, the largest of the three men was already staggering against the rough stone wall, doubled over. The two remaining assailants were circling her with small knives, blood blooming into the fabric along the edges of a half dozen cuts and punctures in their clothing. They were outmatched, King knew, even if they didn't. And the best thing for them to do would be to flee—but this had become a matter of pride. One that they would never settle to their satisfaction, if they even survived.

The angel's rapier flashed in the twilight, like a flare of lightning, and King assessed the ease and the balance with which the woman handled the long-needled blade. Someone, at some point, had given this woman the sort of technical instruction reserved for aristocratic sons. Someone with the sort of wealth and security that allowed one to fight for mere sport and amusement. An indulgent father. A conspiring brother, perhaps. Or maybe a smitten lover.

Yet the black-clad angel also wielded a knife in her other hand, the blade long and curved and stained scarlet along the edge. There was nothing aristocratic about this weapon. It was nothing less than an unadorned instrument of death, and it sat as easily in her hand as the rapier. Someone else had tutored her. Someone who had learned to fight for survival, not entertainment.

Her booted feet made no sound as she circled, keeping a careful eye on the remaining two attackers.

"Whore," the taller of the two snarled, thrusting his knife toward her.

She danced back, her rapier deflecting a similar offensive by the second thug as he lunged at her from the side. "When the occasion requires," she murmured.

King tightened his hand on the smooth silver knob of his walking stick. Her face was expressionless, a mask of concentration, and to intervene now would be dangerous. A distraction could prove her undoing.

The thickset assailant groaned from where he still sagged against the wall and abruptly dropped to the ground.

The woman tipped her head. "Your friend is bleeding. He requires your assistance. Take him and go."

"And you'll pay for that, ye poxy bitch, afore we go anywhere."

"I have no quarrel with you." Her voice was devoid of inflection.

"Ye need to be taught a lesson."

A ghost of a smile touched her lips, but it was chilling. "There is nothing you can teach me that I haven't already learned, I can assure you."

It was the shorter man who moved first, another desperate lunge with a rusty blade that should have gutted her from the side. She twisted, her curved blade sweeping down on his wrist in a flash of quicksilver. The man's knife clattered to the stone as he crumpled, and his pitiful scream was drowned out by the infuriated roar of the man who remained standing. He came at her in a blind charge, his blade raised high above his shoulder.

Fool.

From where he stood, King heard the crunch of bone as the pommel of her knife snapped his head back, blood spurting like a geyser from his nose. She spun, her leg striking down on her attacker's low and hard at his knee. The man collapsed in an ignoble pile next to his consorts, writhing and moaning.

The woman, who looked like an angel but fought like Lucifer himself, stood silently for a moment before wiping her blades on the coat of the nearest fallen man. She sheathed both weapons and, in the pale gray light, caught in profile alone against the cold stone, looked more weary than triumphant.

A strange feeling curled deep through King's chest, peculiar tendrils of...empathy? Longing? He almost took a step forward before he caught himself, swallowing hard against his momentary weakness. A woman such as this did not need empathy.

And he did not need to tarry at the mouth of this stinking cesspool of an alley. He was already late. He should return across the street and to his carriage, which awaited him. In less than four hours he would have the cream of London society in his ballroom, every greedy, grasping peer vying with every other to attain the unattainable. His auctions were as exclusive as they were legendary, and he needed to ensure preparations at his estate had been completed.

Yet he remained right where he was.

The woman started up the alley toward him, her steps unhurried and graceful, with the same efficiency of movement she had demonstrated in combat. She was outwardly beautiful, yes, but that was not what intrigued him. A fair face was never a good measure of motives and convictions, or principles and provocations, and it was these attributes that interested King, man or woman. He did not fool himself into believing he knew all of London's underbelly, but a woman such as this should have caught his attention or that of others long before now—

"Enjoy the entertainment?"

The woman had stopped just shy of him, not looking in his direction nor looking back at the carnage she had left behind. Instead her eyes were scanning the gloomy, sodden street.

"I didn't wish to interfere," he replied. "There was nothing I could do that you hadn't already done."

"Mmm." She looked at him then, studying his face in the waning light. Up close, she was even more extraordinary than he had thought. Skin the color of dark honey, cool silver eyes, and hair like spun midnight woven in a simple plait down her back. "You have my gratitude for that."

"Your gratitude?"

"For not interfering." Her voice was husky, and traces of

an indiscernible accent floated around each syllable. "I did not require your help."

"No," he agreed as he considered her. "You expected a fight."

"Residential hazard."

King glanced at the half-rotting sign swinging from its bracket over the door of the building edging the alley. Four crudely carved cockerels strutted across the graying boards, and King knew the gin to be abysmal inside, the lodgings worse yet. "An odd choice of accommodations for someone new to London," he said.

"New to London?" she repeated. "A bold assumption."

"Not an assumption," he lied.

She lifted a shoulder almost imperceptibly. "The Four Cocks is convenient for my purposes."

"May I ask the nature of those purposes?" He was aware she hadn't confirmed anything yet.

"You may ask. You're a man used to doing as he likes anyway." She was scanning the street beyond them again, her gloved hand resting lightly on the hilt of her rapier. "But I am not required to answer."

King's own fingers drummed on the silver handle of his walking stick as he considered her words. He glanced back down the alley to where her attackers still lay in whimpering piles of agony. "You know who I am?" he asked idly.

The dark angel returned her attention to his face, her gaze impenetrable. "Does it matter?"

His fingers stopped. "That depends."

She smiled at him then, in what looked like genuine amusement. An answering flutter of pleasure stirred within him even as disquiet slid through his veins. He shoved both emotions back down with ruthless efficiency. Emotion had no place anywhere in his world. If one could not detach sentiment and passion from strategy and control, one generally ended up like the three mongrels bleeding in the alley behind them.

Instead King forced himself to consider the utter insouciance she had displayed since he had first set eyes on her. It wasn't fearlessness that she wielded with an icy calm, because he'd always equated fearlessness with stupidity, and only a fool would think this woman stupid. Those who professed themselves fearless had nothing to lose and, thus, nothing of value worth preserving. No true ambition or purpose.

Those individuals had their uses, of course, but they were generally dull-witted and predictable. Nothing like the woman who stood before him. Perhaps it was ambition, then, that this angel wielded with such expertise. Which made her dangerous as well as intriguing.

"Depends on what?" she asked.

"On what it is you came to London for. On what you might require." The need to know who this woman was and why she was here was starting to prick like a sliver that couldn't easily be removed. Insignificant in the larger picture but quickly becoming all-consuming.

"What would ever give you the idea that I require something?" She moved her hand from the rapier's hilt and smoothed her palm over the unadorned lapel of her coat. King had never appreciated men's garments on women, yet these layers that clung to smooth curves seemed to suit her.

"Everyone needs something."

"They do, don't they?" she murmured. "Yet need is a weakness that can be exploited. In the wrong hands, need, more often than not, ultimately leads to downfall." Her smile hadn't slipped, her face still a mask of amused serenity.

King inhaled sharply. He might not know who this woman was, but he knew what she was—one who understood what lurked in the dark corners of the soul. Like recognized like, after all.

"May I have the pleasure of your name?" he asked abruptly.

"Is this something you need?"

He almost smiled. Perhaps her name was something he did need. Given that he still lingered in an alley, asking questions that he would never get real answers to, maybe he was betraying a weakness. Not one that would ever lead to his downfall, of course, but a weakness nonetheless. "Possibly," he replied.

The dark angel tilted her head, her long, ebony braid sliding over her shoulder. She considered him for so long that King didn't think she was going to answer.

"Adrestia," she said finally.

An ancient name steeped in legends of goddesses and divine retribution. It suited her here, in this moment, armed and dressed as she was. But it was not her real name. King would have bet everything he owned on that. Because again, like recognized like. "Thank you."

"I hope it was worth it." She smiled at him again, and before he could say anything further, she simply slipped from the shadows of the alley out into the darkening street.

King did not watch her go but turned on his heel and stalked across the uneven, mucky stones to where his carriage still sat, careful not to look behind him. Litchfield Street was oddly empty at this time, caught between day and night and devoid of the creatures who inhabited both.

Two of his men, who had been watching from their posts, met him as he approached the carriage. They were quick and clever, two of his best.

"Do the bodies need disposing of?" The tallest gestured past him in the direction of the alley.

"No," King said. "They are not dead. Merely stupid. But the woman—she left just before me. Do you see her now? Men's trousers and coat, knife and rapier at her waist."

His men nodded, two sets of hard eyes tracking over King's shoulder. "Yes."

"Follow her. Tell me where she goes. What she does, whom she speaks to."

"Of course."

"Do not let her see you. I can't guarantee she won't gut you where you stand if she catches you."

"Yessir." His men melted into the deepening shadows of Litchfield, and King pulled open his carriage door.

"To Helmsdale?" his driver asked from up top.

King paused, checking his pocket watch. "No," he said. "To Covent Square first."

CHAPTER 2

"Well, isn't this domestic."

The woman looked up from where she sat near the hearth, poring over what appeared to be a heavy ledger. She didn't betray surprise, nor had King expected her to. Whatever thoughts Elise Ellery might possess were hidden expertly behind a mask of bland neutrality. And a moustache. And a wig and a truly awful pair of spectacles.

"King." She closed the ledger and stood, leaning against the edge of the study desk. "I'd say it's a pleasure but it rarely is."

"You look well." He examined Elise's flawless disguise. "Of all your personas, I do believe I fancy this one best. Doddering doctors are always underestimated."

She ignored his comment. "You might consider knocking next time."

"I do believe we've had this discussion before," he said, setting his walking stick by the door and wandering into the study. "You admonish me, I counsel you to improve your security, and in the end nothing changes." He picked up a small card from the pile that rested in a crystal bowl on the desk. Chegarre & Associates. A firm dedicated to managing and shrouding all manner of sordid scandal and other unsavory business for clients wealthy enough to afford its services. A firm in which the woman before him was a dedicated partner.

"What do you want?" Elise set the ledger on the chair behind her.

"Brandy," King suggested. "French, preferably, but I'd settle for Spanish."

She ignored that too. "Ashland is not here."

"Mmm." King set the card back in the bowl and moved to examine the engraved face of the tall clock that ticked away the seconds. As he always did when he spoke with the wife of the man he considered the closest thing he had to a friend, he wondered just how much she really knew about how that friendship had come to be. "I have no business with your husband today, though you might pass along my regards. I came seeking you."

"What for?"

"A job." He turned.

"You employ an army of men to do jobs for you."

"And they are good, but nowhere near as talented as you. Which is why I have previously employed you in matters of delicacy."

"I'm sure I'm flattered." She didn't sound impressed.

"You should be."

She gestured at her altered appearance. "I'm sorry, but as you can see, I'm already engaged to deal with a matter of delicacy for a client. Can't be late."

"You owe me."

The faintest hint of irritation passed across her features before it vanished as quickly as it had appeared. "Indeed? And how have you come to this conclusion?"

"Your brother."

"My brother?"

"Yes, your brother. You know, tall, dark, and troublesome. Owner of a delightful little gaming establishment. Married improbably to a brilliant blond—"

"Stop." She held up her hand. "What does your presence here have to do with Alex?"

"Not so long ago, you requested information on his behalf. Information about murder—two murders, to be precise, connected to the Hutton name. Information that I provided."

"I remember."

"I am here hoping that you might repay the favor in kind."

"You want information on a murder?"

"I'm not entirely sure."

Elise's dark brows rose fractionally over the wire rims of her spectacles. "How very unlike you."

King resumed his travels around the room, stopping in front of a set of towering bookcases. "If she hasn't killed anyone yet, I suspect she might soon."

"She?"

"She's staying at the Four Cocks. Faint accent—French, I believe—black hair, an alarming aptitude with sharp, pointy weapons. Calls herself Adrestia." He withdrew a volume from the shelves and read the title. *Frankenstein; or, The*

Modern Prometheus, published anonymously. He opened it to a random page.

"Clearly, you do not need me if you already know where she is. I shouldn't have to remind you that I specialize in finding those who do not wish to be found. If it's information you're after, you'd do better to ask Ivory."

"The duchess is still somewhat displeased with me."

Elise crossed her arms over her chest. "With good reason. Not so long ago, you kidnapped her sister-in-law and—"

"Oh, for God's sake, I didn't kidnap her, I was trying to keep her safe." The book snapped shut with a report like a pistol. King frowned at the noise. Emotion achieved nothing, and this was the second time today he'd had to remind himself of that. He slid the volume back into its place and moderated his tone. "The foolish girl had put herself in a situation where she could have done far worse than a few days of my hospitality. You're not the only ones schooled in the art of deception. I was trying to make a point she wouldn't soon forget."

"And what point was that?" Elise asked dubiously.

"That one must take great care in whom one trusts. Trust the wrong person and you'll pay for that mistake forever." His words came out with more force than he'd intended.

"I've wondered about that for a long time." A new voice came from the door of the study.

King pivoted to find Ivory Harcourt, Duchess of Alderidge and the founding member of Chegarre & Associates, standing in the doorway. She was watching him with dark eyes, and her expression, like her partner's, betrayed nothing.

"Duchess, you look beautiful as ever."

She ignored his compliment. "I need not remind you that your actions put me in a difficult position."

King lowered himself into one of the chairs by the

hearth and crossed his booted foot over his knee. "Which you handled with the skill and ability I've always admired. Managing difficult positions is what you excel at, and as I expected, you did not disappoint."

"Hmm." Ivory advanced into the study, tucking a stray chestnut curl behind her ear. "Why not tell me this before now?"

King shrugged. "You never asked."

Ivory smiled faintly. "I suppose I didn't."

"I assume you overheard our earlier conversation," King said, returning to the matter at hand and gesturing in Elise's direction.

"Yes." Ivory leaned back against the desk next to her partner.

"Can you accommodate my request?" he pressed. He was aware of the time slipping by.

"This will discharge our debt to you on the Hutton affair?"

"Yes."

"Very well." Ivory pushed herself away from the desk and came to sit in the chair opposite him, rearranging her skirts casually.

"I despise delay, Duchess." King frowned. "You already know where the woman is staying—"

"I too, despise delay," Ivory replied coolly. "I also despise the idea of bloodshed on this very fine rug should my husband return home to find you still here. He has not yet forgiven you for the incident with his sister and still harbors piratical fancies that generally feature him keelhauling you or simply running you through. So in the interest of expediency and the preservation of my decor, you will listen and listen carefully."

King uncrossed his leg, his foot thumping softly on the very fine rug. "You already know who she is."

Ivory steepled her fingers and exchanged an indecipherable

look with Elise. "I am familiar with her work, though she does not often cross the Channel. I cannot speak to why she is currently in London."

"What can you speak to?"

The duchess once again met his eyes with her own. "To start, her name isn't Adrestia."

$\mathscr{C}$HAPTER 3

Adeline Archambault had counted twelve.

Twelve men around Helmsdale House's perimeter, each armed with pistols and blades, and each making no effort to conceal that fact. They were all silhouetted in torchlight and easily visible from the tiny window of her hired carriage, which bumped and swayed toward the looming manor. There were more men, Adeline knew, men who guarded the house and the secrets within but had not been put on display to intimidate the arriving peers. Those men had been harder to count, but her vigilance and patience over the last three days had left her with an accurate tally of those guards as well.

Not that the number of guards would matter in the end. Adeline was not a woman hired for her skills at observational arithmetic. She was engaged to make the sort of well-armed math that surrounded Helmsdale House and all its contents irrelevant.

The owner of Helmsdale, however, was very relevant. Before his unexpected and unwelcome appearance at the mouth of that alley, Adeline had already observed the man called King at a distance a half dozen times in her covert surveillance of the manor. And while his men were never far, King himself was always alone. Outside of brief exchanges and orders to his men, Adeline had not once witnessed him in the company of a kept mistress, a favored acquaintance, or even a regular man of business.

Which didn't surprise her, given his supposed propensity for privacy and the rumors that surrounded him. Facts had been enormously difficult to come by, even through her usual tried-and-true methods involving significant coin. In Adeline's experience, rumor was a poor substitute for fact, but there were always seeds of truth buried in speculation. She'd been told that men who deceived or betrayed him oft disappeared, never to be seen again. That he was ruthlessly capable of finding anything—or anyone—for a price. That he controlled more than half the Kentish coast and the illicit goods that funneled into London from there. That he had as many peers and politicians in his pocket as he did thieves and assassins. Conjecture, all of it, none of it proven.

Yet Adeline had spent far too much time of late wondering which of the terrifying tales about the lord of London's underworld contained those seeds of truth.

Those tales should have unsettled her, especially given King's appearance in that damn alley hours ago. She had made every effort to cloak her presence since she had set foot on English soil, but it had been impossible to discern from their exchange if King's presence had merely been a coincidence or if he had beaten her at her own game and the hunter had become the hunted.

This should have been unsettling, yet their conversation had left her feeling oddly...liberated. As though she had finally met a man who had seen her for exactly what she was and understood it. Though she wasn't fool enough to underestimate him, or his displeasure should she be caught. For brief moments she had considered changing her plan, but she had discarded that idea almost immediately. It was far too late for that. This was merely the final chapter in a story that had been written long ago.

"Halt!"

The shout jarred her from her ruminations. Her hired carriage jolted and jerked to a stop in front of a guardhouse that looked more suited to a fortress than to a manor perched on the edge of London. Two of the hulking guards stepped into the flickering torchlight, snow starting to fall around them. One of them said something inaudible to her driver while the other opened the carriage door. A blast of frosty air and falling snowflakes swirled into the cramped space, sending icy fingers up her legs under the hem of her gown.

"Invitation," the guard grunted, his eyes sweeping the interior of the carriage before coming to rest on Adeline.

She touched the simple half mask that had accompanied the invitation, ensuring it was still firmly in place. As Adeline handed over the expensively engraved missive, she let her cloak fall open to reveal the bodice of her gown, which was a breath away from indecent. This particular gown usually stalled unwanted questions from men like this in situations like this, and tonight was no different.

The guard leered, glancing only briefly at the card, which looked more like an invitation to a coronation than an invitation to an auction. Adeline had considered a stealthier means of accessing the house but, in the end, had decided that this course of action offered the greatest chance of success. Though that was before King had appeared in that alley. And by then the first domino in her plan had already been tipped.

And now the rest would fall as they might.

* * *

Save for the tall fences and gates, Helmsdale House might look like a bucolic country manor from the outside, but Adeline had been in palaces with less sumptuous interiors. As she entered the hall, a golden-haired boy approached and offered her a courtly bow. He was no more than ten, dressed in fine livery and possessing startlingly beautiful features. He whisked away her cloak with nary a word and vanished as another servant, this one a footman in the same livery, offered her a glass of champagne from a gleaming silver tray.

A fire roared in the massive marble-encased hearth, chasing away the December chill and sending a red-orange glow dancing across the polished floor. What looked like ancient Greek sculpture flanked the fireplace, imposing as it was arresting. On a wide canvas mounted above the hearth, a beautiful woman clad in a torn tunic and armed with a bow was forever captured in a bloody battle with an enraged dragon. Yet the display of opulence in the hall paled in comparison to the cavernous ballroom that drew people in through tall, arched doors.

Adeline took a sip of her champagne and allowed herself to be swept into the ballroom in a current of expensively dressed men and the occasional woman, each wearing a copy of the mask that she currently wore. The effect was more macabre than mysterious, but it effectively blurred the identity of each individual, which, she suspected, was the entire point when one was bidding on treasures whose provenance was murky at best.

Adeline continued deeper into the ballroom. Above her head were vast chandeliers, their crystal drops glittering like clouds of diamonds. Somewhere in an unseen corner, a pianoforte was being played, the melody subtle and winding through a hundred hushed conversations. A deserted balcony running the length of the near wall overlooked a low dais that had been set up in the center of the ballroom, no doubt the stage upon which the auction would be conducted.

And scattered throughout the space, lit by a thousand candles, rested the treasures everyone had come to bid upon.

The jewels and smaller antiquities were housed in specially crafted glass cases on the far side, mostly obscured by the crowds that clustered around them. Nearer the entrance, larger sculptures were set up on heavy bases, and on wide easels, paintings that fairly dripped with age and history rested. Adeline wasn't interested in the sculptures or paintings. What she had come for lay in one of those glass cases.

She sipped her champagne and wandered along the near side of the ballroom, forcing herself not to rush. Closest to her loomed a marble statue of a curly-haired man rendered with exquisite detail, the figure leaning on a long staff, gazing down in what looked like contemplation. *Hercules—Michelangelo* was written on a tiny card at the base. A lot number was detailed beneath the title, identifying it as a treasure to be sold this evening to the individual with the deepest pockets. She had no idea where King would have acquired such a piece but such details would be immaterial to those here tonight.

She continued beneath Hercules's silent, unseeing gaze. Her own eyes scanned the ever-growing crowd, but there was no sign of King. She reached the far wall, the items mounted in the polished cases glowing and sparkling on their beds of white satin beneath the abundant light. Clusters of people dressed in lavish evening clothes and extravagant gowns bent over the cases. Muted exclamations of admiration and excitement reached her ears, though she could hear tones of unmistakable greed beneath each word. From a business perspective, Adeline had to admire King's methods. There was nothing like the inevitable rivalries to drive up the value of what one was selling.

Not that she was planning on bidding on anything.

Adeline continued her stroll, casually examining each piece that lay beneath the glass surfaces. She passed a pearl the size of a sparrow's egg, dangling from a chain of lesser pearls interspersed with tiny diamonds. In the next case, a tiara boasting a row of brilliant emeralds sparkled. Beyond that a constellation of rubies blazed where they were nestled in a gold brooch fit for royalty. Adeline continued until she reached the end of the row, each case holding something of extraordinary beauty and extraordinary value.

But what she had come for was not there.

Hiding a frown, she pulled the invitation from one of the pockets concealed in the layers of her skirts and examined the detailed list that had been printed on the back. The lot number was there, along with an abbreviated description, though as Adeline read, she realized that it was not the only thing missing from the ballroom. Two diamonds of almost incomprehensible size—and value—were also absent.

"Dammit," Adeline muttered under her breath, replacing her invitation. Frustration and annoyance pricked. She should have anticipated that prizes like these would not be left exposed to the hordes. They would be presented at the time that bidding would begin, for there would be few who could afford such a competition. What she needed to do now was determine where they were being held.

Adeline pivoted and threaded her way back out toward

the hall. A knot of men moved into her path, speaking in low tones and making notations in small notebooks. She skirted them, careful not to rush and draw attention to herself. The jewels would be out of sight but close. Somewhere they could be easily fetched and transported into the ballroom once the bidding started.

Adeline entered the hall and stopped before the hearth, pretending to study the dragon and the maiden doing her best to vanquish it. Liveried servants continued to scurry and toil as more people arrived, disappearing and reappearing through doors at the front and rear of the hall.

On the far side of the long hall, opposite the ballroom, past the activity and where the shadows set everything into gloom, a different door opened, and one of King's armed men emerged. He had a hatchet-like face, a heavy brow shadowing a forbidding expression. He pulled the door closed smartly behind him and locked it, tucking the key into his coat pocket. Adeline kept her eyes on the painting as he strode toward her, heading purposefully in the direction of the ballroom. As he reached her, she stepped backward, stumbling into him. The guard cursed as he steadied her, champagne sloshing over the rim of her glass and onto his sleeve.

Adeline let out a convincing gasp.

"My apologies, my lady," the guard said, his expression changing from forbidding to uncomfortable. "Are you hurt?"

"No, no," she breathed. "Merely embarrassed."

The guard's discomfort turned to obvious, almost comical, relief. Clearly he had braced himself for a scathing tirade. "Can I get you something?" he asked, brushing at his damp sleeve.

"No, I'm quite fine, thank you." Adeline glanced around her, but no one was paying any attention. "I'll just take a moment."

"You're sure?"

"Quite." She nodded. "Please, carry on."

The guard gave her a brief nod and hurried away. Adeline watched him disappear into the ballroom and turned on her heel. Without looking left or right, she crossed the hall, palming the key she had lifted from his pocket. She wasn't sure how long she had before he realized that it was gone.

She reached the door and unlocked it as though she had every right to be there. She could, for all she knew, be stealing into a linen closet, but it was worth the risk of investigating, for no one, in her experience, ever locked up the linens. She lifted the latch, pushing the door inward. No one shouted, no one hurried toward her. Adeline simply stepped through the door, pulling it quietly closed. And then blinked at her surroundings.

It appeared to be a study of sorts and, as in the hall, a fire burned in a wide hearth, lending heat and a warm glow to the room. The light bounced off the spines of hundreds of books, neatly arranged on towering bookshelves that covered an entire wall. On the other walls, hung on a background of rich, red paper, was a collection of portraits and paintings that surpassed what was currently arrayed in the ballroom. A thick, expensive rug muffled her footsteps, and a massive mahogany desk dominated the center of the room.

And on the gleaming surface of that desk rested three glass cases.

Adeline went directly behind the desk, yanking her mask off and setting the key, her glass, and the mask aside. Her fingers worked the catch of the bulky locket at her throat as she gazed at the cases. Two of the cases before her held an unmounted diamond each, the one on the left a dazzling gray blue that reminded Adeline of a stormy sea, the one on the right sparkling the pale yellow of early sunrise. Both were breathtaking, their worth staggering. Adeline ignored them and instead opened the case in the middle.

The flawlessly cut sapphire gleamed, hues of inky midnight caught in a rich tapestry of cerulean. It had once been mounted in an intricate gold setting, a pool of striking color meant to adorn a graceful neck. The setting had since been pried away, leaving only the stone.

Adeline deftly retrieved the sapphire, placed it into the deep hollow of her locket, and snapped the clasp closed. From her pocket she withdrew a second sapphire, a pretty facsimile made entirely of glass. She placed it in the case and lowered the cover, the hinges making a tiny squeak of protest. The paste jewel would fool no one forever, but she didn't need forever. She needed only long enough.

She straightened, retrieving her champagne glass, and took steady breaths, slowing her pulse. It was done. Time to slip away. From beside the study door, the portrait of a man gazed back at her, a knowing, self-satisfied smirk curling between an elaborate moustache and a pointed beard. Adeline gave in to the urge and raised her glass in a mock toast to the image.

"Not his best work, I think."

Adeline froze, her fingers tightening on the stem of her glass.

"But then, beauty is in the eye of the beholder, is it not?"

The air stirred behind her, accompanied by the sound of a second, hidden door clicking shut. King moved beside her, the superfine of his coat sleeve brushing against her bare arm.

Alarm at his presence was oddly absent, as it had been when she had realized who stood at the top of that alley. Almost as if she had been waiting for this. For him.

"Perhaps," she answered slowly.

King gestured at the bearded man in the portrait. "That is George Villiers, the first Duke of Buckingham, painted by Peter Paul Rubens. Found it hanging in a tavern in Calais, can you imagine? A Rubens relegated to overseeing drunkards."

Adeline took a slow sip of champagne and swallowed, her gaze not leaving the portrait. "A pity."

"On the contrary. I bought it for a case of middling Madeira."

King was still standing close enough that she could smell the starch in his shirt and the richer notes of his shaving soap. The contradiction that was this man struck her anew. The apparent lord of London's underworld, who dressed and spoke like a prince. A man as comfortable in his place among criminals as he was among the aristocratic crowd in his ballroom.

She tipped her head. "The duke looks..."

"Uninspiring?"

"I was going to say vain."

Out of the corner of her eye, she could see King's fingers drumming steadily on the silver head of his walking stick. "You draw that from a single portrait?"

"But it's not a single portrait, is it?" Adeline replied. "It's multitudes of portraits. The duke in fine clothes. The duke as an unstoppable equestrian. The duke as Adonis. If Buckingham thought it would further him, I suspect he would have paid to have himself depicted as Jesus. A man obsessed with portraying himself as something he wasn't."

King's fingers abruptly stopped. He shifted, coming to stand directly in front of her. Like Adeline, he wasn't wearing a mask, and she met his gaze, willing herself to keep her expression neutral even as a crackle of anticipation and awareness raced through her veins, the same way it had when she had faced him in that damn alley.

This was a man who should have been painted by Rubens. Or Titian or Da Vinci or Michelangelo. Or anyone with enough skill to capture the essence of a man who was both compelling and cold at the same time. His red-gold hair was clipped neatly, framing an aquiline face with high cheekbones and a square jaw. He was lithe, not excessively tall or broad, yet exuding a contained power that his tailored evening clothes could not conceal. But it was his eyes that had nearly made her stumble as she had walked up that alley toward him. Eyes that even now made her breath catch in her throat. They were pale blue, icy irises ringed with a deeper indigo. Predatory and remote. Piercing and impenetrable. It would take all her skill to manage this man and escape unscathed.

That thought was far more thrilling than it should ever have been.

King tipped his head to the portrait. "Is it dead dukes or dead artists with whom you're so familiar?"

Adeline almost smiled. "It depends on the duke. Or the artist, I suppose. Though unlike you, I'm far from an expert."

"Unlike me?" A red-gold brow rose ever so slightly.

"Your reputation precedes you as a purveyor of fine...things."

King considered her. "I confess your presence here this evening is unexpected," he said after a moment.

"In your study?"

He held her gaze. "In my home."

"You have a lot of guests in your home this evening," she pointed out.

"Very true." He seemed to be considering his next words. "Each of these auctions is a spectacle of greed. A spectacle that lays bare the true character of the titled and wealthy who circle each other in my ballroom, squabbling over possessions. Yet to a man, they cling to the illusion that they are, somehow, inherently better than those who circle each other in the desperate shadows of London's streets. I know those streets. Fought my way out of those gutters and fought for everything that you see here. And I can tell you that the only true difference between the groups, aside from their tailoring, is that those living on the streets do not cling to illusion of any sort." He paused. "You said it best."

"I beg your pardon?"

"The lengths to which people will go to portray themselves as something they aren't. It used to amuse me, the lies that people tell themselves to help them sleep at night." He still hadn't looked away. "Lately, I've found it tedious and predictable."

Adeline had no idea what she was supposed to say to that, so she said nothing.

King brushed imaginary lint from the top of his sleeve, a ruby set into a gold ring flashing fire. "You are neither tedious nor predictable."

"I'm flattered. I think."

"You didn't crawl through the hedges or over the fence in that gown. And you came without your weapons tonight."

Adeline glanced down at her dress, her breasts straining at the embroidered and beaded edge of her bodice, her voluminous skirts falling away. "Mmm." She made a noncommittal sound.

"Greed, self-indulgence, and umbrage aside, the attendees of this auction all possess an additional three attributes. And those are the familiarity, the means, and, above all, the discretion to purchase what it is I'm selling. Invitations were exceedingly limited."

"They were indeed." She ran a finger along the rim of her glass.

"Perhaps you would share with me who was so careless with theirs?" He paused. "As a courtesy from one...professional to another, if you will."

He might not know exactly who she was, but he knew what she was, to some degree at least. He would, after all, have far-reaching resources, so his words didn't surprise her. What did surprise her was the peculiar ache of longing that caught her unaware as he uttered them. The suggestion, as absurd as it might be, that they were professional allies of some sort sliced through her carefully constructed walls of solitary distance. For a heartbeat she was no longer alone.

And maybe he was manipulating her, and maybe he wasn't, but for just this moment, she wanted to hold on to that feeling of connection.

"Lord Reddingforth," she said, pulling the invitation from her pocket. "His love of art is eclipsed by his love of opium. He's currently insensible on a brothel bed under the care of a madam who has been paid handsomely to keep him thus until dawn."

King reached for it, though Adeline did not release it. Their fingers tangled, and heat shot through her veins. She tried to steel herself against the sensation, but all she could concentrate on was the way his thumb was sliding over the back of her hand.

Adeline dropped her arm, leaving the invitation in King's fingers. "You should have a care in the future," she said. "The next person to exploit Reddingforth's weakness to gain access to Helmsdale may have far less...professional motivations than I."

She could still feel the ghost of his fingers on her skin. Nor did the heat that still pulsed through her body diminish with space.

"Noted," he said, tucking the missive into the inside of his coat.

Adeline hesitated, this dance of questions and answers a complex series of steps. "I have no quarrel with you, King."

"I heard you say that to a man already once this evening before you ran him through." A smile drifted across his lips, and Adeline's mouth went dry. Never had she met a man who was as casually intimidating and as effortlessly provocative at the same time. The combination was far more alluring than was safe.

"I did not run him through. I do not enjoy killing stupid men."

"No, I don't suppose you do."

She swirled the last of her champagne in the bottom of the glass she still held before draining it. "Think of me what you will, I am not an assassin."

"The inescapable," King said.

"I beg your pardon?"

"Your name. Adrestia. Meaning 'the inescapable.' Goddess of retribution and vengeance."

"Most of my clients prefer the term *justice*."

"A much more civilized word indeed." King took the empty glass from her and set it on the desk without looking away. "Be that as it may, your reputation precedes you as well."

"I wasn't aware." She frowned.

"I have excellent sources. Sources who have a great deal of respect for your work administering...justice when all else has failed."

Adeline wasn't sure if King was trying to flatter her into revealing information, but she wasn't about to discuss past contracts with this man or anyone. Now or ever.

"Tell me why you're here, Miss Archambault."

Adeline's heart stuttered, her lungs squeezing the air from her chest. It took all of her willpower to remain still. "I'm impressed," she said, pleased that her voice was steady.

"You underestimated me."

"No. Just your sources. I've never been anything other than Adrestia in my work. I'd prefer it to remain so."

"As you wish," King murmured. "Some say Adrestia was handmaiden to the merciless Nemesis." He set his walking stick against the edge of the desk and stepped closer.

Adeline didn't move. "And some say they were one and the same."

King slipped his fingers under the weight of her locket, a featherlight touch against her skin. "I suppose, in our business, ambiguity and duplicity are advantageous."

Whatever breath Adeline had caught fled again.

"Tell me why you're here," he repeated, his eyes never leaving hers. "For I cannot let you leave with something that is not yours." He tapped the locket with his thumb, and Adeline understood he had been watching her all along. Probably since the moment she had stepped from her hired carriage.

This close, Adeline could see the tiny lines around his eyes, lines not of laughter but of burden. Of living a life in a world that offered survival only to those strong enough to take it. Adeline knew, because she lived in that world too. And had survived.

She reached up and wrapped her fingers around his hand, pressing it against the slope of her breasts, the locket trapped between them. Then she whispered, "This was never yours to sell in the first place."

CHAPTER 4

Adeline Archambault was bewitching.

And breathtaking and daring and possibly mad, and the desire coursing through King right now was unlike anything he had ever experienced. She had trapped his hand beneath hers, and beneath her smooth skin, her heart thumped steadily. The edges of the heavy locket pressed against the pads of his fingers, the gold warm under his touch. All he needed to do, all he had intended to do, all he should do, was yank the locket from her beautiful neck. Take back what was his. Except he couldn't move.

"I do not suffer thieves," he said roughly. "No matter what they call themselves."

"Then we have that in common," she replied. She didn't flinch, didn't cower, didn't plead or beg or dissemble. She simply held his gaze until her eyes dropped to his mouth. A new arc of need flashed through him like liquid lightning, and he shivered.

King released the locket and jerked his hand from hers, stepping away from this woman and the unacceptable longings she stirred within him. He could not put together a coherent thought when she was looking at him like that. He didn't understand her, or her motivations, or her layers.

Worst of all, he didn't understand what she did to him.

King shifted farther away, until the bulk of the desk nudged against the backs of his thighs. The men he had set to following this woman who called herself Adrestia had lost her almost immediately in the twisted maze of London.

At the time King had acknowledged that he might never lay eyes on her again, and an acute and disturbing regret had come with that admission. Until that woman had unexpectedly swept into his hall in a gown fit for a queen, and his disturbing regret had been replaced by an equally disturbing anticipation.

She had dared to steal from him in his own home and offered no apology or excuse, only challenge and accusation. Had she been anyone else, he would have already ordered her escorted out at the very least, or thrown in a dark hole somewhere, or tossed onto the first ship back to whatever corner of the continent from which she had come. Instead he remained rooted where he was, fantasizing about casting her in far more sensual places. Like his bed. Or the desk behind him. Or—

"Make your case before I change my mind and do something I may or may not regret later," he heard himself say.

Adrestia merely gazed back at him, the silver in her eyes reflected in the metallic threads that ran through the pale silk of her gown. The dress was daring, skimming low over her breasts, cinched tightly at her ribs, and then flowing enticingly over her hips in a froth of fine fabric. King grasped the edge of the desk at his sides in an effort to smother the sudden, excruciating impulse to reach out and touch her again.

Jesus, this was insane. He had to stop this.

From the surface of his desk he picked up a small knife, the one he used to trim quills. He turned it over in his hand, allowing the blade to press uncomfortably into his palm. "My patience is not infinite." His words came out harshly. Good.

"The man who sold you this." She seemed impervious to his tone and instead simply touched again the locket where the sapphire was concealed. "Charles Howells. Did he tell where it came from?"

"I don't ask questions I don't need or want answers to."

"Ah." She glanced around at the art that hung from his walls. "No, I don't suppose you do."

King could feel his jaw clench, but he didn't give her the satisfaction of a reply. At the time he had bought that sapphire, it hadn't mattered to him where it had come from. Just as it hadn't mattered that he didn't like Howells. The man reeked of desperation, but so did most of the men who came to him for money. And desperation was always profitable.

Yet the sapphire, impressive as it was, was not as valuable as the two magnificent diamonds that had flanked it. Adrestia could have taken either of those stones. Or taken both and been far richer for it. But he had watched her leave the diamonds where they lay and take only the sapphire.

And King wanted to know why. Needed to know why.

In the wrong hands, need, more often than not, ultimately leads to downfall. Unbidden, Adrestia's earlier words echoed in his mind. And as he had earlier, he dismissed them.

"I'm asking now," he growled, tapping the tip of his knife against his thigh. "Where did the sapphire come from?"

Her full lips thinned. "Spain," she said. "A tiny villa called Canillas de Río. It doesn't exist any longer, of course. It was razed, its livestock slaughtered, its men killed, its women raped, and its contents looted, the most valuable objects shipped back to England by one Lieutenant Charles Howells during Wellington's 1809 campaign. The sapphire was part of that shipment."

"And now you've come to fetch it back."

"That's a rather overly simplistic assumption."

King's jaw hardened. That was the second time today she

had accused him of making assumptions. The worst part of her accusation was that she was right.

"My client," she said, "grew up in Canillas de Río and was thirteen at the time Charles Howells raped her. She might have forgiven him that transgression had he not made her watch his men brutalize each one of her younger sisters first."

King swallowed, dark tentacles of memory rattling their prison walls in the deepest recesses of his mind. Recesses he had ruthlessly buried with time and self-control. With some horror he felt cold perspiration gather at the back of his neck. "Stealing back a family heirloom will not fix any of that. It will not make her forget."

"No," she agreed flatly. "It won't."

And King understood that Adrestia hadn't come just for the sapphire. She'd come for far more.

"You've come to destroy Howells," he breathed.

The goddess of retribution held his gaze, unflinching. "I've come for justice."

"How?"

She considered him, a faint smile playing about her lips. "I think that might fall into the category of questions you do not need or want an answer to."

"On the contrary," King snapped. "Howells destroyed your client's confidence, her security, her future. He stole what was most valuable to her, and I'm not talking about pretty stones. I would know how you plan to return the favor."

Her smile faded, and her eyes held his, measuring, assessing, weighing.

King tensed, wanting each and every one of those words back. This was what happened when one lost control and gave in to emotion. Weakness was exposed, secrets betrayed.

Adrestia opened her mouth to speak and then seemed

to reconsider. She fingered the black ribbon around her neck from which the locket dangled before dropping her hand. "Howells's crippling gambling debts have emptied his family coffers, and he's been reduced to selling what he can." Her voice was toneless, as if she was trying to counter the intensity of his last words, and for that King was grateful. "Aside from selling baubles, Howells has also been selling military secrets. That bit was harder to unearth than the location of a stolen jewel, but desperate people make predictable mistakes." She paused. "Did your men not tell you where they lost me?"

King stiffened. "The Dockyard Inn. And those men have since been dismissed for their ineptitude."

"They were good," she said. "Better than most. You may wish to reconsider."

He ignored her suggestion. "Tell me about the inn."

"Why?"

He twisted the knife in his fingers. "Do I need a reason?"

"I suppose not." Adrestia shrugged. "But since I'm sure you'll read all about it in the papers over the coming days, I'll tell you. The Dockyard is Howells's favorite lodging house, where he goes to conduct his treasonous business and then stays to obliterate his regrets and woes. Usually with gin, occasionally with women. He's been there a half dozen times in the last fortnight. Tonight he's selling information to a Frenchman who is not a Frenchman at all. He will never face justice for what he did in the past, but he can answer for his actions now. If both transgressions were brought before the courts, treason would be considered the more heinous of the two."

"Clever."

"There is nothing particularly clever about an anonymous informant informing of the truth," Adrestia said, and once again King was struck by the sense of weariness that lingered beneath her cool demeanor. "This was by far one of the most artless contracts I've executed."

King understood that weariness, and the exhaustion that came from surviving in a world where honor was scarce and trust scarcer still. A world where the soul standing next to you was more likely to offer a blade in your back than to offer aid. He wanted to tell her that he understood. He had no idea how. Or why he would ever be so foolish as to do so.

Adrestia exhaled. "If you're done asking questions, I'd like to take what I came for and go."

"No." His answer was immediate and unyielding.

"No?"

"No." It didn't matter that there seemed to exist a tenuous, terrifying connection between him and this woman that was as dangerously intoxicating as it was dangerously tempting. If every pretty girl who had ever told him a sad story had been allowed to manipulate him, he would have had his throat and his purse strings slit a hundred times over. That lesson had come early in his unforgiving education, and perhaps the best thing he could do now was offer Adrestia a reminder of the same.

King pushed himself away from the desk and closed the distance between them again. He leaned into her, lifting his hand to trace the midnight silk of the ribbon tied around her neck. "You may go," he said. "Because I understand that you are merely working on behalf of a client and because you seem to have the respect of my colleagues. I'll defer to... professional courtesy. But you'll leave the sapphire here."

Adrestia shifted, yet she didn't move away. "And if I refuse?"

"You can't refuse." It was a ridiculous response, but his

ability to think seemed to have deserted him again. Too late, he recognized the foolishness of his arrogance, and that touching her had been a horrible mistake. His fingers slipped from the ribbon to her neck, sliding up and along the graceful column until they found the softness of her hair. He studied the glossy tresses, the delicate curve of her ear, the angle of her jaw, the shape of her parted lips.

The heady scent of jasmine swirled around him, feminine and foreign all at once. He wondered what she would do if he kissed her. If he settled her on the expanse of his desk and worshipped her the way a goddess deserved to be worshipped.

"You can't refuse because you've stolen something from me," he managed to finally whisper, his voice hoarse.

Like his wits. Like his judgment.

"Then it seems we're at an impasse." Still, she hadn't moved. "I'm not leaving here without the sapphire."

"Bid on it like everyone else." His mind was still sluggish.

"I will not buy what should never have been sold."

King traced the edge of her bodice with the tip of his quill knife. "Things don't end well for those who steal from me." That wasn't what he had wanted to say. But she had backed him into an uncharted corner where his calculated, curated control had long since slipped through his fingers like smoke.

"Again, we are at an impasse. Because I might say the same."

Too late, he felt the edge of her blade pressing against his abdomen beneath his coat. From the pressure and the length of the steel, he knew it was far more substantial than a blade used to trim goose feathers. With a flick of her wrist, she could disembowel him where he stood.

If such a thing had been possible, King would have fallen in love right there.

"That's the third," she murmured.

"Third what?"

"The third assumption you've made. The first one was bold, the second overly simplistic, and this one potentially fatal. I never go anywhere without my weapons." Her lips curled, and King's thoughts scattered all over again. "You should have a care in the future," she continued softly. "The next person to exploit an abundance of skirts may have far less...professional motivations than I."

King gazed down at her, her mouth inches from his. "Noted." His eyes did not leave hers.

The door to his study abruptly opened, the sounds of the crowd and the pianoforte intruding.

King didn't move. Nor did he look away from Adrestia. "Get out," he growled at whoever had entered.

"I beg your pardon, sir." It was the voice of Elliot, his youngest footman. "The Duke of Rotham requires a moment of your time—"

"I don't care."

"But His Grace wishes—"

"I do not answer to dukes." King finally lifted his gaze from Adrestia.

The striking blond boy looked suspiciously between King and Adrestia, though the pressure of her blade had vanished, the knife no doubt concealed neatly back in the abundance of her skirts. "Are you all right, sir?"

"Quite," he assured his footman, lying through his teeth. *I am far from all right.*

"Do you— Blimey, that is Smithers's key," Elliot said, and King followed his distracted gaze to where the key still lay on the corner of the desk.

King swept the key from its resting place and tossed it to Elliot. "Yes. And you can tell Smithers that the next time he leaves his pockets unguarded, he can look for work elsewhere."

The boy caught it effortlessly and regarded Adrestia with something akin to awe. "You bobbed *Smithers*? Blimey—"

"That will do, Elliot," King chastened.

"Of course, sir," the boy replied, not looking chastened at all. "What do you want me to tell the duke, sir? He's arrived with an additional guest who does not possess an invitation," he forged on. "Shall I have them escorted from the premises, or—"

"Jesus." King cursed under his breath. This was the problem with entitled peers. Believing that they could do what they wished with impunity. Yet Rotham, with his bottomless coffers and voracious greed, was good for business on nights such as this.

"Sir?"

"Show the duke in. He has one minute to explain himself." He tipped his head until his lips were a breath away from Adrestia's ear. "But you and I are far from done."

The boy vanished, and King stepped away from her. She retrieved her mask from the desk, swiftly donned it, and retreated to the shadow of the bookcases.

Elliot reappeared. "Sir, His Grace, the Duke of Rotham."

"Another glorious event, King," the portly duke announced as he stepped into the room, flapping his hands like a flightless bird. "The Hercules piece at the entrance is a marvel." He stopped just inside the door, fingers of one hand tugging on the constricting cravat beneath his jowls, the other hand clutching his mask.

King stared stonily back. "Thank you. Though I've been advised that you have brought a stranger to a private affair."

"Not a stranger," the duke said hurriedly. "But an old acquaintance of discerning taste, newly returned to London.

I can personally vouch for his discretion. I'd like to introduce you." Without waiting for a response, the duke turned
and gestured at someone unseen beyond the study door.

King's jaw clenched with impatience and irritation. He
didn't have time for this. This wasn't a bloody ball at
Almack's, and he didn't need introductions to anyone—

King froze as his mind tried desperately to comprehend
what he was seeing.

Whom he was seeing.

A trim, gray-haired man dressed impeccably in rich navy
evening clothes, but without a mask, had entered his study,
his gait marred by a slight limp. He was looking around with
interest, blue eyes lingering on the art and the books and
the diamonds on the desk. He came to a casual stop beside
Rotham, clasping his hands behind his back, his attention
finally turning to King.

The air was sucked from the room, and dark spots danced
around the edges of King's vision. Bile rose in his throat,
and for a moment he thought he might be sick. Prickles of
icy sweat crawled down his spine and more gathered at his
temples. He shuddered, cold and hot at the same time. This
wasn't happening. This couldn't be happening. This man
was supposed to be dead.

"May I present John Westerleigh, the new Baron
Marstowe, recently returned from the Americas." The duke
was talking, though it sounded as if his voice were muffled
by a thick fog.

Shock and incomprehension were giving way to something far darker bubbling up from the deepest parts of his
soul along with a suffocating rage. King was distantly aware
that he was breathing raggedly, old memories of hatred and,
worst of all, helplessness twisting through his chest and
constricting his lungs.

King met the baron's gaze, but there was not a flicker of recognition in the older man's eyes. King wasn't sure if he was relieved or disappointed.

The duke was droning on, presumably making some sort of introduction to the baron, but King didn't hear him. He could only stare, trapped in past memories until he became aware that a silence had fallen. Rotham was looking at him expectantly now.

"Shall the duke and his guest stay, sir?" Elliot prompted from beside King. King didn't remember the child moving.

Only so that I can keep an eye on the devil.

King nodded slowly, still afraid to speak.

"Splendid." The duke was beaming at him, and the baron inclined his head, still without a glimmer of recognition.

But then it had been almost twenty years. And King was no longer a child.

Elliot produced a mask and handed it to the baron with a quick grin. Marstowe smiled back at the boy, and without thinking, King stepped in front of his young footman.

"You are dismissed, Elliot," King said, his voice sounding rough even in his own ears.

"Sir?"

"Go."

"Yessir." Elliot looked confused but did as he was ordered.

"I can't wait to see what other prizes you've managed to procure for our enjoyment this evening." The duke was donning his mask. "Come, Marstowe. You won't be disappointed."

"I am already enchanted," the baron said, following suit.

King watched them leave the study, crossing the room to close the door after them. He returned to the desk and leaned back against the edge, his vision still blackened at the peripheries, rage still making it difficult to breathe.

"King."

Adrestia had appeared directly in front of him, her forehead creased and what looked like concern filling her silver eyes.

"You want the sapphire?" he rasped.

She raised her hand, touching the sleeve of his coat before her fingers slid down to his wrist. "Yes, but I—"

"It's yours."

"I beg your pardon?"

"In exchange, I'm hiring you."

"I see." Her voice was steady. Soothing. "May I ask what for?"

The rage inside him crystallized into cold certainty.

"I need you to destroy someone."

CHAPTER 5

Adeline eyed King warily. He was speaking to her, but she wasn't sure that he even saw her.

She shifted, gently lifting his hand. It was fisted around the small quill knife he'd been toying with, and blood now dripped through his clenched fingers onto the expensive Turkish rug. King glanced down at the rivulets of blood and opened his hand to reveal the knife and the long cut across his palm where the blade had bitten. Silently Adeline slipped it from his grasp and set it on the desk. Without asking she reached up and unknotted his cravat, pulling the linen from his neck and wrapping it around his hand. He didn't seem to notice, and that, for a man for whom control seemed paramount, was exceedingly unsettling.

"Are you sure?" she murmured. "You have your own men who—"

"My men can't do this. I need you." Those last three words were stark.

Adeline swallowed. It wasn't the first time someone had said that to her. But each time, they had meant only that they needed what she could do for them. She was a fool if she believed that King was different. He, like everyone else, didn't need *her.*

I need you to destroy someone.

The man recently back from the Americas. The man recently made a baron. The man who had made this unflinching man flinch.

"My services will cost you more than a sapphire," she said deliberately.

That statement, more than a sharp blade or a soft voice, seemed to bring King back from whatever personal hell he'd tumbled into. "Name your price."

Adeline faltered. She hadn't expected that answer. She'd expected him to negotiate with the ruthless cunning and callousness he was known for.

"Name your price," he repeated.

"Falaise d'Argent," she blurted recklessly.

"What is that?"

"A chateau. Near Lille. In France."

"Done."

"Done?" She laughed, but there was no humor in it. "You don't even know what it would cost to—"

"Money is of no consequence." King glanced down at his wrapped hand. His complexion was still the color of pale linen, though an unnatural flush had stained the edges of his cheekbones. "I will buy you the entirety of Versailles if that is what you require."

"That is not funny."

King looked up at her, his eyes icy. "It wasn't meant to be."

Adeline suppressed a troubled frown. "Perhaps this is something that you would prefer to deal with on your own—"

"If I deal with Marstowe on my own, I will simply kill him. And that would be too kind." His features were a mask of granite. "I want him to suffer."

Adeline moved away from the door, coming to stand in front of a large canvas depicting a resolute Judith beheading a terror-stricken Holofernes. "I'm not sure what it is that your sources have told you, but I do not possess a dungeon full of racks and thumbscrews and burning stakes. I don't torture people, nor, may I remind you, am I an assassin. I recover stolen objects, stolen fortunes, and return them to rightful owners. I bring individuals to justice when and if circumstance allows, as I did Howells. But often, I merely extract monetary compensation by whatever means necessary when justice is not possible—"

"Are you refusing to work for me?"

"Not at all. I am merely suggesting that perhaps you would like to consider this matter further? Take the night, at least?"

"I don't need to consider this matter further."

Adeline shook her head. "My clients engage my services when all other recourse has been exhausted. I'm hired when no one else can or will help them. Once the job is done, I move on. Disappear, so as not to remain a reminder of what was likely the worst moment of their lives." She paused. "Perhaps there are other solutions that you might first—"

"I already told you that I don't need to consider this matter further. Do not make me repeat myself a third time."

Adeline crossed her arms, still studying the curve of

Judith's blade, trying to pick the order of her questions. "What did Marstowe do?"

"He killed someone I cared for very much."

"I see." Not the first time she'd heard that. "Who?"

King didn't answer. A coal shifted in the grate with a loud pop, the only sound in the heavy silence.

"If you are to engage my services, you are going to need to prepare yourself that I will know things. Things that you may not want me to know."

"I don't need you to *know things*," he snarled. "I just need you to destroy Marstowe. I don't care how you do it."

"I can't agree to that."

"Why?" he demanded angrily.

Adeline turned away from the painting to face King again. "Because I don't chase justice recklessly. In Howells's case, I listened to my client and her sisters tell the same story, saw how their lives were altered, witnessed the damage done. I collect facts with diligence and care. I am not a bloodthirsty hound that can be unleashed blindly at the whim of a master."

"I didn't suggest such." King had picked up his walking stick and was leaning on it with his uninjured hand, the tip making a pattern of indentations in the rug.

Adeline approached King. "If I agree to this, then I will start by looking into the dark corners of Marstowe's life. I will have my answers whether you give them to me or not. Because while I do not chase justice recklessly, I will chase truth relentlessly."

King didn't answer.

"What am I going to find in those corners, King?"

King shoved his walking stick aside, and it banged against the edge of the desk. "You will find that John Westerleigh is the younger brother of the late Harold Westerleigh, former

Baron Marstowe. As a young man, John was once destined for an appointment in the church before he sailed for Boston in 1798, immediately after the tragic, accidental death of his nephew, Evan Westerleigh."

"Mmm." Adeline watched King carefully. "Is that whom he killed? His nephew?"

"Yes. Though the account in the *Times*, if and when you go looking in their archives, will say that Evan Westerleigh, young heir to the Marstowe fortune and title, was discovered in the mews of the family's London home. In the absence of witnesses, it speculates that he fell and struck his head or that he may even have been kicked by one of the horses. It describes his death as a tragic accident. You'll find the story is the same in all the papers. It was quite the sensation at the time."

"Why?"

King paced to the bookcase and back. "The old baron enjoyed a fair bit of celebrity in society. He was famous for his lavish events, titillating salons for all manner of artists and writers, and was a significant patron of the theater. He was quite popular. But there was never a mention of John Westerleigh anywhere."

"Then how do you know that Evan's death was not an accident?"

"I was there. I saw him kill Evan."

Adeline frowned. So then there had been a witness. "Yet you did not tell anyone what you saw?"

"I tried..." King hesitated. "And then I couldn't."

An odd choice of words. "Couldn't or wouldn't?"

"The distinction doesn't matter. No one believed me."

"Why?"

He only shook his head, not meeting her gaze, his expression impossible to read.

Adeline waited for King to go on, but he remained mute.

For as much information as he had given her, there was a great deal more he wasn't sharing.

She pressed a different angle. "Tell me, is the baron here tonight to kill you?"

"What?" He looked momentarily nonplussed.

"Given what little you've managed to share about this particular crime, one might call you a loose end," she continued. "I'd like to be adequately prepared for such a possibility."

"That's not funny."

She turned his own words back on him. "It wasn't meant to be."

"No," King said, finally moving. He skirted his desk and came toward her, sinking into the chair, his fingers pressed flat on the smooth surface. "The baron has no idea who I am."

"You're sure?"

"Yes. It happened over twenty years ago. I was a child."

"I see." That explained a great deal. The word of a street urchin would never have stood against the word of an aristocratic gentleman destined for the church.

"I was eleven. I should have—" He stopped abruptly and didn't finish.

"You didn't expect to see Marstowe here tonight."

King went eerily still. "I thought he was dead. I was told that the ship he was on sank off the coast of Massachusetts. At the time it was a small comfort. But if I had known he was alive—" He stopped again.

This time, Adeline knew the end to that sentence.

"Who was Evan Westerleigh to you?" she asked.

"He was my best friend." His words were barely audible.

Adeline sighed. The boundaries of class should have made such a relationship impossible, but children were rarely bothered by such details. Adeline would know. "I'm sorry."

"For what? You weren't there. You couldn't have done anything. At least not then," he added pointedly.

Adeline bit the inside of her lip. If this had been any other person, she would most likely have walked away. A client who refused to provide information was impossible to serve. And yet...

Falaise d'Argent.

Named for the dark-silver cliffs against which it nestled, the small château and its vineyards had belonged to her family for over two centuries before it had been stolen. To Adeline it represented the roots she had never been able to put down, the only tie she had left to a family long gone. It was a promise of constancy, of a place where she might finally rest her weary soul. She had despaired of ever being able to recover the land, but now, in a single moment, the possibility dangled before her.

It was too much to turn away from.

"Very well," she said.

"Very well?" King repeated. "What does that mean?"

"I agree to your proposal. Though I will verify the merit of what you have asked me to do."

"The merit?" His voice was a growl. "That's not—"

"That's my offer to you," she interrupted him. "The same offer I make to every potential client until facts can be corroborated and proven to my satisfaction."

King gazed at her, his chilling eyes once again remote and unreadable. "Fine."

Adeline touched the locket at her neck. "I will return to London immediately after I deliver—"

"You can't leave."

Her hand fell away, her fingers curling in her skirts. "You

may control the darker side of London and everything in it, but you do not control me. I have property to return to its rightful owner. A contract to finish, a promise to keep."

"I will see it done."

"I beg your pardon?"

"I will have the sapphire returned. Provide me with your client's direction, and it will be delivered immediately."

Adeline frowned.

"You doubt my word?"

"No," she said truthfully. "It is your motivations behind such an offer that are opaque."

"As I said, if I am left alone with him, I will simply kill him and regret that kindness later."

"And keeping me in London will prevent you from doing that?"

"No. You misunderstand me." King paused. "You will stay here. At Helmsdale."

CHAPTER 6

Adeline did not stay at Helmsdale.

The demand had surprised her, but she hadn't bothered arguing—really, where she slept was an insignificant detail when cast against the possibility of recovering Falaise d'Argent. She would collect her belongings from the Four Cocks when she was able and eventually return to Helmsdale, but right now, Adeline had work to do.

The end of King's auction had prompted a mass exodus of attendees, similar to the emptying of a theater, its patrons all drunk on spirits, gossip, excesses, and the entertainment provided by all three. Adeline had slipped from the house, her hired carriage still waiting exactly as she'd instructed, and it hadn't been difficult for her to follow the Duke of Rotham's flamboyant equipage as he and Baron Marstowe had departed Helmsdale.

Adeline had spent the entirety of the auction alternatively observing Marstowe and observing King observing Marstowe. The baron had bid on nothing and had appeared to be more interested in imbibing from the trays of expensive liquors that footmen had circulated through the ballroom than in examining the treasures surrounding him. Aside from Rotham, he'd generally avoided those around him and made little effort at conversation. The baron had sought no further interaction with King, even though the owner of Helmsdale had been easily visible as he'd watched the spectacle alone from the ballroom balcony, his expression cold and grim.

Adeline had no idea where Rotham and Marstowe were headed now but had simply instructed her driver to follow the pair. As they went deeper into London, the empty spaces and orderly squares soon gave way to a jumble of twisting streets, hemmed in on all sides by looming buildings. The darkened cobblestones were punctuated only by light spilling from the occasional street corner or from the windows of businesses that did the bulk of their trade in the hours long after the sun had set.

Rotham's carriage eventually rolled to a stop in front of a nondescript brick building, light seeping from the edges of its covered windows, carriages and their bundled drivers lining the street beyond. The two men disembarked and disappeared into the building, the two large lanterns blazing by the door making it easy to observe.

Adeline's own equipage stopped a short distance away,

and she hopped out, shivering against the winter air that stabbed at her with icy fingers. The snowfall that had started earlier had become heavier, and a thick layer of pristine white covered everything, though the streets would be a mucky morass come morning.

"What is this place?" she asked her driver.

"Lavoie's," he replied. "A gaming hell, but the exclusive kind that caters to rich toffs with fat purses wishing to amuse themselves. Their ladies too."

"Mmm."

"You planning on gambling?" her driver asked.

"Something like that." She pulled her cloak more tightly about her body.

"You need me to wait?"

"Thank you but no. You've spent enough time in the cold—"

"I reckon you've 'bout paid me enough this evening to wait for you till Christmas. 'Tis no trouble."

"There's no need." If she didn't return to Helmsdale, she'd simply lodge back at the Four Cocks after she was done here tonight. She could return to Helmsdale on the morrow, King's directives be damned.

"Very well." The driver tipped his hat and pulled away.

Adeline brushed at the snowflakes that clung to her cloak and started toward the gaming hell, the promise of light and warmth beckoning.

A man stepped into her path before she could reach the door, and Adeline's hand immediately dropped to her skirts, her fingers brushing the handle of her blade. She did not wish to fight in skirts, but she'd done it before—

The man stopped and leaned casually on his walking stick.

Adeline cursed under her breath. "This is starting to become tiresome, King," she said.

"Define *this*," he said, sounding unconcerned.

"You, skulking in alleys, waiting for me."

"I don't skulk. And this is more of a street."

"You followed me here."

"Of course I did. I am protecting my investment. London is a dangerous place at night. If you die in one of these rotten alleys, you will be of no use to me."

"I thought we established that I am hard to kill."

"*Hard* is not the same thing as *impossible*."

She ignored his words. "I also thought we'd established that you are my client and that I was to work on your behalf. I'd like to do so without you spying on me or otherwise interfering with my ability to do my job."

"Spying implies a level of subterfuge, which this encounter most certainly lacks. And I haven't interfered with anything."

"You're interfering now. Marstowe and Rotham—"

"Are inside, very likely partaking in a bottle of very excellent French brandy that has never seen the inside of a customhouse and, knowing Rotham, getting drunker by the minute. I am supposing you are here to take advantage of that."

Adeline's jaw hardened. "I'd like to get a better measure of Marstowe."

"You could have spoken to him during the auction—"

"Did you think me incapable when you hired me?" she interrupted.

"Not at all."

"Do you think me incapable now?"

"Of course not. I just would have preferred if you had advised me of your intent to leave Helmsdale this evening."

Adeline gaped at him. "Advised you? You—" She closed her eyes, forced herself to picture the sun-drenched vineyards of a French château, and collected herself. "You are neither my nursemaid nor my keeper," she said, opening her eyes. "Did you honestly expect me to remain locked up in your towers to magically spin straw into gold?"

"What does that mean?"

"The tale of Rumpelstilzchen?" Her breath misted in the cold air.

"I'm not familiar."

"A wretched story meant to entertain children in which a woman becomes a pawn of her foolish father, then a vicious king, and finally a cruel little goblin."

"Then she should have killed them all," he said darkly. "And you weren't locked up."

"I refuse to be your pawn, King."

"I can't imagine you've ever been anyone's pawn."

The wind gusted, and Adeline shivered. This was ridiculous. She stalked toward the door of Lavoie's. "Just leave, King," she said. "Go back to Helmsdale, get some rest, and let me do my job. I'll keep you abreast of my findings."

He fell into step beside her. "You have no idea what Marstowe is capable of."

"That is rather the point here, King. To determine exactly that, since you are hardly a fount of information."

"You already know that there are two types of people who exist in this world," he said. "Wolves and sheep. Predators and prey. Marstowe is a predator of the most monstrous sort."

"There are shepherds too," Adeline said irritably.

"The shepherds." King made a dismissive sound. "Those fools spend their lives exposed to the worst of the elements, trying to protect creatures too dumb to understand that they need protecting or understand what the shepherd risks on their behalf."

"Are you insinuating I'm a fool?"

"If you recklessly risk your safety."

"Well, since we're still speaking in similes here, I will remind you that sometimes those shepherds hide dogs within their sheep. Clever, cunning animals that do not fear wolves."

"Now you're a dog?"

Adeline threw up her hands in disgust. "You were right the first time. I am a fool, but only for trying to have this conversation with you."

He didn't answer, and Adeline took three more steps before she realized that he was no longer at her side. She stopped and turned to find him standing motionless, studying her intently. With his pale eyes, fair coloring, and seeming imperviousness to the snow swirling wildly around him, he looked a little like some sort of avenging Nordic god.

"I will not leave you," he said quietly.

She should be furious. She should cling to healthy frustration that this man insisted on meddling in her craft. Yet...

I will not leave you.

The way he said those words made her knees wobbly and sent a tide of longing flooding through her. It filled the vast caverns in her soul that had been carved out by too many years of loneliness. Everyone left her eventually, through choice or circumstance, but in this moment she wanted to believe him. In him.

He closed the gap between them, his footsteps muffled by the snow. "I'll not interfere, merely observe. I need you to..." He trailed off, clearly struggling for words.

Her eyes dropped to his mouth. A snowflake landed on his upper lip, starting to melt almost instantly. She wondered what it might feel like to kiss this man. To press her lips to the place where that snowflake had disappeared. To run her hands over his skin, feel the hard strength of his muscles as he moved against her—

She tore her gaze from his mouth, aware her breathing had become somewhat erratic. She met his eyes and then forgot to breathe altogether. He was looking at her with a heat that should have melted the snow where they stood. Those icy-cool eyes of his had ignited into blue flames, pinning her where she stood.

He was going to kiss her, she thought hazily, right here in the middle of this snowy street. The anticipation made her entire body thrum with want.

Her fingers brushed the sleeve of his coat. "You need me to what?" she whispered.

King started and suddenly stepped back. He shook his head, as if trying to clear it. "You need to remember what is at stake here," he said harshly. "And you need to remember that you work for me."

Whatever fantasies Adeline had been entertaining burst like a bubble.

"I have not forgotten," she said, turning toward the door to hide the uncomfortable flush that was burning across her cheeks. She had never, in all her life, mixed business with pleasure. She would not start now, no matter how enthralling or provocative this man might be.

Adeline reached for the door and yanked it open. She was immediately enveloped in a welcome heat laced with tobacco smoke and perfume. The club opened before her, and while the outside of the building was unremarkable, the inside was anything but. Gleaming floors were almost invisible beneath a wide arrangement of gaming tables surrounded by laughing, chattering crowds of expensively dressed gamblers. Richly papered walls framed two opposite hearths, each with a blazing fire. Liveried servants circulated with silver trays of bottles and glasses.

"You're going to want this." King's voice came from behind her as something soft slid over her eyes.

She managed to resist the urge to spin and yank the offending object from her face. Instead she remained frozen as he adjusted the mask carefully, his fingers working the ribbons at the back of her head. His breath was warm against her exposed nape, the backs of his fingers lingering gently along her neck as he finished.

That simple touch sent currents of desire rippling through her. It made her want to discover just what it might take to ignite the heat that smoldered beneath that cool exterior of his. But she could not afford this sort of distraction if she was to focus on the task at hand. Starting with the fact that she was now wearing yet another mask.

She raised her hand to her face. It was not the same type of mask that she had worn for the auction—this was a decorative affair, feathers affixed to the side, and covered only the upper part of her face. She frowned in confusion. "Does no one in England show their faces in public any longer?"

"The female guests prefer to wear them here. Gambling, especially in an establishment such as this, is not always considered a suitable pastime for women of genteel birth." His voice was low in her ear.

Adeline glanced at the women in risqué gowns, realizing that the tops of their faces were also covered with ornate and dramatic masks. "Credible deniability," she murmured.

"I've not heard it stated as such, but yes." King seemed to find that amusing.

Without hesitating, his hands slid down her neck to her throat, deftly working the ties of her cloak. Adeline felt the burn of his touch all the way through her, making her muscles clench and her breath catch. The woolen garment slid easily from her shoulders as he passed it to an approaching footman.

He had to stop touching her. She couldn't think clearly when he did.

Adeline stepped away from the man at her back and headed out onto the gaming floor, the snap of cards and clatter of dice occasionally audible over the conversations. Her gaze danced over the crowd, seeking the new Baron Marstowe, and she finally found him sitting at a vingt-et-un table. The Duke of Rotham was with him, both looking significantly worse for wear since she had last seen them at Helmsdale. A nearly empty bottle of what looked like brandy sat between them. Perfect. Next to coin, liquor was often Adeline's greatest ally.

Within minutes she had found a footman and procured a new bottle of French brandy, along with another glass. She approached the table and found King leaning casually on his walking stick with one hand, presumably observing a game of piquet being played nearby. His outwardly laissez-faire deportment would fool most, but it did not fool her for a second. She could almost feel the tension rolling off him in waves.

Rotham and Marstowe had their backs to King and were unaware of his presence, while he'd be able to hear everything being said. Adeline looked away. When King had promised to merely observe, she had assumed that it would be with a larger measure of discretion. Served her right. Assumptions were perilous things, after all.

Adeline slid silently into an empty chair between the baron and the duke. Neither man seemed to notice her, absorbed as they were in their game. She glanced at the dealer, somewhat surprised to discover that it was a woman who sat opposite the players. She was blond, dressed in a gown and mask the color of the Mediterranean shallows, and sharp blue eyes assessed Adeline. Adeline gazed back until the dealer returned her attention to the game that was still in progress.

The duke was rubbing his forehead above reddened eyes as he contemplated the seven of hearts and the ten of spades that lay in front of the dealer. He was, as King had predicted, utterly foxed, his movements clumsy and slow. The baron appeared somewhat less inebriated, or perhaps he was simply concealing it better. He had a look of fierce concentration on his face as he stole another look at the cards trapped beneath his palm on the green felt.

Up close, Adeline studied Marstowe's soft hands, his manicured nails, his tailored clothing, his carefully trimmed gray hair, and his upright posture. He looked every inch the well-groomed, well-dressed gentleman, as one would expect of a man of his station. He didn't look like the sort of killer portrayed by caricaturists, with pointy teeth and a forked tail, but then none of them ever did.

Adeline slowly filled her glass as both players asked for another card and both went over twenty-one.

Rotham threw his cards down in disgust. "Goddammit," he swore. "You better find your pocketbook fast, Marstowe, 'cause mine's not goin' to last long at this rate."

The baron slapped his cards down beside the duke's. His face was flushed with heat, frustration, or anger—or maybe all three.

"S'posed to distract me from my troubles, no' remind me," he groused. "An' I'm working on it."

"Work faster." Rotham drained the last of his brandy and reached for the almost-empty bottle. "Goddammit," he cursed again. "We're out."

"May I?" Adeline pulled her chair closer to the table and set down her glass on the edge, lifting her brandy bottle in invitation.

The duke and baron seemed to notice her for the first time. Rotham leered at her décolletage while Marstowe merely shoved his cards away and slid his glass in her direction.

"God, yes," the baron slurred.

Adeline poured, aware of the men's eyes on her.

"I don't know you," Rotham said with the slow, exaggerated deliberation with which the very intoxicated spoke. "We've no' met."

"No." Without asking, Adeline reached for the duke's glass and filled it as well.

"I am th' Duke of Rotham," he announced with all the pomposity he could muster.

Adeline tried to look duly impressed.

"Marstowe." The baron downed half his brandy.

"Marstowe," she murmured as if searching her memory. "Ah. You're just recently back from the Americas, if I've heard correctly."

The baron grunted.

"That he is." The duke's eyes hadn't made it up past her chin yet. "Mebbe you could welcome 'im back properly. Wha's your name?"

Adeline suppressed a shudder. "You may call me Adrestia."

"Greek name," Marstowe mumbled into his glass.

"It is." Adeline pretended to be delighted. "Are you familiar with the language?"

"Mebbe." He took a large gulp of brandy.

"'Course he is," Rotham chortled. "Taught Greek an' Latin fer twenty years for Will'am an' Mary in the backwoods."

"For whom?" Adeline tried to untangle that statement.

"College in the godforsaken colonies. Can't imagine what they need Greek fer in Virginia." He slapped Marstowe on the shoulder. "Don' know why you stayed s'long either."

"Would you like to be dealt in, my lady?" the beautiful dealer asked smoothly.

Adeline shook her head. "I do not know how to play," she lied.

"Not mus' of a game for women, an'ways," the duke said, leaning toward her. "Maths, you know. Hard for you to unnerstand."

"Of course." Adeline glanced with no little irony at the woman dealing the cards, who only gazed back impassively. "Would you mind if I watched?"

"S'long as your French friend stays put," Marstowe mumbled, gesturing at the bottle by her elbow.

"What made you decide to go to the Americas, my lord?" Adeline asked guilelessly.

Marstowe didn't answer or even cast a glance in her direction. He only picked up his glass and took a healthy swallow.

Adeline tipped her head in consideration. Interesting. Not that she'd expected him to confess that he'd killed a child and had had to flee, but her fawning ingenue approach almost always yielded better results with men deep in their cups.

The duke, however, did not disappoint. "The kind o' opportunity the church don' give," Rotham answered for him instead, his eyes straying once again to Adeline's bodice. "His father wanted 'im to join th' church but we've been frien's since Eton an' Marstowe would 'ave made the worst sort o' cleric." He sneered. "Bloody bunch o' thieves, the church—"

"I heard that the ship you were on sank in a terrible storm

off the coast of Massachusetts," Adeline interrupted, facing the baron and putting a hand to her chest. "How terrifying that must have been."

The baron's head finally came up. "How'd y'know that?"

"One hears things," Adeline said.

"You never tol' me that, Marstowe," the duke protested. "Yer ship really sank?"

"It was a goddamn packet," the baron mumbled. "Goddamn pig o' a ship captained by a half-wit. Blew off course in th' wind."

"You sailed on a packet?" Rotham asked, sounding suitably horrified. "How primitive."

"S'what was available." Marstowe picked up his first card.

"That's what happens when you kill someone," Adeline said with a forced chuckle.

The baron's hand jerked, the card bending in his grasp. His face drained of color. "What did y'say?"

"You must have killed someone. That's why you were in such a terrible rush to leave England," she continued gaily. "Desperate enough to sail on a packet."

"Jesus, Marstowe, careful wi' th' damn cards." The duke elbowed him. "She's no' serious." He accepted two cards from the dealer.

The baron clutched his glass and drained the rest of his brandy in a single gulp.

Rotham turned and grinned sloppily at Adeline. "I know some Greek too, my lady."

Adeline ignored him, watching Marstowe. His color was starting to come back, though he hadn't relinquished his grip on his glass.

"I bought Hercules tonight," the duke announced, his eyes once again straying south to lodge at her breasts. His hand followed his gaze, his fingers reaching for the embroidered edge of her bodice. "Mebbe you'd like t' be my Hippolyta an' show me yer girdle—"

"Heracles." A new voice broke into the conversation and stayed the duke's wandering fingers. "It was Heracles who was Greek."

*C*HAPTER 7

As the shock of seeing John Westerleigh had subsided over the course of the evening, the knowledge that the man still lived and breathed had become like a festering sore that could not be ignored. However, King had managed to rein in the rage and revulsion that had dictated his actions in that study and blinded him to good sense. The time that had elapsed since coming face-to-face with a dead man had also allowed King the opportunity to think more clearly, and he'd come to the very uncomfortable realization that he should have heeded the goddess of retribution.

Adrestia had urged him to either take the night to think or simply deal with the situation on his own. But he hadn't listened. Hadn't *thought* beyond his all-consuming need for revenge. And he hadn't really comprehended just how many layers of his own life would inevitably be peeled back and exposed once she started chasing the truth.

And that intrusion into his privacy and his past was unacceptable.

King settled himself into a chair beside the duke. Adrestia was glaring at him now through her mask. She was breathtakingly beautiful, even when furious, or maybe more so because of it. The mask only added to the alluring air of mystery that surrounded her. It didn't, however, conceal the fact that she was a threat to his privacy and, more alarmingly, his control.

He forced himself to look away from her.

Rotham had straightened and was regarding him with a bleary sort of wariness, as if he had just discovered a tiger amid a room of house cats. "King. What're you doin' here?"

"I do like to get out from time to time." King waved at a passing footman and a glass of amber liquor appeared in front of him. "Hercules was a Roman hero, adapted from the Greek Heracles," King continued from his earlier comment, tracing a lazy pattern on the green felt with his fingers. "But it was Heracles who fell to madness and killed a child."

Marstowe hadn't said a word yet, his eyes fixed firmly on the damaged card in his hand. King looked away before his animosity and revulsion became obvious.

The duke blinked at King and then shrugged. "Roman, Greek, no matter. What matters is it's sculpted by Michelangelo hisself." He looked back at Adeline and waved his glass at King. "Didn' think he'd find such a thing. But I shoulda known better 'cause this man is famous fer findin' the impossible—" He abruptly stopped. "That's it." He gave Marstowe another jab with his elbow. "He can find it."

"What?" Marstowe didn't look up, only asked for another card from the dealer.

"The money. Your money. He could find it for you."

King took a small sip of his brandy and forced himself to remain still. The duke had made a comment about money when Adrestia had first sat down, but King hadn't given it much credence. He was certainly paying attention now, because what the blundering duke was alluding to was a fair sight more than a missing pocketbook.

Marstowe glanced at his new card. "I don' think—"

"Yer damn solicitors 'ave been looking fer an age," the duke whispered in a voice that was far from a whisper. "King might be yer best chance."

The baron looked unconvinced.

Adrestia had suddenly become absorbed in a loose thread on the shoulder of her gown.

"May I ask what it is you seem to have lost?" King asked Marstowe. He was careful to keep his expression blank.

"Money," the duke told him.

Marstowe grimaced, the muscles in his neck flexing.

"I see," King said, trying not to imagine snapping that neck. He adjusted his grip on his walking stick where it rested against his thigh. "Money from your personal coffers or money tied to the barony?"

The baron hesitated.

"Oh, fer God's sake, i's not like it's a secret," Rotham grumbled. "Least not fer much longer. An' I can't keep payin'."

Marstowe stared into his empty cup.

"The barony," Rotham told King impatiently.

"How much?" King inquired.

"All of it." The duke sat back with a thump.

King stared at Marstowe. He knew that there was no land associated with the barony, only the expensive town house in London, but Marstowe's great-grandfather and his grandfather had each made an obscene fortune from their very unfashionable obsession with trade. For that much money to have disappeared...

"Gambling debts?" he asked as evenly as possible. "Poor investments, malicious blackmail, diabolical mistresses, or failed ventures?"

The baron only glowered and reached for the brandy beside Adeline.

"No," Rotham answered for him. "The damn estate lawyers think mebbe his brother gave everything t' the church. I tol' you, thieves, the lot o' them," he finished, banging the table with the flat of his hand.

"Indeed?" King pushed his glass back and forth across the felt with his fingers, watching the brandy splash gently against the sides. The loss of the entire Marstowe fortune should please him. Yet he didn't feel pleased. There was no amount of money lost that could equal what King had lost. "An inopportune donation to the church can be verified."

"How?" Marstowe finally found his voice.

"Leave that to me." He glanced at the baron. It was hard to look at the man and not feel nauseous. "I'll take twenty-five percent."

"I beg your pardon?" Marstowe nearly pitched from his chair, gripping the edge of the table to regain his equilibrium.

"Twenty-five percent of whatever I find and recover," King repeated. "That is my offer to you, Marstowe. It's not negotiable."

Rotham was looking wide-eyed between the baron and King.

"You're a goddamn thief," Marstowe hissed.

The duke went ashen. Even the dealer paused.

"Because you are newly returned to England and, it seems, under some duress, I will let that…comment slide for now. But I am a businessman, Marstowe." King shrugged and crossed his boot over his knee. "And currently, you are nothing but a pauper." The now-familiar rage and revulsion coiled within him like angry snakes, constricting his chest and squeezing the air from his lungs. His gaze collided with Adrestia's, and inexplicably it became a little easier to breathe. "You do not need to agree to the terms," he said.

The baron stared at King, and then his expression cleared. "Very well then," he sneered. "Don' much think you can fin' what the lawyers and Runners haven't an'way."

"Meet me at the St James churchyard on Piccadilly," King said. "Tomorrow at two o'clock."

"What? Why?" the baron demanded.

Because that is where Evan is buried, King wanted to snarl. *And I want you to look upon what you did.*

"Seems like a good place to start if the church really does possess your fortune, no?" King said instead. "It is, after all, where your family used to attend services."

Marstowe stared at King. "How would y'know that?"

"You might be surprised by what I know." He lifted his glass to his lips. He saw the baron's gaze catch on the band of gold that circled his little finger and the ruby that glowed in the light.

"Where did y'get that ring?" Another card was being convulsively crushed in Marstowe's grasp.

King set down his glass and held up his hand, examining the ring. "A gift." And King had hidden Evan's gift almost immediately, knowing how angry the old baron would have been if he had known that Evan had given away an heirloom that was meant solely for the Marstowe heir. It had been another decade before King had been able to go back for it, and he hadn't taken it off since.

"To be honest, I never did care for the setting," he said, "though the ruby is spectacular. And I've always had an affection for rubies. They have been, after all, a talisman of passion and protection throughout the ages. Did you know that there are those who believe that a ruby can warn its wearer of impending danger?" He turned the ring slightly so that the elaborately engraved *W* could be seen on the side.

"Jesus, Marstowe, wha'd I tell y'bout the cards? 'Ave a care," Rotham scolded his companion with a grunt.

The baron jerked his attention back to his hand, trying to smooth the crushed cards.

King relaxed his grip on his walking stick, his hand stiff.

"Are you going to finish your game?" Adeline asked into the silence, sounding for all the world like a spoiled, bored debutante. "All this whispering is tiresome. I want to see who wins," she complained.

King knew very well she had heard every word uttered.

"I'll stay," muttered Marstowe.

The dealer's deft hands laid out a series of cards before her. An eight of spades, a five of clubs, a two of diamonds. She hesitated before turning over a final card. A six of spades. "Twenty-one," she said.

Marstowe cursed loudly and smacked his cards on the table. He stood, his chair scraping back and toppling with a loud clatter. "Bloody fixed game," he barked, pounding his fist on the two tens he had just discarded. He lunged unsteadily over the table in the direction of the dealer, who hadn't moved. "Bloody cheatin'—"

He stopped abruptly, his eyes bulging.

Adrestia had stood as well, and King took a savage satisfaction in knowing that the steel of her blade was undoubtably pressed discreetly against the baron's belly. Or possibly lower.

"You're drunk, my lord," Adrestia said clearly. "And lady luck has not graced you with her presence tonight. I think it's best if you retire before good sense and honor desert you as well."

A man dressed in Lavoie's livery and roughly the size of

an ox had started toward the table at the first sound of the disturbance, his expression set in thunderous, determined lines. He stopped, however, just shy of the table as the dealer held up her hand.

King estimated Marstowe had less than ten seconds before the ox man reduced him to an afterthought or the goddess of retribution ended her fact-finding mission early by simply running him through. King wondered if perhaps either of those possibilities wouldn't be for the best.

The baron swayed and gripped the edge of the table, and Adrestia shifted, her blade vanishing back into her skirts.

"My lord?" Adrestia prompted.

"Take your friend home, Rotham," King said coldly. "Before Alexander Lavoie discovers such a disappointing lack of judgment. He is somewhat fond of his vingt-et-un dealer and somewhat... unpredictable when it comes to cup-shot fools threatening her."

"Yes, yes. Come, Marstowe, mebbe we should retire." With a look of alarm, Rotham heaved himself unsteadily to his feet and staggered before catching himself. "I's late."

The baron smoothed a hand over the front of his coat and frowned, first at Adeline and then at the duke, as if he was unsure what had just transpired. In that moment King almost wished that the man would do something foolish. Something that King could react to with a swift, unyielding violence that would release the hatred and wrath pounding through his veins. Every muscle in his body was tense.

"Jenkins will escort you to your carriage, Your Grace," the dealer said, nodding at the ox man. "To make sure no one bothers you on your way out, of course."

The liveried man stepped forward and, with a firm, polite precision that indicated he had done it many times, shepherded the duke and the baron back through the crowd in the direction of the door.

King remained where he was and took a deliberate sip from his glass, once again trying to detach emotion from good sense.

The dealer was gathering the cards with deft movements, and if she was at all flustered by the disturbance, she didn't show it. "That was very well done," she said to Adrestia. "I must have a conversation with my modiste about modifying my skirts."

"I have no idea what you're talking about," Adrestia replied.

"Of course you don't." The dealer smiled faintly. "Allow me to introduce myself. Angelique Lavoie. Lady Angelique if you feel you must."

Adrestia stared at her.

"Lady Angelique does my accounting," King said, uncrossing his legs and standing. An uncomfortable restlessness was crawling through him.

"Your accounting?"

"She also owns this establishment," he added.

"With my husband," Lady Angelique clarified before transferring her attention to King. "Who is hardly unpredictable. Your presence on my gaming floor at the moment, however, is highly irregular."

"Perhaps I wanted to play a hand of vingt-et-un."

"And I am the queen of France." Lady Angelique's gaze went back to Adrestia. "A bottle of brandy that you poured liberally but did not take a sip from. An expensive investment, but in my experience—and, I think, yours—nothing clouds a man's judgment or loosens his tongue more than vast amounts of liquor and a cleverly tailored bodice. The duke and the baron were your marks."

Adrestia remained silent.

"I am in your debt for your...restrained assistance." Lady Angelique set the deck of cards aside. "And aside from poor judgment and ill-advised wagers, nothing gets traded more often in a gaming hell than rumor and gossip, usually in front of our dealers and servers. Perhaps I can assist if it is information you are after."

"Yes," said Adrestia.

"No," said King at the same time.

Both women frowned at him.

"You were after information about Marstowe's money," Lady Angelique speculated. "Or the missing money, as it may be."

"You already knew about it," King remarked.

"Of course I did. I have some experience with missing fortunes." Lady Angelique gave a small shrug. "But more to the point, we make it our business to know who can honor their vowels." She picked up the cards again and absently shuffled them. "Or in Marstowe's case, who might honor them for him. That's just good business."

"Do you know where the money is?" Adrestia asked.

Lady Angelique shook her head. "No. The late baron was not well in the year before his death. He withdrew from society and began acting erratically. Dismissed the staff, sold the horses and equipages. He'd wander the city, especially the London dockyards. Became a common sight prowling the London Docks and buying drinks for the Portuguese captains, of all people. Many friends tried to reach out in concern but were met only with suspicion and fear, and wild claims that he had to atone."

"Atone for what?" Adrestia asked.

King looked away, another wave of wrath almost suffocating him.

Lady Angelique shrugged again. "He barely made sense on the best of days. He was a complete recluse by the end. He had a single visitor the day that he died, and that was the rector of St James's. So yes, the working theory is that he gifted every Marstowe shilling to the church, but no one has been able to confirm this."

King kept his breathing steady as the brandy churned in his gut. He really was beginning to wish Adrestia had simply eviscerated Marstowe when she'd had the chance. Then they wouldn't be standing here, talking about the Westerleigh family and everything it might have to atone for.

"What about the late baron's wife?"

"The baroness died five, maybe six years before him. Unlike her husband, she was not overly sociable. She was always a very religious person but became a zealot after the deaths of her sons. One in some sort of stable accident, and the younger one to illness not long after. The grande dames of society couldn't get away from her fast enough."

The hate and horror slithered out again, thick and noxious, an icy perspiration pricking King's temples. Before tonight, he had thought that he was immune to such memories. Yet in the space of a single evening, the mere mention of what had transpired that day reduced him to that terrified, helpless eleven-year-old, cradling Evan's bloodied body and betrayed on all sides by those who were supposed to believe him.

"The new baron has been back in London for barely a sennight," Lady Angelique said. "Apparently it took the estate lawyers a while to track him to Virginia. But I'm afraid that that is the extent of my knowledge."

"Do not trouble yourself," Adrestia said. "This was productive. Thank you."

"And we should be going." King didn't care if he sounded desperate, and the air seemed to have become stifling, and the space seemed to have shrunk. He needed to get away from here. He signaled a footman and within a minute Adrestia's cloak had been delivered. "It was lovely to see you again, my lady." King offered Angelique a brief bow. "My regards to your husband."

"I'll pass them along." The gaming hell owner was watching him thoughtfully. "You can find your own way out?"

"We'll use the back."

"Certainly."

King offered Adrestia his arm, and she took it without hesitation, her hand steady. As before, it suddenly became easier to breathe. Unlike before, he was now very aware of the feel of her body as it pressed against his. And maybe this night, with all its emotion and revelations, had exhausted him more than he had wanted to admit, because he leaned into her, drawing strength from her presence.

She squeezed his arm but didn't look at him. Instead she only paused, turning back to speak to Lady Angelique.

"When you speak to your modiste, spend the money on a quality leather lining," Adrestia said, gesturing at her skirts. "Otherwise your blade will cut you to ribbons."

Lady Angelique smiled, though she was still considering King. "I have no idea what you're talking about."

CHAPTER 8

The ride back to Helmsdale was completed in utter silence. Though Adrestia said nothing, King was keenly aware of the weight of her gaze from across the confined space. She watched him steadily, her hands folded neatly in her lap, her expression unreadable. King gazed back, doing everything in his power to appear unaffected by her scrutiny. He looked away only when the carriage creaked to a stop in front of Helmsdale.

They disembarked and, in continued silence, King led Adrestia up the wide stone steps and into his now-deserted hall, dimly lit by the subdued fire in the hearth. He should be relieved to be home and anxious to retreat to his rooms, his private sanctuary away from this woman who had already seen far too much. But with every step, he became more aware of the heat trapped beneath Adrestia's hand where it rested on his arm, the soft rustle of her skirts where they brushed against his leg, and the scent of jasmine that swirled around him.

He stopped at the base of the stairs and put a hand on the banister, strangely reluctant to ascend. "I selected rooms for you upstairs and had them prepared," he said stiffly. Rooms not far from his own. Another inexplicable, impulsive decision from that evening.

The very few times he tolerated a guest, voluntary or otherwise, they resided in the small cottage near the stable. Close enough that his men might observe their presence and control comings and goings, and far enough away that they did not threaten King's privacy.

Adeline Archambault threatened far more than his privacy. He had no idea what he had been thinking, other than that he hadn't been. But to change his mind now and send her to a dark, freezing cottage would not only be callous, it would make him look like a fool.

"You should find the rooms comfortable," he continued, as if he had beautiful, bewitching women stay in his home regularly. "If you—"

"Was that you?" she asked, the first words she had spoken since they had left Lavoie's.

"Was what me?"

"Marstowe's missing fortune. Did you do that?"

"No."

"Mmm. I didn't think so. The timing didn't make sense, but I needed to hear you say it. Do you know where it is?"

"Not at the moment." King gestured up the stairs. "If you'd like to get settled—"

"And your ring?" She gestured at the ruby.

"A gift from Evan. The last thing he gave me before he died."

"Ah."

"You will not be disturbed in your rooms. My staff are only allowed access to the upper floor at my explicit direction—"

"I will meet Marstowe tomorrow," she interrupted quietly. "Alone."

"Absolutely not. I will handle Marstowe."

She shook her head. "You hired me for just this reason. You're going to have to trust me at some point."

"I do trust you." He just didn't trust himself.

"But not with the secrets that hurt you the most in the past. The secrets that cause you pain even now." Without warning, she stepped toward him and caught his hand in hers, turning it over and running her fingers over the proper bandage that had been applied over his palm. He should pull away from her touch, hide his bandaged hand under his coat. But he couldn't seem to do it.

"You did not follow me tonight because you were protecting your investment," she continued, her fingers winding through his.

He couldn't answer because her touch was sending a firestorm of heat through his veins.

"You followed me because you've reconsidered," she said into the silence.

"I beg your pardon?"

She sighed. "You regret your decision to engage my services." It wasn't really a question.

"No," King lied instantly. To admit that very regret now would be to admit failure on his part to preserve control. "We reached an agreement, and I gave you my word. Of all the things that I have lost in this life, the integrity of my word is not one of them. I will not renege on our agreement." He just needed to manage the outcome.

"You're not the first to discover after engaging me that some secrets are better left buried," she said. "And like the others who have come to reconsider, I release you from whatever promises you made regarding our agreement. I will not think less of you. But the sapphire stays with me."

She was giving him the perfect escape. He should seize her offer. He would simply say goodbye to Adeline Archambault on the morrow, and his secrets would remain safe. Wasn't this exactly what he had just wished for, sapphire be damned?

Yet he couldn't say the words. He couldn't let her go.

"No," he said, hating the weakness that his answer had betrayed.

"No?" She sounded less than convinced. "I will not judge you for reconsidering your decision. Your pain and your secrets are not commodities that I am entitled to but things that you may entrust to my care should I stay."

He looked away, aching with the strange longing that he had felt the first time he had laid eyes on her. He wished that she would rant and hurl accusations at him. He needed her angry. This gentle dissection of his soul was disquieting.

"And what if I had reconsidered?" he demanded harshly. "If I told you that I will simply kill Marstowe for what he did? What then?"

Her fingers tightened around his. "That would be your decision, of course."

"Jesus. I don't think you're hearing me. I could have killed him tonight. Thought about it more than once." His voice echoed loudly in the empty hall.

"Yet you didn't."

"I could have."

"And so could I. You don't scare me, King."

"I should scare you," he growled. "I am not a good person."

"Then what does that make me?"

"What?" Her question caught him off guard.

"I pulled a blade on the baron tonight, and you did nothing. Weren't even troubled."

"I knew exactly what you had done. Why the hell would I be troubled? You are magnificent with both your wits and your weapons."

She made a funny little noise. "But that's just it. You are the first person to make me feel...seen."

His gaze came back to hers. She was still watching him, her expression even, her eyes like pools of quicksilver. The urge to kiss her, to make her feel far more than merely seen, was overwhelming. This woman deserved so much more. She deserved to feel treasured and adored and respected.

But not by him.

He'd had women in the past, brief physical interactions that left both sated but that had never, ever involved emotion. Those interactions had barely involved kissing, or even much undressing, for God's sake, much less conversation or the surrender of secrets. Adrestia deserved a man as honorable as she was.

He should walk away from her right now.

Instead he lifted his free hand, pulling at the ties of her

cloak for the second time that night. The wool slipped off her shoulders and pooled at her feet. He ran his fingers along the edge of her jaw, tipping her chin up. He could feel the warmth of her breath against his hand, the softness of her skin beneath his fingertips.

Her eyes dropped to his lips, and whatever rational thoughts he was still clinging to scattered. He took a step forward, closing the gap between them. "Adrestia—"

"Adeline," she whispered. "Call me by my real name."

His breath caught, and for a wild, insane moment, he wished he could offer her the same. Because she made him feel seen too.

And that realization was terrifying. Even worse, he couldn't seem to muster the wherewithal to care.

"Adeline," he repeated, and her shiver as he uttered her name almost brought him to his knees. His thumb drifted over her bottom lip, and she closed her eyes. He backed her up a step against the wall. Desire licked through him, and he—

"Sir?" A door on the far side of the hall creaked open, and light flared. King stumbled away from Adeline and turned to find Elliot gripping a small lantern while rubbing his eyes sleepily. He was still dressed in his livery from the auction.

"What are you still doing up?" King asked. *Besides saving me from doing something monumentally stupid.* He'd already capitulated to weakness and lost enough control for one night. He could not afford to lose any more.

"Waiting for you, sir." His bright green eyes slid past King. "Your belongings are in your room upstairs, miss," he told Adeline. "I collected them from the Four Cocks for you."

"You did wh—" She stopped. "Thank you," she replied politely.

"How did you do it?" he asked, his face brightening. "How did you buz the key from Smithers?"

King groaned. "Elliot—"

"Assumptions," Adeline said, smiling at the boy.

"Assumptions?"

"When Smithers looked at me, he wasn't looking at a thief. He assumed I was a wealthy, refined lady, there by invitation. Had we been anywhere less, had I been wearing anything less, had I been acting as anything less, his assumptions would have differed, and he would have had his guard up. Costuming and presentation make all the difference, and they're worth investing in."

"Where did you work most?" Elliot asked eagerly.

"The Paris cabarets," she answered easily. "And gardens similar to the pleasure gardens you have here in London."

"Do you think that maybe you could show me—"

"Go to bed, Elliot," King interrupted. Because if he let him, Elliot wouldn't stop talking, judging from the besotted look on the boy's face.

"But—"

"I have an appointment at the St James's Church tomorrow afternoon at two. First thing tomorrow morning I need you to make the arrangements to have my carriage ready to ensure I am able to leave on time."

"Yessir."

"Now go to bed. It's late."

"Yessir." Elliot's face fell and he dutifully slipped back across the hall, vanishing back through the narrow door at the end.

"You sent a *child* to the Four Cocks?" Adeline asked as the door closed behind him.

King kept himself a careful distance from the seductive siren that was Adeline Archambault. He used to sneer at the stories of hapless sailors, thinking them weak and pitiable, without willpower. In retrospect, his naivete suddenly seemed laughable.

"Do not let Elliot's appearance fool you," he told her, seizing the safe subject she offered. "He probably has more sharp, pointy blades hidden on his person than you do. He is an opportunistic viper in the guise of a cherub. Worked the Finish for four years before he came to work for me."

"The Finish?"

"A coffeehouse in Covent Square. It's popular with gentlemen trying to correct the previous night's bad choices with coffee. A rich hunting ground for those with clever hands and clever blades. The two of you can compare notes tomorrow."

"And why does he work for you now?" she asked.

Because boys like Elliot generally died by their twelfth birthday, killed by their prey or fellow hunters. Because Elliot reminded him of Evan, not just in looks but in the way he defended those whom he cared for.

"Because I did not wish to see such talent wasted in the rookeries." He cleared his throat and started up the stairs. "You should retire. It's been a long night."

"I should what?" She was behind him, sounding somewhat incredulous.

"I believe I will retire as well," he continued brusquely, ignoring her question and reaching the long, narrow hallway above lit intermittently by sconces. He paused at the second door on his left and pushed it open. "Your rooms," he announced. "We can discuss our business arrangement further on the morrow." Not now, and certainly not standing in the hall outside her bedroom with soft light playing across her skin.

Adeline stepped into the room but stopped and turned

almost immediately. "We have unfinished business, King. I think we need to talk about what you—"

"I have nothing further to say to you tonight." It sounded cold, but he didn't trust himself with a woman who stole his breath, his composure, and his control merely by looking at him. Unlike earlier, King recognized the danger of allowing weakness and emotion to dictate action. He had survived unspeakable things on his own. He would survive this too.

"King, I—"

"Good night, Adeline." He closed her bedroom door.

CHAPTER 9

The snow that had been falling earlier had stopped, leaving a blanket of white over the grounds beyond the tall windows. Moonlight reflected off the sparkling crust and filtered through the diamond-shaped panes, filling the room with an eerie silver light. A massive bed dominated the far-right corner, a darkened door beyond leading into what was likely a dressing room. A small desk sat at the end of the bed, a discarded book resting on a simple wooden chair. In a near corner, a chaise longue was situated, a coat and waistcoat tossed over the brocaded back, a pair of boots abandoned at its feet, the polished toes gleaming dully in the light from the nearby hearth.

But all these details were insignificant, her attention riveted on the figure at the pianoforte on the far side, his back to her. And for the first time since she'd slipped into King's rooms, Adeline wondered if she'd made a mistake.

King was seated on a bench, his fingers flying over the

keys, his head down. Music filled the room, reaching a crescendo before becoming subdued, only to rise again in a haunting, stirring rhythm. Adeline's mouth went dry at the sight of his lean power illuminated in the moonlight. He'd stripped down to his shirt and trousers, his sleeves shoved to his elbows. The muscles in his forearms flexed as he swayed and bent, his shirt stretching across his shoulders, his red-gold hair falling just over his forehead as the music and his movements became more frantic.

The urge to push that hair away, to put a soothing hand on his back, was overwhelming. He was playing like a man possessed and, in essence, he was—held captive by the demons that had emerged from his past with the return of John Westerleigh. Which was why Adeline would not let him alone anywhere near Baron Marstowe tomorrow. A man who slew another in broad daylight in the middle of a churchyard would hang, no matter who he was.

She moved into the center of the room. "We need to talk."

His head snapped up, a discordant crash of notes ending his exertions, but the rest of him remained motionless. "There are locks on my doors."

"Not good ones."

"On the contrary." Still he didn't turn around. "You could have knocked."

"You wouldn't have answered."

"You can't be here."

"What's at the St James churchyard?" she asked.

"A church."

"Don't be obtuse."

His head dropped, his hands gripping the edge of the keys. He looked like a man caught in a struggle that only he could see. She'd had glimpses of that struggle in Lavoie's, in the carriage ride home, in the hallway outside her bedroom.

A man fighting his memories, fighting his emotions, fighting his instincts, and fighting her.

"It's where Evan is buried."

Adeline took a few more careful steps closer. "Thank you."

"What do you want, Adeline?" he demanded, turning around but remaining seated on the bench. He crossed his arms over his chest, his forearms flexing, and for the first time, she noticed his scars. They were old and faded, thick bands of discolored skin that circled both wrists. She had seen scars like that before.

In places where men and women spent their lives chained to walls.

She swallowed and dragged her gaze away from his scars and back to his face. His cool eyes impaled her, and she felt the force of that stare all the way through her body.

"I want to know the price you wish John Westerleigh to pay that will give you peace." She asked the question that she needed the answer to the most.

Even in the shadows, the anguish that tore across King's carefully cloaked features was easily visible. Adeline had seen that before too—a soul forced to relive a moment from which it had never truly healed.

King stood, stalking away from the bench and coming to stand in front of the windows. The curtains hadn't been drawn, and King was silhouetted by the ghostly white gardens beyond. Adeline followed him, her own shape a reflection in the glass as she came to stand beside him.

She had changed out of her dress, pulling on her black trousers and coat for both warmth and practicality.

"Marstowe's money is gone," she said. "Is that enough?"

"No. There is no amount of money that is worth Evan's life."

Adeline sighed. She hadn't expected a different answer.

"Would you see him lose his seat in the House? See him publicly accused? Imprisoned?"

He put one hand against the glass, his other clenched at his side. "I want him to know fear. I want him to feel what Evan felt in those moments before he stole his life. I want him to know what it's like to be thrust alone into a nightmare from which he cannot wake."

Adeline chose her next words carefully. "Revenge is a dangerous mistress. Sir Francis Bacon once wrote, 'A man that studieth revenge keeps his own wounds green, which otherwise would heal and do well.'"

"You think that I should just forgive and forget?"

"I didn't say that. No one can ever truly forget. And forgiveness—well, that is something that I cannot determine for anyone. I'm only saying that, in some cases, the need to right the past comes at a high price to the future."

King remained motionless. "Sir Francis also wrote, 'Revenge is a kind of wild justice' and 'If we do not maintain justice, justice will not maintain us.'"

"He did." It would seem the bookshelves in King's study were not there for decoration. "But it's a fine line, that which lies between justice and revenge. And neither can bring back the dead, nor undo past wrongs."

"I know that."

"Good."

"Why do you do this?" he demanded.

"Do what?"

"Seek revenge—justice for those you don't even know. For people you do not care about."

"What?" She heard the edge to her question.

"They're nothing but clients, Adeline."

"They're people first," she said. "And I care very much about each person."

King made a sound in the back of his throat. "Even me?"

The man who seemed to understand and accept her more than anyone had?

"Especially you." Her answer was barely a whisper.

She didn't really see him move. One second she was standing beside him, the next he was in front of her, her chest almost brushing his, her head tipped back so she could see his face.

"You can't be here," he rasped.

"You've left me little choice."

"You should go."

"No."

"I need you to leave."

"Tell me why."

His hand came up, and his fingers drifted along the side of her jaw, tangling in her hair. One by one, he pulled the pins from the back of her head, each falling to the floor, allowing her hair to spill over her shoulders. She shivered.

"You and your damned questions," he murmured.

"Tell me why," she said again. "And tell me the truth. And then I'll go."

"Because you make me weak." He sounded almost angry, even as his fingers were tracing the top of her ear with exquisite care, dropping down to her lobe and then her neck.

The absurdity of that statement registered only dimly. Her entire body was a fiery mess of nerves, each stretched taut, yearning to discover where his fingers might go next. "You are not weak, King."

"I needed you earlier tonight." His words were stilted. "I still do."

"Good," she whispered.

"No." He shook his head and brushed his thumb over her lips. "Needing people makes one weak. But you..." He trailed off. "I need you. And I can't stay away from you. I keep trying but—"

"Then stop trying." It was a reckless thing to say.

He groaned softly and dipped his head, his lips finding the spot on her neck just behind her ear. A decadent throb ignited at the junction of her legs.

"Perhaps I need you just as much," she managed to gasp.

He caught her earlobe with his teeth, tugging gently as his hands slid over her shoulders and down her arms. "I am not what you need."

Adeline's head tipped back. "Let me be the judge of that."

His hands slipped to her lower back, pulling her against him. Her breasts pressed against his chest, heavy and aching, the friction against her nipples sending currents of pleasure burning through her.

His lips hovered just over hers, not taking, only asking.

Adeline slid her hands up his arms, over his shoulders, and cupped his face in her hands. The short stubble on his cheeks was rough beneath her fingers, his skin warm. "Kiss me," she said.

Very slowly, he brought his mouth to hers. It started gently at first, her lips tasting his, teasing and exploring the feel of him. One of his hands slid up her back, pulling her more firmly against him as he deepened the kiss. She parted her lips instantly, reveling in the heady feel of his tongue stroking hers, the heat and rhythm of his kiss making the pulsing throb between her legs intensify into an unbearable ache.

Her hips tipped involuntarily, wanting to feel more of him.

He groaned deep in his throat, a raw, unguarded sound that made her pulse skip. His unmistakable arousal was thick and hard beneath the fall of his trousers, pressing against her lower abdomen. That he was just as vulnerable to whatever this was between them was electrifying.

"I've wanted to kiss you from the moment you stepped into my study," he said roughly. He nudged his thigh in between hers, pressing her back up against the cold glass of the window. With smooth motions he pulled her coat from her shoulders and let it drop, tracing the ridges of her collarbones beneath her shirt.

Adeline closed her eyes, letting the sensation of his touch flood through her. His hands dropped to cup her breasts through the worn linen of her shirt, his thumbs gliding over her nipples. She moaned softly and arched, pushing herself more fully into his hands. His mouth drifted along her jaw, leaving embers over her skin in their wake.

Adeline dropped her own hands, her fingers yanking the hem of his shirt from his waistband and then pushing the fabric up to explore the planes of his abdomen and chest. His muscles contracted beneath her touch, and his breath hissed in her ear.

He shifted, and then his hands were cupping her buttocks, lifting her against him. Adeline gasped and wrapped her legs around his waist, the bulge in his trousers now pressed exactly where she needed it most. She twined her arms around his neck as he kissed her savagely, surrendering her mouth to his.

This time it was King who rocked his hips into her, his tongue and his body once again keeping time.

"Yes," she gasped against his mouth. "Don't stop."

There was something incredibly devastating about being wrapped around this man as he slowly took her apart, kiss by kiss, touch by touch. As if there were no real break to determine where he ended and she started.

He dropped his head, dragging his tongue over the hollow at the base of her throat, and Adeline moaned again. He nuzzled lower, and Adeline tipped her head back, and then his mouth was on her nipple, sucking through the threadbare linen. His teeth grazed the peak, sending a bolt of fire through her, and she bucked against him.

"Please," she whispered.

He did it again, this time paying homage to her other breast as his hips rolled steadily, bringing her to the brink. His hands gripped her hard against him, and that perfect pressure sent her tumbling over the edge.

Adeline curled her fingers into the back of his hair as white-hot pinwheels of ecstasy exploded behind her eyelids. Her entire body bowed, every muscle clenching as bright, blinding pleasure streaked through her, pulsing and pounding. King held her the entire time, pressed relentlessly to him as she rode out each wave, without giving her quarter.

Adeline's head fell to his shoulder, panting. He had just unraveled her fully clothed against a damn window. And holy hell, she wanted to experience that all again, but this time with him buried deep inside her. This time with nothing between their bodies.

"Take me to bed," she whispered. "Now."

King made a feral noise and spun her away from the window, carrying her over to his bed. He set her down on the coverlet, one knee between her legs, one hand braced at her shoulder. His eyes were blue flames again, his breathing ragged, his arousal undeniable.

Adeline sprawled on the bed, breathless and aching, her clothing in disarray and her hair jumbled around her. She had never felt so gloriously feminine. So gloriously powerful.

She lifted her arm and trailed a finger down his chest and abdomen, stopping at the waistband of his trousers. "Let me see you," she whispered. "All of you."

King stared down at her, unmoving, his breath still coming in shallow gasps. He seized her wrist with his other hand. "No."

Adeline froze. Her heart stuttered. "No?"

"I can't."

"You can't." She was dimly aware she was repeating him like a half-wit, but honestly, what the hell was happening here? There was pain and regret in his voice, but Adeline didn't understand why.

"I won't," he said hoarsely.

"You won't what?" Adeline tried to sit up, but he wouldn't let her. Instead he crawled into the bed beside her, pulling her against him so that her back was pressed to his chest. His arm was like a steel band over her waist, his erection still hard against her buttocks.

She arched against that hardness, wanting this man with every fiber in her body. Wanting to feel him move inside her, wanted to watch as she took him apart as he had her. "King—"

"I won't fuck you simply because I'm weak. Because that would make me no better than the man who tries to obliterate his regrets and woes in women or gin."

"That's not at all what this—"

"You deserve better, Adeline. A man so much better than I." His voice was raw, yet he kept his arm tightly around her.

She tried to turn but he wouldn't let her. "Let me decide who—"

"Don't. Please."

Adeline exhaled and closed her eyes in frustration. "You're not—"

"Who taught you how to fight?" he whispered raggedly.

"What?"

"Will you tell me who taught you how to fight?"

Adeline shifted her head on the pillow. She didn't fully understand what was going through King's mind, but she understood that, at this moment, this man needed something different. Something far more intimate than just her touch.

"My father." She found his hand with hers, covering it gently. He didn't pull away. "Who taught you about art?"

He drew in a sharp breath. "That's not how this works."

"Do you want me to stay?"

His fingers grasped hers, and she could almost hear the war being waged in his head. "Yes," he finally said, making Adeline's heart expand with something that was almost as painful as it was tender.

"Good. Because I don't want to leave. Who taught you about art?"

He might have chuckled, though it came out as more of a muffled groan. "Very well. Art was Evan's passion even from a very young age. He taught me what he knew. The combined galleries and palaces of Italy taught me the rest."

"You've been?"

"Many times. I highly recommend the Uffizi if you have not had the opportunity to experience it."

"I have not. But I'd like to."

"Then I'll take you there one day," he said in Italian.

Adeline didn't react. She hadn't spoken Italian in years, but she understood what he had said, and she wasn't sure if it was his unexpected mastery of the language or the vow he made that had her heart skipping.

And it was far too easy to desperately want to believe that such a journey might one day be possible.

He cleared his throat. "Your family was titled," he rushed on, switching back to English.

"What makes you think that?" She let him change the subject.

"Your speech suggests an education that extends far

beyond what a common pickpocket working the Paris cabarets might have expected."

"As does yours."

"I never worked the Paris cabarets," he said. "And aside from your speech, your skill with that rapier suggests that your teacher was also very skilled. Thus, I can only conclude that your father was trained by the best. And the best is expensive. And exclusive. I'm not sure it was your father who taught you to fight with that knife, however. No gentleman learns that."

"*Mon Dieu*, all that from a single alley skirmish." This time, she spoke in French.

"Tell me if I'm right," he replied in the same language.

Adeline twisted and turned to face him, propping herself up on her elbow. He gazed up at her, one hand behind his head, the other resting easily on her hip. He looked rumpled and devastating and as unguarded as she had ever seen him. Her stomach did a slow flip through a storm of butterflies, and a soft warmth flooded through her. She looked away from his face, afraid that if she didn't, she would give in to the impulse to kiss him again.

She reached for his hand at her waist, her fingers tracing the thick band of scar tissue. "Yes," she said. "My parents were the Comte and Comtesse de Chadonnet. In the absence of a son and anything that resembled a conventional upbringing, my father taught me about rapiers and politics, and my mother taught me about history, languages, and maths. What are these scars from?"

He tried to yank his hand from hers but she held fast.

A muscle was flexing in his jaw. "I was imprisoned for nine years."

She had heard harrowing stories about London prisons, Newgate in particular. That he had survived nine years in such conditions was as horrifying as it was astounding.

"What happened to your family?" he asked.

"They died." An unwelcome pang of grief stabbed her. "What were you in prison for?"

King tipped his head back, his eyes sliding from hers. He seemed to be gazing at something only he could see. "For trusting the wrong person," he said finally.

Adeline wanted to press him further but stopped herself, afraid that he would shut down completely. "I'm sorry."

"Don't be. Because there is absolutely nothing in this world that can scare me any longer. I lived through hell and survived." He cleared his throat. "How did your family die?"

Her fingers traced the muscle of his forearms up to his elbow. There were other scars there too, pale white lines mixed with darker ones that suggested defensive wounds from blades. Adeline had a few herself. "My parents lost everything in the Revolution. Their Paris home, and the château and vineyards. They fled only with what they could carry. And me."

"Where did you go?"

"Italy at first. Spain later. We moved around a great deal over the next decade, staying where we could, pretending to be people we weren't. But my parents longed to return to Paris. When the nobility was revived with limited privileges in 1805, they immediately returned to reclaim their birthright. I went with them." She stopped, struggling and unsure why. It had all happened so long ago. "They were killed two days later by a man shrieking, 'Remember Robespierre, death to aristocrats.' He shot both my parents in the middle of rue Saint-Honoré while we were walking to the market."

"Jesus. I hope he paid—"

"He was never caught."

His forehead creased. "You never got justice."

"No." She shook her head. "I never did."

"Is that why you do what you do?"

"Maybe. Probably." She bit her lip. "Yes," she decided. She lay back down beside him, staring up at the ceiling. "I know what it feels like to have no one on your side. To feel lost and helpless and angry. I never got justice for my parents, but I could get it for others."

"That's very—"

"Selfish," she finished for him. "It was selfish. It was easier to focus on others who were suffering so that grief didn't consume me whole. It started with small things—writing appeals and petitions on behalf of those who couldn't in exchange for food or clothing. Later, slightly bigger jobs like recovering a set of molds stolen from a chandler in exchange for payment. My...reputation grew from there, as did the gravity of the injustices I was tasked with addressing."

He shifted, moving his arm from behind her head to slide around her shoulders and pull her close. Her head came to rest against his chest.

"And now?"

Adeline listened to his heart beating steadily, his voice rumbling low. "Now it's all I know."

"You can't keep taking on everyone's pain and making it yours, Adeline. That is too much to ask of one person. You can't live like that."

"Secrets lose their power when they are shared. Grief loses its burden when it is shared." She hated how defensive she sounded.

"And whom have you shared your secrets with? Whom have you grieved your losses with?" he asked.

You, she almost said. She hadn't shared any of this with anyone outside of this tiny cocoon of candor. A tear slid down her cheek. Horrified, she wiped it away before it could fall.

"How did you get out of prison?" she asked abruptly.

His body tensed beside her. "I escaped. How did you come to learn how to survive in Litchfield alleys?"

"The same way you did," she said. "The hard way. My education was swift and brutal. I imagine the streets of Paris are not so different from the streets of London."

"But surely your parents would have had friends or family who would have—"

"All dead or scattered in the Terror. At the time, raised on stories of the mobs and given what I witnessed, I believed it safer to simply disappear on the streets." She paused. "How did you escape?"

His hand tightened around her shoulder. "I trusted the right person. Still trust him."

"Was he a prisoner too?"

"Yes. He saved my life. And I repaid that debt not so long ago."

"And now?"

King's chest rose and fell beneath her cheek. "Now he's a duke."

Adeline played with a button of his shirt, her fingers circling the smooth edge. "I'm glad you have this duke."

"He's not my duke."

"Will you trust me the way you trust your duke?"

King reached over her and drew the coverlet across their bodies. "I am trusting you not to kill me in my sleep," he said. "I'm trusting you not to steal the Rubens from my wall downstairs. And I'm trusting you not to give Smithers another apoplexy by filching his key again."

But I don't trust you with my secrets, Adeline finished for him silently.

"Will you let me come with you to the churchyard tomorrow?" she asked.

"Go to sleep, Adeline," he whispered, pressing a chaste kiss to the top of her head.

And when Adeline woke the next morning, sunlight pouring through the windows, King was already gone.

CHAPTER 10

The sun was blinding in its brilliance against the snow.

It wouldn't last long, King knew, before the newly fallen ground cover surrendered to mangy patches of melted snow and ice. But for now, the churchyard looked a little bit as he imagined heaven might, every surface glistening with an unmarred mantle of dazzling white.

There were a handful of people in the churchyard, including a small knot of mourners who were just now departing from a newly dug grave. Two men who had been sweeping the gravel paths stepped respectfully out of the way, though none of the mourners spared them a second glance.

King walked through the rows of headstones, his boots leaving deep imprints. On some of the stones, the snow had obscured the inscriptions, but that didn't matter. King came here often. He knew where he was going.

He reached the northwest corner of the churchyard, the collection of Westerleigh headstones arranged in a neat row along the path. At the edge, the familiar stone with its sculpted angel rose from the ground.

> EVAN WESTERLEIGH
> BELOVED SON
> 1785–1798

King knelt on one knee and set the small posy down atop the headstone, the brilliant yellow burst at the center of each flower ringed by white and then an ever-deepening amethyst. Against the snow, they were like a spray of gems.

"Those are lovely," a voice said behind him. "What are they?"

King rose from where he had knelt, brushing the snow from his trousers. He knew that voice as well as he knew his own. It had delivered him from moments of overwhelming despair and kept hope alive during the nights that would not end.

"Heartsease," King replied. "In the Renaissance they represented remembrance, memory, and spiritualization. Evan always liked painting them."

Noah Ellery, the Duke of Ashland, joined him, a yellow hothouse rose twirling gently between his gloved fingers. Both men looked down at the headstone, neither speaking. The clatter of hooves and rattle of wheels echoed outside the churchyard from Jermyn Street and Piccadilly. Nearby, a young boy's voice rose, peddling the newest edition of a scandal sheet to pedestrians hurrying by.

"I used to love winter," King said idly, tucking his bare fingers into his sleeves. "I would find Evan on street corners or garden squares trying to paint the city under snow. I'd tease him because he could never quite finish before the snow melted if it was too warm, or his paints froze if it was too cold. At the time, I never understood his need to capture individual moments." He nudged the snow with the toe of his boot. "Now I wish I could have just one of those moments back."

The duke was silent, listening with the same quiet intensity King had come to associate with the boy he had been in those first awful years and then later with the man he had become. Incarceration had not broken Ashland. Nor had it changed the inherent goodness that had always dwelled within him. King could not say the same of himself.

"Would we have been friends?" King asked abruptly. "You and I? If we had not been cast into hell together?"

"Why do you ask this now?" The duke touched a thorn on the rose's stem.

"Of late, I've reflected on lost moments, I suppose. Moments where a different choice, a different action, a different twist of fate would have changed everything."

Ashland looked down, once again turning the rose over in his fingers. "Yet all of those moments are gone. You can remember them or forget them, like them or hate them, but you cannot change them. Only the moments to come can be changed."

King exhaled, his breath a silvery cloud in the air. "Evan would have liked you. Neither of you ever said much, but when you did, it always seemed to be maddingly sensible." He paused, tilting his walking stick so that the silver handle gleamed in the sunlight. "Why are you really here, Ashland?"

"I think the better question is, Why are you?"

"I've come to pay my respects."

"Hmm." The rose in Ashland's fingers stilled. With great care he bent and placed it on top of Evan's grave next to the heartsease. His charcoal-colored coat stretched across his wide shoulders, his light blond hair falling over his eyes. Slowly he brushed away the snow clinging to the decorative scrolling engraved above Evan's name.

"Say what's on your mind, Ashland," King said wearily.

The duke straightened, his green eyes regarding King. "What do you need?"

"I beg your pardon?"

"I am a damned duke, King. And with that title comes a shocking degree of power. Power in places that even you do not have it, despite rumors to the contrary."

"Your point, Ashland?"

"If you need something, ask. I do not wish to see you do anything rash."

King stared at the flowers on top of the stone, the snow sparkling like a mantle of tiny diamonds in the light. "Like kill a baron on the grounds of St James's Church?"

"Like kill a baron on the grounds of St James's Church," Ashland agreed.

King reached the obvious conclusion. "Lady Angelique spoke to you."

"Lady Angelique spoke to my wife. And Elise spoke to me."

"How quaint. Did you all trade gossip over tea and cakes?"

Ashland ignored his barb. "She seemed to think that you've hired a new assassin. A very beautiful, very clever assassin."

"She's not an assassin. But yes, she is beautiful. And clever."

"She also seemed to be of the opinion that you are . . . rather taken with this particular assassin."

"Did you not hear me? She's not an assassin." King didn't address the other part of Ashland's comments. Mostly because he couldn't deny it, and Noah Ellery would see right through him. He wasn't taken, he was bewitched.

"Is she here? In the churchyard?"

"Yes." King hadn't seen her here, which meant only that. He would be deluding himself if he thought she was anywhere else. That knowledge, instead of being irritating, was like a soothing balm to his soul.

"Did you ask Marstowe here to kill him?" Ashland asked. To his credit, he sounded merely curious. But then, Ashland had known his share of violence long before he had become a duke.

"If I were to kill the man, I most certainly wouldn't do it here with a half dozen witnesses." He gestured at the bundled people scattered throughout the churchyard. "Though the convenient proximity of a burial ground does hold some appeal."

"So the men who have been sweeping the same stretch of pathway for the last quarter hour are not yours."

King glanced at the two men with the brooms. They were brothers, their features too similar to mark them as anything else. Both were wearing somber colors, nothing so rich nor so ragged as to draw attention. "No. Those are the Darling brothers. And they work for themselves."

"And who are the Darling brothers?"

"Purveyors of fine medical specimens."

Ashland gave him a blank look.

"Resurrection men. They sell to medical schools in Scotland. Edinburgh, generally. I have used their services on occasion. They are very good at making bodies vanish into thin air."

Ashland stared hard at King. King stared back.

The duke cleared his throat. "That night you saved my life and killed—"

"Credible deniability, Ashland."

"What?"

"Credible deniability. A little something I learned from my assassin who is not an assassin. And it's what I'm giving you here."

"Did you ask them here today?" the duke demanded. "Thinking that there would be a body you'd need to make vanish?"

"We've already been over this, Ashland. No."

"King—"

"I wish he had died." King knocked the snow from the edge of the grave in a violent blizzard. "I wish the twisted fuck had died aboard that packet off the coast. He's sick." He pulled out his pocket watch, ignoring the way his fingers were white around its edges. "He's also late."

Ashland merely clasped his hands behind his back. "Perhaps your assassin has already done her job."

"For the love of God, she's not an assassin."

"Hmmm." He unclasped his hands. "Did you find Marstowe's money?"

"My my, Lady Angelique really was effusive."

Ashland ignored that too. "Did you?"

"Not yet." King tucked his watch back into his pocket. "The rector swears he has no idea where it is. I believe him."

Ashland pinched the bridge of his nose. "Why?"

"I suggested that he keep his mistress at a better address. Currently she lives in a hovel near the Dials. It's a dangerous area. One never knows what may happen to an unsuspecting woman who travels alone at night to meet her paramour."

"You blackmailed him and threatened his mistress?"

"I did nothing of the sort. I merely offered him some good advice. Free of charge, I might add."

"How could you possibly know he had a mistress?"

"Because I generally don't visit this churchyard during daylight hours. Neither does she." He paused. "The rector did tell me, however, that the late baron called him to his house right before he died and offered him fifty pounds to take whatever measures were necessary to make sure that his family's graves in the churchyard were not disturbed. Someone, it seemed, had disturbed the grave of the younger Westerleigh brother just before the old baron's death."

"Resurrection men?" Ashland glanced at the Darling brothers.

"No, grave robbers, more likely. Corpses need to be fresh for the medical folk."

The duke made a face. "Perhaps the money is truly gone."

"*Tsk.* Nothing is truly gone, Ashland. One just needs to know where to look. I think your wife might agree with me. She found you, after all."

"King—"

"Go, Ashland. Go be a good husband and a good duke and do all the good things that I never have and never will."

"I could take the matter to the courts—"

"And risk exposing your secrets as well as mine? Not a chance, Ashland. I am not that selfish. I will handle this."

"Don't do anything rash. Please."

"Do not worry," King said. "When I do decide what it is I will do, it will most certainly not be rash."

CHAPTER 11

King found Adeline sitting in the wide chair behind his desk, considering the depiction of Judith beheading Holofernes. That she had beaten him back to Helmsdale did not surprise him. He had stayed in that churchyard in front of Evan's grave long after Ashland had departed. Long after it had become clear that Baron Marstowe was not going to appear.

"There are locks on my doors," King said for the second time.

"Not good ones," Adeline replied again without turning around. She was dressed in her black trousers and coat, her rapier sheathed at her side, her curved knife held absently in her hands. "Who painted this?"

"Caravaggio." A faint draft swirled through the study as he shut the door behind him. "I had the version Rubens painted but I sold it. I much prefer this one."

Adeline ran her fingers along the smooth surface of her knife. The light from a half dozen sconces that had been lit against the encroaching darkness danced off the steel. "Tell me, is Judith a good person?"

"I beg your pardon?"

"Judith." Adeline gestured at the painting with the tip of her knife. "Is she a good person?"

"I don't understand your question."

"Look at her. She is assassinating a general without remorse. She has his hair wrapped in her fist, his head wrenched back, and her blade deep across his throat. She displays neither revulsion nor fear, satisfaction nor pleasure. She merely looks..."

"Stoic."

"I was going to suggest *determined*. But then I suppose all assassins should be both stoic and determined."

"Judith wasn't an assassin."

"She was that day."

The desk creaked as King settled his weight on the corner. "She didn't have a choice."

"No?"

"Bethulia would have been destroyed, her people slaughtered. She saved those she loved."

"So she was a good person. A good person who was

forced to do an awful thing to make sure she and those she cared for survived."

King opened his mouth and abruptly closed it again. "I know what you're doing."

Adeline's head tipped back, and she gazed at the painting for a long time in silence. "I envy Judith," she said eventually.

"Why?"

She jabbed her knife in the direction of the painting. "She's not alone." She laughed softly, though there was no humor in it. "Her maid is there to help her kill Holofernes."

"Her maid only conceals and carries the severed head in her basket."

"A task Judith could have easily done," Adeline replied. "The maid is not just carrying a head, she's carrying some of Judith's burden." She was still gazing at the painting, a note of sadness creeping into her words. "Her maid already knew what it would cost Judith to kill a man, and this was the only way she could lessen that burden. She didn't want Judith to be alone in her task."

King pushed himself off the desk and came to stand near Adeline, wishing he could smooth away the sorrow and weariness that had settled across her features. But to touch her now would be folly because he wouldn't just offer her a token of comfort. He would take her in his arms and kiss away her sadness and tell her that everything would be all right. And that was absurd because inane platitudes never made anything all right, and they both knew it.

"I'm tired," she said. "Tired of fighting alone," she clarified, looking up at him. "Of not belonging to anywhere or anyone. Of not having that one person who will put severed heads in baskets so that you don't have to."

You could belong to me as I fear I already belong to you.

He swallowed the words before he could make a fool out of himself.

"You need a partner, then," he said instead, trying to sound objective.

"Are you volunteering to be that partner?"

A peculiar ache settled like a vise around his chest. For one terrifying second, he wanted to say yes. He shook his head hard because there was no point in entertaining an idea that would never come to pass. "I must decline," he said with all the cavalier wit he could muster. "As much as I might enjoy transporting severed heads, I hear the hours are wretched."

She tried to smile but it didn't reach her eyes. "Then perhaps it's just time for a change."

"The château."

"It was always my father's dream that he could one day reclaim it. Make the vineyards productive again."

"And is that your dream too?"

"Maybe. I'd like the chance to find out."

"And what does a goddess of retribution know about wine making?" he asked.

"Almost nothing," she admitted. "But in Italy and Spain I loved watching the men and women in the vineyards we saw. Entire generations of families that had the ability to coax something from the earth, to grow and care for it and make it into something wonderful..." She trailed off. "I envied that. I feel like maybe Falaise d'Argent is a place where I could find the remnants of my own familial roots and grow them there. Finally find the place I belong."

"And what happens to Adrestia?"

She smiled faintly. "She'll always be there. Just in case."

"You will have your home in France." King spoke quietly, not remembering making the decision to tell her this. "Along with the man heading to Spain, I sent a man to Lille this morning. He'll take care of the paperwork and payment for Falaise d'Argent to be yours."

Adeline looked up at him, her eyes wide. "But I haven't found justice for you yet."

"You will. We will."

"But I—"

"You're here right now, and that's enough." But she wouldn't be here forever. She would leave, and he would be alone—

He rubbed his face with his hands. Jesus, he sounded positively maudlin.

"The man who was with you in the churchyard. Was he your duke?"

He stilled. "My duke?"

"The one you spoke of—the one who was imprisoned with you?"

"What makes you think that?"

"You didn't guard your emotion with him."

King didn't answer right away. He had known that she would be there watching for the baron. He hadn't considered how carefully she might have been watching him. "Yes."

"Does he know what the baron did?"

"Enough." But not all. No one knew it all.

"Was he there to talk you out of murder?"

"Yes. He's a good man. Noble and honorable."

"And he really thought you might kill a baron in a church-yard full of witnesses?" she asked. She was making a clear effort to keep her voice light, but it sounded forced.

"The thought had crossed his mind."

"Where was he today?" she asked. "Marstowe?"

"I don't know."

Adeline uncrossed her foot from her knee, her boot

thumping softly to the rug. "I tried the Marstowe house in Hanover Square, but he wasn't there."

"Perhaps he simply refused to answer the door."

"I didn't knock, exactly," Adeline told him. "The house was deserted, as were the stables in the mews around back. It was clear he does not yet have a staff, probably because servants and horses cost money. A groom further down did tell me that he's seen Marstowe use Rotham's carriage from time to time."

King frowned faintly.

"There are reasonable explanations for his failure to meet you this afternoon, of course. Perhaps he was too drunk to remember the conversation last night. Or he was too much of a coward to meet you and is on another packet back to Virginia as we speak." Very carefully she set her knife on the surface of the desk and stood. Without warning she brushed a stray piece of hair from his temple, her fingers lingering against his skin.

"How did he kill Evan?" she asked.

He had known the question would come eventually, had prepared answers in his head that would satisfy her without giving away too much. Yet right now, he couldn't seem to think of those answers. Not with her silver eyes watching him, her touch unapologetic.

"He hit him," King heard himself say. "A blow to the head that killed him instantly." King made a fist with his injured hand, and the resulting sting of the wound across his palm was a welcome pain.

"Tell me why." Adeline's tone was businesslike, devoid of pity, and King was grateful for that small mercy.

"Why?" he stalled.

"Tell me why he killed Evan."

"To gain access to the title." That was one of his prepared

answers. An answer that kept the true horror of that day at a safe distance.

Adeline's hand dropped and her eyes glittered. "Don't do that."

"Don't do what?"

"Lie to me."

King sucked in a breath. It was terrifying how easily she seemed to be able to read him. It was equally terrifying just how much of the truth he wanted to tell her.

King swallowed. He would need to give her some of the truth. "Marstowe—" He stopped. God, after everything that he had seen, everything that he had survived, speaking of a single, violent moment in a life full of violence should not have been this difficult. He was letting weakness creep in again.

King cleared his throat. "Marstowe had a fondness for young boys. I suspect he still does."

Adeline was silent.

"Evan resisted his advances. And paid for that with his life." He braced himself for her response.

"That's better. Thank you for the truth." Again there was no pity, just a steady acceptance of what he had told her.

It took a moment for the realization to sink in that Adeline Archambault was only the third person to whom he had ever told that truth.

And she was the first person to believe him.

"Why didn't you just tell me this at the beginning?" she asked.

"Because I was there and I couldn't stop it." Not the whole truth, but close enough. "And I hate myself for not saving him." That was real.

"You were a child."

"That may have been an excuse then, but I am no longer a

child. What he did to Evan he'll have done to someone else. He'll do it again now that he's back. And I won't allow that to happen," he said roughly. He felt unaccountably shaky, as though he had just run a footrace to the point of exhaustion but a hundred stone had slipped from his shoulders along the way.

Adeline picked up her knife and slid it back into the sheath at her waist. "I think we should have someone watch his house," she said slowly. "To do a better job of keeping track of his movements. If he...if he tries to abuse another child, we will be able to stop him before it happens. You and I can't do it by ourselves. Do you have men who might be able to observe in a rotation so that they are not so conspicuous?"

King mentally berated himself for not doing this last night. Like everything else, he'd blame the oversight on the loss of his wits in the face of meeting a dead man. "Yes. I can have Smithers organize that."

"What will you tell him?"

"Nothing. My men are not friends entitled to explanations. They are paid to obey orders and not ask questions." King reached for the tasseled bellpull and gave it a yank. He'd tell Elliot to fetch Smithers immediately. The man would be in a hurry to redeem himself.

A minute later, a sharp knock sounded on the study door before it opened. Smithers appeared in the doorway, key in his hand, his narrow gaze skidding away from Adeline. "Yessir?"

King frowned slightly. It was Elliot's responsibility to answer summonses, though Smithers's presence saved some time.

"I need you to watch a residence," King said briskly. "From now until midnight. And I'll need to arrange a scheduled rotation of men to continue after your shift. I want him watched every minute of every day."

"Of course." Smithers nodded curtly. "Anything in particular we should be looking for?"

"I need to know when the owner of that residence goes out, where he goes, and what he does. Do not let him out of your sight. You or any of the men are fully encouraged to intervene in the event that he puts another's life or well-being in danger."

"Intervene?" Smithers asked. "To what degree?"

"To whatever degree is necessary to make him stop."

"Understood."

King knew that Smithers did.

"Who is it that you'd like us to follow?" Smithers inquired. "And where is the residence?"

"Baron Marstowe," King replied. "His address is in Hanover Square."

Smithers frowned, his sharp features becoming even more pinched. "I don't understand, sir," he said.

"What is it you don't understand?" King demanded. Smithers was usually one of his more incisive—

"Marstowe was here this afternoon. Perhaps an hour ago?"

King heard Adeline's sharp intake of breath.

"What did he want?" she demanded.

Smithers glanced uneasily between King and Adeline, and the hairs on the back of King's neck stood up.

"What did he want, Smithers?" King repeated.

"He said he was working with you to recover some money. He confirmed that you had met at the St James's churchyard, but that you were in need of further assistance and had asked the baron to fetch Elliot." His hands were clenching and unclenching. "Was that not the case?"

"No," King managed to say. "It is not the case at all."

He dragged in a laboring breath, feeling as though he were underwater. "Did Elliot go with him?"

"Yes."

King couldn't even answer. Jesus Christ. This was his fault. He didn't know if Marstowe had come for the boy because he believed King had something to do with his missing fortune or if the baron knew who he truly was, or if he simply wanted Elliot for his own twisted purposes. Regardless, King had overplayed his hand. He should have kept his distance and let Adeline handle the baron.

Or he should have simply killed Marstowe at the very beginning.

"Sir, Elliot may be small, but he can take care of himself."

Smithers wasn't wrong. Elliot was indeed small, and he could take care of himself provided he saw the danger coming. But he wouldn't be looking for it. Not from Marstowe.

Because King had admitted Marstowe to his auction, and by doing so sent a message to Elliot that the man need not be suspected of anything but being another greedy, predictable peer. The boy's guard would be down, especially if he believed that he was on his way to assist King.

Smithers was twisting his key in his hands. "I can send—"

"No." King would fix this. He would finish this. Once and for all. "Did the baron speak to you?"

"No, sir. He was in the Duke of Rotham's carriage and never came into the house. Spoke directly to Raul and Levrett at the gate."

"Did he say anything else?"

"Only that you had reached an agreement of twenty-five percent and that Elliot would help serve to recover his portion of that."

King put a hand out on the desk to steady himself. As on the first time he had come face-to-face with John

Westerleigh in his study, dark spots danced before his eyes. He would take Marstowe apart piece by piece.

"Where are they?" It was Adeline who was asking urgently. "Do you know where they would have gone? Where he would have taken him?"

King's vision abruptly cleared, an icy calm crystallizing in his veins. "Somewhere where there are no servants or staff to witness his depravity. Where he will have all the time in the world to indulge himself without disturbance." He spun, heading for his stable. "He'll have taken him home."

CHAPTER 12

The ride from Helmsdale to Hanover Square was a desperate one, the thunder of the horses' hooves and the screaming wind in Adeline's ears blocking out the small voice in her head that was mocking her for her failures. Failure to be at the baron's house at dawn, prepared to follow the man wherever he went. Failure to remain at the baron's house after he did not show at the churchyard. She had failed in the single job she had been tasked with, and now a boy who had done nothing save possess an angelic face and a sense of loyalty was very much in danger.

Evening had settled firmly upon the city, only moonlight and the pools of lantern light on the street corners offering respite from the darkness. Traffic became lighter as they wended their way toward the elegant squares of London, the wealthy not yet emerged for the evening's entertainments and their servants having long ago completed their outdoor tasks in the daylight.

Adeline's cheeks were frozen, tears from the wind were crystallized in her lashes, and her fingers were aching with cold. King hadn't said a word since he had bolted from his study, his expression dark and his eyes as glacial and remote as she had ever seen them. He led them unerringly toward Hanover Square, reining his horse to a stop in front of Marstowe's home.

The town house was the first one in a long row of pretty, terraced residences that formed a neat square around a central garden, but unlike its neighbors, no lights glowed from within, its windows dark and empty.

King dismounted and took the stairs two at a time to the front door. For the second time that day, Adeline swiftly picked the lock and pushed the door open. They entered the cavernous interior, lit weakly by the gaslights from the pavement outside. King stalked through the entranceway and into the center of the hall, and a moment later, a candelabra flared to life. Holding it before him, he strode through the space, checking each darkened room, his steps as sure and unerring as if he had been here a thousand times before.

"Upstairs," he grated, but Adeline was already on her way up.

Two flights of stairs, three floors of rooms, and all of them filled with nothing but the ghostly shapes of furniture sheeted against the dust. King and Adeline returned to the ground-floor hall.

"The mews," Adeline said.

They hurried out the back of the townhome, into a fallow kitchen garden still covered with snow. Across the expanse of garden, the row of stables and living quarters above that belonged to the neighboring townhomes were as well lit as the houses themselves, both the animals and their keepers at their evening meals. The stable on the end that belonged to the baron was not blazing with light, though wavering candlelight glowed in a window.

Adeline started forward, only to be caught by a hand on her arm.

"You should go," King said to Adeline. "You don't have to be here."

"I beg your pardon?"

"You are not an assassin. You don't need to be a part of this."

"I am already a part of this."

King stared at her.

"I'm not leaving you," she said, repeating the words he had once said to her outside a gaming hell. Without considering what she was doing, she kissed him hard. "Besides," she whispered, pulling back, "someone has to hold the basket with the severed head."

King caught her face with his, crushing his lips to hers with the same urgency she had felt, and then turned, hurrying over the snow-covered ground.

A crash sounded from within the stable, and a string of muffled curses rose before it was abruptly cut off. Adeline and King were running now, yanking open the stable door and pounding down a dusty, stall-lined alleyway that hadn't seen horses in years. At the far end of the stable, where the space opened up into a room that would have at one time housed harnesses and saddles, Marstowe had Elliot by the collar of his jacket, the boy struggling in his grasp.

The baron struck him on the side of the head with his fist and Elliot staggered, going to his knees. He shook his head, and his small hand reached into the top of his boot, withdrawing something. He stumbled back to his feet, and in the weak light Adeline saw a blade flash forward. The baron screamed and released Elliot, lurching back against the wall, clutching his upper leg. Blood was blooming on the inside of his thigh at an alarming rate.

Adeline and King reached the end of the stable as Elliot scrambled back, only to fall to his knees again. For the first time, Adeline noticed the chains affixed around the boy's ankles, secured to a heavy iron hook set deep into the wall near the center of the room. The child's face and clothes were filthy, his livery jacket torn. He had a large lump at his left temple with dried blood crusted on the broken skin and staining his fair hair. Fresh blood trickled down his chin from a split lip that was swollen and bruised.

Across the room the baron had collapsed against the wall, still gripping his thigh and making mewling sounds. Marstowe was coatless, and his shirt was untucked and bunched around his waist, the top buttons at the fall of his trousers open. Blood was pulsing steadily through his fingers and pooling beneath his leg, turning his buff breeches dark.

"He stabbed me," he keened. "Dear God, he stabbed me. The scaly bastard attacked me. Tried to rob me. I'll see him hanged."

Elliot climbed to his feet unsteadily, the chains clanking. He shook his head, his complexion waxy, his eyes bright with panic. "No, no," he croaked. "That's not—" His hand was shaking where it still gripped the knife. "His Lordship toppered me senseless, and when I woke, it was dark and I was chained like this. And he was going to...and he was trying to—" Elliot stopped. "I was only defending myself."

"He's lying, the little vermin," Marstowe shrilled.

"I'm not lying." Elliot's small voice cracked.

King walked into the room and retrieved Marstowe's coat from where it had been hung high on a peg. With unhurried movements, he rifled the coat's pockets until he found what he wanted. He let the coat drop to the floor and tossed a key to Adeline.

"Unlock the boy."

Adeline crouched and released the fetters, and Elliot scrambled back.

"You chained a child to the wall," King commented in a tone so chilling that it sent shivers down Adeline's spine.

"I had to," Marstowe wheezed. "He deserved it. He's a thief—"

"No." Elliot was shaking his head miserably. "I didn't steal anything. Honest, I didn't—"

"I believe you, Elliot," said King. "And I know exactly what the baron tried to do."

Elliot's eyes went wide.

"I believe you," King repeated. He had returned to the wide entrance of the room and was looking around him, almost absently, as if trying to remember if he had misplaced something in its confines. "Go with Adrestia now, Elliot," he said.

Adeline stared at King, though he did not meet her gaze.

"Should I fetch a doctor, sir?" Elliot asked.

King gently extracted the knife from the small boy's fingers. "You will find my horse in the square in front of this townhome," he said. "Take it and go to the Lion's Paw. Do you know where the tavern is?"

Elliot nodded.

"Good. When you get there, ask for the Darling brothers and tell them that I require them to attend me at this address."

"How d'you know they'll be there?"

"They are always there at this time of night when they are in London."

"Are they doctors, sir?" The child was still shaking.

"This man is not going to need a doctor," King murmured to Elliot. He crouched in front of the boy and straightened his jacket, brushing a stray piece of straw and dust from his shoulder. "I am going to take care of this so that what this man tried to do to you, he will not do to anyone else. Ever. Do you understand?"

Elliot nodded.

"Good. Now wash your hands and face in the snow before you go out front," King instructed.

Adeline's throat tightened at the careful gentleness of his words and actions.

He straightened and guided Elliot out of the room, pointing him down the alley toward the wide stable door. "Your instructions, Elliot," he said. "What are they?"

"Go with Adrestia. Wash. Then horses. Then the tavern and the Darlings. Tell them to come here." His voice was stronger, some of his color returning.

"Very good. But I do not want you to come back in these stables under any circumstance. Do you understand?"

"Yessir." He started toward the stable door.

King finally met her eyes.

"You're sending him on a fool's errand," she whispered. "Marstowe will be dead long before anyone can be fetched. He is bleeding from a major vessel in his leg."

"I know. The Darlings will be counting on that."

"Oh." Adeline bit her lip.

He put a hand to her face, touching her cheek. "Take care of Elliot. Please."

Had he said anything else, Adeline would have fought him. Instead she nodded. "Of course."

She caught up to the boy at the end of the alleyway, stepping out into the night air, the wind biting at her exposed skin.

"You need to go back," Elliot said the second the door closed behind them. "You can't leave him."

"He asked—"

"He sent me away, and we both know why. What he's gonna do." The child who suddenly didn't sound like a child at all was looking up at her, his expression fierce. "But he asked you to stay."

"No, he asked—"

"Not right now," Elliot blurted, sounding almost impatient. "Before. At Helmsdale. He's never asked anyone to stay." He poked her in the chest with a small finger. "Ever."

Adeline stared at the boy.

"You can't leave him now."

Slowly Adeline nodded. "You're right."

Elliot jerked his head. "I know. 'Sides, I don't need no damn nanny to ride a horse to the Lion's Paw." He spun and vanished into the night, heading across the gardens toward the townhome.

Adeline watched him go for a moment before she turned and silently let herself back into the stable. She crept through the gloom, her weapons ready in her hands, coming to stand in the shadows just beyond the edge of the harness room.

Marstowe was still slumped against the wall, a sheen of perspiration across his forehead. "Where is it?" he was demanding.

"Where is what?" King asked.

"My goddamn money. I know you took it. You're a goddamn criminal who sells stolen art and smuggled liquor and God knows what else. And I know you stole my money."

"You sound sure."

"You know too much about my family."

"Lots of people know about your family."

"Do you think I'm stupid? You're wearing my brother's

goddamn ring!" Marstowe shouted before sagging back against the wall. "I need a doctor," he groaned.

"Mmm." King wandered to the wall opposite the baron. With the toe of his boot, he brushed aside a mouse-eaten rug. He bent, pulling open a small hatch door that was set into the floor. Adeline frowned. How would he have known that that was there—?

"It's been a while since I was here," King said.

"What the hell are you talking about?" Marstowe rasped. "Get me a goddamn doctor." He lifted his hand briefly before clapping it back over the wound as blood pulsed. He made another pathetic sound.

"Evan and I used to hide all of our treasures here," King said. "We played in the stables all the time. And it was where you brought Evan."

The use of Evan's name seemed to have caught Marstowe's attention.

From the hidden recess, King withdrew a faded peacock feather, a slingshot, a skull that might once have belonged to a deer, and a carved deity that looked as though it had traveled from a land far to the east. "The baroness forbade dirty, impure things in her house. Me included, though I was more difficult to dispose of. After Evan died, they couldn't keep me, as immoral as I was, not without admitting that they had sired such wickedness. So they quietly put me away in a place where no one knew who I was and no one believed a word I said."

Adeline fingered the handle of her knife uneasily, a strange awareness stirring deep in her subconscious. Because it sounded as if he was saying—

"Do you know who I am?" King asked, putting the feather and the skull back and holding the carved deity in his palm.

Marstowe's breathing was becoming ragged. "You're a goddamn criminal."

"When required," King agreed.

"A goddamn criminal who thought he was entitled to a piece of my fortune."

"It's not just a piece of your fortune I'm entitled to," King said so quietly Adeline almost didn't hear. "In truth, I'm entitled to all of it."

Adeline grasped the edge of the stall door as comprehension crashed through her subconscious and into the forefront of her mind. It had all been there before her, had she only chosen to see. His speech, his education, his knowledge, his memories, and the intense power those memories held. God, she had censured this man for making assumptions while she had been unforgivably guilty of the same. King hadn't been a street urchin or an unlikely best friend.

He had been Evan Westerleigh's brother.

Marstowe seemed to have reached the same realization. "Joshua Westerleigh died of fever when he was eleven. He's buried at St James's. Everyone knows that." His words were belligerent, but Adeline could hear the underlying fear.

"They do, don't they?" King shrugged and tucked the little carving into his pocket. "It was very well done, really. How else to explain a child who simply . . . ceased to be?"

"You're lying."

Adeline had stepped out of the shadows and crossed the floor to stand beside King. He didn't glance at her, but if he was surprised at her presence, he didn't show it.

"Who th' 'ell are you?" Marstowe wheezed. His face had taken on a gray pallor in the low light, and his words had started to run together.

Adeline simply gazed back. "At the moment, Judith's maid."

King exhaled, his eyes closing briefly.

"G'me a doctor, girl," Marstowe demanded, perspiration still beading on his forehead.

Adeline only sheathed her blades.

King bent again, this time picking up a smith's hammer from a jumble of tools tossed into a bucket.

"You'll remember this, I think, Uncle," he said, hefting the hammer in his hands. "It's what you used to kill Evan when he tried to pull you off me. Because he knew what you were going to do to me. Because you'd been doing the same thing to him for years, until he became too long in the tooth and I became the more tempting of the two."

The baron swayed as he tried to focus on King. "Devil spawn," he slurred. "Tempting the unwary with your evil ways." He shifted against the wall. There was a wide pool of blood beneath his leg now. "You can't prove I did any of that."

"I suppose I can't. Any more than I could prove my innocence back then either," King said. "In the breath it took for you to utter a handful of words, I became an unnatural killer." He stepped closer to the baron and stopped in front of him. "And against your word, mine was powerless."

"Then what? You're goin' t'kill me now?"

"That ship has long sailed," King said. "Or at least, that is what my smugglers in Dover would say in a situation like this." King tossed the smith's hammer to the side with a deafening clatter.

"I shoulda killed y'too," the baron garbled.

"Perhaps you should have. But you didn't."

"Y'can't leave m'like this," Marstowe panted.

"Alone, you mean? The way I was left after you killed my brother? After you told my father and my mother that it was I who had wielded that hammer in a fit of jealousy?" King stepped back and extended his arm to Adeline.

She took it without hesitation, and he covered her hand with his other one, gripping it as if he was afraid she might disappear.

"Goodbye, Uncle."

CHAPTER 13

King knew when she had slipped into his rooms by the ghost of movement reflected in the dark windows.

He didn't stop playing, just let the music wash over him, his fingers moving of their own accord. While Evan had been the artist, King had been the musician, the notes flowing effortlessly from his mind to his hands. When he'd been four or five, the baron and baroness would trot him out from time to time to play for guests, the collection of people making all the right noises of approval as he dutifully executed a preselected piece. As he got a little older and his parents had become impatient with his frivolous obsession with music over more suitable pursuits like Latin and maths, riding and fencing, he'd been forced to sneak in time at the pianoforte whenever he could. And then after, when he'd been taken from his home in Hanover Square, there had been years and years when there had been no music at all.

It was why, when he'd bought Helmsdale, he'd had a pianoforte installed in his bedroom. It was a Broadwood grand, enormously expensive, and King would have paid five times that amount for the luxury of playing whatever he wished whenever he wished, uncensored and undisturbed.

Yet when Adeline sat down next to him on the long bench, he didn't feel disturbed. He simply finished the sonata, drawing out the waning notes.

He rested his fingers on the ivory keys. "I have locks on my door."

"That weren't locked tonight." She placed a finger on a key in front of her and pressed down, a single note reverberating through the room. She was wearing a loose, belted robe the color of the sapphire she had once tried to steal, the neck snug at her throat, the sleeves almost too long for her arms. The simplicity of the garment was more evocative than anything else she had ever worn.

"No," he agreed. "They weren't."

She withdrew her fingers from the keys. "The Darling brothers departed with their cargo an hour ago for Edinburgh," she said.

King nodded. "There will be a rumor soon that the baron returned to Virginia, humiliated and defeated by his inability to find his missing fortune." He traced the edge of a key with the pad of his finger. "I thought that this part would be easier. I thought that the rage and revulsion would be replaced with...satisfaction. Elation. But being back in those stables with him was like living everything all over again, and all I could feel—all I can feel now—is grief."

Adeline's hand came to rest gently on his leg, but she didn't speak.

"It was my fault Evan died," he said. "He died trying to spare me from what he had endured for years."

"It wasn't your fault," Adeline said fiercely. "You were a child. And you were betrayed by the very people who were supposed to keep you safe."

"I told them," he said. "My mother and father. Told them what had happened when they found me with Evan, covered in his blood, my clothes torn, my breeches ripped." He covered her hand with his. "They told me that I must be touched by the devil to make up such blasphemous lies. That if I didn't recant, then I would sacrifice my soul and be denied salvation."

Adeline closed her eyes.

"Perhaps I did. Sacrifice my soul," he whispered. "Because I did not recant. And they cast me into hell."

"Bedlam."

"Yes. A never-ending nightmare of mad-doctors, purges, starvation, and torture."

"But you survived."

"No. Joshua Westerleigh died there," he said. "The boy who once believed in the goodness of people died. King survived. A merciless man who does whatever awful things are necessary to keep surviving."

"You're wrong."

King clenched his fist and brought it down on the keys. He was rewarded by a jarring jumble of notes.

"What you did for Elliot tonight were not the actions of a merciless man. They were the actions of an honorable man."

"Jesus, I did nothing except send him to fetch men who could make the evidence of what happened disappear. I am everything Marstowe said I was. Don't try and...redeem me, Adeline. I do not wish or deserve to be redeemed."

"I'm not redeeming you," Adeline said. "I'm seeing you. I saw a man who sent a child away so that he wouldn't know that it was his blade that killed a man. Elliot doesn't need to carry that with him. Not yet. Maybe not ever. You let him believe that you killed Marstowe for what he tried to do."

King looked away. "So? I've killed men before."

"So have I."

He turned slowly.

"I've killed because I did not wish to die," she said in a whisper. "I've stolen because I did not wish to starve. Will you punish me for those things the same way you're punishing yourself? I am merely a survivor of circumstance and fate, the same as you."

King couldn't look away from her.

"Kiss me," she said.

Her words seared right through him, making his blood heat and stirring arousal instantly. "You don't want this, Adeline. You don't want me. In a fortnight you'll be in France, where you'll find a good man—"

"Stop talking."

King's mouth snapped shut.

"You left your door unlocked for a reason."

"I left my door unlocked because locking it is pointless." It sounded feeble even in his own ears. "You don't want this. I don't want this." *I can't want this.*

Her hand settled on his chest, over the left side where his heart might once have been. "I don't believe you."

His fingers fell from the piano keys.

Adeline extricated herself from the bench and stood before him, the fire dancing across her features and putting flames into the darkness of her hair. She reached for the belt at her waist.

"Stop." He surged to his feet, the bench nearly tipping behind him. His blood was pounding in his ears, right in time to the throbbing in his cock.

Her hand paused.

He should walk away from this. It was what an honorable man would do, the sort of man that she thought he was. That he might have been.

But he wasn't honorable. And he wasn't strong. And he wanted her so damn badly. So, so badly.

"Have you reconsidered?" she asked in French, the beautiful lilt to her words caressing him and raising gooseflesh across his skin.

Very deliberately he grasped the hem of his shirt and pulled it over his head, letting it fall to the floor. He saw her swallow, saw her eyes flicker over his naked torso.

With the same deliberation, he unbuttoned the fall of his trousers, stepping out of them. He was entirely naked, every muscle in his body rigid, every fiber longing for her. She would be able to see the scars on his wrists and ankles, and the scars across his arms and chest. She would be able to see every act of violence that had followed him through Bedlam and then the streets of London. She would see everything that he was.

And she could still leave. Back away from what he was.

Except she wasn't leaving. Instead her eyes were doing a slow dance over his body, her mouth parted slightly, her silver eyes smoky with arousal. If he had been hard before, he was like granite now, carnal need roaring through his veins.

"I haven't reconsidered anything," he growled.

"Yes, I can see that," she said with a small, self-satisfied smile, and that sultry confidence was the most beautiful thing he had ever seen.

She stepped forward, her hands hovering just above his shoulders. He forced himself not to move. Not to push himself into her touch as her hands settled on his skin, her fingers traveling over his chest first and then his abdomen, tracing each scar. Her fingers skimmed his ribs, her palms sliding over his hips and around his backside.

She hummed in the back of her throat, and it was all the

warning that he got before her lips grazed his jaw, moving down to trace the same path across his chest that her fingers had just taken. Her mouth moved across his skin, her tongue swirling around one nipple and then the other, and the pleasure that tore through him almost made him stagger.

She straightened again, her lips finding his, and he deepened the kiss before she could pull away. He caught the sides of her face with his hands, tipping her head back to give himself better access to her mouth, and there was nothing gentle about his kiss. It was hot and greedy, as if he could funnel all the desperate need that she'd incited within him into it. He wanted to drown in her, sink into all her strength and courage and beauty.

Her hands slid from his backside, one hand closing over his erection, the other cupping his balls. He shuddered, groaning into her mouth. She stroked him once and then again, and his head dropped to her shoulder, dizzying pleasure sizzling through him. Her thumb drifted over the head of his erection, and he nearly came out of his skin. He stepped away from her, knowing that she would undo him where he stood if he let her continue. And he didn't want to come without her. He needed to be inside her when she came apart, needed to feel her wrapped around him.

He reached for the belt of her robe and pulled on the loose bow, watching as the belt slid to the floor and her robe fell open. He pushed it from her shoulders until she too was standing naked.

He swallowed, his mouth gone dry. In the firelight her honey-kissed skin glowed, her breasts topped by peaked nipples, the line of her waist curving gently before flaring over her hips. Just as visible in the soft light were the scars that covered her own body. A long mark that slashed down her shoulder to end by her elbow. Small streaks of pale skin crisscrossed over her forearms. A wide, puckered gash that had healed badly near her hip. He would ask her about that one. But not now.

Instead he sank down on the pianoforte bench, tugging her forward so that she stood directly in front of him. He bent his head and placed a slow kiss at the ruined skin at her hip, his hands sliding up her ribs to cover her breasts. This time it was Adeline who moaned softly. He rolled her nipples between his fingers, and her hands found his shoulders, her fingers digging into the muscle.

His hands dropped, one sliding over the curve of her buttocks, the other caressing the inside of her thigh. She was trembling, her legs not entirely steady, and this pleased him to no end. He wasn't the only one being undone. He slipped a finger between her legs, stroking through her wet folds.

She gasped, her fingers tightening on his shoulders. "I need more. I need all of you."

He stroked her again, and she made another small, desperate sound, and his cock twitched in response.

His hands slid around her hips, and this time he urged her forward so that she was straddling him. "Take what you need."

Her eyes locked on his as she took him in her hand, guiding him to her entrance. She tilted her hips, the tip of his erection sliding into her heat.

"Don't look away," she whispered, and seated herself fully.

Pleasure exploded like a lightning storm, crackling through his body and straight up his spine. He thrust hard up into her, unable to help himself, and she whimpered.

He froze. "Did I hurt you?"

"Never," she breathed. "Do it again."

He rocked his hips, and this time she met him. Her inner walls clenched around his erection as he slid rhythmically inside her wet heat, setting a hard pace. She laced her fingers across the back of his neck, holding on to him tightly. King caressed her breast in one hand, dipping his head to catch her nipple with his mouth. He sucked gently and was rewarded with a tortured moan.

"I could die right here, right now, and die happy listening to the sounds you make," he managed.

"Don't die yet," she panted, her fingers leaving his neck to tangle in his hair.

He sucked again, and Adeline cried out softly. He slipped his other hand between them, finding her swollen bud where their bodies were joined. He stroked it lightly with his thumb.

"Yes," she hissed. "Right there. Just like that."

King closed his eyes and fought for control against the storm of sensations gripping him as he stroked and worshipped his goddess.

"Look at me," Adeline said breathlessly.

He opened his eyes. Her silver gaze was lust-filled and hooded, her lips kiss-swollen and parted, her skin damp and flushed. She was achingly, unbearably beautiful, and in this moment, she was all his. With deliberate movements, King shifted the angle of his hips and thrust twice more.

"Joshua," she whispered as every muscle in her body convulsed.

Her fingers curled into his scalp, and small, sensual sounds escaped her lips. He kept thrusting, watching the rapture on her face as pleasure consumed her until he could no longer fight his own release roaring down on him.

He grasped her hips and pulled out of her, his throbbing erection sliding against her abdomen. He reached for his cock, but she beat him to it, fisting him in her palm and stroking him from crown to base.

Her name tore from his lips as he came, intense pleasure such as he'd never known wiping his mind of everything save the feel of this woman. His hips still moved relentlessly, but he couldn't stop, couldn't pull away from her touch, couldn't pull away from her.

Eventually his movements slowed, and Adeline collapsed against him, both of them breathing hard. Neither said anything for a long time, the air cooling their skin. But his pulse hadn't slowed. If anything, his heart was thundering even faster against his ribs, an unnamed ache gripping his chest and squeezing the air from his lungs. Bits and pieces of the last minutes floated back to him in a haze. The feel of Adeline's body, the sound of her voice, the words she had spoken.

Ribbons of unease wound through him.

Jesus, what had he done?

CHAPTER 14

"You called me Joshua."

He had tensed, the muscles in his legs beneath her like steel, his entire body stiff.

"Yes." She lifted her head, but he didn't meet her eye. "That is your name."

He twisted and snatched his shirt from the floor. He wiped his seed from her skin before he tossed the garment to the side.

"It's not." He still hadn't met her gaze, and she could feel him retreating from her as surely as if he were running for the door. "Joshua Westerleigh is dead."

"Joshua Westerleigh did not die. He simply survived the best way he knew how, and I, of all people, will never judge you for that. But he is not a prisoner anymore. Not of his name, not of his life."

"You're wrong."

Adeline slid from his lap with a sigh. Her body was still humming with the aftereffects of the last minutes, but a familiar frustration was beginning to creep through her. She retrieved her robe and drew it over her shoulders.

"I am what I am now," he continued, his voice rough and wooden. "I can't be who you want me to be. Who you think I am. I can't just...change."

"Change?" Adeline said, trying not to let anger color her words but failing. "I don't ever want you to change from who you are—"

"I am a criminal. A thief. A killer."

"Yes. All of those things. But you are also a friend. A lover. A protector."

"A protector?" He stood and fetched his trousers, yanking them on in angry motions.

"Yes. Of Elliot. Of your duke. Of me."

"And yet I was unable to protect the one person who needed it the most," he sneered. "I will never go back to being...helpless. Powerless. Vulnerable."

"And is that what I make you? Vulnerable?" She pulled her robe around her more tightly.

"No." King stared at her before bracing his palms against the edge of the piano. "You make me—" He stopped and stared down at his hands, as if suddenly comprehending what he had been about to say and not liking the answer.

"Afraid," she said quietly.

He recoiled. "I've already told you I'm not afraid of anything."

"And you lied. You're afraid to trust. You're afraid to need."

"Fine words from a woman who once said that need leads to downfall."

"I said in the wrong hands, need can lead to downfall. But needing and trusting someone who—" *Loves you*, she almost said before she caught herself. She pressed her fingers to her lips, fighting the ache blossoming inside her heart. "Needing someone who cares about you," she amended, "does not make one weak. It makes one stronger."

King scoffed derisively.

"I understand that you were betrayed in the most heinous manner. But this facade you maintain, this reputation of being merciless and ruthless and unfeeling, is not all that you are. You're so much more than a facade."

"That facade keeps the blades out of my back when I least expect them," he snarled. "So have a care."

"No, I don't think I will, because that makes you no better than the Duke of Buckingham, demanding Rubens to portray him as something he's not."

He straightened. "I beg your pardon?"

"That might have been your past. But what about your present?"

"What about it?"

"The ruthless, merciless lord of the underworld would tell me that he feels nothing for me. He would tell me that what just happened was you simply fucking away your regrets."

He flinched.

"I don't want you to change," she said softly. "I want you to take a chance."

"On what?"

"On yourself. On me. On the possibility of us."

"There will never be an us."

She had thought herself prepared for those words, but hearing them sent pain lancing through her heart.

"I want to know what the man standing in front of me has to say. King, Joshua, I don't really care what it is you wish to call yourself. Tell me what you need. What you feel."

"Don't make me do this." His arms were rigid at his sides.

"I will never *make* you do anything. This is your choice."

He cursed and turned away from her, bracing his hands on the edge of the piano. "Then I want you to do no less than what you do for all your clients."

"Which is?" she asked in some confusion.

"Disappear, so as not to remain a reminder of what was likely the worst moment of their lives."

She was clenching her jaw so hard she thought her teeth might shatter.

"Your words. Not mine," he finished. "You have to go, Adrestia."

"It's better to send me away before I have the opportunity to betray you, is that it?" She forced the words through her lips.

"In the end, everyone betrays you." His head dropped, and the muscles across his back flexed.

Adeline swallowed hard against the ache that had risen in her throat and the gaping emptiness that had once again opened in the center of her chest. She could not force her love on a man who did not want to be loved. She could not give her heart to a man who would never take it. She could not make him love himself enough to accept love from another.

Adeline walked to the door, pausing with her hand on the latch.

"Goodbye, Joshua," she said before pushing through the door. She did not look back.

CHAPTER 15

King stood in the frigid churchyard, the moonlight that flooded down bright enough to cast long shadows across the ground. The snow had long since melted, and Evan's headstone glowed an ethereal white, save for the new blooms that sat on top of the stone. They were the same flowers that King had always brought on the same day of the week during the same small hours of the morning. Except nothing was the same, really.

Adeline Archambault had left a void in his life—in his entire existence—that he didn't know what to do with. King had thought that he would simply move on after Adeline left. That in her absence he would go back to the life he'd known before she'd broken into his study, seized a sapphire, and made him question everything he thought he knew about himself.

He hadn't moved on at all. He hadn't even played his damn pianoforte in a sennight because all he could think about was—

"You look terrible."

King started. He had completely lost his edge. He hadn't heard Ashland approach.

"And it's a pleasure to see you as well," King replied irritably, most of his ire directed at himself. "What are you doing here? It's freezing and long past midnight."

"I was looking for you. I stopped by Helmsdale earlier but you weren't there. Your young footman told me where to find you." The duke gazed down at the headstone. "In hindsight, I should have looked here first."

King grunted. He would speak to Elliot about discretion later. "Why were you looking for me?"

"Marstowe is gone."

"Yes. I heard he left England," King said with complete honesty.

"I heard the same." The duke paused. "Your assassin is also gone."

"For the last time, she's not a bloody assassin. And she certainly is not mine." Though she had been, once, for a tiny sliver of time. Regret lanced through him, sharp enough to make him feel slightly ill.

"King—"

"She didn't kill Marstowe, if that's what you're asking."

"Did you kill him?" Ashland's breath misted in the cold air.

"No." Also true.

"Do you know where he—"

"Stop asking questions you neither need nor want answers to," King snapped.

The duke fell silent.

"I'm sorry." King leaned on his walking stick, the point spearing some remnants of frostbitten vegetation. "That was uncalled for."

"You're angry. Would you care to tell me why?"

"I'm not angry." Another truth. He was bereft. Miserable. Alone. "And it doesn't matter. Forgive my lack of civility."

The duke tipped his head, his expression merely thoughtful. "You've always done that."

"Done what? Lost my composure?" King pinched the bridge of his nose with his gloved fingers.

"Protected me."

King's hand dropped, an ache stirring in his chest.

Adeline had once called him a protector. And he had sneered at her.

"I haven't done anything of the sort," he said harshly.

"You did it in Bedlam. Bore the worst of the cruelty to spare me the same. Kept me alive on the streets of London in those first years after we escaped."

"That's not—"

"I'm not done," Ashland interrupted. "You've shielded me from the truth of what happened the night you saved my life. Credible deniability, you called it, and you're doing it again right now. Protecting me by keeping secrets."

"Perhaps," King said. He didn't have the will to argue the point.

"But she knew everything, didn't she?"

"I beg your pardon?"

"Your assassin. She knew all your secrets. The secrets in your past that you have never even told me."

King gripped the silver handle of his walking stick, the leather of his gloves stretching uncomfortably taut across his knuckles. The hoofbeats of a lone horse on the cobblestones beyond the churchyard echoed through the stillness of the night and then faded. "Yes," he finally allowed.

"She saw you, then. All of you. The man behind this myth you've so carefully curated. And she didn't run." The duke stepped in front of him. "She didn't run so you sent her away."

"You have no idea of what you speak." King's free hand curled into a fist. "You have no right to—"

"And you didn't send her away to protect her," Ashland pressed on, ignoring him. "You sent her away to protect yourself."

The ache in King's chest intensified into something more unnerving.

"You are a great many things, King, but I never took you for a coward."

"Watch yourself," King snarled. "Before you say something you regret."

The duke appeared unmoved. "Tell me, did you fall in love with her?"

"What sort of question is that?" He despised how defensive he sounded.

"The only one that matters."

King stared at the man still standing before him.

"You're going to have to choose the moments you want to define you," Ashland said, and there was a hard edge to his voice that King had never heard before. "The ones in the past or the ones yet to come. You deserve happiness, but you must choose it."

"I—"

"Yer purse or yer life!" A rough voice cut off whatever King might have said. At the same time he became aware of the muzzle of a pistol pressed against his lower back.

A movement behind Ashland betrayed another thief, this one no doubt holding a similar weapon on the duke. King's jaw slackened. Goddammit, this was intolerable. His distraction had kept him from noticing these two fools approaching, and his inattention had left him and Ashland exposed.

King shifted, the anger that had been absent earlier suddenly rising with a potency that made him light-headed. It was bad enough that these cretins should dare accost him here, in a place he considered sacred. But the anger directed at himself was something else altogether.

He'd been standing in this churchyard drowning in regrets and self-pity because he'd been a coward. Ashland had been right. King had let the woman who saw him, who completed him and who was his equal in every way that mattered, walk away. No, not walk away. He had cast her away because he couldn't bring himself to admit that in the end, she had been right too. She did make him vulnerable and afraid.

But she had not made him weak. At his side, she had only made him stronger.

"I said, yer purse or yer life," the thief repeated, and this time there was a wild note of desperation in his demand. He jammed the pistol into King's back again. "I'll shoot you right here, don't think I won't."

His accomplice, just visible over Ashland's shoulder, nodded vehemently, his eyes wide below unkempt hair. "Yer money. Or I'll shoot 'im too."

King shifted and grasped the silver handle of his walking stick. With his other hand, he gripped the ebony staff.

The Duke of Ashland caught his eye and winced. "Please don't do anything rash, King."

"I believe we've had this conversation before, Ashland," King said through gritted teeth.

"Bloody hell." The duke sighed.

"Stop talking an' give us yer fecking money." The pistol at King's back wobbled.

In a swift movement fueled by fury and practiced many times over, King drew the blade hidden in his walking stick and spun, slashing at the offending pistol and then driving the silver handle of his weapon into the thief's horrified face.

He heard bone crunch as the man collapsed in a pile at the foot of Evan's grave. The tip of the needlelike sword came to rest at the man's throat. King glanced at the thief's hand, only to discover that what he'd thought was a pistol wasn't a pistol at all but the blunt end of a short shovel. It now lay next to the gasping, whimpering man, the rusty tool dull in the moonlight.

Grave robbers. Who had thought to try their hand at fleecing living victims instead. Jesus, this night was getting better and better.

King glanced behind him and found that Ashland had also disarmed his would-be attacker. The man was facedown on the cold ground, and the duke had a boot planted squarely across the back of the man's neck. He was tapping the blade of a small but lethal knife across his gloved palm.

"I'm glad to see a duchy hasn't rendered you completely helpless."

The duke rolled his eyes.

King returned his attention to the thief at the end of his sword and increased the pressure at the tip fractionally. "Give me a good reason why I shouldn't kill you," he said.

The man's eyes bulged, blood streaming from his nose. "Didn't mean it," he babbled. "Were goin' to just dig around some but then we saw you an' yer fine clothes and thought—"

"Yes, I know what you thought."

"We jes' made a mistake, is all."

"You did," King agreed coldly. "I do not like being threatened, and I do not suffer fools. I suffer fools who threaten those I care about even less."

The man under the duke's boot writhed helplessly. "Please don't kill us," he croaked. "I beg you."

"No one is killing anyone," Ashland said with a pointed look at King.

"It would make me feel better," King growled.

The thief whimpered.

Ashland snorted and glanced down at the hapless man. "You'll have to excuse my friend. He's having a wretched day."

"What?" the man wheezed against the frozen ground.

"He's in love," the duke informed him rather smugly. "With an assassin."

The grave robber sprawled on Evan's grave hiccupped loudly. "Oh, sweet Mary, we're goin' to die."

King scowled fiercely at Ashland and tightened his grip on his blade, anger and frustration and regret still singing through his veins. The urge to lash out at the imbecile who'd dared threaten him only to spare himself the effort of digging among the dead for a few coins or baubles—

King froze. "Give me your shovels and I'll let you live," he said, his mind racing.

"What?" The man's throat worked convulsively under the point of King's blade.

"Or I can simply slit your throats and take your shovels. Your choice."

The ragged man eased out and away from King's blade, and, when he found himself still alive, scrambled to his feet. He kicked the shovel in King's direction and backed away. "They're all yers," he panted.

"Take your friend with you. And don't ever return to this churchyard. I won't be so charitable next time."

The man shook his head and, without waiting to see if his accomplice was following, turned and fled. The duke released his thief, and King watched both men scramble frantically over the church wall.

"While I am pleased you didn't kill anyone, what the hell was that about?" Ashland demanded.

King sheathed his blade and set his walking stick aside, picking up the shovel. The seed of suspicion that had sprouted was growing with each passing minute, pieces of the puzzle that was Marstowe's missing fortune sliding into place.

He walked past Evan's grave and stood in front of the smaller headstone next to it. There was no ornate scrolling, no decorative swirls, and no declarations of adoration. *Joshua Westerleigh, 1787–1798* was carved into the surface in plain letters.

"The rector told me that, on the day he visited my father, the old baron asked him to protect these graves," he said slowly. "Because someone had disturbed this one."

Ashland was frowning. "So? Fools like the ones we just dispatched are not uncommon."

"True. But even those fools, looking for jewelry and gold, would not ignore the grand graves of barons and baronesses and dig up the resting place of a lowly child." King's shovel blade hit the hard earth. It was packed but not frozen.

"What the hell are you doing?"

"Digging up my grave."

"Because you think someone robbed it?" The duke sounded incredulous.

"No. I think someone put something in it." He turned over another shovelful of earth.

"I beg your pardon?"

"Are you going to help or watch, Ashland?"

The duke made an exasperated sound but bent and retrieved the second shovel and set to work beside King.

The box, when they found it, was buried not far below the surface. It was made of wood and smaller than the child-size coffin that presumably lay somewhere below, but larger than a case that might hold a fine pair of long dueling pistols. King dropped his shovel and awkwardly wrested the heavy box from the cold earth.

Wordlessly Ashland passed him his knife, and King pried open the latch. He set the knife aside and lifted the lid, already knowing what he was going to find.

"Bloody hell," Ashland breathed beside him as the moonlight illuminated the contents.

"Indeed," King agreed. He closed the lid and rested his hands on the surface.

The duke pushed himself to his feet. "Well, then. I won't ask what you're going to do with them because I know you won't tell me." He sighed. "Credible deniability and all that."

"No," King said quietly, looking back at his brother's headstone. "I will tell you. I will tell you everything because the whole truth is what you deserve." He straightened and met the Duke of Ashland's gaze.

"You don't have to."

"I do. Because I trust you. And because you've never run either."

"Not even when you asked me to dig up your grave," Ashland said wryly. He retrieved King's walking stick and handed it to him, his expression becoming serious again. "And what about your assassin?"

King gripped the familiar silver handle.

"It would seem I owe her a truth as well."

CHAPTER 16

The sun was hot on her skin.

Adeline tipped her face up to that warmth, the rich scents of sun-baked earth and flourishing vegetation mingling on the breeze. She lifted her heavy braid off her neck, gazing at what months of hard work had wrought. While the grand old château hadn't survived the fiery destruction of the revolutionary mobs, the cellars and equipment sheds had been spared, along with the handful of workers' cottages that sat on the edge of the property. The important things that were making Falaise d'Argent whole again had survived. Including her.

Before winter had ended, Adeline had hired a foreman and a dozen workers, men and women who had toiled in vineyards like this one their entire lives. They'd been willing to teach Adeline everything they knew and share what information they could. Including the assurance that, two summers from now, they would be able to harvest their first grapes from the rows of new, tender vines that were now growing under a warm French sun. Adeline's days became a cycle of hard work, ending only when she collapsed into a satisfied, exhausted slumber at the end of each day.

Which was what she wanted—no, needed—because there were still too many moments when her hands and her mind were idle that she thought of King. She dropped her head, the loss that she had thought would get better with time still cutting deep. She might have found a home here, a place where she belonged, surrounded by honest, simple work, but she hadn't been able to forget the man she had left behind. The man to whom she belonged.

She hefted her basket from the ground over her arm.

"I hope there's not a head in there," a voice said from behind her.

Adeline set her basket back down, the disorienting surge of emotion that raced through her followed quickly by the irrational fear that she was hearing things.

"Not today," she replied. "And that's a rather macabre way to greet a woman."

"Yes, but you're not just a woman. You are the goddess of retribution, the inescapable, and an avenging angel who wields her weapons as well as she wields her wits."

"Then I'm afraid you'll be disappointed. Because today I'm just Miss Archambault. Pulling weeds in a hot field."

"I will never be disappointed, Adeline."

Slowly she turned around. King stood before her, his coat as immaculate as ever, his breeches spotless, his boots polished to a high shine. He was leaning casually on his walking stick, the silver handle gleaming in the sun.

"I feel a little underdressed," she said inanely, because she had no idea what was happening. Or why he was here.

"And by underdressed, you mean you're not wearing your weapons?" He held up a hand before she could speak. "And that was a question, not an assumption. I don't know where vintners hide their weapons under their clothes. Perhaps, if I don't ruin what I've come to say, or you don't run me through for utter stupidity, I might get the chance to ask. And yes, I know you do not enjoy killing stupid men, but there might always be an exception."

Adeline found herself wanting to grin, a terrifying sense of hope daring to rise. "I'll restrain myself for the time being."

"You look beautiful," he said suddenly. "Beautiful and happy."

"I've discovered that I like growing things and that I'm reasonably proficient at it. I've discovered I like teaching reading and writing and fencing to the children who live here. I want to build a school as soon as I am able. I like working alongside others toward a common goal with dirt under my fingernails and the sun on my skin. These are all things that make me happy."

"I'm glad." He smiled, the corners of his ice-blue eyes crinkling. The sight took her breath away. "I'm sorry it's taken so long for me to come. I had some affairs to put in order first."

"What are you doing here?" she asked, unable to help herself any longer.

"I came to find you. You left me."

"You told me to go."

"Yes. And that is the profound stupidity of which I speak." King set his walking stick carefully against a trellis.

Adeline stared at him.

He reached into his coat and withdrew the locket that had once housed a Spanish sapphire. He held it out to her, the heavy locket swinging on its black ribbon. "You were right. I was afraid. Terrified, in fact, to allow myself to be vulnerable."

"King, I should never have—"

"Open it."

Adeline took the locket from his hand, careful not to touch him. She tried to ignore the way her fingers were not quite steady. With some effort, she managed to release the catch. Nestled in the interior was not a blue sapphire but a ruby pendant on a delicate gold chain, the deep crimson burning like fire from within. She put a hand to her mouth.

"What have you done?" she whispered.

King moved forward and took the pendant and chain from inside the locket. "Turn around."

Adeline did as she was bid. He lifted her braid over her shoulder, and his hands brushed the sides of her neck, sending currents of awareness crackling over her skin the way they always had. Her eyes fluttered closed. The pendant slid from her throat to rest at the tops of her breasts, his fingers working the catch of the chain at her nape.

"There." His breath was warm against her skin. "That's where it was meant to be. It looks much better on you. I was telling the truth when I said that I never did care much for the setting."

Adeline turned, her eyes searching his. "This was a gift to you from your brother—"

"And now it's a gift from me. I want you to have it. Evan would have wanted you to have it."

"I can't accept this." Her throat had closed, making speaking difficult.

"Yes, you can. You took the worst moment in my life and helped me find a measure of..."

"Justice?"

"Healing. Peace."

"But I—"

"You also can't refuse because you've stolen something from me."

Adeline recognized the words he had uttered a lifetime ago. "What?"

"My heart, Adeline. You've stolen my heart and my soul, and I don't want them back without you. I need you, Adeline. With my entire being."

Adeline blinked, the backs of her eyes burning.

"I understand now that needing you never made me weak. It made me stronger. I know that I am not the man you might have imagined that you—"

"Would fall in love with?" she asked.

His breath stilled.

"I love you," she said. "All of you. The dark parts and the light parts because they match mine too. You've always seen me, King."

"Joshua. Call me Joshua."

Emotion flooded her heart, joy spilling over.

"I left King behind in England. He'll certainly still be useful in business matters, but here, with you, I am Joshua."

Adeline stepped into his arms, and he caught her tight,

claiming her lips with his. It was a messy, passionate kiss, the world around them dropping away so that only the two of them existed.

"You are the most magnificent woman I've ever known," he said presently, not releasing her. "I love you. And I should have told you that a long time ago."

"Thank you for your trust," she whispered.

His arms tightened around her. "Thank you for seeing me."

They stood like that for a time under the sunlight, until Joshua drew back. "I was thinking of traveling to Italy," he said. "But only if you might consider joining me. In the winter, of course. I once promised a beautiful woman I'd take her to the Uffizi."

"I remember," she replied, tipping her head back with a slow smile. "Are you asking to court me?"

"No." He brushed a piece of hair back from her face and tucked it behind her ear. "I'm asking for more than that. I'm asking for your days and for your nights. I'm asking to be the partner you deserve."

Adeline could barely breathe. "Yes," she managed.

Joshua kissed her softly.

"Where would we live?" she asked.

"England. France. Italy. All three of those places or none of those places. Anywhere you wish, really. My home is with you."

"What about your business in London?"

"The best art and the best wine are not in London," he said. "Which made me think that perhaps I need to expand my business. And as it turns out, I have a newly procured fortune that requires investing."

Adeline started. "You found the missing Marstowe money."

"Of course I did. Again, nothing is truly lost. One need only know where to look."

"And where was that?"

"Do you remember what Lady Angelique told us? That before his death, my father was seeking out Portuguese captains in the London dockyards?"

"Yes," she replied slowly.

"It bothered me, that seemingly incongruous remark. But it got me thinking. Aside from what little spice trade the Portuguese cling to, they still import another commodity that is highly desirable."

"What?"

"Diamonds. From Brazil, through Goa. I find it almost humiliating that it took me as long as it did to come to such a realization, given I deal in diamonds often. Easy to transport, easy to conceal, and accepted as payment the world over."

"The old baron converted his fortune to diamonds?"

"Yes."

"Why would he do that?"

Joshua shrugged. "I can't give you a good answer. And I can't tell you what was going on in his head when he buried the entire cache under the headstone he had once laid for his child who had not died. Perhaps he believed that I was still alive and that I would one day find them? Perhaps he simply did not want his brother to inherit the fortune? Guilt and remorse are powerful sentiments." He touched the ruby at Adeline's neck. "Of course, it might have simply been delusion. Or just plain insanity."

Adeline covered his fingers with hers, pressing them against her skin.

"I don't need the money," he told her. "But I'd like to see it used for something good. Use it to build your school. Use it to help those around you however you wish."

"However we wish," she corrected. "We're partners in this."

"We," he agreed with a smile. "And speaking of partners, I don't suppose you'd know a vintner who might like to engage in a business venture? My ships coming back across the Channel through Dover are often a little lighter than I'd like. Good French wine is always in demand."

"I might. If the terms were agreeable."

"And what would those terms be?"

"Well, to start, you could kiss me."

Joshua bent his head and did exactly that. Thoroughly, without hesitation, until Adeline was breathless.

"And then?" he asked.

"And then," she said slowly, pressing her lips to the hollow at his throat, "I think it would not be remiss if you were to spend some time discovering exactly where vintners keep their weapons hidden under their clothes."

ABOUT THE AUTHOR

Kelly Bowen is the award-winning author of the Lords of Worth, Season of Scandal, and Devils of Dover series. She won RITA Awards for *A Duke to Remember* and *Between the Devil and the Duke*.

Kelly grew up in Manitoba, Canada, and earned a master of science degree in veterinary physiology and endocrinology from the University of Manitoba.

But it was Kelly's infatuation with history and a weakness for a good love story that led her down the path of historical romance. When she is not writing, she seizes every opportunity to explore ruins and battlefields.

Currently, Kelly lives in Winnipeg with her husband and two boys, all of whom are wonderfully patient with the writing process. Except, that is, when they need a goalie for street hockey.

You can learn more at:

KellyBowen.net
Twitter @KellyBowen09
Facebook.com/AuthorKellyBowen

*Looking for more historical romances?
Fall in love with these sexy rogues
and darling ladies from Forever!*

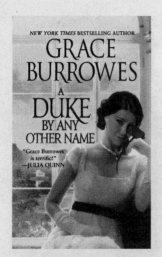

A DUKE BY ANY OTHER NAME
by Grace Burrowes

Lady Althea Wentworth has little patience for dukes, reclusive or otherwise, but she needs the Duke of Rothhaven's backing to gain entrance into Society. She's asked him nicely, she's called on him politely, all to no avail—until her prize hogs *just happen* to plunder his orchard. He longs for privacy. She's vowed to never endure another ball as a wallflower. Yet as the two grow closer, it soon becomes clear they might both be pretending to be something they're not.

THE TRUTH ABOUT DUKES
by Grace Burrowes

Lady Constance Wentworth never has a daring thought (that she admits aloud) and never comes close to courting scandal...as far as anybody knows. Robert Rothmere is a scandal poised to explode. Unless he wants to end up locked away in a madhouse (again) by his enemies, he needs to marry a perfectly proper, deadly dull duchess, immediately—but little does he know that the delightful lady he has in mind is hiding scandalous secrets of her own.

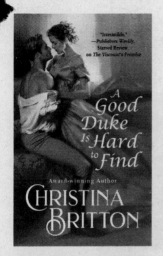

**A GOOD DUKE
IS HARD TO FIND
by Christina Britton**

Next in line for a dukedom he doesn't want to inherit, Peter Ashford is on the Isle of Synne only to exact revenge on the man responsible for his mother's death. But when he meets the beautiful and kind Miss Lenora Hartley, he can't help but be drawn to her. Can Peter put aside his plans for vengeance for the woman who has come to mean everything to him?

**ANY ROGUE WILL DO
by Bethany Bennett**

For exactly one season, Lady Charlotte Wentworth played the biddable female the *ton* expected—and all it got her was society's mockery and derision. Now she's determined to take charge of her own future. So when an unwanted suitor tries to manipulate her into an engagement, she has a plan. He can't claim to be her fiancé if she's engaged to someone else. Even if it means asking for help from the last man she would ever marry.

THE HIGHLAND LAIRD
by Amy Jarecki

Laird Ciar MacDougall is on a vital mission for Scotland when he witnesses a murder—and then is blamed for the death and thrown into a Redcoat prison to rot. He never thought he'd be broken out by a blind slip of a lass and her faithful hound. He soon learns that Emma Grant is just as fierce and loyal as any clansman. But now they're outlaws on the run. And as their enemies circle ever closer, he will have to choose between saving his country or the woman who's captured his heart.